Praise for the Rhona MacLeod series

'Lin Anderson is one of Scotland's national treasures . . . her writing is unique, bringing warmth and depth to even the seediest parts of Glasgow. Rhona MacLeod is a complex and compelling heroine who just gets better with every outing'

Stuart MacBride

'From Glasgow's real underbelly, Lin Anderson's *Sins of the Dead* will have you biting your nails and wondering why you ever bought a telly. Inventive, compelling, genuinely scary and beautifully written, as always' Denzil Meyrick

'Hugely imaginative and exciting'

James Grieve (Emeritus Professor of Forensic Pathology)

'Vivid and atmospheric . . . enthralling' *Guardian*

'Shades of *The Wicker Man*, with a touch of Agatha Christie. Superb' *Daily Mail*

'The bleak landscape is beautifully described, giving this popular series a new lease of life' *Sunday Times*

'Greenock-born Anderson's work is sharper than a pathologist's scalpel. One of the best Scottish crime series since Rebus'

Daily Record

'Guaranteed to grip the reader's imagination. Lin Anderson writes at a cracking pace . . . Very readable. Every last word'

Herald

By Lin Anderson

Driftnet
Torch
Deadly Code
Dark Flight
Easy Kill
Final Cut
The Reborn
Picture Her Dead
Paths of the Dead
The Special Dead
None but the Dead
Follow the Dead
Sins of the Dead

NOVELLA

Blood Red Roses

Sins of the Dead

are all consuming . . .

LIN ANDERSON

PAN BOOKS

First published 2018 by Macmillan

This paperback edition published 2019 by Pan Books
an imprint of Pan Macmillan
20 New Wharf Road, London N1 9RR
Associated companies throughout the world
www.panmacmillan.com

ISBN 978-1-5098-6620-5

1 3 5 7 9 8 6 4 2

A CIP catalogue record for this book is available from the British Library.

Map artwork by Hemesh Alles 2018

Typeset by Palimpsest Book Production Limited, Falkirk, Stirlingshire
Printed and bound by CPI Group (UK) Ltd, Croydon, CR0 4YY

This book is dedicated to the many Harley-Davidson motorcycle owners who together form the H.O.G. Dunedin Chapter Scotland (9083). This group and their partners organize Thunder in the Glens in Aviemore each year.

SLEEP CLINIC
ASHTON LANE
BYRES ROAD
GLASGOW UNIVERSITY
RIVER KELVIN
HEMESH· ALLES

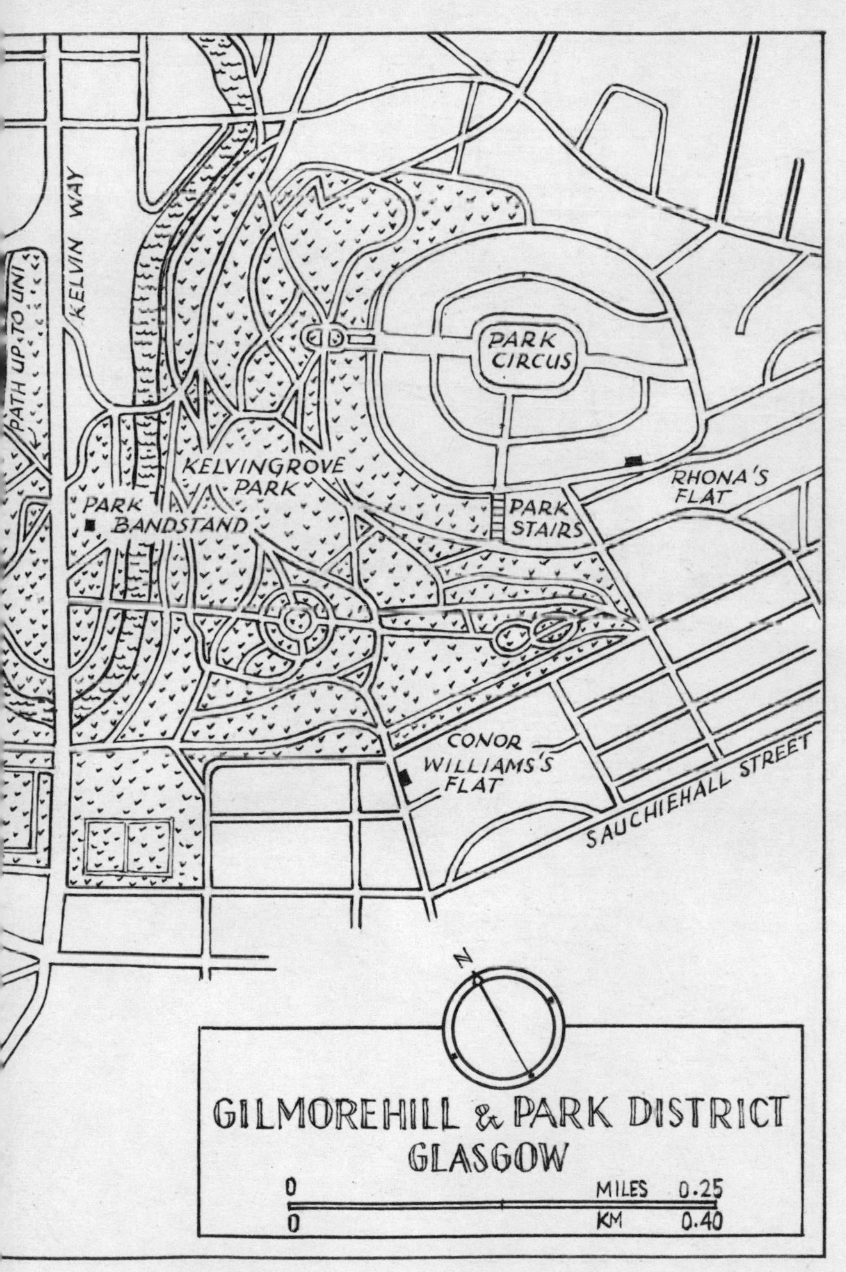
KELVIN WAY
PATH UP TO UNI
PARK CIRCUS
KELVINGROVE PARK
PARK BANDSTAND
PARK STAIRS
RHONA'S FLAT
CONOR WILLIAMS'S FLAT
SAUCHIEHALL STREET
N
GILMOREHILL & PARK DISTRICT
GLASGOW
0
MILES 0.25
0
KM 0.40

It was happening again. The crushing weight on his chest suffocating him, the paralysis of his limbs and his voice. Fear was the only thing that moved, surging through him like a bolt of lightning, tingling his skin. He tried again to open his eyes. If he could do that the night paralysis would end.

His eyes finally sprang open on darkness and the realization that something was still wrong. Usually once the bond was broken, he could move again. He would be shaking with shock, but around him the normal images of his bedroom would take form and reassure him.

Not this time.

This time his eyes had opened on something entirely different.

A figure was crouched next to him, formed by shadows, but he still recognized it as human.

Then the figure turned and he saw the face, and with horror he remembered.

1

I do not focus solely on the *why* of my endeavours any more, but increasingly on the *how*, as evidenced by the books I surround myself with and the various classes I take to assist me.

Her lectures are the best. I note the audience of around sixty participants – police officers, mortuary assistants, social workers – all of whom hang on her every word. The scene reminds me of an Indiana Jones movie where Harrison Ford, as the famous Professor of Archaeology, faces a class of entranced students. One girl blinks in order to show him the words on her lids . . . *I love you*.

I do not know if there is a similar wannabe lover among the current contingent, but I imagine there will be someone, other than myself.

The course is approaching completion. I have considered whether I should submit the required paper to gain a diploma in forensic medical science. I like the idea of adding that to my list of qualifications. Should I decide to do so, then I think the topic will be 'Buried and Hidden Bodies', a speciality, I know, of Dr MacLeod.

But I haven't decided, because the sins of the dead take up so much of my time.

2

Izzy shone the torch on the padlock. Vertical to the gate, the metal gadget required a four-digit combination. Fortunately, Izzy's relationship with the minder of the entrance was still going strong. Ellie sometimes wondered if it was sex, true love or, on Izzy's side at least, a sacrifice required for her one true love . . . her Harley.

They could of course have shone their beams rather than the piddly torch, but that would have alerted local residents to the fact they were entering the tunnel. With tenements on one side and the car park of Paradise, Celtic's home ground, on the other, they'd even pushed their bikes the last hundred yards rather than roar in.

Someone else had been inside the outer cordon recently, probably having dreeped the wall on the Paradise end. This was evidenced by a cluster of beer cans, empty Buckfast bottles and a rather splendid new gang slogan adorning the brick wall which sealed the tunnel they were intent on entering.

The combination complete, Ellie smiled at Izzy as the gate clicked open.

'Sex still good?'

'Looks like it,' Izzy said.

The other two wheeled their bikes out of the darkness

to follow them. Immediately they were through, Ellie locked the gate behind them.

The next barrier was the steel door set in the brick wall. Ellie felt in her pocket for the Yale key, a copy of which had also been acquired from Izzy's playmate. The newly painted gang slogan, pure white and outlined in black, had seamlessly included the steel door in its indecipherable message.

Reaching the door, this time the key had to be wriggled back and forth before it finally conceded, which did cause some consternation among the four women. The steel door free, now came the hardest part – manoeuvring the heavy bikes through the opening.

When the door finally clanged shut behind them and the smell of the tunnel hit their nostrils, a cheer went up as four sets of headlights blazed on.

'Fucking hell.' Izzy gave Ellie a wide grin. 'I'm looking forward to this.'

The old railway tunnel ran in a virtual straight line, about 400 yards short of a mile, under the East End of Glasgow. It was, according to legend, the original link between Parkhead South station and Bridgeton Cross, having been closed down in 1964, although since then there had been talk of using it to provide a second circle for the Glasgow Subway. A favourite with urban explorers, it had eventually been bricked shut by the council to keep them out.

But not us, Ellie thought as the roar of four engines punctured the silence.

Closed to the public years before they'd started racing here, the tunnel offered a selection of obstacles to circumvent at speed. It was, Ellie thought, a bit like playing a computer racing game, but for real, complete with the smell of petrol.

Ellie had been brought up with a similar scent, although speedway bikes ran on ethanol. Her father had been a rider with Glasgow Tigers and she'd spent her formative years alongside a speedway track. Trouble was, women didn't ride speedway, not back then and rarely now, so she'd decided if speedway riding wasn't an option, then a real motorbike was.

Her father's face had been a picture at that decision.

It would be even more of a picture if he knew I was down here.

The three women with her shared the same love of bikes, or more precisely, Harley-Davidson bikes, all being frequent visitors to the HD shop where Ellie worked. Although all four were welcome among the mainly male Harley riders on the various club outings, they'd fancied doing their own thing.

Which is why they were down here.

Now lined up, engines revving madly, at the agreed signal they took off, their back wheels throwing up a shower of stones. The race, Ellie knew, would be dominated by her and Izzy, although Gemma had vastly improved in her control of the bike since they'd made their first visit here. Mo was the beginner, her fear factor still too high to take the chances required, especially when negotiating the route.

Ellie felt a surge of pleasure as her thighs gripped the bike, her eyes focused for the sudden emergence of obstacles in her headlights which had to be avoided. The faster the ride, the swifter the encounter. She gave an excited shout as she swerved just ahead of Izzy and only just in time to miss the frame of an old pushbike.

Izzy was behind her but only just. If she fucked up again, Izzy would overtake. Something Ellie definitely didn't want. Being leader of the pack meant you had to win – or expect a demotion. The races were supposed to be friendly, but you didn't enter to lose.

The next major obstacle was the old Ford Sierra Cosworth, a classic car of the nineties which had found its way down here, probably to race like they were doing now. Stripped of its dignity, it sat across the tunnel with just enough room on one side to pass. Whoever got there first would take the lead.

They were now running neck and neck. Without looking, Ellie knew what the expression on Izzy's face would be. Gallous, determined, Izzy in moments like this had no fear.

Ellie urged the bike on with a sudden blast of the throttle. As it jumped forward, like a stallion running free, she whipped the handlebars round so that, like a speedway bike, the back end swung round to block her opponent's path. A dangerous move, but one that Izzy would have attempted had she had the chance.

The tunnel wall reared up on her left, the Sierra Cosworth to her right, and by the skin of her teeth she was through.

Now the way was free, though Izzy wouldn't be far behind. The race wasn't over yet. The route ended at the next obstacle, a discarded oil drum, just short of the air vent. A quick turn about that, then back the way they had come.

Izzy was good on this stretch and she could still overtake her.

Ellie glanced behind, expecting Izzy to be tight on her tail. Yet she wasn't. Had she got stuck passing the Cosworth? Just as she skidded towards the oil drum, a flashing torch beam from the tunnel ahead caught Ellie full in the face before being swiftly extinguished.

Fuck, was someone down there with them?

Realizing Izzy hadn't followed her, Ellie slowed and turned the bike to face back the way she had come, only to discover the other two had roared up and were parked alongside Izzy, who'd already dismounted just short of the Cosworth.

Had they spotted the torch beam too? Was that why they'd come to a halt?

In her headlights, Ellie saw that Izzy appeared to be checking out the wreck, albeit from the other side.

So it wasn't the possibility of someone else down there that had stopped them, but something about the Cosworth.

Starting up again, Ellie cruised forward, her heart skipping a beat, not from excitement, but from what she now saw.

'Tell me it's not what I think it is,' Izzy demanded, her voice sharp with fear.

Ellie doused her engine and a sudden and ominous silence descended. She shot a quick glance behind her, but if someone had been down there, they had gone or at least had turned off the torch.

Here the Cosworth and its associated horror were illuminated in the Harley's headlights. From her side at least there was no doubt what she was looking at.

It was the body of a male, fully clothed, stretched out alongside the wreck as though in sleep.

Dismounting, Ellie approached, the wide-eyed trio opposite watching her every move.

Ellie held her breath, having no wish to smell death, and, quickly hunkering down, reached for the exposed neck.

*

They'd retreated as far as the frame of the abandoned push-bike, keen to get away from their view of the Cosworth.

'Well?' Izzy demanded.

'There's no blood, but I think he's dead,' Ellie said, glancing down the tunnel, wondering if she'd imagined the torch beam and whether she should even mention it.

'Maybe it was suicide?' Mo suggested, almost hopefully.

'Or he was murdered and dumped down here?' Gemma said.

'What the fuck do we do?' Izzy's raised voice bounced back at them from the walls.

Ellie studied the three frightened faces in turn, then answered Izzy's question.

'We go now and quietly,' she said, trying to keep her own voice calm.

Izzy said, 'Do we call the police and tell them?'

Ellie didn't know the answer to that. For once, it appeared her decision-making process had ground to a halt.

All she could think was, if he had been murdered maybe whoever had flashed the torch in her face had killed him.

They'd probably stashed the body here, because they thought no one would find it. It was, to all intents and purposes, buried.

Except they'd been here and seen it, and if they reported it they would become potential witnesses.

Did that, could that, put them in danger?

Ellie had been born and brought up in Glasgow. She knew its underbelly as well as its face. This part of the city had been regenerated. The Emirates Stadium built for the Commonwealth Games was just along the road. That didn't mean the gangs had deserted the place or had moved to only artistic pursuits like the graffiti on the bricked-up entrance. If it was a gang killing . . .

'We go,' she said, 'as quietly as we arrived.'

'And hope no one's watching.' Izzy's nose studs glittered in the single light they'd left on, wishing to avoid any further image of the Cosworth and its contents. At that moment the defiant piercings seemed at odds with her fearful expression.

Ellie suddenly felt sorry for Izzy, for the others, for the person that lay beside the car.

'We go now,' she stressed. 'We'll decide once we're clear.'

Ellie remembered how earlier she'd been worried about losing her position as leader of the pack, yet wished now that she had. Then Izzy might have taken the lead on this and made the decision.

Turning their backs on the nightmare, they headed in silence for the exit.

3

Rhona stood for a moment just inside the doorway. The air that met her face was cold and dank, in contrast to the warm stickiness of an August heatwave above. The throb of a generator indicated a source of power had been supplied for the arc lights, the bright beams of which were visible in the near distance.

The call-out to attend a crime scene had come late into the night. She'd been out, hence her arrival here dressed inappropriately. That had been dealt with via the boiler suit she now wore, although the high-heeled shoes had proved a problem, eventually solved by their removal and a double helping of forensic boots. The tunnel floor, however, which had apparently once housed a railway line, was a mix of mud and the sharp stones of old ballast, which wasn't easy on the feet. Fortunately, the dedicated path had already been laid.

As Rhona stepped out across the metal plates that would be her stepping stones, a thought fleetingly crossed her mind.

If I'd just said I'd had alcohol, they would have found someone else to attend.

But she hadn't been drinking, although she almost wished she had. Then she could have blamed that for her stupid decision of earlier.

Instead, I have no one to blame but myself.

Acknowledging this, Rhona then banished those thoughts from her mind. She was here now, and concentrating on the job meant she could forget everything else. Mistakes in her personal life included.

Reaching the locus, she took in the scene. The brick tunnel was, at an estimate, twenty-five yards in width. On the walk here, Rhona had observed nothing but scurrying rats, decaying rubbish and a rusted bicycle frame. Now, sitting horizontally across the tunnel, was a car. Or, more correctly, the body of a car, its skeleton shape suggesting it had come from a previous era.

How such a vehicle had got down here, she didn't know.

Then again, in Rhona's experience, if folk wanted in somewhere, however tricky or even dangerous, they generally managed it. Certainly, at some time in the past, someone had driven through here in what DS McConnachie, crime scene manager at the entrance, had knowingly informed her was a Ford Sierra Cosworth, once the car of choice for criminals because they could outrun any cop car.

'One gangster who had his stolen put it about that if it was brought back by the next morning, the thief would be allowed to live.' DS McConnachie had told her a tale as illustration. 'Next day there were three Cosworths outside his door,' he'd finished with a grin.

The famous model, classic or not, was now little more than an empty shell and, it seemed, marked the final resting place of the victim she'd come to examine.

Male, approximately five foot eight or nine, and at a guess in his mid to late twenties, he lay on his back, hands together on his chest. From where she stood, his face appeared unmarked and there were no obvious wounds or blood. He was dressed in a dark padded jacket, blue jeans and brown leather pointed shoes. His auburn hair was styled longer on top, shaved at the sides, and he sported a three-inch beard, shaped and trimmed.

He was in fact a good-looking young man who would have blended in at any Merchant City or West End drinking establishment – had he been alive, that is.

Rigor mortis was still present, although on its way out. Said to start between two to six hours following death, the stiffening began with the eyelids, neck and jaw. In this case the peak had passed and gradually the body was becoming flaccid again as decomposition set in, but, as Rhona knew, standard rigor patterning was a poor indication of time of death.

Rhona was also aware that locations such as this, before they'd been sealed off, had been a magnet for urban explorers, who ventured below ground to catalogue and photograph a forgotten Glasgow. The entrance itself had recently been a hangout for a gang, as indicated by the fresh bottles, cans and graffiti between the gate and the door, but once inside, she'd seen nothing to indicate the gang had gained access to the tunnel.

The victim's mode of dress didn't suggest a gang member or an urban explorer, but then appearances could be deceptive.

Rhona stepped away as a team of SOCOs began raising the tent. She was suddenly aware of the throb of the portable generator resounding off the tunnel walls, like an echo of itself, suggesting earplugs would be a good idea.

The dead always had something to say to her, but rarely out loud.

*

Detective Sergeant Michael McNab joined the other vehicles parked alongside the football stadium. Despite the circumstances, viewing the giant images of key figures in the history of Celtic football club displayed at the entrance, in particular the statue of the Big Man Jock Stein, always brought a smile to his face. McNab took a moment to salute the former manager's genius before heading down the slope to the big metal gate, which stood open and guarded by a uniformed officer.

McNab flashed his badge. 'Who's scene of crime officer?'

'DS McConnachie, sir.'

The gate, McNab noted in passing, had a combination padlock, the inner door a standard one.

'Were these unlocked when we got here?' he asked.

'When I got here, yes.'

The rank smell of damp and disuse met McNab as he stepped through the open doorway. Glasgow had plenty of these subterranean tunnels, which had provided, in the past at least, a good place to hang out, get drunk and on the odd occasion shag. He'd frequented a few such locations in his own heady youth. This one, so close to Paradise Park, being a favourite. Back then, though, they hadn't been gated and padlocked.

Kitted up now, he approached the tent, in which he knew he would encounter Dr MacLeod. Not something he was looking forward to for a variety of reasons, including what had taken place earlier that night.

McConnachie met him halfway, looking surprised to find him there at all.

'Wasn't expecting you, Sergeant?' he shouted above the generator noise, his big jowled face puzzled.

'I was about when the call came in and I know the area.' McNab glanced around. 'And this location in particular.'

McConnachie acknowledged his look. 'Ah. A teenage haunt?'

'I always got lucky when Celtic won at home,' McNab told him with a smile.

Pleasantries over, he signed his name on the scene log and headed for the tent.

Rhona had her back to him and didn't turn on his entry. McNab knew that would be for two reasons. She was likely wearing earplugs against the noise from the generator and, more importantly, she was fully focused on what she was doing. McNab stood quietly, waiting for her to sense his presence, aware that her reaction to his arrival wouldn't be positive.

Eventually she turned and, registering him, stood up. Above the mask her eyes met his and McNab flinched under their penetrating gaze.

'What are you doing here?' she said in what he acknowledged was a far from welcoming tone.

And who could blame her?

McNab wasn't as glib with the explanation for his visit a second time. In fact he found himself momentarily incapable of coming up with a suitable answer.

Rhona's response to this was to release her gaze and move a little to one side, to allow him a view of the corpse.

Considering the area, McNab had been expecting one of three sights. A bloodied knife victim, common enough in Glasgow. Alternatively a shooting, which was increasing in popularity, especially among the drug barons. Or maybe just some poor homeless bastard who'd taken shelter here and hadn't managed to find his way out.

None of these was what he was looking at now.

Coming from an Irish background, McNab had been to wakes where the coffin had been left open, so that the deceased, in all their Sunday best, might be viewed. As a child, he'd found the tradition unnerving. As an adult, he still felt the same, but at his age he could drink copious amounts of whisky before viewing Great Aunt Marie, or her male equivalent, lying like a waxwork doll, hands clasped together, make-up on. Some relatives, he recalled, had looked better in death than life.

The young male victim here might be missing a coffin, but the seemingly unmarked body was arranged as though he lay in one. With no obvious evidence of a violent death, McNab's first thought was that the guy had committed suicide, although he didn't voice it.

'Any ID?' he tried.

'Nothing in his pockets to tell us who he is, no wallet, no mobile phone,' Rhona said.

That was weird, McNab decided, although suicides often ditched their identities before carrying out the act, as though wiping out their past together with their future. And, if it turned out to be a homicide, then the perpetrator might not want the identity of their victim known.

'Did he die here?' McNab asked.

Rhona threw him a look that suggested he should know better than to imagine that she would give her opinion on that before studying the evidence.

McNab knew there were folk, guys for the most part, who liked to photograph hidden Glasgow. The victim, he supposed, might be one of those, although his mode of dress suggested something other than a stroll through a disused railway tunnel.

'Take a look inside the car,' Rhona suggested.

Crouching, McNab did so.

A white cloth the size of a large napkin had been spread out on the remains of the back seat. On it, surprisingly, was a half glass of what looked like red wine, and a chunk of bread, partially eaten.

'His Last Supper?' McNab quipped.

By Rhona's expression his attempt at a joke either hadn't registered or hadn't been appreciated.

'There are no visible signs of a struggle or a wound. And no blood. And the positioning of the body is very precise,' she said.

McNab decided to try the suicide angle. 'People can be quite ritualistic about taking their own life.'

Rhona acknowledged that with a nod. 'But,' she said, 'someone may have been down here with him.'

'And you know this how?'

She indicated the area alongside. 'There's an impression, a heavy boot by the pattern. It's a smaller size and doesn't match his footwear.'

Her explanation was interrupted by McNab's mobile ringing. Surprised that he even had a signal, he checked the screen to find Ellie's name.

'I'd better take this,' he said, but Rhona had already turned her attention back to the body.

Nevertheless, McNab chose to wait until he was well away from the tent before answering.

'Where are you?' Ellie's voice sounded shrill, which immediately put him on his guard. That, and guilt about his movements earlier in the evening.

'At work,' he said, exasperation in his voice. When she didn't respond, McNab added, 'Is something wrong?', hoping there wouldn't be, because he didn't want to deal with any more relationship shit tonight.

'No, it's fine,' Ellie said, as though mustering herself. 'Everything's fine.'

As she fell silent again, McNab suddenly registered why she might be calling. In a post-coital moment of madness he'd agreed to accompany Ellie to the next speedway meeting, where Ellie and a group of fellow female enthusiasts were to lead the teams out on their Harleys.

When she'd invited him to tag along, McNab had been initially quite taken with the idea, but his enthusiasm had since waned, especially when he'd learned that Ellie's father, an ex-speedway rider, would be there.

Already planning his excuses, McNab bit the bullet. 'About the speedway tomorrow night—' he began, before being interrupted by Ellie.

'You don't need to come,' she said.

This surprising response flummoxed McNab, and he found himself swithering between relief that he didn't have to turn up at Ashfield and meet her father and the sudden thought that he might get dumped if he didn't.

A real boyfriend would keep his word, his conscience told him, but then again he was a shite boyfriend. 'Can I call you about it tomorrow?' he tried.

McNab decided on his way back to his car that Ellie's subsequent reply of 'okay' was definitely not okay. Something was obviously wrong. *But what?* There was no way Ellie could know he'd met with Rhona earlier, unless she was tailing him. Which she obviously wasn't.

Things had been going well with Ellie, at least until recently, and better than any of his previous attempts at a relationship. Usually by now he'd fucked things up via too much work, too much drink or sheer bloody-mindedness.

They'd met in the tattoo parlour where she had her second job, her first being in the Harley-Davidson shop where she fitted up the bikes with extras. McNab, a former motorcycle cop, had been seriously impressed by both lines of work, especially the Harley connection.

Ellie had seemed to take the fact that he was a detective in her stride, and, he realized, until this moment she had never sounded fearful of anything. The opposite in fact. McNab, trying to imagine again what a real boyfriend would do, glanced at the mobile, wondering whether he should call her back, but knowing that wasn't going to happen.

A car drew in as he approached his own, a quick glance in at the driver's window alerting him to who had officially been sent to check out the scene. DS Clark's expression when she spotted him was a picture.

He and Janice went way back. They were even friends, despite the fact he'd made more than one play for her, which she'd summarily rejected. As he'd been promoted to DI, she'd risen to DS, then he'd met her on his way back down, with his demotion after the Stonewarrior case.

The very case that had resulted in tonight's issue with Rhona.

'What are you doing here, McNab?' Janice sounded exasperated as she shut the car door.

McNab gave his rehearsed speech of earlier.

'I thought you were off tonight?'

'I was. I heard it through the grapevine,' he said, being suitably vague.

McNab could almost hear the silent words, *like hell you did,* being muttered as Janice studied him intently.

'Is Dr MacLeod here?' she finally said.

McNab mustered himself and said, 'She is,' before quickly changing the subject. 'Any idea who placed the call?'

Janice shook her head. 'Anonymous and muffled, the operator said.'

'You need a key to get in the steel door and a combination for the padlock on the outer gate,' McNab told her. 'You should check with the council who has access.'

Janice threw him a withering look. 'You trying to tell me how to do my job?'

'Not brave enough for that,' McNab admitted.

Watching Janice head for the tunnel, McNab spotted a message sprayed on the retainer wall behind the leafless bushes.

Mikey is a wanker.

4

Ellie flung the mobile on the bed.

Calling Michael had been a bad idea, especially when she'd had no idea what she was going to say to him. *And he was immediately suspicious.* She'd had some forlorn hope that hearing his voice would help her decide what to do. Then, when she'd realized he was out on a job, the full impact of him being a policeman had descended and she'd lost her nerve. Even more so when he'd started talking about coming to the speedway tomorrow night.

What if he linked the four of them riding round the track with the tyre impressions in the tunnel?

Ellie shuddered at the thought, however unlikely.

She and Izzy had come back to her flat, telling the other two girls to go home and keep quiet about what had happened.

'But shouldn't we call the police anonymously?' Gemma had tried before she'd departed.

'They can trace calls,' Mo had reminded them, her face still fearful.

'Reporting something doesn't make you guilty,' had been Izzy's response.

When Mo and Gemma had finally gone, she and Izzy had discussed it further.

'Maybe he'll never be found?' Izzy had tried.

The idea of waiting and watching the papers and news for such a thing had freaked Ellie.

Seeing her hesitation, Izzy reinforced her line of thought. 'If the police do go down there, they'll find the tyre tracks. They can do stuff with tyre impressions. Maybe even trace them back to us.'

'Shut up!' Ellie had fired back, even though she knew what Izzy had said was true.

Izzy had thrown her a belligerent look. 'I don't want to get involved,' she'd said sharply.

'Neither do I.' Ellie had softened her tone in an attempt at reconciliation. Whatever they did must be agreed upon.

'Dougie'll shite himself about this,' Izzy had said.

'He doesn't have to know.'

'So he's not going to think it weird we're not using the place any more? And what about when he goes down himself?'

'How often does that happen?'

'I've no fucking idea, but he does have to check it out now and again. *And* he knows we were down there tonight. So if he finds the body, he'll know that we did too, and didn't report it.'

'But he won't tell the police that, because then he'd have to admit to giving us a key,' Ellie had reminded her.

'So do I keep having sex with him?' Izzy had demanded.

'Do you want to?'

'He gets a hard-on just thinking about me riding my bike through his tunnel,' Izzy had said. 'When I wanted to keep the key that was fine. Now I'm not so sure.'

Ellie had realized at that moment that they hadn't even told a lie yet, and a web of deceit was already being spun.

Izzy had come back in then. 'The walls are running with

water so, over time, the tyre tracks will fade, won't they? There'll be no connection with us and the bikes if we just wait. So,' she had come to a decision, 'I'll break it off with Dougie and give him back the key.'

She'd stood up at that point, her mind made up. 'That's what we do. Agreed?'

Ellie had nodded, but alone now, she realized that she wasn't convinced. The dead guy was bound to be reported as a missing person. She had barely looked at him, but even a swift glance had told her he wasn't a poor soul living on the streets. He would have a family, a girlfriend or boyfriend, and workmates. They would need to know what had happened to him.

She hadn't wanted to touch him, to check for life, yet knew the others expected her to. She'd had to force her finger to meet his neck, all the time telling herself he had to be dead. He had to be, but . . .

The horror of the scene replayed in her mind. He'd looked so peaceful lying there. Nothing had suggested he'd been attacked. Then there was the strange arrangement behind him in the car. Bread and wine? How bizarre was that? When she'd mentioned it to Izzy, she'd agreed with Mo that it had to be a weird suicide.

That thought brought a wave of emotion, because it hadn't been the first time Ellie had viewed a suicide. She definitely didn't want to relive those memories. *But what if her wee brother Danny had just disappeared? Would we all have preferred that, rather than discovering that he'd killed himself?*

Ellie knew the answer to that one, for her anyway. She could have survived for years in the hopeful belief that Danny had finally gone on that world trip he'd always talked about. Instead they'd had to face the fact that her little brother had been so sad and desperate that he'd taken his own life.

I should have told Michael what we were doing down there and what we found.

That thought was immediately accompanied by a flurry of others. If she had done, all four of them would be called for interview. They might even be suspects. The press would jump on the story of them racing in the tunnel. They'd be in the papers. *Jeez. Dougie might even lose his job for giving them the key.*

No, if she was to tell the police, it would have to be anonymously.

Ellie decided to wait at least until the morning. Maybe, by then, she would have decided.

5

Rhona checked her watch. It would soon be morning, although down here there was little chance of seeing daylight. Left alone in the tent, she'd worked throughout the night. They wouldn't move the body to the mortuary until she indicated she was satisfied she'd collected as much evidence as possible from it *in situ*.

A thorough taping of the clothing and accessible body had resulted in a selection of fibres, including one from the victim's nostrils. From the neck area she'd lifted a partial print. This, coupled with a heavily ridged footprint, smaller than the victim's, and a tyre impression, painted a picture of someone on a motorcycle being in the vicinity of the dead man, either before or after his demise.

The decision on whether to remove the clothing at the locus was always a tricky one. In this case Rhona had worked the clothes here, rather than strip them off and bag them. They'd be removed at the autopsy and further examined in the lab, but she had wanted to be sure that nothing would be lost in transit. She'd bagged the head, feet and hands, after she'd taken samples from all three areas. The covered parts of the body would have to wait until the PM.

From what she'd observed, there were no outward signs that he'd been attacked, just as she'd told McNab. She'd detected no drug traces on the body or in the immediate vicinity, although that didn't mean he hadn't died of an overdose. Had he planned suicide, then he would have come here with the means to accomplish that. Since he hadn't attempted to hang himself, the likelihood was he'd swallowed something or injected it, although she hadn't located an injection point in the visible skin or a syringe in the area.

DS Clark had joined her just after McNab had departed. Rhona wondered if Janice was aware that McNab had been there. She didn't have long to wait to find out.

'I met McNab in the car park. He said he'd heard about this on the grapevine,' Janice had said.

'He heard it from me.' Rhona had put Janice straight, without enlightening her as to the circumstances.

Janice's 'Oh' in response had been, Rhona thought, a question in disguise. She was a detective after all. Plus DS Clark was well aware that there was history between McNab and Rhona. Sexual as well as professional. Janice had also been involved in the Stonewarrior case, so knew things had been bad between them after that.

But only McNab and I know the full story.

Rhona hadn't needed to change the subject at that point, because by then Janice was more interested in taking a closer look at the crime scene, after which she'd quizzed Rhona about her take on it. Rhona repeated her earlier interchange with McNab.

'And this has all been recorded?'

'The full works,' Rhona said. 'Three-hundred-and-sixty-degree video recording and my own photographs.'

'If his death wasn't self-inflicted,' Janice indicated the contents of the car, 'could this be a signature?'

An organized killer had a modus operandi, the manner

in which they chose to end the life of a victim. In a case of strangulation, the ligature chosen and how it was used was regarded as the killer's signature. There was no evidence yet that the body here was a murder victim. Should that turn out to be the case, the strange arrangement of food and drink alongside the body might well prove to be a signature. Rhona said so.

'Should we bring in Professor Pirie?' Janice asked.

That thought had crossed Rhona's mind. The last case the Professor of Forensic Psychology had worked on with her had been in Orkney, where Magnus was originally from. He'd been invaluable then, bringing both local knowledge and a psychological understanding of the perpetrator.

'I could make these images available to him?' Rhona suggested.

'How much longer are you going to be with the body?'

'Another hour should do it.'

'I'll give Magnus a call,' Janice said, 'ask if he's free to come down and take a look before we move it.'

When DS Clark left the tent to check on the SOCOs working the perimeter, Rhona settled down next to the body to write up her notes, a habit she'd acquired early in her career for two reasons. No one else wanted to be in there, so she had peace to concentrate, and more importantly, it was her way of paying her respects to the dead.

Magnus reached out, hoping to find the other side of the bed still warm. Pulling himself upright, he realized with regret that any hope of warmth was as unlikely as the coupling he'd just imagined in his sleep. The woman of his dreams wasn't here and, he acknowledged, unlikely ever to be.

Rising, he padded to the French windows to drink in the dawn sky and the wide expanse of the River Clyde. He never tired of this view of his adopted city, but often imagined it as it had once been. The distant shore alive with the clang of metal, the shouts of the men who'd built the great ships. There was still evidence of this in the shining beacon of the last giant crane just downriver from him, the regeneration of the city personified by the nearby needle-like structure of the Science Centre, a favourite with Glaswegians of all ages.

This morning the sky was so clear Magnus could make out the distant rise of Glennifer Braes to the west and Cathkins Braes to the east. Not quite in the same league as his view across Scapa Flow to the island of Hoy from his Orphir home, but at least he was as close to the water here in Glasgow as he was to Houton Bay in Orkney.

After setting up the coffee maker and popping a bagel in the toaster, he checked his phone to find a voicemail had arrived while he'd still been asleep and fantasizing. Recognizing the name and number, Magnus immediately called them back.

'DS Clark,' he said, tempering the excitement in his voice.

The truth was he hadn't been called upon by Police Scotland since the Sanday murder, and he was missing the challenge of a real live case.

The unearthing of a grave in one of the most northerly islands in the Orkney archipelago had brought both Rhona and DS McNab north. DS McNab, Magnus remembered with a smile, had been more than a little uncomfortable in such a location.

'Sorry to be in touch so early . . .' she began.

'No problem,' Magnus quickly assured her. 'How can I help?'

Minutes later, he was dressed and ready to go. Carrying his coffee and bagel down to the low-level car park, Magnus reminded himself that relishing the prospect of a case wasn't the same as wanting someone to die in suspicious circumstances so that he might be called upon to offer his advice.

Exiting the building, he took the riverside route. He was already familiar with the East End of Glasgow and some of the tunnels that lay beneath that part of the city. The first case he'd been invited by DI Wilson to participate in had centred on the Molendinar Burn, which ran in a beautiful brick-built culvert close to where he was now headed.

The memory of his contribution to that case brought with it a swift rush of embarrassment.

I really screwed that one up, he thought. *It's a wonder I was ever invited back.* DI Wilson had a forgiving nature, Magnus acknowledged, although his team not so much.

Drawing his mind away from such painful thoughts, he contemplated what DS Clark had told him, which wasn't much. An anonymous call from a muffled voice, indistinguishable as male or female, had led them to a disused railway tunnel near Parkhead, where a body was discovered in suspicious circumstances. Then the really good news. Dr Rhona MacLeod was already on the scene and would like Magnus to take a look in person, before she authorized the transport of the remains to the mortuary.

Rhona had been involved in the Molendinar case too. In fact, that was where they'd first met. Magnus grimaced at the thought of how badly that had gone for her, mainly because of his own actions.

But she forgave me too.

At this time of the morning the traffic was light, and he was soon drawing into the car park next to the football stadium. Parking his car next to the line of police vehicles, Magnus made his way under the outer cordon and down the concrete ramp that led to the bricked-up entrance. He took a moment or two to observe the area around the tunnel entrance, registering the gang slogan and photographing it. From his experience, many of the gangs now had a presence online, often through their graffiti. It wouldn't hurt to check out this one.

The scene of crime officer, whom he didn't know, had obviously been warned of his visit because he swiftly waved Magnus in, kitted him up and sent him along the designated path in double-quick time. On entry, Magnus's highly developed sense of smell had alerted him to petrol and, as he strode across the metal treads, he noted that two SOCOs were busy taking casts of what looked like tyre impressions.

Further in and nearer the tent, the scent changed to diesel, obviously caused by the portable generators which supplied the lights. Around the tent, concentric circles had been marked out and the team of SOCOs had reached the outer ring on their dedicated search.

Magnus halted at the entrance to the tent, glancing down into the further darkness of the passageway, wondering where else someone might gain entry, if not by the way he had used. By the quality of the air minus the diesel, he concluded that there had to be air vents further along the tunnel, if not an open exit.

He found Rhona inside the tent, seated by the body, busy writing up her notes. Her smile when she spied him was welcoming, although he could tell this only by the way it shone in her eyes, above the mask.

'I'm pleased you got here in time. We've taken video and stills but . . .'

'There's nothing like seeing the real thing,' he finished for her.

As they both lapsed into silence, Magnus moved closer to the remains. First impressions were often the truest. The immediate presence of death, its scent, its appearance, imprinted on the brain emotionally as well as physically.

Magnus took in the image and processed it. The clasped hands, the partial rigor mortis, the apparent absence of violence. He dropped to his knees for a closer look and saw the strange arrangement on the back seat of the car, whereupon a similar image immediately sprang to mind. An uncomfortable image, which provoked a sudden but fleeting memory.

'What is it?' Rhona said, registering his alarm.

Magnus shook his head. 'Not sure, but the Last Supper connotation certainly suggests something.'

'McNab made a similar comment,' Rhona said.

'The sergeant's here?' Magnus looked around in surprise as though expecting the tall, auburn-haired detective to stride in.

'Not officially,' Rhona said. 'But you know McNab. He doesn't like anything going past him and this is his neck of the woods.'

Magnus found himself rather sorry that DS McNab wasn't on the scene. They'd had their differences, mainly around the fact that McNab thought Magnus a charlatan due to his profession and wasn't afraid to say so.

Forensic Psychology wasn't rated highly amongst the

police rank and file, who preferred to rely on years of experience coupled with gut feeling. Magnus was inclined to agree with them, although he thought of their intuition as real psychology in action.

Something Magnus wasn't inclined to voice to McNab.

'The picnic appears highly symbolic,' Magnus said. 'Is it wine in the glass?'

'Yes,' Rhona told him.

'If it *is* a homicide,' Magnus offered, 'the bread and wine would be significant. But then again it could be important in a suicide too.' He paused. 'I wonder who ate the bread.'

'Whoever it was will have left their DNA on it,' Rhona told him.

Magnus suddenly recalled what the image of the body, the bread and the wine had reminded him of.

'What?' Rhona said, catching his look.

'Have you ever heard of a sin-eater?'

6

After departing the crime scene, McNab had made for home, planning a few hours' sleep before he was back at work. As he'd undressed for bed, he'd contemplated calling Ellie. Now he was far enough away from Rhona, common sense was beginning to rear its head again.

He had no wish to break up with Ellie or to have her break up with him. As far as he was aware, their relationship had been exclusive up to now, and on both sides. Contemplating the late and peculiar call from her, plus her hesitancy, had made him think she was about to finish with him. And the closer to home he'd got, the more he began to believe this.

Better not to give her a chance, had been his final decision as he'd rolled into bed. Unfortunately his brain had got hold of the idea and had replayed such a scenario numerous times during his troubled sleep, so that by the time he surfaced at seven, he even believed it to be true.

Now, under the shower, McNab mulled it over again. It would be best to meet Ellie face to face. She'd been direct with him up to now, so this was an aberration. If he saw her in person he would know for sure. And that could happen tonight at the speedway meeting. McNab decided to ignore his concerns about her father being there. It wasn't as though he was going to be a future son-in-law.

Arriving at the station, he was greeted by the desk sergeant who blithely reminded him that he was due at the funeral parlour ten minutes ago. Sergeant Drew McIvor was a character suited to his post on the front line, and well known for his unique sense of humour.

McNab gazed back at him, awaiting the punchline, which would probably have something to do with the way he looked from lack of sleep. Now that he was on the wagon, the remark couldn't refer to a hangover.

When nothing was forthcoming, except a steady grin, McNab eventually said, 'What are you on about, Sergeant?'

'Bodily interference with a cadaver.'

McNab was none the wiser. When that became obvious, the sergeant filled him in.

'Marshall's, the funeral directors? They've reported that someone's been messing with their bodies.'

'What the fuck . . . that's hardly my department.'

'The boss said you were to go along and get the story.'

McNab had been about to declare that this was a job for a uniform, but once DI Wilson's name was mentioned, he shut up. The repercussions from the last major investigation had seen him, if not grounded, then shackled, which was probably why DS Clark had got the heads-up on the tunnel body.

McNab turned on his heel without a response. Best way to play this was to do as told, in the hope he would be back in business sooner.

7

The funeral parlour wasn't open for business yet. Claire liked this time of day as much as the evening after she'd locked up, when she was alone with her charges. People thought working in a funeral parlour was a weird job, but she loved it. When she'd applied for the post, it had been out of necessity. Three weeks late with her rent and with most of her savings gone, she'd had to accept the first job on offer, even if it was with the dead.

She hadn't done that well in the interview and had no experience of the work, but Mr Marshall had given her a chance – he told her later it was because he thought she seemed kind and that's what people needed when they came into the shop. Claire's mantra from then on had become just that.

Be kind. It could be you walking through that door.

She'd thought the work would be sombre, but instead she'd found it joyful. There was much laughter among her fellow workers and Mr Marshall himself had a wonderful sense of humour.

Strangest of all, she found she liked being with the dead. She'd thought she would be afraid of them but she wasn't. She greeted them when she came in and talked to them as she worked. It was surprising that without life they still had characters.

And she had her favourites.

Like Mr Munro who'd wanted to be buried with a photograph of his dog, Bella, who'd gone before him. Claire had really missed Mr Munro when he went. Some made her sad, like Chloe, the young girl who'd hanged herself. Claire had talked to her a lot, and to her family. She'd done her make-up and Chloe's mum had asked her to paint her daughter's nails. Even brought in the polish, a lovely purple colour.

Claire had discovered it wasn't easy painting the nails of someone lying in a coffin. She'd been worried she would drip the polish as she leaned over the side, but had finally solved the problem by asking Chloe if she would hold the bottle. Sensing she was happy to, Claire had propped the bottle in her clasped hands and completed the task. She'd even told Chloe's mum how she'd done it, and the poor woman had smiled, a little light coming into her troubled eyes.

'Chloe would have liked you,' she'd said.

'I think she does,' had been Claire's own genuine reply.

Some bodies were cantankerous even in death. Where Chloe had been sweet, Mr Martin had been an awkward cadaver. Claire wondered if he had been the same in life, but when no one came to view him, except one man who, having looked at the body, declared Mr Martin wasn't who he thought he was and had promptly left, Claire wondered if it hadn't been loneliness that had made Mr Martin the way he was. After that she was more patient with him.

Claire cherished her charges, which made what had been happening to them personal as well as terrible. At first Mr Marshall had been sceptical, but she'd at last convinced him with the before and after images, even though she wasn't supposed to take photos of the deceased.

It was the crumbs she'd spotted at first. Mr Martin's red waistcoat had been sprinkled with them. Initially she'd suspected a mouse. Now that had scared her. She didn't fear the dead but was less sanguine about live rodents. Then she found red wine splashed on a white shirt worn by Mr Robertson, a lovely old man whose daughter was quite distraught at losing him.

'He was a real stickler with his shirts,' she'd told Claire. 'Used to iron them himself.'

So there was no way Mr Robertson would have a blood-red wine stain, dead or not.

It was at this point Claire had spoken to Mr Marshall, convinced now that it wasn't forgetfulness or carelessness on her own part. He had drawn his bushy eyebrows together and declared he had never met anything quite like this in his thirty years in the job.

'Are kids sneaking in?' he'd said.

Claire wondered why everyone, including nice Mr Marshall, always blamed the young for the bad things that happened in life.

'Could whoever it is be getting in during the night?' she'd suggested.

That had been the trigger for the phone call to the police station, which had resulted in Claire ready and waiting for a policeman, who was already late, to arrive.

8

McNab pulled up on a yellow line in front of the funeral parlour and stuck an ID on the window, indicating he was on duty. The shop front was glossy and black with gold lettering spelling out the name MARSHALL'S FUNERAL HOME.

McNab had never set foot in such a place before. When his mother died, the priest had handled everything and McNab had paid for it along with a generous donation to the church. His mother had appeared in her casket, chosen by Father Donovan, in the chapel as required. Father Donovan had said the mass, then she'd been taken to the graveyard and buried. McNab had no memory of which funeral director had made this all possible.

He hesitated now at the entrance, feeling by entering he was courting death. It was, he accepted, a stupid thing to think, but it didn't make any difference. Stepping over the threshold felt like entering the underworld. He was therefore surprised at who awaited him there.

Being met by a young female, not dressed in sombre black, but in a summery dress and with a welcoming smile on her face, had McNab nonplussed, so much so that she spoke first.

'Are you the police?'

Her voice, McNab noted, was warm and welcoming, and

he suddenly realized that she might be employed to make it easy for people to come in here.

He showed her his ID. 'Detective Sergeant McNab, miss.'

'Claire Masters.' She offered him her hand to shake and McNab did so. 'You're a detective,' she said, looking impressed. 'I assume you've come about the interference with the deceased?' she checked.

Her description of the crime worried McNab as it brought to mind a sudden image of some bastard sexually molesting a cadaver. Something that did happen. If that were the case, he would have preferred talking to Mr Marshall about it rather than the girl.

'Yes,' he said, stalling for time. 'Is Mr Marshall here?'

She shook her head. 'He's out with the hearse. Anyway, it happened on my watch,' she told him determinedly. 'And I have photographs to prove it.'

McNab glanced about, looking for cameras. She must have guessed this because she said, 'I took them with my mobile.' She hesitated for a moment. 'I think you should come in the back with me and I'll explain.'

As she ushered him through a set of heavy velvet curtains, any noise audible from the busy main street was immediately extinguished. *The silence of the grave,* McNab mused. Something that obviously didn't worry the girl.

'I prepare the deceased. They like to look nice for their loved ones.' She smiled her pleasure at this. 'Make-up, even for the men. Death drains the face of colour, you know.' Spotting McNab's expression, she added, 'They don't want to look like a ghost.'

McNab, for once, was lost for words. Seeing this, Claire continued, 'That's how I know exactly what they look like when I leave them. And how I know when they don't look the same when I come back next morning.'

'You believe someone's been breaking in?' McNab said.

'How else would they manage to spill crumbs on Mr Martin's waistcoat and red wine on Mr Robertson's lovely white shirt?'

McNab had been waiting to hear about disturbed clothing, maybe a semen stain, so the bread and wine had come as a surprise. 'Bread and wine?' he checked. 'Consumed over a dead body?'

'I don't know if it was actually consumed *over* the body,' said Claire, obviously a stickler for accuracy.

'But it was consumed in the vicinity of the body?' McNab tried.

She nodded, willing to accept that.

'Do you keep food and wine on the premises?' McNab asked, somehow confusing the lying in state with an Irish wake.

Claire shook her head. 'Definitely not.'

'So whoever broke in would have brought these things with them?'

'Yes.'

'Show me the photographs and then let's take a look round the premises and try and work out how our intruder gained entry.'

When Claire went to fetch her mobile, McNab took stock of his surroundings. The entire room was draped in blue velvet, which made him think of the Hollywood movie of that name in which sexual perversion and death went hand in hand. Not a comfortable thought. As for the Last Supper connotations . . .

Claire arrived as he'd reached this stage in his thoughts,

and held her mobile up for him. On the screen was an open casket in which lay an elderly man she called Mr Martin, who looked almost ruddy and definitely not dead. Wearing a tweed suit and a rather splendid red waistcoat, he cut a dashing figure. If this was Claire's work then McNab was impressed.

'Look more closely at his waistcoat,' Claire demanded, enlarging the image.

Now McNab could see the waistcoat was splattered with crumbs, some of them smeared in, turning it into a child's bib.

'I had to brush out the coffin and sponge his waistcoat down. He wasn't happy about that,' Claire declared indignantly.

She swiped the screen again and another gentleman appeared. Mr Robertson, as she referred to him, was the elder of the two, his crinkled face serenely calm. He too was smartly dressed as though about to go to a wedding, with a bright white shirt and maroon tie. The next photograph showed the damage. The shirt was ruined by splashes of a dark-red liquid, which Claire said smelt like wine.

'Obviously I had to change his shirt. I was embarrassed to tell his daughter in case she thought I did it, so I went out and bought a new white shirt, ironed it and put it on.' Claire looked distressed by the subterfuge she'd employed.

'That was kind of you,' McNab found himself reassuring her.

She looked mollified by that, then said what McNab had been thinking: 'Why would anyone do that, Detective? Why would anyone so disrespect the dead?'

McNab shook his head. 'I don't know, Claire.' He paused. 'Let's see if we can work out how they got in to start with.'

9

'Shouldn't you be in bed?' Rhona's forensic assistant, Chrissy, asked in an accusatory manner.

'I have been,' Rhona responded, without mentioning how little time she had spent there.

Chrissy regarded her with suspicion, but chose not to say anything further. An unusual occurrence for the colourful and garrulous Glasgow girl that she was.

'Coffee, strong?' she offered instead.

'Please.'

'I've sent out for two filled rolls.' Chrissy glanced at the clock. 'They shouldn't be long.' Her admission made it clear that regardless of how much time Rhona had spent with the body, Chrissy knew she would be at the lab first thing.

Five minutes later, Rhona was sitting at her desk nursing a coffee that would have made even caffeine-addict McNab's eyes water, with a breakfast roll that contained the full works – bacon, egg and black pudding topped by a potato scone.

Silence was maintained as they scoffed this particular Glasgow delicacy, Rhona's minus tomato sauce, Chrissy's with copious amounts of the stuff.

'So,' declared Chrissy after wiping the smeared ketchup from her mouth. 'What's with this body under London Road?'

As Rhona began her résumé of the previous night's proceedings, she became aware from Chrissy's expression that her assistant's personal grapevine had delivered much of this information already.

'I spoke to Janice this morning,' Chrissy admitted. 'I wanted to check when you'd finished up last night.' She gave Rhona a knowing smile. 'I believe our handsome Viking is on the job.'

'He is,' said Rhona, fully aware of Chrissy's soft spot for Magnus, his Orcadian accent in particular.

'What does the Prof have to say about it then?'

'He didn't elaborate.'

In the interim, Rhona had set up her laptop. 'Want to take a look?' she offered an eager Chrissy.

Video footage was never a substitute for being at a scene. It was like watching a documentary, rather than being a participant in the story. And an image was odourless, where smell was forensically important. Context was everything and being inside that tunnel was completely different from viewing it on a laptop screen. Nevertheless, Chrissy was engrossed. She sat in silence until the end, then asked to have it repeated.

'I've been down there,' she finally said. Chrissy pointed at the wreck. 'To see that car. It was famous, or infamous, back in the day,' she explained.

Rhona assumed Chrissy was referring to her teenage years, when, according to her assistant, she'd been intent on being more of a delinquent than her brothers, albeit briefly.

'Was the tunnel bricked up then?'

'Well, I didn't go in via that ramp,' Chrissy said, remembering. 'We used the air vent along the road near the new

Emirates stadium.' Noting Rhona's surprise and relishing it, Chrissy continued, 'Someone has to lift the heavy grid, but below there's a metal ladder leading straight down.'

'Is there another entrance apart from the vent?' Rhona asked.

'I think you used to be able to climb over the wall at the old Bridgeton Cross station, which was on that line. Don't know how accessible the London Road stretch is from there, though, and the air vent's closer to the Cosworth.'

Rhona considered whether the Cosworth itself might be significant in the death scene, other than somewhere to lay the bread and wine. 'Might the dead guy have gone down there because of the car?'

Chrissy smiled, knowing her prompting had led Rhona to that point. 'It's a possibility. You get Cosworth spotters. And he doesn't look like an Urbex to me,' she added with a further glance at the screen.

'What's an Urbex?' Rhona asked, bemused.

'An urban explorer,' Chrissy informed her.

Rhona contemplated this. If the death was a suicide, placing himself next to the car suggested it meant something to him. If it was a homicide, maybe the perpetrator lured their victim down there using the car as bait.

Chrissy was reading her thoughts, as she often did. 'So, when do we know if it's a homicide?'

'The PM's this afternoon.'

'You're going?'

'I want to know how he died,' Rhona told her.

10

Ellie hadn't slept, except for a short spell between two and four during which she'd found herself paralysed by fear, unable to move her limbs or cry out. She'd imagined herself buried alive, the roof of the tunnel she'd ridden through earlier descending relentlessly down on her. Although her mind had known it was a dream, nothing she had done could break that spell.

Plucked free at the last minute by unknown hands, her eyes had sprung open on the familiar scene of her bedroom, the light of the street lamp like a beam sent from heaven to save her.

Sweating and shaken, she'd forced her trembling body out of the bed and, heading for the kitchen, poured herself a glass of water. Even her throat seemed paralysed as she'd forced the liquid down.

The remainder of the night she'd spent in the chair wrapped in the duvet, rousing herself if she dozed, desperate not to succumb to the nightmare again.

Now, standing under the shower, she made herself face the reason for the tortured dream. No matter what she'd agreed with Izzy, she would have to tell the police what they'd found inside the tunnel. Anonymously, at least. Once she'd decided this, she felt a little easier. Then she remembered the motorcycle tracks, and Izzy's reminder that she had touched the body.

'Only his neck,' Ellie had protested. 'To look for a pulse.'

'Every contact leaves a trace,' Izzy had told her. 'Don't you watch crime dramas?' That had been Izzy's parting shot just before she'd banged the door on her way out.

Ellie looked down at her hands as though they'd become a foreign body.

'How would they know they were my prints?' she said out loud. She'd never been in trouble with the police. Had never had her prints taken. She halted there, remembering the break-in at the Harley shop just before last Christmas when three prize bikes had been stolen, and how they'd all had their prints taken to eliminate them from the enquiry.

Shit. Would her prints still be on record? She had no idea.

I could ask Michael, she thought, *but he would be bound to wonder why.*

Dressed now, she spooned coffee into the cafetière and added boiling water, her hands shaking. Reaching for the remote, she flicked on the TV. It was still on silent from last night when she'd used it as background for her traumatized state. The headlines ran along the bottom, at a speed her brain could barely assimilate, until a sudden image of Parkhead appeared, the stadium car park busy with police vehicles, crime scene tape stretched across the ramp they'd silently rolled their bikes down last night.

Ellie grabbed the remote and turned up the sound.

It took seconds for her recent plan to evaporate as the newsreader indicated that the police had been called to a tunnel at Parkhead. There was as yet no news as to why.

A sudden flash of the cold white face, seemingly frozen under her hands, brought back the terror of that moment.

They've found him.

She felt a sense of relief as she put distance between herself and that discovery. She wouldn't have to report the body now, because someone else must have done that. Then a thought, and not a pleasant one.

Had the person who reported the body been in the tunnel while they were there? Was that who had flashed the torch at her? If it had been, then they would have seen and heard the bikes. Might they think that those riding them had been responsible for the body?

From thinking she was off the hook, Ellie now realized this didn't make things better, but maybe worse. Her mobile's ring startled her even further. Glancing at the screen, she saw Izzy's name.

'They've found him,' Izzy announced triumphantly. 'So you can stop worrying.'

Izzy was fearless, but she didn't think of potential problems. Ellie wondered if she should outline them for her or just allow Izzy to stay unaware and happy. When Ellie didn't immediately respond, Izzy came back in.

'Maybe your boyfriend will keep you posted on what happens now.'

In the present uneasy situation between herself and Michael, Ellie couldn't imagine that happening, even if she asked him.

'See you later,' Izzy said brightly.

With a jolt, Ellie remembered that they were supposed to be leading out the two speedway teams at Ashfield tonight.

Masking her concern, she attempted a cheerful goodbye and ended the call.

The TV's trailing news bulletin had moved on from the

Parkhead tunnel to a scene of devastation and death somewhere else in the world. Ellie switched it off. A quick glance at her watch reminded her that if she didn't get a move on she'd be late for work. She was due at the Ink Parlour this morning and, from memory, had a client booked in for nine o'clock. On her way out the door, her mobile rang again. This time it was an unidentified caller. Ellie swiped to ignore it and, slipping her phone into her pocket, headed out of the flat.

11

> Her skin shines naked and cold, the threading of blue veins beneath the surface resembling a spider's web. The open eyes see nothing from their clouded irises. She lies on her back on the hard surface of the table, her hands resting on her breast. Around her is spread a feast, cooked meat and fowl together with ripe fruit. A decanter filled with red wine sits next to a partially eaten loaf of bread. Before all of this sits the sin-eater.

The description of the painting made Magnus's skin crawl as much as the image itself. It was this picture he'd recalled on seeing the body in the tunnel, although he hadn't told Rhona.

It had taken him hours to locate it on his return from the crime scene. His initial thinking that he had found it online had proved false, only established after much searching. At that point he'd suddenly remembered the book he'd bought when he'd been writing a paper on 'Psychology and Art'. The book of illustrations had been too tall for the shelf so he'd laid it flat on top of the bookcase.

Retrieving it, he'd placed it on his desk and began flipping through, even then unsure if it contained the image he sought.

Eventually, he'd found it. The power of the painting was as he remembered. Even now it struck him like a blow in the stomach and he almost recoiled. Rendered by an unknown artist sometime during the earlier part of the nineteenth century, it depicted a medieval sin-eater, an elderly man who sat by the body of a young woman, bread and wine clasped in his gnarled hands.

The juxtaposition of the young woman, still beautiful in death, and the ancient goblin-like creature, alive and breathing beside her, was horrible. Even more so was the idea that he was symbolically devouring her sins.

Magnus pushed his chair away from the desk, distancing himself from the disturbing image, but contemplating what it might offer to their understanding of the scene in the tunnel. The ancient concept and role of a sin-eater was found all over Europe, in both folklore and Christianity.

In former times, should someone die suddenly with no opportunity to confess their sins and therefore receive absolution, a sin-eater was required to sit with the recently deceased and partake of food and wine next to the body, symbolically consuming their sins to allow them to enter heaven.

The practice was said to have died out in the early twentieth century, although there was still evidence of it after that in the New World, in particular the remote Appalachian Mountains, probably brought there by immigrants from Europe.

A sin-eater was a necessity for a community that believed in eternal damnation, but whoever adopted the role wasn't permitted to dwell among the inhabitants. The sin-eater was essentially an outcast, usually living alone on the outer reaches of society, and called upon only when required.

No doubt a strange and lonely occupation, although in medieval times at least, a busy one, when death assiduously courted both young and old, and hell was the only alternative to absolution.

The positioning of the body in the tunnel had appeared to Magnus like the laying-out of a corpse. The nearby bread partially consumed, plus the wine, was definitely significant in some form. Those considering suicide rarely involved anyone else in the act. So the victim himself would have ritualistically partaken of the bread and wine. Something no doubt Rhona would provide proof of.

If it was a homicide, however, the bread and wine might well turn out to be the signature of the perpetrator, and perhaps provide a DNA profile of them.

Unless the perpetrator is forensically aware.

Most murders happened on the spur of the moment, usually fuelled by drink or drugs, and carried out for the very human reasons of anger, jealousy or revenge. Killers in this category, having not anticipated the outcome of their actions, had no plan as to how they would avoid detection.

An organized killer, on the other hand, had a detailed plan to follow, a logical reason for their kill, and often boasted a signature.

They wanted to make their presence known. They wanted to signal their existence. And organized killers rarely killed only once.

12

McNab accepted the mug of what he could smell was strong coffee.

'Just the way I like it,' he told Claire.

They had gone over the funeral parlour together, checking all the places that might have allowed entry by person or persons unknown. There were, to McNab's eye at least, no signs of a break-in.

'Who holds keys to the place?'

'Me and Mr Marshall.' She paused there. 'I suppose maybe the hearse drivers, but I'm not sure. You'd have to ask Mr Marshall,' Claire added, like a mantra.

McNab figured in that moment there were multiple keys among the staff. Probably spares sitting about too. It was obvious that Claire's boss trusted his workforce, and had no reason to think anyone would want to gain entry for nefarious purposes.

'When will Mr Marshall be back?' he asked.

Claire shook her head in apology. 'Maybe not until tomorrow.'

Since both the bodies involved had already gone to their eternal rest, plus the place had obviously been cleaned and polished after the said events, McNab didn't think they would discover any evidence of an intruder, not even a fingerprint. The best he could do was try to ensure it didn't happen again. He told Claire so.

'Have Mr Marshall change the locks as a precaution,' he suggested. 'And get back in touch if anything suspicious happens again.'

Claire's look of determination suggested it wouldn't if she had anything to do with it.

McNab departed the funeral parlour and looked around for the nearest place he could buy another coffee. Once ensconced in a booth with a double espresso, he contemplated what would happen next.

DI Wilson's obvious desire to keep him tethered meant that if he returned to the station, he would be given a desk job. No doubt important, but mind-bendingly boring. He appreciated the boss's efforts to keep his DS out of range of disciplinary eyes until the previous case he'd been involved in went to court, considering McNab's former pal Davey Stevenson was one of the accused.

McNab felt his anger burn fresh again at the thought of what had gone down then with Davey, and elsewhere in that investigation. He'd gone out on a limb on that one and was paying for it now.

And, he acknowledged, he'd do it all again, despite the consequences.

That thought brought back an image of Davey's wife, Mary, formerly Mary Grant, someone McNab had carried a torch for, for years. The last time he'd seen her in hospital after her accident, he'd promised to keep in touch.

I haven't kept my promise.

It would be so easy to text her now. Check how she was. Yet McNab knew he wouldn't do that, probably ever.

It's better if I stay out of her life, he thought, knowing he really meant it would be better if she stayed out of his. Still, his fingers lingered over her name on his contacts list, as though, given the slightest encouragement, they would urge him back there.

McNab set the mobile on the table and moved his thoughts back to last night – not what had happened between himself and Rhona on a personal level, but what he had viewed in the tunnel. It didn't look as though the boss was inclined to make him part of that investigation, even should it prove to be a homicide.

Unless . . .

DS Clark listened in a manner only she could. It was at times like these she reminded him of Rhona, and both women could spot drivel being spouted at a hundred yards. As Janice narrowed her eyes – not a good sign – McNab awaited her dismissal of his theory, and with it his chance of escape from a desk.

'I think you should run that past Professor Pirie.'

Fuck's sake, the Viking was already on the job?

Janice was awaiting his reaction.

McNab swithered about agreeing to do as suggested because that meant he would be in on things, the downside being he would have to listen to Magnus Pirie and whatever nonsense the so-called forensic psychologist would spout at him.

The current conversation was a result of his returning to the station from the undertaker's, and being promptly given another job he didn't want, scheduled to begin as soon as he'd filed his report on the situation at Marshall's.

A way out of this predicament had then presented itself in the form of the impatiently waiting DS Clark.

McNab tried to look on the bright side. If he did what Janice suggested, she might, with a little luck, be persuaded to go to the boss and ask for McNab's assistance on the tunnel enquiry, which would be a definite improvement on his situation.

Mustering himself, McNab nodded as though in complete agreement with her suggestion, and managed a 'will do'.

Despite his attempt at thoughtful reasonableness, he caught a gleam of amusement in Janice's eagle eye. She had seen through him without a doubt, but, he decided, he would keep up the pretence anyway. Her next remark proved his theory true.

'The PM's at two o'clock,' she said in what McNab read as a veiled invitation to tag along.

Janice knew full well his feelings on autopsies. Viewing dead bodies, however messy the circumstances, was one thing. Watching them being sliced open was another.

'I take it you're going along as SIO?' he said testily.

She nodded, waiting.

'I'll check with the Prof first,' McNab managed. 'If the timing works out, I'll be there,' he said firmly.

She gave a small smile, which suggested she'd seen right through his prevarication.

Once out of earshot, McNab made the Pirie call, his hope of getting voicemail swiftly shattered when the Viking himself answered. Not only that, he actually sounded pleased when he heard who was calling him.

'Can we meet?' McNab interrupted the ensuing attempt at pleasantries. 'It's about the guy in the tunnel. Or maybe more about his last supper.'

There followed a studied silence. McNab found himself

recalling Pirie's expression when he was forming his supposedly deep insights based on what exactly? McNab had spent the last fifteen years wading through the output generated by criminals. When he'd joined the force he already believed that evil existed. The Church had made sure of that. Humans were sinful, all of them, all the time, but some excelled at it. Nothing he'd met on the job had changed his mind about that. The soul was a dark place. His own included. He didn't require a criminal profiler to tell him that.

'When do you want to meet?' the Prof was saying.

'As soon as possible,' McNab told him.

'Okay.' Then came a pause. 'Could you come to the university? I have a lecture starting in five minutes, but we could talk immediately after that.'

McNab had no wish to visit the university. As he began his rejection, Pirie interrupted him. 'There's material here I think you should see.'

McNab had never been a student, unless the Police College at Tulliallan counted, where he'd done his training. His mother had wanted him to go to university. She'd saved up for it. The thought of constant studying, even subjects he was interested in, and good at, hadn't appealed to the teenage McNab. Or, he hadn't wanted his mother scrimping for another four years to fund him swanning around with student wankers.

Once that was decided, he'd entertained a passing interest in joining the army, having flirted with the cadets in high school. He'd enjoyed the training, but not getting bossed around. Then, when a few of his mates did join up and subsequently came back from foreign parts either in a body bag or generally fucked up, McNab had decided against the army as a career.

And so he'd joined the police, which hadn't been an all-out success, if you measured it by progress up the ranks. But it was here McNab recalled the reason why he'd stuck with it. It was undoubtedly the boss, DI Bill Wilson. The man who had faith in Professor Magnus Pirie as well as his DS.

'Okay,' McNab heard himself say.

'Come to my office.' Pirie sounded relieved – or even pleased? 'I'll see you there.'

13

The pathologist on this occasion wasn't Dr Sissons but a younger man, who Rhona didn't recognize. The larger mortuary in the new Queen Elizabeth hospital, nicknamed the Death Star by Glaswegians, could hold up to two hundred bodies in a national emergency. A super hospital, it required enough staff to service it. So it wasn't surprising to meet a new face.

Rhona wasn't sure if she was sorry it wasn't the acerbic and self-promoting Dr Sissons in charge of this one, but since two pathologists were required at an autopsy in Scotland, she wondered if he might yet show up.

In this she was right.

'Dr MacLeod,' Sissons appeared to welcome her with an arched eyebrow. 'I assume you processed the body at the scene and you now wish to know what myself and my new colleague, Dr Walker, make of it?'

Rhona found herself looking into the mischievous blue eyes of Dr Walker above the mask. It appeared the new recruit was already taking the measure of his master.

'Nice to meet you, Dr Walker,' she said formally.

'You too, Dr MacLeod.'

'Are we expecting an SIO?' Sissons queried.

It was protocol for the Senior Investigating Officer to

attend the PM of a suspicious death, so Rhona had expected to find Janice there.

'Maybe DS Clark is running late?' she suggested.

'Then let's get started,' Sissons declared, waving the team into place – the photographer who would record the proceedings in their entirety, two SOCOs to tape each item of clothing and the naked body beneath for hairs and fibres, and Dr Sissons's APT, or anatomical pathology technician, effectively his right-hand man or woman.

The mortuary was a crowded place nowadays, hence the increased spaciousness required in a new building.

Rhona recognized the majority of suited figures in the room, except for the APT. Expecting Ronnie's solid figure and brown eyes, she found a taller, blue-eyed replacement instead, who gave her a swift nod before moving on to his duties.

As the body was gradually unclothed, Rhona was immediately struck by how perfect it was. Used as she was to viewing death as the outcome of a violent attack, the image before her was of someone who had simply fallen asleep, reflecting the impression she'd had in the tunnel.

She listened as Sissons recorded the formal measurements, giving the victim's estimated age at mid to late twenties, then detailing the sex, build, height, ethnic group, weight, nutritional state and skin colour of the subject.

'No obvious scars or wounds,' Sissons said. 'The only identifiable marks are a one-inch-thick black tattooed band on the left lower arm and a similar one round the right thigh.'

'You'll find they all seem to have tattoos these days,' Sissons informed Dr Walker. 'These, I have to say, are plainer than I'm used to seeing. What about you, Doctor?'

Rhona watched as the young doctor tried to read the question. Was his superior asking if he had a tattoo or if everyone he examined had? Rhona smothered a smile behind her mask and decided to help him out. 'It's a popular past-time being inked,' she offered.

'Ah,' Sissons said. 'Is Dr MacLeod admitting to having one too?'

Rhona didn't answer, but she did acknowledge Dr Walker's silent thank you.

'So,' Sissons said, looking to his co-worker. 'What Dr MacLeod really wants to know is how did he die? And whether it is a homicide or a suicide.'

Dr Walker glanced over at Rhona, as if expecting her to respond, which she didn't. One thing he would swiftly learn was that although the chief forensic pathologist often asked questions out loud, he seldom welcomed answers to them.

'There was no evidence of drugs in the vicinity of the body?' Sissons said, this time seeking an answer.

'None,' Rhona told him.

At that point the door opened and a suited figure, who wasn't Janice, entered. Rhona recognized the figure immediately, and the eyes above the mask proved her right.

'Sorry I'm late,' McNab offered on approach.

A lesser man would have flinched at the look Sissons shot him, but not McNab.

'We were expecting DS Clark,' Sissons said.

'She sends her apologies.'

The sound Sissons made indicated the substitution wasn't to his liking, but he could do little about it, other than ignore the newcomer.

McNab took up his place alongside Dr Walker and sensibly

kept quiet, not even attempting to catch Rhona's eye. Dr Walker, no doubt sensing the animosity that had recently entered the circle, focused solely on his boss.

A wise move, Rhona thought.

'You've studied the photographs.' Sissons addressed Walker again. 'Context is everything. The layout of the limbs, the positioning of the body, where it was lying.' He looked to Rhona. 'In your opinion, was it the deposition site or the site of the assault?' he said, studying the pattern of lividity on the body, which could point either way.

Rhona explained about the soil on the soles of the victim's shoes. 'It looks like material from the tunnel floor, but that's still to be verified by a soil scientist.'

'So you think he walked in there?'

'It's a probability.'

'Have we any idea why?'

At Rhona's mention of the car, Sissons's eyes lit up. 'An old Cosworth, how interesting. Might have to take a look myself.'

He was taking swabs now, first the perineal skin, then the anus was probed by a proctoscope. Sensing Rhona's eyes on him, McNab grued behind his mask. He'd admitted to her once that watching that being done had the same effect on him as eyeballs being popped out.

'You found no evidence of a sexual encounter?'

'I detected no semen on the clothes, the face or the mouth,' Rhona responded.

'So it doesn't look as though he was down there to have sex, although as we know, locations such as that offer a certain frisson for some.'

McNab's eyes suggested he might unwisely comment on this, so Rhona deflected that possibility.

'There was a piece of partially eaten bread and a glass of red wine on a napkin on the rear seat of the Cosworth,' she said.

Sissons acknowledged that he'd noted this on the video recording of the scene. 'I'm not equipped to comment on the psychology behind that feature. However, if our subject did partake of this last supper shortly before his demise, we'll find evidence of it in his stomach contents.' He paused. 'But, before we cut him open, let's see if we can discover if either poison or drugs could have entered his system in another manner.'

Rhona dropped the oversuit in the receptacle provided and headed for a cubicle. The scent of death was hard to get rid of and the sooner you tried, the better.

Standing under a hot shower, she registered that what had happened in the mortuary had likely given the police enough evidence to progress the case as a homicide, although there might still be room for dispute. It wasn't always the case that a pathologist's verdict on a death matched that of the police investigation.

McNab had stayed to watch the stomach contents being examined, keen as he was to find out if there was any evidence that the subject had partaken of the Last Supper.

It seemed he hadn't.

According to Dr Sissons, the victim hadn't eaten solids close to his death and certainly not that bread. So it was likely that a person or persons unknown had consumed the bread at the scene, and probably drank some of the wine.

Perhaps that same someone had used the injection site they'd discovered in the back of the left thigh. Difficult to distinguish in the band of black ink, and only spotted by an eagle-eyed Dr Walker.

Dried and dressed now, Rhona made a swift call to Chrissy to let her know the news. When she emerged from the changing room, McNab was waiting for her.

'I don't know how you wangled coming here, McNab,' she began before he interrupted her, his voice as testy as her own.

'DS Clark asked me to attend the PM because of what transpired at my meeting with Professor Pirie,' he declared.

Why the hell were you meeting Magnus? Rhona's expression clearly said. After a moment she added, out loud this time, 'Well?'

'There's been an incident that might be linked to this case, and Magnus agrees,' McNab added for effect. 'Can we get a coffee and I'll explain?'

14

'I have to give a lecture on the diploma course in less than an hour,' Rhona told him.

Catching her expression, McNab said quietly, 'Look, can we put what happened last night behind us? Please.'

He could feel the nerve twitching just below his right eye, a sign of a lack of caffeine or the fact that everything about sitting here with her was freaking him out.

'Then stop stalking me.'

'I'm not,' McNab said, baffled by the accusation.

'Then why come to the tunnel? DS Clark was given responsibility for that. Yet you turned up, knowing that was where I was headed.'

He couldn't deny that. He had no business following her there. Despite this, he came out fighting.

'Just as well I did.' McNab laid his mobile in front of her. 'I was called out to Marshall's Funeral Home this morning. The girl there, Claire, thinks someone's been tampering with their bodies. Eating bread and drinking wine over them.' McNab flipped the image from the crumb-covered waistcoat of Mr Martin, deceased, to the wine-soaked white shirt belonging to Mr Robertson.

Rhona took control of the mobile and had another look at both images.

'Are the bodies still in the funeral parlour?' she finally said.

'Unfortunately not. One's buried, the other cremated. Anyway, according to Claire, she cleaned them up, even changed Mr Robertson's shirt before his daughter saw it.'

'Does she still have the shirt?' Rhona said swiftly. When McNab didn't answer, Rhona came back in. 'Call her and see if she has.'

McNab did as she asked, knowing he should have checked that himself. Maybe if he'd seen the painting earlier he would have.

It was Claire's voice that answered. 'Sergeant McNab. Did you find the man?' McNab didn't correct her on her assumption that it had been a man, but asked her about the stained shirt. There was a moment's silence that felt like embarrassment.

'I do,' she finally said. 'I was planning on putting it in the laundry and giving it to a charity shop. It was very good quality,' she added. 'I can't really give it back to his daughter, because then she would know.'

'But you haven't washed it yet?' McNab checked.

'No. It's in a bag here at the shop.'

'I'll come and pick it up.'

When he rang off he could tell by Rhona's face that she didn't require an explanation. 'It's a long shot forensically,' he offered as way of an excuse.

Not a wise move, he realized, as Rhona gave him a look that suggested he should know better.

'And this is why you met with Magnus?' she asked.

'Janice suggested I did, and at that point she hadn't seen this.' McNab flipped forward to a new image and offered back the mobile. He gave Rhona a moment to study the painting before he said, 'It's called *The Sin-eater*. The old guy fucking eats your sins. I must say I prefer that way of getting to heaven, rather than through abstinence or the confessional,' he added.

Rhona didn't acknowledge either the title, the explanation for it or McNab's attempt at a joke, but continued to study the picture intently. McNab could almost hear her brain working.

He waited as long as his patience would allow. 'Well?' he said. 'That's too weird to be a coincidence, don't you think?'

'I have to get to my lecture,' Rhona said. 'Can you bring the shirt to the lab? I'll warn Chrissy it's coming.'

McNab agreed, noting as she rose in preparation to leave that he didn't want her to go. She'd accused him of stalking her. He wasn't. Well, not physically anyway, but she was on his mind a lot.

Heading for his car, McNab castigated himself yet again for what had happened the previous night. Things between him and Dr MacLeod had seen a slight improvement since the Stonewarrior case. He'd even managed to blot the reason for their major fall-out from his mind, but he was never sure that Rhona had. It was like a big black mark on his copy book. One that she might try to live with, but that she would never forgive him for.

'Fuck it!' he said for the umpteenth time as he forced his way into the line of traffic, incurring the wrath of the car immediately behind.

Claire was waiting for him in the reception area, a worried look on her face.

'This won't be in the papers?' she said. 'Mr Marshall wouldn't like that. And I don't want Mr Robertson's family to find out that someone did that to him.'

'No,' McNab promised, taking the bag she offered. 'But I'd keep this between you and your boss.'

A flicker of further concern crossed her face.

'You've told someone else?' McNab said.

'My boyfriend,' she admitted. 'I had to talk to someone about it. It was Taylor who made me tell Mr Marshall and you.'

'Taylor sounds like a sensible bloke, but tell him not to share the story with anyone else.'

She gave him a searching look. 'The person who did this, have they done something else?'

McNab considered how long it would be before the tunnel murder hit the headlines. Not long, he suspected. Once it did, the press would have a field day with the Last Supper references. As for the sin-eater . . .

'Let's just concentrate on what they did to Mr Martin and Mr Robertson,' McNab said.

Claire seemed placated by this and gave him a firm nod. 'Okay.'

McNab threw the bag onto the passenger seat and jumped in the car. As he headed for the lab and Chrissy, he contemplated how long the story of the shirt and the funeral parlour would go unmarked by the tabloids, knowing it wouldn't matter whether there was a direct connection with the tunnel death or not. Claire, he suspected, was about to discover how persistent the press could be.

15

The place is packed. It always is when she gives a lecture. I never miss one of hers, nor the guest appearances by the Professor of Forensic Psychology. He has an amazingly soothing voice. I can imagine him interviewing me, probing my secrets.

Know your enemy.

If I know how he thinks, then I know how to thwart him.

As for her, it's all down to knowing the science. Which is the reason I'm here.

As she enters, I feel a frisson of pleasure. It's interesting that I haven't yet involved sex in my project. Nor a female subject. But it's early days.

I was expecting more on the tunnel death on the news before coming here, but there was no detail as yet, which was disappointing. Then I remembered, when discussing her work at a crime scene, she clearly stated that she might be up to twelve hours with the body before it was removed to the mortuary.

I picture her in the forensic tent in the tunnel. Did she find what I left for her? There had been the possibility that she wouldn't be the one they called out to the scene. So I followed her to make sure.

And saw her with the detective.

That image comes to mind, unsettling me, but I dismiss it as she approaches the lectern. The voices around me dissipate, and I focus entirely on her. Notebook open, ready to begin.

16

Rhona realized as she opened the door that, though often in a mortuary, she had never been inside a funeral parlour before, even when she'd been arranging the burial of her parents.

Jamie McColl, the latest McColl to work in the family business, had come to their cottage on Skye to discuss the arrangements for the last funeral, her father's. He'd sat in the kitchen with a mug of coffee and they'd exchanged stories. Even laughed at some of the memories of her parents that they both shared.

'My father sends his condolences,' Jamie had said. 'I hope you don't mind, but I asked to be the one to come, seeing as we know one another from way back.'

'I'm glad you did.'

She and Jamie had spent many holidays in each other's company when her family had come to the cottage during the summer months from Glasgow. They'd shared shifts in a local cafe. Swum together off the nearby beach and got drunk among the rocks.

The tall gangly youth back then had become a handsome, steady man, Rhona acknowledged.

If I hadn't met Edward at university, things might have been different.

'You vowed that last summer that you'd do anything

rather than become an undertaker,' Rhona had reminded him.

'I did, didn't I?' he'd said with a smile. 'I was so keen to leave the island, never to return. You told me I was lucky to live here. We fell out about it, as I recall. I stayed, but you stopped coming back?'

He'd waited then, hoping for an explanation, and Rhona had almost told him. How she'd got pregnant and hidden it from her parents. How she'd given Liam up for adoption immediately after his birth.

In that moment with an old friend, when her guard was down, and she'd been distraught at having denied her parents the right to know that they'd had a grandchild, Rhona had almost revealed her most closely guarded secret to Jamie.

Even now, she could picture his expression, knowing she wanted to tell him something important, but not pushing her.

Then the moment had passed, *although the guilt never had*.

Past sins rarely do, Rhona said inwardly, thinking again of the recent scenario with McNab.

'May I help you?'

The young woman who'd appeared from behind the draped velvet curtains fitted McNab's description of Claire, whom he'd interviewed. Rhona was struck immediately by her pleasant voice and demeanour. Whoever had given her the job of working with the bereaved had made the right choice.

'Claire?' Rhona said to make sure.

When the girl, a little surprised by the rendition of her name, nodded, Rhona introduced herself, an act which brought a flush of concern to the young woman's face.

'I gave the shirt to Sergeant McNab.'

'Yes,' Rhona said. 'Thank you for that.'

It was obvious by the girl's expression that she couldn't imagine, having done so, why Rhona should be there at all.

Rhona's decision to come had been fired by the lecture she'd just given. They had been concentrating on Locard's principle, *Every contact leaves a trace*. Although everyone in that room had some rudimentary knowledge of the principle and what it meant in practice, few were aware of how all-encompassing it could be.

'I wanted to chat to you about the incidents you reported to DS McNab,' she explained.

Claire was examining her. After a moment, she said, 'Has something else happened?'

It was unlikely that the fuller details of the tunnel death would escape the evening news, although the signature feature of bread and wine definitely wouldn't be one of them.

'I'm here because of what happened to your . . .' Rhona hesitated, unsure what term to use for the victims.

'My charges,' Claire saved her. 'For the short period they're with me, I think of them as in my care.' At this point she appeared to come to a decision. 'It's probably better if we go through to the viewing room where it all happened. There's no one due to come in and, if someone does, they'll ring the bell on the desk.

'I told Sergeant McNab a fib when he asked if I'd laundered the shirt,' Claire volunteered, almost as soon as they were ensconced in the heavy-draped silence of the viewing room.

Rhona waited, sensing her discomfort at having to admit to this.

'I did try to get the stain out by rubbing it under running water,' she explained. 'It didn't work, so I gave up.'

The look on Claire's face indicated how traumatic that had been for her. It could also affect what forensics they might retrieve from the shirt, but Rhona didn't mention that, instead asking, 'How did you clean up the crumbs?'

'I tried brushing them up, but some landed in the coffin.' She pulled a face. 'I eventually had to hoover them out.'

Rhona's spirits lifted a little. 'You used a vacuum cleaner?'

Claire nodded. 'A hand-held one from my car.'

'Have you emptied it since?'

Claire indicated she hadn't. 'I hardly ever use it. I'm not fussy about my car.'

Internally, Rhona gave a cheer at that news.

'What about the brush?'

'It's here, in the back.'

'Can I see them?'

Keen to show willing, Claire disappeared and returned with the said items.

The brush was of soft bristle, and from a quick glance, Rhona could see crumbs among the hairs. She carefully slipped it into an evidence bag.

The vacuum, she indicated, she would take intact.

Rhona stowed the items in the boot of her car, pleased now that she had visited and spoken with Claire. It wouldn't be the first time she'd extracted valuable forensic material from a vacuum cleaner or a brush.

As she drove to the lab, she contemplated what Claire had said as she'd departed. It was something that had occurred to Rhona too.

'I don't think either the mess of crumbs or the spilling

of the wine was an accident,' she'd said. 'Someone wanted me to know they'd been here.'

Rhona was inclined to agree.

17

'What is it between you and McNab?' Chrissy asked on Rhona's return to the lab.

'You mean apart from all the times he's pissed me off?' Rhona tried to make light of the question.

'Apart from that,' Chrissy challenged.

'Nothing,' Rhona lied.

'Yeah.' Chrissy shot her a disbelieving look. 'If you don't tell me, I bet he will.'

By that statement, Rhona guessed Chrissy had had no luck so far, which meant McNab was keeping as silent as she was. She changed the subject by asking about the shirt.

Chrissy, registering this, seemed to accept defeat, but, Rhona thought, it would only be for the moment.

'McNab delivered it and gave me the backstory. Is there a chance the funeral parlour was a practice run for the real thing?'

It was a possibility.

'How are you doing with the body evidence?' Rhona said.

'Come see,' Chrissy ordered, her face lighting up.

Chrissy had been examining the mix of both individual and class evidence Rhona had removed from the victim's clothing and exposed skin. Individual items such as fingerprints, DNA and footwear impressions had a high probability of being linked to one source. Class evidence like hair and fibres had common characteristics, although uniqueness might be found in wear or stain patterns on the fibres from clothing items.

Rhona settled down at the microscope. 'What am I looking at?'

'The fibre taken from his nostril. Wait till you see what it's come from.'

It took some moments for Rhona to register the reason for Chrissy's excitement.

The fibre on view had been built in such a manner that it wouldn't shed easily. In fact, the material it had come from was designed that way, with an outer coating preventing this.

However, should the integrity of the inner side become compromised, such as coming into contact with sharp stones like the ballast in the tunnel, fibres from the exposed cut *might* become detached.

Which had obviously happened in this case.

'I checked it against the fibre database,' Chrissy said, before Rhona could ask. 'It's definitely what we think it is.' She made a 'wow' face at Rhona. 'How the hell did that get there?'

Up to now, they were tending towards the locus being the assault site. Now Rhona wasn't so sure. And if they were right about the source of the fibre, it changed everything.

Chrissy was watching her, following Rhona's thought process, verbalizing it for her.

'The soil samples on his shoes suggested he walked through the tunnel,' she reminded Rhona.

True, but as yet unconfirmed. And there were other ways the soil could have got on his soles.

'What if the car in the tunnel wasn't the assault site, but the deposition site?'

It was the question Rhona was asking herself.

And, if so, what part had a forensic suit played in either scenario?

18

Unbeknown to Rhona, McNab had caught the latter part of her earlier lecture. She was, McNab had decided, as impressive at the lectern as she was at a crime scene. And she had her fan boys and girls, by the reaction of the audience.

He'd also realized, while scanning the crowd from his place at the back, that pretty well everyone in the audience was younger than him – which had been a dispiriting thought. There had been, he'd noticed, a fair percentage of police officers in the sixty-odd crowd, plus other professionals who worked alongside them.

The diploma course was open to law-and-order professionals and members of the general public, so there would be a scattering of folk in here who just fancied knowing more about forensics. The university's reasoning behind this being that anyone might end up on a jury and be presented with forensic evidence by both defence and prosecution. To understand that evidence, it helped to have some basic knowledge of the subject.

McNab held quite the opposite view. Knowledge was power and it was difficult enough to catch criminals without them knowing as much about the art of detection as he did.

He was even further convinced of this in the area of forensic psychology, which, according to Janice, was just as popular with the general public. Who needed psychopathic nutters learning how to avoid being recognized as such?

Then there were all the crime dramas on TV. He'd never watched any of them, but there were always folk in work discussing the latest one, usually round the coffee machine. DS Clark was a fan of foreign stuff in particular and had tried to get him interested. *No fucking chance.* As far as McNab was concerned, the previous case involving Norwegian Inspector Alvis Olsen was enough foreign crime for him.

Although, McNab silently acknowledged, *I do owe Janice.* If she hadn't spoken to the boss on his behalf, he would have been frozen out of the groundwork on this case and been spending his time in front of a computer screen.

Not that folk who did that weren't important.

As though on cue, a text came in from Ollie in IT, who McNab liked to think of as his own personal screen watcher. It seemed that Ollie of the owl-sized eyes and keen appetite wanted a word with him. McNab thought to ignore the request at first, but Ollie was both an asset and someone who'd put himself on the line for McNab on more than one occasion, so McNab texted back with a promise that he would come by soon, but he had another appointment to deal with first.

There was a sudden burst of laughter from the audience, the reason for which he'd missed in his engagement with the mobile.

She has them in the palm of her hand, he thought as silence fell again and Rhona continued with her talk.

Why exactly he'd come here, McNab wasn't certain, although it hadn't been to learn more about bloody forensics. He'd been delivering the wine-stained shirt to Chrissy at the lab, as ordered by Dr MacLeod, and found himself not that far from the building where the lecture theatre was.

If Chrissy knew I was here, had been his next thought.

Rhona's forensic assistant had already given him a grilling about 'what was going on with him and Rhona'. For a brief moment, McNab had thought Rhona might have told Chrissy what had happened the previous evening, then dismissed it.

Once Rhona gave her word . . .

McNab had brushed Chrissy's concerns aside with a *Fuck all,* although he wasn't sure she'd bought that, and had switched to the sin-eater story, which Chrissy had eagerly lapped up.

Suddenly realizing Rhona was bringing her lecture to a close, McNab now moved swiftly towards the exit. Due to present himself in DI Wilson's office in twenty minutes, he had no wish to blot his copy book by being late.

Making his way back to the car through a throng of undergraduates, McNab noted that this was the second time in one day he'd had to endure being among Glasgow's student population. That morning, at the rival Strathclyde campus, when he'd been waiting for the professor, and now here.

He'd arrived at the earlier gig in just enough time to witness Pirie pontificating about the psychological approaches to lie detection. It seemed that the detection of lies was a skilled and rare talent. Something that McNab actually agreed with.

It was the statement that had followed that he'd taken umbrage at. According to Ekman's Theory of Detection, experienced police officers were no better than the general public at detecting lies, and no better than new recruits. Since that was in essence his job as a detective, and he also thought he was rather good at it, that statement had pissed off McNab.

Pirie of course had greeted him in his usual pleasant but searching manner. It was the role of a policeman to believe everyone guilty until proved innocent. McNab always had the impression Pirie was doing the same with him. Rhona had once compared them to stags at bay and she wasn't far wrong. McNab wasn't sure exactly where his own antagonism came from. Pirie had messed up spectacularly on his first case, but the boss had forgiven him that, so why couldn't he?

It wasn't as though he always got it right.

Just as Pirie had invited McNab to follow him to his office, a blonde female undergraduate had approached. McNab had tried not to be jealous of the way she'd looked at the Viking. He might be her professor, but there was little doubt that she fancied him like mad. Magnus, seemingly oblivious to this, had swiftly answered her question, then led McNab on, without comment.

Whereas a normal bloke would have at least shared a joke about it, McNab had decided. That thought had been swiftly followed by another, more honest one. *Maybe I'm just jealous of his magnetic attraction.*

That attraction had been further demonstrated by two more interruptions en route to the office, both female, both encounters playing out in a similar manner.

At that point McNab had realized that he'd never seen Pirie with a female on his arm, although he was pretty sure the Prof fancied Rhona, which in all honesty was probably the real reason for his own dislike of the man.

'In here.' Pirie had broken that train of thought by ushering McNab into his office and flicking on a sign that said he was busy and not to be disturbed.

McNab had been at Pirie's flat on a previous occasion to discuss a case, but he'd never been in his place of work before.

All places of learning made McNab uncomfortable and Pirie's office was no exception. A quick scan of the bookshelves, filled with titles like the one Pirie had quoted from in his lecture, had just served to irritate him further.

Pirie's offer of a strong coffee had eased things a little. McNab had drunk his swiftly and requested a refill before they got down to business.

After that things had become interesting. McNab's own disquiet at the sin-eater image had been surpassed by Pirie's reaction to Claire's photographs of Mr Martin and Mr Robertson.

'How long before the discovery of the tunnel body did these attacks happen?' had been Magnus's immediate response.

'They occurred on two adjacent nights, three days before the body was reported.'

'Who was first?'

'Mr Martin with the bread,' McNab had told him. 'Claire cleaned that up, but didn't tell her employer. Then came the wine found on Mr Robertson.'

'Spilt on purpose to ensure she had to report it,' Pirie had said almost to himself.

'Whoever did it wanted Claire to call us?' McNab said.

'I suspect so.'

DI Wilson didn't look up as McNab entered, which might or might not be a bad sign. His relationship with the boss was a turbulent one, on McNab's side at least. Most officers complained about their superiors; few did about this man. He was regarded as the bulwark between those below and those above. He had certainly proved to be McNab's defence on more occasions than one.

DI Wilson's compassionate leave while attending his dying wife had, McNab realized, left him like a boat without its rudder, which signalled that if, or when, the boss gave up or retired, McNab would have to change his own modus operandi. That meant either leaving the force to become a security guy or maybe returning to undercover work, where it was easier to do your own thing.

With that abiding thought, he realized the boss wasn't ignoring him, but was engrossed by whatever was on his laptop screen. He turned it towards McNab to reveal the images of Mr Martin and Mr Robertson side by side in their coffins.

'I want you to follow up any leads on the break-ins at the funeral parlour. Speak to the families, find out if there was any reason these two men were targeted.'

McNab opened his mouth then shut it again. To do what the boss was asking would involve revealing what had happened to the deceased's families and put Claire in the firing line, which he had led Claire to believe wouldn't happen.

'Well, Sergeant?'

The boss listened as McNab explained about the shirt, the clean-up operation and Claire's role in all of this, but it was clear from his expression that what McNab had said changed nothing.

'Professor Pirie believes there's a strong possibility of a connection between whoever was involved in the tunnel death and events at the undertaker's. He'll outline this at the strategy meeting tomorrow morning. Find out everything you can before then.'

The final remark was both an order and a dismissal. McNab hesitated but only for a second before saying 'Yes, sir' as though he meant it.

DI Wilson held him with a commander's eye. 'And don't disappear on me this time, Sergeant.'

19

McNab, feeling very much the interloper, joined a sea of Tigers fans walking swiftly from the parking lot to the nearby stadium. He'd been lucky to get one of the last parking spaces available. If he'd arrived any later, he would have had to seek a spot somewhere in the surrounding streets and probably would have missed Ellie's ride-out.

Most of the fans obviously held season tickets, because there was virtually no queue at the box office. McNab paid up and headed inside past a shop full of red regalia and a neat little bar, busy with punters buying their pint for the match.

McNab passed by reluctantly, because downing a pint would have helped him face the prospect of meeting Ellie again. He'd spent the time between his interview with the boss and coming here looking for excuses not to turn up. Why? Because he was a coward where relationships were concerned.

Yet here I am.

McNab found himself a second-row place next to a pillar and texted Ellie that he'd arrived, muttering under his breath that it was too late to back out now.

The stadium, he noted, was pretty full, the atmosphere friendly. Plenty of families, he guessed, as he surveyed those around him, and an almost even split of women and men. Something you didn't see at a football match.

McNab had been a keen Celtic supporter as a teenager, hence his knowledge of the area round Paradise, but once he became a police officer he'd stopped going to matches, because, when there, he couldn't pretend not to be an officer of the law, especially when he ran up against arses.

No problem with that here, he thought.

There was a crowd of kids on the centre grass taking part in some sort of running game. Regardless of who won, it seemed they all got sweeties. McNab began to relax.

Hey, this wasn't so bad.

Once the kids all got back to their parents in the stand, the loudspeaker announced that the Harley-Davidson girls would lead out the teams. Six Harleys appeared in the far right corner and over the megaphone came the riders' names. First up was Ellie. Seeing her roar onto the track, McNab relived the moment when he'd first learned she was a biker chick, and suddenly remembered how lucky he was.

You're a prick, he told himself as a cheer went up from the crowd on Ellie's approach to the main stand. Caught up in the excitement, McNab waved wildly and bawled her name as she waved back to the crowd.

'Ellie, as you all know, is the daughter of Tiger veteran Willie Macmillan.'

This announcement was greeted by an even bigger roar of approval, signifying Ellie's father's fame, which resurrected McNab's doubts about being here.

Next time round the circuit brought the speedway riders themselves, kicking up a shower of shale against the barriers as their uncovered back wheels swung round the bend in the circuit. When the scent of ethanol hit his nostrils,

McNab questioned why the fuck he'd never tried out a bike like that for himself.

Then Ellie was back for her second circuit. All six female riders were waving to the fans and McNab was pretty certain Ellie had spotted him beside his pillar, then realized that the guy in front of him was blowing her a kiss.

Fuck that!

McNab stepped down alongside the guy for a closer look. He was about the same height as McNab, had a build that suggested he worked out, a hipster beard and the usual haircut to go with it.

'You a friend of Ellie's?' McNab said, putting the emphasis definitely on *friend*.

The guy looked as though he might take offence at McNab's belligerent tone, then changed tack.

'Wish I was, mate,' he smiled. 'I take it you are?' When McNab nodded, he added, 'Lucky man.'

The Harleys were leaving the arena. McNab kept an eye on his mobile, hoping there would soon be a response from Ellie to his earlier text. When there wasn't, he sent another urging her to meet him in the shop.

Ten minutes later, with no response from either of his attempts, he began castigating himself.

You've messed up, mate. Big time.

Shouldering his way through the crowd keenly watching the first race, McNab headed for the bar, empty now of punters. He would have gladly ordered a beer, but settled instead for a large black coffee. He'd fucked up enough, he decided, without resorting to drink as well.

'Michael.'

McNab turned at her voice. She was still in her leathers, her face flushed with either excitement or embarrassment.

'You were great,' McNab immediately said. 'I was waving like mad.'

She gave a small smile that didn't reach her eyes.

'Can we talk?' McNab was aware his own voice held a pleading tone.

'Let's go out front,' she said, making for the door that led to the entrance area.

McNab followed, rehearsing his words in his head, realizing they wouldn't sound any better when said out loud.

She'd loosened her hair, which had been tied up under her helmet, and it now hung round her face. She looked, he thought, lovely and fearful.

Was she afraid of him? Why?

'I only have a few minutes,' she said.

'I'll stay,' McNab offered. 'And meet you at the end.'

She was struggling with this. He could see that on her face.

'There's a get-together afterwards. My dad . . .' She trailed to a halt.

'Okay,' he said cautiously, registering the fact that she didn't want him there. 'What about tomorrow night? We could get something to eat.'

'I thought you'd be working,' she blurted out. 'I . . . I saw the news. The guy in the tunnel?'

So the discovery was out there. McNab fell silent, wondering if that's what had frightened her.

'I'm not involved in that,' he fibbed.

'Oh.' She looked relieved.

'So we on for tomorrow night?'

As she considered her response, a girl appeared behind her. Also dressed in leathers, he assumed she too had been one of the lead-out riders.

'Hey, Ellie. Is this your policeman?' A pair of green eyes sized McNab up. 'Aren't you going to introduce us?'

Ellie didn't look as though she wanted to do that, so McNab helped.

'Michael McNab,' he offered with a smile. 'But don't tell the entire world I'm a cop,' he whispered.

'Izzy McElroy,' she offered, accepting his proffered hand.

Ellie made a point of checking her watch. 'We'd better go,' she told Izzy. 'I'll ring you later,' she promised McNab as she whisked the bold Izzy away, leaving McNab a little puzzled by their interchange.

Ellie had clearly not wanted a meeting between himself and Izzy. That had been obvious enough by the look she'd worn from the moment her pal had arrived.

McNab hadn't considered that maybe having a police officer as a boyfriend wasn't as acceptable as Ellie had initially made out.

Well, you thought you were about to get dumped. Seems you were right.

McNab heard a roar as the race finished. Someone had won here, but it definitely wasn't him.

'Shut up,' Ellie said under her breath. 'Just shut the fuck up, Izzy.'

Izzy adopted a belligerent look, but didn't do as requested. 'You need to stick with him. Find out what they're doing about the bike tracks down there.'

'He won't tell me,' Ellie insisted. 'He's a fucking detective and I don't fuck someone to get their secrets.'

'No, but you got me to fuck someone for their keys.'

'It was your idea,' Ellie reminded Izzy.

'You wanted to race down there.'

This was going nowhere. Ellie tried to still her trembling hands. She should have ignored McNab's request to meet in the shop. She should have broken it off, not stalled him until tomorrow night. It was Izzy's arrival that had prevented her.

Ellie walked away, afraid she'd say even more to regret later. Izzy was a friend. A long-time friend. They shared history. They shared a love of bikes. Izzy would be there long after McNab had gone. And he would go. Ellie knew that. The job was everything to him. And the job would win, every time.

We were lucky to get this far.

Admitting she'd been in the tunnel and had seen the body would only hasten things, even if she'd said they'd intended calling it in, only to discover someone else had. Michael always played the detective, even when he was trying not to. He assumed everyone was lying until they were proved innocent.

And she wasn't innocent.

20

Stanley Robertson's last abode had been with his loving daughter and her husband.

Harry Martin, on the other hand, hadn't been so lucky. It seemed he'd spent his final years in a council-run nursing home.

Having been summarily dismissed by Ellie, McNab had driven to the Eventide Home, mindful of the boss's orders to be prepared for tomorrow's strategy meeting. At the home he'd learned that Harry had been 'a crotchety old bugger' who'd proved difficult to please. He also hadn't mixed well, thinking himself above the other residents because, according to Harry at least, he had a millionaire son living in Hong Kong.

'Who, sad to say, didn't care about his father,' had been the verdict of the young Polish nurse McNab had spoken to.

Aleksandra had made McNab a strong coffee and they'd sat in her office where she'd seemed happy to answer his questions concerning Harry.

'He didn't get visitors or phone calls. When I contacted his son to tell him Harry was dead, he said that was a shame and asked us to organize the funeral, as he wouldn't be coming back for it. I was the only one there,' she added, 'apart from that nice girl from the undertaker's. She was quite upset.'

McNab could see Claire doing that. Kind to the end and way beyond the call of duty.

He had explained about the break-in and asked if Harry had had any enemies.

'Harry pissed people off with his superior manner,' she said, 'but in truth he did it because he was lonely.' She'd smiled a sweet smile at McNab then and added, 'Most people are, you know.'

At another time, McNab would have asked for her mobile number. Even as he left, he'd wished he had. After all, he reasoned, he was about to get dumped.

I can always call back, he consoled himself.

The Robertson story proved to be the opposite of Harry's.

Stanley had lived out his final years in the bosom of his family, or at least in the grandpa flat they'd had built for him. When McNab apologized for visiting in the evening, Stanley's daughter had dismissed his concerns, more interested in talking about her father than the reason for McNab's appearance.

'We miss him every day,' she told McNab, tears welling in her eyes.

At this sight, McNab wondered again how he might raise the subject he'd come about. How did you say that some fucker messed with your dad while he lay in his coffin? Any idea who that might be?

They were seated in Stanley's small sitting room surrounded by framed photographs of his late wife, his three children and numerous grandchildren.

'We're investigating a break-in at the funeral parlour around the time your father and another gentleman were there,' McNab began. Before she could react, he hurried on. 'We believe it had something to do with the other man,' he lied, 'but we have to check with you about your dad.'

As her face creased in concern, McNab continued before she could ask for details.

'Can you think of anyone who might have held a grudge against your father?'

'A grudge?' She looked horrified. 'God, no. He was the kindest of men.'

McNab was on a hiding to nowhere here and knew it.

The daughter was thinking, perhaps dredging up memories she'd rather forget. McNab waited, mildly hopeful.

Then she shook her head.

'No,' she repeated. 'My dad made a point of not falling out with anyone.'

There was, McNab realized, no one here willing to speak ill of the dead.

'Did he go out much?' he tried, hoping for some connection outside the family circle.

'He wasn't that mobile. He did a lot on his laptop – free courses in subjects that interested him.'

'Such as?'

She wrinkled her brow. 'The courses the university offered. MOOCs he called them,' she added, obviously having no idea what that meant, much like McNab himself.

'Do you still have his laptop?' he asked, wondering if Stanley's blame-free life was as good as stated.

'I do.' She rose and went to a desk near the window, extracting a laptop from the drawer.

'May I take this with me? Just to check,' McNab said.

She hesitated, then nodded. 'You will bring it back?'

'Of course.'

'What about the other man?'

'We're asking the same questions of his family.'

McNab parked his car at the flat and walked back to the pizza place, deciding for once to sit in and eat rather than order a takeaway.

He'd been avoiding an evening alone in the flat with nothing but his thoughts. Something that had been happening increasingly of late. It was always the same at this stage of a relationship. The moment when he began to withdraw, or she did.

He should be used to it by now, because it always played out the same way.

And whose fault is that?

At least the job didn't change. It never improved and it often got worse, but it was always there and he knew how to do it. At moments like these McNab understood perfectly why men might be drawn to join the forces. There the path was mapped out for you, and you could put personal stuff on the back burner until you came back. Or maybe forever.

'Detective Sergeant McNab. Long time no see.'

Marco had spotted him from the kitchen and had come to the counter, behind which the pizza bases were being stretched and hand-spun by a young guy who was obviously showing off to a group of girls nearby.

'No home delivery tonight?' he queried.

'I fancied eating in style,' McNab said, indicating a nearby booth, one of the few that were unoccupied.

'Of course.' Marco waved him in. 'What are you having?'

'The usual, and a bottle of red wine,' McNab said, deciding that was preferable to hitting the whisky.

'I could recommend one?' Marco offered.

'Good idea,' McNab agreed.

McNab laid his mobile on the table out of habit. Not so long ago he would have been looking forward to a text or a call from Ellie. Maybe making one himself. Neither was likely tonight.

The four girls at the neighbouring table were acknowledging his presence. McNab wondered if they'd heard Marco announce him as a detective and hoped they hadn't. They were chatting amongst themselves, throwing him encouraging looks.

McNab smiled back, which caused an explosion of giggles, suggesting much wine had been consumed there already.

Marco arrived with the pizza and a serious-looking bottle of red wearing a gold label.

'From my region. The French think they can make good wine.' He made a *poof* sound of dismissal. 'Italian is better.'

McNab waited as the bottle was opened and a glass poured, then tasted it with a flourish, which was obviously required. It wasn't whisky, but it would do.

He now set about his meal, glad that he had come here rather than go back to an empty flat. Glad too that he had never brought Ellie in here or he would have had to endure questions from Marco about where she was now.

Maybe that's why I never did. So when it was over, which it most surely would be, I didn't have to explain.

He was on his second espresso when the mobile did ring. Startled, McNab checked the screen to discover Ollie's name.

'You said you were coming by?'

'Sorry, I got caught up in stuff.' McNab waited. When

Ollie didn't respond, he said, 'I'm at Marco's having a pizza. Will it wait until tomorrow?'

'It's about the guy you took the photograph of on Sanday. The one you thought you recognized?'

Months ago now, so McNab took a moment to remember what Ollie was talking about. 'Oh, yeah. Any luck with that?'

'I found him.'

'And?' McNab waited. When he'd been introduced to DI Erling Flett's live-in lover, Rory, it had been at the annual bonfire on Cata Sands on Sanday. McNab had had no wish to attend, but Rhona had persuaded him, plus there had been free food and drink, and their investigation complete, they were heading home next day.

But there had been something about that bloke, McNab remembered. *Something familiar*.

'His real name is Dean Watters . . .' Ollie said.

That name didn't ring a bell. 'So not Rory, then?'

'No. Shall I send you details?'

'Anything bad in there?' he checked.

'A few priors, some years back.'

'Okay, send them through. And, Ollie, I have a laptop here I want you to take a look at.'

'Drop it by tomorrow.'

Ollie rang off, and shortly afterwards McNab heard a ping as an email downloaded. He refilled his wine glass and contemplated opening it.

Did he really care who Detective Inspector Erling Flett was shacked up with? Did it even matter if the Scouser who called himself Rory wasn't who he said he was? Flett wouldn't be the first police officer who'd found himself in a relationship with someone less than desirable.

I can vouch for that.

McNab pocketed the mobile. It would keep, whatever it was. He was unlikely ever to be back in Orkney. In fact he would do his best never to return. So why the fuck should he care? Back when he'd asked Ollie, the super recognizer, to check out the said Rory, he was still messed up by what had happened on his trip to Sanday.

But that was then, and this was now.

There was an explosion of laughter at the neighbouring table as more wine arrived. The girls were making a night of it.

McNab checked his own bottle to discover it was verging on empty.

Maybe he ought to buy another? Take it home with him.

Or else find someone to share it with?

21

The evening air was moist and warm, an earlier heavy shower now rising in steam from the trees and thick undergrowth that encircled the university hill.

Emerging from the shadowy cloisters, Rhona stood for a moment, seeking her favourite landmarks – the golden dome of the nearby Sikh temple and the skeleton beauty of Glasgow's last giant crane – before turning towards the gate and the path that dropped steeply downhill towards the River Kelvin.

Stopping on the bridge, Rhona gazed down at the water, rushing brown and swollen with the recent rain. August had been warm and humid, with occasional downpours of torrential rain, reminding the city's inhabitants that, although it was considered summer, they were still living in Scotland.

The discovery of the fibre, she acknowledged as she walked on, had altered her perception of the crime scene. True, PPE suits could be bought freely online, as could many of the items required for forensic work, but there was no escaping the fact that if a PPE suit had been used in whatever capacity, it suggested forensic awareness.

Offenders wise to the DNA trail had been known to try and destroy evidence, or even plant it to incriminate others. What they rarely appreciated was how difficult it was to do that successfully. Nor how advanced the techniques available to the police now were.

The easiest thing was to hide the body. No body, no evidence that a crime has been committed. People disappeared all the time and were never found. Some didn't want to be, others were dead. The male in the tunnel could have lain undiscovered for months, maybe longer, but he hadn't really been hidden.

He was there to be found, like the mess at the funeral parlour.

At that moment, Rhona was startled out of her reverie by the swift approach of a bicycle, its rider head down and seemingly oblivious to her presence on the path. Realizing they were on a collision course, Rhona stepped out of the way, but not quite quickly enough. The rider, suddenly catching sight of her, swerved abruptly, the bike hit the verge and he was catapulted off onto the grass.

Rhona went swiftly to his side.

'Are you okay?'

He groaned a little and pulled himself up. 'My fault entirely. I was going too fast and not paying attention.' He gave her the once-over. 'I hope I didn't hurt you?'

Rhona assured him he hadn't.

'Good.' He pulled up the bike and shot her a wide blue-eyed smile from beneath the helmet. Catching her amused look, he quickly removed the said helmet to display a head of dark curly hair to match the stubble on his chin.

'You often walk through the park,' he stated as though suddenly recognizing her.

Rhona nodded. 'I work nearby.'

'Ah.' He was trying to push his bike onto the path and Rhona got the impression the front wheel was no longer in the correct position.

'Your wheel's buckled.'

'I believe it is.' He shook his head ruefully. 'More hurry, less speed.' He nodded ahead. 'Looks like we're both on foot now.'

They walked together for a bit, their brief conversation being about the park and their mutual affection, like most Glaswegians, for the nearby Art Gallery and Museum. Five minutes later they had parted company, the man heading towards Sauchiehall Street, Rhona climbing the hill towards home.

As she approached her building, she spotted a piece of paper stuck under her car's windscreen wiper. Assuming a flyer of some sort, she pulled it free, only to discover it was a note urging her to check the pressure on a front tyre.

On closer inspection, her good Samaritan, whoever it was, was proved right. The tyre was virtually flat. Rhona opened up the boot and brought round the pump, and blew it up again. Chances were she had a slow puncture. If it was down again by tomorrow morning, she would take it round to the garage and have them take a look.

On her way upstairs, she pondered who had left the note. It could of course be someone living in her building. She knew most of them by sight and would offer a hello, if passing on the stair, but there had been a big turnover in the flats over recent times and only she and Mrs Harper were long-stay residents.

And thank goodness for Mrs Harper, Rhona thought as she opened the front door. Without her, Tom the cat would be seriously neglected. It was Mrs Harper who supplied his food and affection when Rhona was away on a job, although Sean had been known to step in too, when required.

The aforementioned Tom made no appearance on her

entry. Moving into the kitchen, Rhona wondered if he'd taken advantage of the window she often left open for him and accessed the roof for a wander about. Calling his name through the window, she listened for his answering meow. When there was none she checked the rest of the flat for him.

The spare room, Sean's domain, was strewn with clothes but empty of his saxophone, suggesting he was already at the jazz club. Rhona stood for a moment, catching his scent in the air. They weren't operating as a couple any more and Sean only stayed over on occasion, yet he was a benign presence in the flat when she allowed him to be.

What is it with the two of us? Rhona thought.

She imagined the Irishman's response to such a question. *Can't live with me, can't live without . . .* he would no doubt say with his characteristic Irish charm.

Rhona dismissed such a thought and double-checked among the pile of clothes for the curled body of the cat. If Tom wasn't here, on her bed or anywhere equally comfortable in the sitting room, he must be on the roof.

Rhona returned to the kitchen to put the kettle on, then heading for the shower, she swiftly undressed and stepped under the hot spray.

Like a walk in the park, the beat of the water on her head usually helped the thinking process, but instead of contemplating the day's events at the lab, she found herself revisiting her collision with the fast-moving cyclist.

The man who'd nearly knocked her down had introduced himself as Conor Williams who was carrying out research at the sleep clinic at the university. Rhona had given him her own name, omitting her professional title, but indicating she worked at the same university. Revealing she had anything to do with the police or forensics usually resulted in a conversation she didn't seek.

Conor had then surprised her by asking how many hours' uninterrupted sleep she got a night.

'Never enough,' she'd replied with a laugh.

'I'll get less too, with my bike off the road,' he'd said. 'I'll have to get up earlier and walk to work.'

After that, they'd discussed his frequent visits to the Art Gallery, a favourite place of his, and Rhona had related how her father had taken her there as a child and she'd loved it ever since. That discussion over, she'd caught him checking her left hand for, she assumed, a ring.

Did people still do that?

Then, as he'd suddenly announced he was heading in a different direction from her, Rhona had had the distinct impression he was about to ask if he might have her number. She would probably have turned him down, but she was still a little put out when he walked away without asking for it.

I must be losing my knack, she'd thought at that point.

Fifteen minutes later, she'd ordered a pizza and was awaiting its delivery when she heard a sharp meow as Tom squeezed through the open window and presented himself to her in a flourish of leg rubbing. The affectionate welcome was, however, short-lived. Merely seconds later, he headed to his dish in the hope that some fresh titbit had been added, and when that proved untrue, he deserted her for the window seat to survey his domain through the glass.

He spends a lot more time sooking up to Sean than me, Rhona acknowledged. And since the cat had stayed at Sean's flat when she'd been away on the Norwegian case, Rhona had gained the impression that Tom was merely putting up with her until he could get back there, and to Sean's cooking.

Opening her door shortly afterwards to the delivery boy, Rhona was presented with a warm and fragrant pizza box, and a wine bottle bag.

'I didn't order wine,' Rhona said, puzzled.

'It was outside your door when I arrived. I take it you're Rhona?' He showed her the gift tag with her name on it. When she nodded, he grinned. 'Looks like you've got an admirer.'

Her hunger greater than her curiosity, Rhona left the wine in the bag and started on the pizza. Three slices later, she lifted out the bottle to find it was an expensive-looking red, wearing a winner's label.

Rhona immediately checked her mobile, in case there had been a text from Sean, the red-wine connoisseur, warning her of its imminent arrival. It was the sort of thing he would do.

But why not sign it? And why was it left outside the door?

She couldn't answer the first question, but the second was easier. With the shower running, she could easily have missed the doorbell.

Rhona examined her name again, then a thought occurred and she fished in her bag for the note she'd found on her windscreen to compare them. She was no expert, but the handwriting looked similar.

Maybe the delivery boy was right and I do have an admirer other than Sean.

Rhona fetched the corkscrew. She wasn't a big fan of red, despite Sean's continued efforts to educate her palette, but she could always try.

22

She was running from something or someone, but had no idea who. Suddenly the thick undergrowth parted and she saw the tree.

Ugly, obscenely so, its trunk warped and raw as though it bled. Stunted, twisted branches reached out to her like mangled limbs.

Then came the smell. One she knew too well. A hand caught her in its deathlike grip and suddenly she was below ground, looking up into the web of branches, earth falling into her open mouth.

'Rhona.' Sean's voice came from far away as the paralysis gripped her limbs.

'Rhona. It's okay.'

Her eyes, finally released from the stranglehold of the nightmare, sprang open to find him looking worriedly down at her.

'I thought I came in quietly, but I must have disturbed you,' he said.

'I was in a wood.' Rhona immediately recalled the vividness of the scene. 'There was a dead body.'

'That sounds like a normal day for you.' He was making light of her fear, trying, Rhona knew, to reassure her.

'Apart from the bit where I was being buried alive.'

Even as she said it, the stagnant taste of earth was back in her mouth, the suffocating smell of death in her nostrils.

Rhona dragged herself up in bed, seeking solace in the familiar-shaped shadows of her bedroom. She wasn't prone to nightmares, even after copious amounts of alcohol, and she had drunk only half the bottle of red wine.

'What time is it?' she said.

'Around three.' Sean looked at her. 'If you're okay, I could go back to my room?'

Rhona didn't want that. 'No. Stay,' she said.

Sean pulled back the duvet and slid in beside her.

His hair, brushing her cheek, smelt of wet night air, and for a horrible moment she was back in that wood.

'You're shivering.' Sean pulled her to him, enveloping her in his radiant warmth.

'Did you send me a bottle of wine earlier?' Rhona checked.

'You mean that rather nice vintage on the kitchen table?'

'It was left outside the door. The gift tag just said "Rhona".'

Sean drew back to catch her eye. 'A secret admirer. Should I be jealous?'

'I don't like red wine, remember?' Rhona said, pulling him to her.

23

McNab's face was like fury. 'Claire called me first thing, terrified. Fucking press banging on her front door.'

'Any idea who contacted them?' Rhona said.

'Claire and the boyfriend knew about the break-in, plus Mr Marshall. She swears no one else did and I believe her,' McNab said.

'You've questioned the boyfriend?'

'First thing. He's like the male equivalent of Claire. They're well matched. I'd swear he wasn't lying. As for her boss, he's got publicity, sure, but the kind that'll fuck his family business.' McNab shook his head. 'We are being played by the fucker who left that body in the tunnel.'

Rhona had arrived for the strategy meeting to find the room already packed. She was due to be called on to say her piece, but at that moment DI Wilson had been leading the fray. She'd spotted McNab nearby with Janice, his face like thunder. And had soon learned the reason.

The tunnel body had been prominent in the morning headlines. Unfortunately, so too had the matching story of the break-in at Marshall's funeral parlour, along with the feature of the bread and the wine.

Rhona, like McNab, couldn't imagine that Claire had contacted the press. If they eliminated Mr Marshall and the boyfriend from the leak, that left the possibility that a police insider had given the story to the newspapers – or that the perpetrator had.

'Who else knew about the funeral parlour incident?' Rhona said.

'I was convinced the boss gave me that job to keep me grounded. The only other person I spoke to about it was Janice. Then, of course, Pirie.'

Rhona ignored McNab's belligerent tone. There was no way Magnus would reveal anything to the press and he knew it.

Bill was calling the meeting to order again. As the noise died down, a photograph of the victim appeared on the screen, identified now as Andrew Jackson, a male model, working for a Glasgow agency. Last seen at a photo shoot in the afternoon prior to his body being discovered.

It seemed Chrissy had been right when she'd suggested he wasn't a typical Urbex.

Details of possible entry points to the tunnel followed, none of which were well covered by CCTV, so no luck yet on how or why he'd gone down there.

As Bill signalled to her, Rhona rose and made her way to the front, knowing that what she was about to say would probably confuse matters still further.

'The autopsy was inconclusive. The pathologist found no evidence of foul play,' Rhona explained. 'A puncture mark was located on the left thigh, but Toxicology revealed nothing through the standard tests we requested. That doesn't of course mean that he didn't ingest poison in some form.'

They couldn't test indiscriminately. There had to be something that pointed them in the right direction, she explained, like in the recent case of the drug addict who'd committed suicide by injecting himself with ricin, a highly toxic, naturally occurring protein produced in the seeds of the castor oil plant. Not an everyday occurrence and only discovered when IT had indicated that the victim had been purchasing the seeds of *Ricinus communis* online.

'So it's still not clear if we're dealing with a homicide or a suicide?' Bill said.

'Correct.' Rhona brought up the scene photos. 'Lividity suggested that he died at the scene or was moved there swiftly after death.' She paused to let that sink in. 'We've established that the victim's stomach contents did not contain the bread or the wine found partially consumed in the car. A footprint near the body wasn't that of the victim, plus I lifted a partial print from the victim's neck which also wasn't his.'

Rhona paused here. 'Evidence also suggests that motorbikes have used the tunnel recently, although when exactly we can't say. But perhaps the most significant evidence taken from the body was this.'

Up on the screen came the magnified image of the fibre taken from the victim's nostril.

They'd moved to Bill's office. Rhona accepted the coffee Janice was handing out, her head thumping again, the paracetamol she'd taken at breakfast having worn off. She was beginning to suspect she was coming down with something. Either that or a night in the London Street tunnel, plus last night's poor sleep, was the reason for the splitting headache.

McNab's countenance was still like thunder and, having accepted a coffee, he'd quickly drunk it and looked for a refill. Whatever was up with him also involved not meeting her eye. Rhona suspected he was annoyed she hadn't told him about the PPE fibre before she revealed its existence to the assembled team.

Magnus had followed her performance with one of his own, which might in fact be the reason for McNab's ugly mood. Now the entire team was aware of the possible sin-eater aspect to the tale of bread and wine. Rhona wondered just how long it would take for the press to find out about that. The tabloids in particular would have a field day.

'So,' Bill was saying to Magnus, 'do we exploit the sin-eater story or suppress it?'

Magnus took time to think before answering. 'If we assume this is a homicide, or at the very least an assisted suicide, then up to now the perpetrator has been doing the running. If we release this information then control of the situation moves back to us.'

Rhona glanced at McNab, but it was almost as though he wasn't listening.

'But,' Magnus continued, 'I don't think we should make public our thoughts on the signature. I suspect that's what the perpetrator wants us to do. After all, that's the point of a signature, to claim ownership and its associated notoriety. If we don't mention it, then it's likely he or she will be driven to broadcast it themselves in some form, which might offer us a lead.'

Dismissed, they began to troop out. Rhona tried to catch McNab before he made what looked like a quick getaway, but was prevented from doing this when Bill called her back.

'There's a forensic team heading to the victim's flat. I'd like you to check the place out. If he did orchestrate his own death, you're the one most likely to spot evidence of it.'

24

Rhona's mobile rang as she climbed into the car. Glancing at the screen, she found Sean's name and immediately knew what he was calling about. So much so she almost didn't answer.

'Are you okay?' were his opening words.

'I'm fine,' Rhona assured him.

'I heard you this morning in the toilet.'

Bugger it. Sean never woke much before eleven when he'd had a late night at the club. And she had tried to keep her retching as quiet as possible. Her stomach had been really weird, and as for the headache . . . *You would have thought I'd been downing Tequilas instead of a couple of glasses of wine with a meal.*

'It was the wine,' she said. 'Red sometimes disagrees with me.'

'Any better now?' He sounded concerned.

'Yes,' she lied, having taken a further two painkillers before leaving the police station.

'When are you home?' Sean asked.

'No idea,' Rhona said honestly.

'I'll put something in the slow cooker then, and see you when I get back from the club.'

This arrangement where Sean was sometimes at her flat, sometimes at his own, had been a feature since she'd returned from Norway. How long it would last was yet to be decided.

'Maybe go back to your place tonight,' Rhona said, with a sudden desire to have the flat to herself.

'Okay,' Sean agreed, a little too readily, which made Rhona wonder if that had been the plan in the first place.

Having rung off, Rhona sat for a moment, concentrating on the ache in her head and calculating how long she had until the painkillers kicked in. As for her stomach, the nausea had retreated a little, but not enough to consider food or coffee. She'd accepted a cup in Bill's office for appearances' sake but had swiftly abandoned it, even the smell causing her problems. *It's just as well,* she thought, *that I'm not about to sample the smell of death again.*

The SOCO team were already at the victim's flat, as evidenced by their van parked outside. Rhona brass-necked it on a yellow line with the pool car she'd signed out, and asked the officer stationed at the front door to assure any patrolling parking attendant she was there on police business.

The stairwell she entered was clean and recently washed, given the faint smell of antiseptic still in the air. A scent Rhona's queasy stomach thankfully didn't react to. Andrew Jackson's flat was on the fourth floor of the upmarket tenement. On each level, ornate stained-glass windows complemented the colourful tiling of the stairwell.

It was a classy address.

Situated just off the top of Sauchiehall Street, the building looked north across the green stretch of Kelvingrove Park to the university beyond. Had she been at home right now, Rhona realized that she could probably have picked out this building from her own front window.

Andrew Jackson had been a Westender, like herself, so how did he end up in a disused tunnel in the East End of the city?

Kitted out now, Rhona made herself known to Joyce, the SOCO team leader.

'DI Wilson said you were coming. Not sure why?' Joyce looked perturbed, as though she hadn't been seen to be doing her job properly.

Rhona reminded her about the guy who'd killed himself using ricin from his own carefully tended castor oil plant.

Joyce nodded. 'No plants here of any description. But if he was sourcing something online, it would be easier if we had his electronic devices.'

'So no mobile here?' Rhona said.

'No laptop either,' Joyce confirmed. 'I take it IT are looking for an online presence?'

Rhona had already had a quick look herself. It wasn't difficult to find a male model once you had a name. It seemed Jackson had had a flourishing career via the Alpha bureau – hipster gear and branded underwear a speciality. She told Joyce so.

'They're following up the male model link, according to McNab, but nothing there explains why he was in the tunnel.'

Rhona checked with Joyce what she'd found up to now in the flat.

'It's been thoroughly cleaned and recently. The guy liked doing housework or he had professional help. No dirty stuff in the washer. The bed sheets were fresh on. Dishes all washed. Fridge empty, apart from some low-fat milk still in date. New liner in the bin, no carry-out cartons anywhere.' She took a breather here. 'I'm assuming he ate out most of the time. He has a decent stock of wine, mostly red, in a rack in the kitchen. Sounds like the life I would like,' she added wistfully.

'Did he live alone?'

'Looks like it. All the clothes and shoes are the same size and for a male. No evidence anywhere of a female.'

They'd stepped out onto the landing so that they might talk with ease. Now, pulling up the hoods and masks, they went back inside where Rhona, despite having had the lowdown from Joyce, set about her own examination.

The apartment, although obviously refurbished, had retained many of its original features, including the stripped and varnished floorboards and the original black cast-iron fireplaces. The sitting room was tastefully furnished with an L-shaped couch facing a large TV screen mounted on one wall. Below the screen were shelves housing a selection of computer games.

Rhona took a moment to imagine the man whose body she'd examined under London Road living in this place. Without talking to those he knew or worked with, she had only the forensic facts of his life and death to try and understand Andrew Jackson by.

And that isn't enough.

She had the distinct feeling that, despite her careful analysis, she was missing something. Something important.

Toxicology reports had indicated that both the wine and the portion of bread left at the scene were safe for human consumption. However, neither the cup of wine nor the bread had provided a DNA profile of whoever might have sampled them, despite the fact that Chrissy had identified indentations on the bread in the shape of teeth marks.

She and Chrissy had spent some time trying to work out

how this had been achieved, her assistant finally settling on a straw being used for the wine and a covering of cling film for the food. Both explanations plausible, and a further reinforcement, if needed, that the perpetrator had forensic knowledge and was putting it into practice.

Rhona, now on her knees at the cupboard under the kitchen sink, backed away with a groan, the smell of cleaning products having upset the delicate balance of her stomach. Sitting down, her back against the kitchen unit, she brought a plastic evidence bag to hand just in case and waited for the feeling to subside.

The flat was too warm, aided by the weather outside, but the bigger problem was the PPE suit she was wearing. Feeling sweat trickling down inside her clothes, Rhona decided she would take another break out on the landing to get some cooler air.

The kitchen, like every other room in the flat, was spotless. Either Jackson had never used it or someone had been busy cleaning up in here too. Discarding the evidence bag, she put a hand down to help her rise, and felt something gritty against her gloved palm.

Rhona slowly raised her hand and turned it over.

Three green pine-like needles were stuck to the surface of her latex glove. She contemplated them for a moment, then reaching for the evidence bag, she brushed the needles inside. Rhona checked the floor again. The original floorboards had been resealed, but there was still a gap between them.

Rhona crouched, angling her torch.

There were at least two more needles visible. Using tweezers, she extracted and bagged them with the others. Rising from the floor, she now took a closer look at the kitchen surfaces. A mortar and pestle stood next to a wooden chopping board. Rhona bagged both items.

'You found something interesting?' Joyce appeared, her voice muffled by the mask, her cheeks reddened by heat.

Rhona shrugged. 'Possibly.'

'Good, because we definitely haven't.'

The outside air was clammy as though a thunderstorm was on its way. Rhona, free now of the suit, breathed in deeply, thankful that her headache had eased and her stomach had stopped churning. In fact she was beginning to feel hungry.

Finding her vehicle unticketed, she thanked the officer responsible.

'No problem,' he said. 'You finished up in there?'

'For the moment.'

As she headed back to the lab, the dark clouds amassing overhead thundered into action, a jagged line of light cutting through them. Then the rain began to fall in grey sheets, so forcefully that Rhona decided to pull in to the side of the road, aware that her wipers weren't up to the onslaught.

While she waited for the downfall to ease, she did a Google search on her phone.

The image wasn't perfect but probably sufficient to confirm the identity of the needles she'd found in the kitchen, especially when she was already fairly sure which tree they'd come from.

Taxus baccata, more commonly known as the English Yew.

25

'You don't look so good.' Chrissy gave Rhona the once-over. 'Big night, last night?' she added, in an envious tone. Chrissy didn't like to miss a party.

Rhona glanced in the nearest mirror, only to confirm that Chrissy was right. She looked like shit. Pale as a corpse, with eyes like a panda.

'I only drank half a bottle of red wine,' she told Chrissy.

'Wow. Was it laced with something?'

'It was vintage, according to Sean.'

'And he would know.'

Rhona was aware that her assistant harboured a not-so secret admiration for Sean Maguire, their mutual Irish Catholic background being a factor in that.

'I have rolls . . .' Chrissy offered.

'Dry bread only,' Rhona said firmly. 'Nothing fried on it.'

Chrissy pulled a face. 'God, it's that bad?'

Rhona's expression conveyed that it was.

After a tentative bite of the roll and a couple of mouthfuls of coffee, Rhona kitted herself up, this time choosing a cooler theatre suit and headgear rather than a forensic suit, then questioned Chrissy on any results that had come in.

'Still waiting for the response on the DNA sample from the fibre. Luckier with the footwear database,' Chrissy told her. 'The pattern next to the body was made by a size six, Men's Harley-Davidson Biker Boot called "Clint". Harley boots have distinctive orange sole patterns and the HD symbol embossed on them.'

'And the tread impressions?' Rhona tried.

'The movement patterns suggest up to four bikes, all with individual tread designs,' Chrissy said. 'I'm checking them out. The bikes definitely couldn't have accessed the tunnel via the air vent I told you about, nor been lowered over the wall at Bridgeton station.'

Exactly what Rhona had been thinking. 'One set of tracks ended just past the wrecked car. They must have entered via the slipway.'

'Which means they knew the code on the main gate and had a key to the padlock on the door.'

It would have been easy for a motorbike to deposit the body in the tunnel. Especially if the driver had had help.

Rhona recalled McNab's expression in the meeting and his quick getaway afterwards. There were plenty of motorbike enthusiasts in Glasgow, but, she suspected, his mind would have been on the one he knew. Maybe the Harley community would know who'd been using the tunnel as a race track.

'How's things with Ellie and McNab?' Rhona asked.

Chrissy pulled a face. 'Not good, I fear. I asked, when he came by with the shirt. Normally he acts like a guy who's getting it. Not this time.'

The mention of the shirt reminded Rhona to ask if Chrissy had had any luck with the items she'd brought from the funeral parlour.

'Unfortunately, as you said, Claire had tried to wash the wine stain out. I did extract crumbs from the Hoover and the brush.' Chrissy paused. 'The fragments are from the same type of artisan bread as you found in the tunnel, but I have nothing on where it was purchased.'

Rhona shook out the needles she'd found in the flat.

'Okay . . .' Chrissy looked quizzically at her. 'You're still finding needles from last year's Christmas tree?'

'These aren't pine. They're yew needles. I found them tucked between the floorboards in Andrew Jackson's kitchen.'

'The graveyard tree?'

'Aptly named, considering all of it is poisonous, the needles most of all.'

Rhona extracted the wooden board from its bag and handed Chrissy a magnifying glass. 'It looks like someone was chopping them up on this.'

Chrissy took a closer look. 'Jesus. You think he poisoned himself?' she said. 'Like the castor-oil-plant guy?'

'It's got to be a possibility.'

26

McNab had had a suffocating need to get out of the boss's office after the strategy meeting. He'd been aware Rhona was keen to have a word as he left, but he had no desire to talk to her.

At least, not yet.

He headed for the Tech department, keen to offload the laptop he'd taken from the Robertson house. He didn't expect anything on it to link the old dead guy to the sin-eater, but the boss had given him that job, and he was doing his best to stick to orders.

On the surface anyway.

He couldn't get out of his head how shitty Rhona had looked in this morning's meeting. She'd given her piece about the autopsy okay, but he'd watched the colour drain out of her face in the office afterwards. She either had a hangover or something else was making her nauseated.

Rhona wasn't in the habit of getting wasted, not like him, so he was inclined to dismiss the hangover theory, which meant she was ill or . . .

A brief but searingly awful thought entered his head. She and Sean were back together. The Irishman had been staying at her flat, just like old times. Maybe they were planning to be a permanent feature after all? Settle down and all that went with it? McNab cut that thought off right there, not wanting to progress it any further.

Cosy domestic bliss didn't fit his image of Dr MacLeod. Nor did he want it to.

Reaching his destination, McNab looked for Ollie in his usual spot in the far corner. The room hummed with digital sound, just like the main operations room. McNab didn't like being in either of those spaces. Blue screens and digital noise made his brain hurt.

Ollie looked up as he approached. 'Hey, Sergeant. You okay?'

McNab wondered what was wrong with his face that would prompt such a look on Ollie's.

'Great,' he emphasized, handing him Stanley's laptop. 'Belonged to one of the old dead guys from the funeral home.'

Ollie's face lit up the way it did when McNab brought him bacon rolls. 'I saw it on the news. Weird, that. Messing with dead bodies. Are you going to exhume them?'

'Why would we do that?'

'You only have the girl at the undertaker's word that the bread and wine was all that happened to the bodies. Maybe the perp's DNA is on them.'

McNab didn't like Claire's word being questioned, but bit off his angry retort because what Ollie said was true.

'One was cremated, so that DNA went up in smoke. The laptop belongs to the buried one, Stanley Robertson.'

'So he could be resurrected, if I find anything useful?'

'We would have to have something really concrete to get permission for that to happen,' McNab reminded him.

Ollie nodded. 'Did you check the stuff I sent you on the Orkney guy?'

'I did, thank you. I've decided to leave well alone.

Ollie appeared a little put out by the lukewarm response. 'I had to look through a hell of a lot of footage to find what I did.'

McNab clapped Ollie on the back. 'I'll buy you a pint sometime.'

Ollie looked disappointed. 'I'm not much of a drinker.'

McNab realized he hadn't seen Ollie hanging out with them in a pub after hours. Somehow, he never imagined Ollie anywhere else but here. True, he had spent a night in Ollie's flat on a couch in a room that closely resembled this one, as Ollie had searched for information for him.

Recalling that he might have need of Ollie again in such circumstances, McNab tried to respond accordingly. 'Then I'll treat you to a pizza instead.'

That offer seemed to suffice.

'I'll get back to you about the laptop,' Ollie said, returning to his screen.

And with that McNab was summarily dismissed.

He needed to talk to DS Clark, but he wanted to think through what to do about Ellie beforehand. He hadn't fully registered the bike aspect of the investigation until Rhona had outlined it in more detail at the strategy meeting. McNab wasn't surprised that motorbikes had been using the tunnel, probably to race – something he would have liked to do himself.

The question was, had Ellie known about it? Was that why she'd been so freaked out?

McNab recalled her weird phone call the night they'd found the body, and Ellie's reaction to him since then. She'd announced when they'd first met that she didn't mind that he was a police officer because she had nothing to hide. At the time he'd found her declaration of innocence a definite turn-on. Mainly because there was no one, even among police officers, who didn't have something to hide, himself included.

Then again, maybe she was acting weird because she'd simply gone off him. Something that had happened often enough with women before now. She'd certainly attempted the brush-off at the stadium. If the other girl, Izzy, hadn't come into the shop, McNab suspected it would have definitely happened. Yet the pal had seemed relaxed, even pleased to see him, before Ellie had rushed her away.

Weighing up both scenarios, McNab's gut feeling told him that Ellie did know something about the bikes in the tunnel. Although that didn't mean she wasn't also planning to break up with him.

And there was one way to find out if he was right.

McNab pulled up her number before he could change his mind. As he heard it ring out, he rehearsed asking Ellie out tonight for a pizza at Marco's. Now that would be commitment. Once there, he would await a suitable opening for the tunnel question.

'Hi. This is Ellie. Please leave a message.'

McNab could picture Ellie as he listened to her recorded voice. The smiling, funny, fearless Ellie he'd sat behind on the Harley. Not the one he'd met last night at the speedway track.

McNab cut the call, not wanting to leave a message. If Janice hadn't already sent someone down to the Harley shop, something she was bound to do, then he would volunteer to go. Today was one of the days that Ellie should be there.

27

'Phone call for you.' Chrissy motioned to Rhona through the intervening glass.

When Rhona mouthed back *who?,* Chrissy shrugged her shoulders and just waved her into the office to answer it.

On entering, Rhona registered that Chrissy had set up the coffee machine and acquired a box of iced doughnuts. Thankful that the sight and smell of food no longer repelled her, Rhona smiled her thanks as she picked up the phone.

'Hello, Dr MacLeod here.'

'It's Dr Conor Williams from the sleep lab. We met in the park, when I almost knocked you over.'

'Oh, yes. I remember,' Rhona said.

'I apologize for the call, Dr MacLeod, it's just that one of the volunteers on the research project is taking the forensic diploma course and mentioned your lectures. I put two and two together and found your lab number listed in the internal directory.' He paused for a moment as though his planned speech had come to an end and he wasn't sure now how to proceed.

Rhona helped him out. 'You should have been a detective.'

'It may be a police matter I'm calling about. I was about to contact the number given on the news regarding the body found in the London Road tunnel. Then the same volunteer said that you were working on that case, so I thought I'd run it past you first.'

'Okay?' Rhona said, intrigued now.

'The victim, Andrew Jackson, contacted the sleep clinic some months ago. He was suffering from sleep paralysis and was pretty desperate about it,' Conor said. 'I wondered if his condition might have contributed to his death.'

The quadrangle was bathed in sunshine, the tall tree that stood in the middle of the well-tended lawn casting a waving shadow. A few folk sat on the neighbouring benches, enjoying the sunshine. Resits would be due to start at the end of the month. Then the faces surrounding the courtyard weren't likely to be so cheerful.

Following the directions given by Dr Williams, Rhona headed out of the main gate, taking the route along University Gardens. It was a path she used often, usually when heading to the jazz club for a drink after work.

Following the phone call, she and Chrissy had discussed her plan of action over the doughnuts and coffee.

'So,' Rhona had said, licking raspberry icing from her lips, 'what do you think?'

'About the handsome Dr Williams?' Chrissy had given a nod to the photograph of the doctor she'd found on the internal staff system. 'Or his theory about the dead guy?'

'Both,' Rhona had admitted.

'Well, I'd accept an invite to visit *his* lab any time,' Chrissy had told her. 'As to his theory, if Jackson was as desperate as the doc said, then maybe he did kill himself.'

Dr Williams had indicated that he was on duty in the sleep lab, so couldn't leave his patients unattended. He'd asked Rhona to advise on whether he should go ahead and phone the police with his concerns or else talk them through with her first.

'You're going?' Chrissy had apparently read her expression with ease.

'I am,' Rhona had declared. In truth, she'd been intrigued by Dr Williams's call and was keen to find out more, particularly since they'd discovered chopped-up yew needles in the victim's kitchen.

'So, I'll catch you later at the club for an update?' Chrissy had said.

'You will,' Rhona had promised.

The sleep lab was tucked in behind the School of Computing Science, near the Centre for Cognitive Neuroimaging. A list of buttons at the entrance indicated it was on the top floor. Rhona pressed the buzzer and a woman's voice answered and asked her business. When Rhona told her, she was let in.

She met no one on the way up the stairs, although she did hear the lift ascend or descend as she climbed. Emerging on the top-floor landing, she discovered Dr Williams awaiting the arrival of the lift and, Rhona assumed, herself.

'Dr Williams.'

He turned on his name with a surprised look. 'Few of my visitors climb five flights of stairs,' he said, impressed. 'And please call me Conor.'

'Okay, Conor, and you may call me Rhona.' She studied him for a moment. 'You look different minus the bike.'

'Better dressed and without the daft helmet?' he smiled.

'That could be it,' Rhona admitted.

He gestured her to a nearby open door, beyond which was a carpeted corridor with glass sleeping cubicles along one side. Rhona's first impression on stepping into the area was one of a deep silence.

'I take it none of your participants snore?' she said.

'Oh, they do, mostly because they're required to be in a supine position for us to observe their REM sleep.' Seeing her expression, Conor explained in more detail. 'The unique phase of sleep that features random movement of the eyes, low muscle tone and propensity to dream.' He paused. 'Like when you see your dog's eyes twitch behind closed lids.'

'I have a cat, but I know what you mean,' Rhona said.

'REM sleep is essential for our well-being and our imaginative ability,' he went on. 'It's reported that Albert Einstein discovered relativity in his sleep and Paul McCartney composed entire songs while sleeping.'

'Really?' Rhona could certainly relate to forensic problem-solving during sleep and told him so. 'Though it would be a miracle if I wrote a song.'

They'd reached the end cubicle, wherein a man lay asleep, his head festooned with wires attached to a variety of machines.

'Leo's the reason I have to stick around here this evening,' Conor explained. 'And why I couldn't go into the police station and give a statement.' He smiled. 'So I'm grateful you agreed to come here instead.'

He steered her towards a small office and offered her a seat. 'Coffee?'

'Please. Black, no milk or sugar,' she added.

'Good,' he said. 'Then you can appreciate the real taste.'

As he poured two small cups from the jug, Rhona took a quick glance around the room, noting the numerous shelves laden with books and the absence of any personal photographs, family or otherwise.

Seemingly interpreting her thoughts, Conor said, 'I'm married to my work, I'm afraid. What about you?'

'It feels that way at times,' Rhona answered honestly.

Accepting the proffered cup, she sniffed at the fragrant aroma.

'A French Arabic blend,' he told her. 'A favourite of mine.'

Rhona took a mouthful of coffee, which was hot and strong.

'Okay?' he asked, almost anxiously.

'It's delicious,' Rhona assured him. Now the niceties were over, she asked him about Jackson.

Taking a seat alongside her on the leather sofa, Conor placed his cup on the low table and began.

'As I mentioned on the phone, Andrew contacted us because he was suffering badly from sleep paralysis, where your mind is aware, but you're unable to move.' He looked to Rhona as though to assure himself she knew what he was talking about.

When she nodded, he continued, 'Some people describe it as a living death. Andrew's attacks were accompanied by vivid and terrifying hallucinations.' He paused, and Rhona registered his concern. 'So severe that Andrew had taken to avoiding sleep at all costs, which in turn led to higher anxiety and more extreme hallucinations, such as seeing shadow men.'

'Shadow men?'

'Black amorphous shadows that the victim interprets as a living humanoid figure, come to attack them.'

28

Conor rose and, pulling up a second chair behind his desk, he now beckoned Rhona over.

Moving to sit next to him, Rhona caught the rapid beat of his neck pulse and knew that whatever Conor was about to show her was the reason for his call. Around them the room had dropped into shadow and her imagination was already playing with the shapes that made.

'Andrew suffered from a feeling of intense pressure on his chest, which prevented him from breathing,' Conor told her. 'And that pressure manifested itself in what he called his demon.'

Conor sat back to allow Rhona a clear view of the screen.

The painting was of a pale and beautiful young woman lying supine on a curtained bed, her eyes closed. Clad in a white gauze robe, her naked body was clearly outlined below. On her breast squatted a black goblin-like creature staring malevolently out at them, as though daring them to interfere with its intentions.

'Henry Fuseli's *The Nightmare*,' Conor said quietly, 'painted in 1781 and inspired, it's thought, by just such a sensation during sleep paralysis.'

Rhona felt a wave of disgust wash over her and for a moment the nausea returned and with it the acrid taste of strong coffee. She sat back from the screen, keen to distance herself from the image and its connotations.

'It's horrible.'

'I agree,' Conor said. 'There's evidence that a strong belief in not being able to breathe in such circumstances can trigger cardiac arrest in severe cases. Literally frightening people to death.'

Rhona recalled her own experience of the previous night. The terrible sense of suffocation. Of being buried alive.

It must have shown on her face, because Conor immediately said, 'You've experienced sleep paralysis yourself?'

'I would have called it a nightmare,' Rhona said, 'but I definitely couldn't move during it.'

'If it's any consolation, up to fifty per cent of people are reported to have experienced night paralysis at some time in their life,' Conor told her with a sympathetic look.

'Do we know why it happens?'

'Well, traditionally it was linked with a subconscious guilt or supposed sin on the part of the sufferer, hence the religious symbolism in the images associated with it.'

Rhona had assumed her own experience had been linked to working round the clock with the addition of the red wine, but then a memory of McNab dragging up their shared guilty past presented itself . . .

Her thoughts must have shown on her face, because Conor asked if she was all right.

'The image just reminded me of that feeling of being unable to move,' she told him, not untruthfully.

'It's a memory that's hard to forget,' Conor agreed.

Rhona changed the subject. 'Did Andrew ever mention the tunnel?' she asked, thinking if he'd planned his suicide down there, the location must have meant something to him.

'I wondered that myself. We did talk a fair bit, but he never mentioned the tunnel or gave an indication that he might choose to take his own life.'

Rhona shot Conor a look. She had given no indication that suicide, assisted or otherwise, was being considered.

'I'm sorry,' Conor said. 'The news report didn't indicate how he'd died, but in view of the circumstances and his condition, I did wonder . . .'

It was a fair response.

'I haven't been much help, I'm afraid,' Conor said as he walked her to the door.

'On the contrary, building up a picture of the victim is always a help,' Rhona told him.

He nodded, looking relieved.

'Shall I summon the lift?' he offered.

'I'll take the stairs. They're even easier on the way down.'

As she took her leave, Conor hesitated, as though there was something further he wanted to say.

Rhona helped him out by offering her card. 'If you think of anything else, feel free to call me. And do go and give a statement as soon as you can.'

He smiled and nodded. 'Will do,' he promised.

29

'Looking for a particular model?' a voice enquired.

The guy with the shaved head and silver earrings was eyeing him as a potential customer. At that moment McNab definitely was one. *Jeez,* he would love to own any of the bikes on show before him, although where the money to buy a new Harley might come from, he couldn't imagine.

'Any recommendations?' he said.

'We all have our favourites. Mine's a Sportstar Custom. Gemma over there,' he indicated a girl behind the counter, 'she's a Fat Bob lover.' Gemma gave him the thumbs-up to indicate what he said was true. The guy looked McNab up and down. 'You've ridden a Harley before?'

McNab had been on the back of Ellie's but didn't know its name. *Maybe he should have asked.* Momentarily stuck for an answer, he spotted a poster which offered a solution to his problem.

'A Street Glide,' he offered.

The guy gave him a knowing smile. 'Excellent choice.'

McNab decided it was time for honesty. 'I'm a friend of Ellie's. I really came here to see her.'

The guy's face clouded over, indicating he wasn't comfortable with that admission. He shot a quick glance towards a door in the back wall, before muttering, 'I'll check if she's in yet.'

He disappeared into the back, leaving McNab to contemplate the change in his demeanour, plus the uneasy look Gemma was now giving him.

Had Ellie contemplated his visit and warned the staff? Fuck's sake, were things that bad between them?

Moments later, another man emerged and came towards him. For a moment McNab couldn't place the figure or the face, then he remembered. It was the guy from the speedway, only this time he was the belligerent one, not McNab.

'What d'you want with Ellie?' he said, a scowl on his face.

'I'd prefer to tell Ellie that,' McNab responded sharply.

'She doesn't want to see you.'

The smug look on the guy's face suggested he saw himself as McNab's replacement.

McNab made to sidestep him, only to discover how fleet of foot the guy was.

'The back shop is out of bounds to anyone but staff, sir,' he added sarcastically.

McNab gritted his teeth, knowing what he was about to do was a mistake. Nevertheless . . .

He brought out his warrant card. 'What about the police?'

Now the guy was the one wrong-footed, suggesting Ellie hadn't told him that part of the equation. He floundered, his mouth opening and shutting like a goldfish. He didn't look nearly so confident or cool, which pleased McNab no end.

'She's not here,' he finally admitted. 'She called in sick.'

'I'd like to see that for myself,' McNab said, sidestepping this time without interference.

The back shop was larger than he'd imagined. If Ellie

was hiding out among the packed shelves or the bikes in the process of being repaired or refurbished, it wouldn't be easy to spot her. Even as he contemplated this, McNab felt sick at the thought that Ellie was afraid to see him.

What the fuck had he done wrong?

'Ellie,' he called out. 'I just want a word with you.'

McNab waited, wishing and hoping to see her slight, tattooed figure emerge. He'd never conceived of Ellie being afraid of anything up to now, and definitely not him.

He pulled out his mobile and rang her number. Waiting, hoping to hear it ring out nearby.

It didn't.

'I told you so,' the bodyguard said. 'She called in sick.'

'Detective Sergeant McNab. Is there an office where we can talk police business, Mr—?' McNab said, assuming his official tone.

A flicker of concern crossed the guy's face. 'Roddie,' he said. 'Roddie Symes.'

'Are you the manager?'

Fear leapt between his eyes. 'Supervisor.'

'Then let's talk. Mr Symes.'

Once he was finished with Symes, McNab took himself round the corner and tried Ellie's number again, getting the same message. She could, he acknowledged, be simply choosing not to answer when she saw his name on the screen. Then again, Symes had stuck to his guns with the 'she called in sick' story. Even after he'd been quizzed about members of the Harley Club using the tunnel as a racing circuit.

McNab went for his car, already formulating a plan to visit Ellie at home, using the excuse that he wanted to tell her about the possible Harley connection.

Which was true enough.

When he'd approached DS Clark and proposed a visit to the Harley shop, she'd pointed out that they hadn't identified the tracks as being made by a Harley. She wasn't sure that that was even possible.

'I just wondered if Ellie or anyone in the shop might have an idea who was using the tunnel,' McNab had told Janice honestly. 'The motorbike fraternity are a pretty close-knit community.'

She'd studied him for a moment before answering. 'And Ellie would tell you if she knew?'

It was a valid question. Most folk didn't like ratting on their friends whatever the circumstances.

'She gave me the heads-up on the Davey Stevenson case,' McNab had said, reminding Janice how he'd known where to find a vehicle used in a hit and run.

'And you kept schtum about where you got that info.'

'I told *you*,' McNab had protested.

'Okay, go see Ellie. Find out what you can. After which you can chase the council and find out who has keys for the tunnel.'

McNab had smiled an okay, because both tasks were infinitely preferable to watching CCTV footage captured in the vicinity of Paradise Park, although it now looked as if he would have been more useful doing exactly that.

When he reached Ellie's block, there was no sign of her bike outside. McNab had adopted a frame of mind that said if he could only meet Ellie face to face and alone, they would talk things over. He would make her laugh again and . . .

We'll fuck and all will be well.

It was, even McNab could recognize, a decidedly male solution to the problem, but it was the only one he had.

He tried the buzzer a couple of times. When that didn't work he tried someone else's buzzer, pressing each of them in turn until he got a response.

'What?' an angry voice finally said.

'Police. I need into the close.'

The response was a frightened 'Fuck' after which the door buzzed open.

McNab took the stairs two at a time, keen to get this over with. Ear to the door, he listened, hoping for some indication that Ellie was inside, but heard none. He rapped on the door and waited, wishing now he'd agreed to have a key when Ellie had offered him one.

At the time, he'd feared accepting it would mean he would have to furnish Ellie with one for his own flat, so he'd jokingly turned her offer down. Not one of his best moves.

He could, of course, force an entry, should he so wish, but that would be unlikely to endear him to Ellie.

He turned from the door, accepting that, if in there, she had no wish to have a visitor, but preferring the explanation that since the bike was gone, so was she.

The question was, where?

30

Ellie opened the bedroom door and stepped into the hall. All was silent, apart from her heart that was thumping fit to burst in her chest.

She hurried to the sitting-room window and cautiously took a look outside.

Michael had gone. Ellie leaned against the wall and, slipping down to sit on the floor, hugged her knees.

How she'd longed to open the door to him, to have his arms round her again, and to tell him why she was behaving like this. And she would have done so, if it hadn't been for the phone call.

'I know what you did,' the voice had said.

'I didn't harm him.'

'No, but you felt a pulse. You felt something.'

'He was cold. He was dead.'

'But you're not sure of that, are you?'

And the voice was right. She'd touched him so briefly that she hadn't been sure, but paralysed by fear, for a moment she'd seen Danny's face again. Was that why she'd told the others that he was dead and made them leave and not tell anyone? She'd even argued with Izzy, putting the blame for their silence on her.

'You could have saved him if you'd called the police. You could have saved him.'

And the voice was right.

'I know what you did.'

Ellie dragged herself up from the floor, feeling the weight of guilt on her chest.

I did it again, just like with Danny. I let him die.

In the tunnel, it had been a possible faint flicker of a pulse she had ignored. With her brother it had been much more than that. All the signs were there.

He didn't tell you outright, but he tried. Oh, how he tried. And you ignored everything. You pretended it wasn't happening. That he wasn't taking drugs. That he wasn't taking chances. That he didn't care if he lived or died. That he might kill himself.

He told you in unspoken words and looks and actions.

And still you let him die.

Ellie buried her head in her hands. She'd believed the dark desert that she'd inhabited after Danny's death had finally gone. But in one moment, in that tunnel, the sand had swept in to drown her yet again.

She extracted the mobile from her pocket. It was still turned to silent. She checked her voicemail and found Michael's message. She'd never heard him sound like that before. She'd heard him being funny, sarcastic, evasive, tender, loving, but never with an edge of fear in his voice.

I can't tell Michael that I panicked and ignored the possibility that he might just be alive.

If she did, then she would have to explain about Danny and she couldn't do that. Ever. Even afterwards when her parents had tortured themselves with the idea that they had seen nothing to warn them he was taking drugs, she had said nothing to relieve their pain. Even when their marriage had disintegrated in grief.

I said nothing then. I can say nothing now.

She would go away, she thought. Climb on the bike and just go. She'd called the shop and the Ink Parlour and feigned sickness. They'd seemed to buy it. She'd also told Roddie at the shop that she didn't want to see Michael.

He was pleased about that.

Ellie imagined what might have happened had Michael gone to the shop. It wasn't a pretty thought.

God, what a mess.

It would be better to make herself scarce for a few days. Let things cool down. When she returned, she would make things right. She just needed time and space to think, and the open road would let her do that. It had saved her before. It would do so again.

She began packing. Just enough for a few days. She'd parked the bike a couple of streets away, hoping, should Michael come here, should anyone come here, they would think her gone.

She would go west, she decided. At this time of year there were always strings of motorbikes on Highland roads. She would just be one of many.

Her mobile vibrated on the bed, where she had laid it. On the screen was the empty outline of a figure and the unknown caller ID. She had made the mistake of answering it once.

She wouldn't do that again.

31

Ashton Lane was busy, outside tables being the favourites in the late sunshine. Rhona skirted these and headed downstairs into the shadowy interior of the jazz club, knowing Chrissy rarely if ever chose to visit the recently revamped beer garden out back. Apparently its mainly student clientele made her feel old.

'Plus, they listen in to our conversations.'

Rhona wasn't sure that the latter part of Chrissy's complaint was true, although, since the two of them often discussed forensic business, it was better not to be overheard.

Making her way down the stairs to the main room that housed the stage, Rhona found it virtually empty apart from a few customers who preferred the dark interior. Among those was Chrissy, seated at her usual place at the bar.

'I ordered for you.' She indicated the glass of white wine on the counter. 'Didn't think you'd want red.'

'You were right.'

'So,' Chrissy said conspiratorially. 'Tell all.'

'God, I have so many sins that need forgiven,' Chrissy declared, after listening to Rhona's story of the sleep lab. 'Why don't I suffer from sleep paralysis?' She sounded disappointed.

'Perhaps because you go to confession?' Rhona tried.

'I haven't been regularly since wee Michael was born.' Chrissy looked a trifle guilty at that. 'Although I did go when McNab disappeared at New Year.'

'So it's your fault he always comes back,' Rhona said.

'See,' Chrissy said triumphantly, 'I knew you two had fallen out *again*.'

Rhona didn't contradict her.

'So I texted him. Asked him to join us.' Chrissy glanced at the door as though McNab was about to appear. 'We can find out what's happening with Ellie.'

The idea of mixing McNab with Chrissy *and* alcohol didn't appeal to Rhona. Who knows what she might say, seeing as the sins of the past seemed to be getting an airing. Rhona finished her wine and got off her stool.

'Where are you going?' Chrissy demanded.

'Home, to eat,' Rhona declared. 'Sean put something in the slow cooker for me and I'm ready to find out what it is.'

Ignoring Chrissy's protestations, Rhona said her good-byes.

32

The aroma of the promised stew met Rhona on opening the front door.

The flat was silent, indicating Sean had already gone. His room confirmed this. He'd even made up the bed. The tidy image of his departure, plus the aroma of the prepared meal, instigated a brief feeling of guilt, which Rhona quickly dismissed.

She hadn't asked Sean to cook for her, and she hadn't invited him to stay here permanently either.

They'd tried living together once before and it had failed spectacularly.

Things were better the way they were now.

Tom failed to greet her entry, preferring, it seemed, to remain stretched out along the back of the settee in the sitting room, basking in the final rays of the sun.

Taking herself into the kitchen, she found a note from Sean alongside the slow cooker. It simply said, 'Enjoy'.

Rhona spooned a large helping onto a plate and took it to the window seat.

Below her, the neighbouring convent garden was already dappled with shadow, the setting sun partly obscured by the surrounding buildings. Two nuns sat on a seat next to the herbaceous border, chatting. Perhaps sensing Rhona's watchful eye, the younger of the two looked up and gave her a friendly wave, which Rhona returned.

The views from both front and rear windows had been the primary reason Rhona had bought the flat. Back then, the long terrace of stone tenements that overlooked the park had been a little rundown, her neighbours decidedly more eclectic than now, both features endearing the place to Rhona.

More recently, however, property developers had recognized the area's potential and had begun to buy up neighbouring buildings that had once housed offices and were redeveloping them into luxury flats, which were selling for high prices. Hence the turnover of residents in her own building.

Rhona was fairly philosophical about that, *except,* she thought, *if the convent were to move, I might have to go too.* The view from her kitchen window had sustained her through many of the darker moments in both her personal and professional life. She wasn't religious, but there was something comforting about the quiet certainty of the female community she looked out on.

Her hunger assuaged, Rhona now noted that the corked wine bottle from last night still stood on the kitchen table, its contents slightly depleted (or had she in fact drunk more than she'd realized the previous night?). Beside the bottle sat a brown paper bag which, she now discovered, contained a loaf of bread, partially consumed, an edible organic label attached with the name 'Henrietta's' on it.

Which I was supposed to eat along with the casserole.

If Henrietta's was a local shop, Rhona didn't recognize the name. Then again, Sean was the food and wine connoisseur. She, in contrast, existed mainly on Chinese and

Indian takeaways and, of course, the ubiquitous Italian pizza, delivered and eaten at odd hours.

Popping the loaf in the bread bin and turning off the slow cooker, Rhona moved through to the sitting room, taking her laptop with her, intent on checking for any forensic results that might have come in since she'd departed the lab earlier.

The air in the room, she noted, was redolent of the heat of the day and something else, a sharp scent, of what she wasn't sure. All the time she'd been in the kitchen enjoying the kind of food Tom usually went mad for, he hadn't moved from his favoured spot on the settee.

Sean, to Rhona's mind, was inclined to overindulge the cat with titbits while he cooked, which she assumed was the reason for Tom's disinterest in her own meaty meal.

'Tom?' Rhona said, approaching to ruffle his ears, an action he was particularly fond of.

He stretched a little under her touch, but then relaxed back into what resembled the sleep of the dead. He was usually like this after he'd been on the roof chasing and sometimes consuming the small birds that dared to land or nest in the vicinity, but there was no evidence via discarded feathers that he had brought one inside for his supper.

'Tom,' she said again, looking for a response which didn't come.

As Rhona crouched beside him, seeking an opening eye at least, the acrid scent grew stronger.

Had the cat been sick?

A little perturbed now, Rhona raised Tom's head, to discover a patch of drool beneath, accounting, she now realized, for the smell.

It wasn't the first time the cat had vomited up things he

shouldn't have eaten, but she'd never seen a reaction like this before. Rhona let go of his head and it lolled alarmingly, so much so that he would have fallen to the floor had she not caught him.

Weighty now in her arms, and unresponsive, it was obvious the cat was in something more than a deep sleep.

Rhona laid him out on the couch and checked for a pulse, her own heart racing.

33

The list of foods toxic to cats was comprehensive. Rhona ran her eye down her mobile screen, but could see nothing on it that Tom could have found in the kitchen. The stew had had onions and garlic in it, both on the list, but if Sean had given the cat a taste of the casserole, surely it would have been a piece of meat?

The most likely of the items listed would, she decided, be mouldy food, possibly discarded by seagulls on the roof rather than rifled from her kitchen bin.

Maybe Sean could give her a clue?

Sean's mobile rang out unanswered, so he either couldn't hear it in the noise of the club or else he was playing and had turned his mobile off.

Rhona switched tack and checked online for the nearest 24-hour vet service. The first one to appear was near Charing Cross, not too far away. She couldn't tell them what the cat had eaten, and for most poisons there wasn't an antidote anyway, but they could perhaps monitor his organs until the effects subsided.

Rather than try to load the cat into the carry basket, Rhona fetched a towel and, wrapping it round Tom's inert body, carried him down to the car. It wasn't until she opened the rear door to lay him along the back seat that she remembered the tyre.

God.

She had done nothing about having it fixed and it was flat again.

Rhona contemplated whether to call a taxi, but doubted whether they would accept an obviously ill cat in their cab. Maybe if Tom was in his carrier?

Should she go back for it?

Rhona went for the pump instead.

As she fitted it to the tyre, her mobile rang. Hoping it was Sean returning her call, Rhona answered without checking the screen.

'Rhona?'

It took her a moment to register who was calling her at this inopportune moment. 'Sorry, Conor. I have a bit of an emergency. I have a sick cat to take to the emergency room, and I've got a flat tyre.'

He responded immediately. 'I'm just leaving the clinic and have the car with me. Can I help?'

The tyre, despite her efforts, didn't appear to be inflating. Rhona swore with some force.

'Where are you exactly?' Conor said.

When Rhona told him, he came back with, 'I'll be with you directly,' and rang off.

Rhona tried refitting the pump to the valve. It didn't make any difference. Either the pump wasn't working or else the air was exiting as quickly as it could enter.

Just as well Conor proved true to his word.

Rhona looked up with relief as minutes later a car drew alongside her and Conor jumped out.

'If you sit in the passenger seat, I'll lift him in to you,' Conor offered.

Rhona did as suggested. Tom's body felt so lifeless when

Conor passed him to her that Rhona searched for a pulse again.

'Forget the pump,' she ordered, locking the car remotely from where she was. 'Let's go.'

She gave him the address, then called the emergency number to warn them she was on her way and the reason for their visit.

'Not sure it'll taste like coffee, but it's hot and black.' Conor handed Rhona the cup. 'Any word while I was at the machine?'

'They'll monitor him overnight. The vet says I can go home.'

'He'll pull through?'

'They seem to think so.'

Conor looked as relieved as Rhona felt. 'Have they any idea what he ate?'

'No, and without a pointer, they wouldn't know what toxins to test for,' Rhona said. 'It's the same with humans and poison, although a human can hopefully tell you what they consumed.'

'And if they can't?'

'Trickier.'

'So they might die and you wouldn't know why?' Conor looked horrified at the thought.

'Context is everything,' Rhona said. 'That's why reading a crime scene is so vital.'

'And why you hang around in those tents for so long?'

'Exactly.'

'But surely a pathologist can discover the cause of death at the autopsy?'

Rhona had met this conversation before, in her lectures in

particular. The general public believed anything was possible, probably from watching too many episodes of *CSI* and associated TV dramas.

'With an obvious injury, usually, yes. In the case of poison, there are so many tests Toxicology could be asked to do. We need a clue to point us in the right direction,' Rhona said.

Conor was obviously processing what she said.

'I was worried that Andrew's sleep paralysis might have contributed to his death, but what if . . . ?' Conor halted. 'The news just said an unexplained death – do you really not know how he died?'

'We're working on it.' Rhona wasn't saying anything that hadn't been said on air. She observed Conor's troubled look. 'Is there something else?' she encouraged him.

'After we spoke, I went back through the notes of my conversations with him. In retrospect, he may have been suicidal.' Conor scrunched up the empty coffee cup and tossed it in the bin. 'I failed him.'

'You're not a psychiatrist. You weren't responsible for his mental health.'

Conor didn't look convinced.

'When are you giving your statement to the police?' Rhona asked.

'Tomorrow morning. That's what I called to tell you earlier,' he explained.

Rhona finished her own coffee and disposed of the cup. 'I'm glad you did. Your help probably saved Tom's life,' she said gratefully.

Her words seemed to cheer him a little. 'Shall we ditch the car and get a drink?' he suggested.

Rhona agreed. It was the least she could do in the circumstances.

34

Tracking down all those with possible access to the London Street tunnel would take longer than twenty minutes, which was all he'd had before the council offices were destined to close for the night.

'If you come back tomorrow . . .' The woman on the desk had given him a pleading look at that point. The last thing she'd wanted before home time was the job McNab had just requested.

'I don't have access to that information,' she'd explained further, 'I'd need to talk to maintenance and,' she'd given a small apologetic smile, 'they've knocked off already.'

It had been a futile trip, he'd known that before he'd embarked upon it. If he'd come straight here after the Harley shop instead of heading for Ellie's flat . . .

Exiting the building, McNab took himself over the road and into George Square. The outside tables of the pub next to Queen Street station were packed with office workers, enjoying an after-work drink in the sunshine. McNab contemplated joining them, but knew he couldn't abandon the car in the city centre and expect to find it still there tomorrow morning.

Instead, he found an unoccupied bench, and sat down. The text from Chrissy encouraging him to come to the jazz club had arrived as he'd entered the council buildings and he had yet to respond.

He had to admit he was attracted by the idea.

Plus parking was free in the nearby side streets and if he headed there right now, he might just get a vacant spot before the nearby residents returned from work and commandeered all the spaces.

On the other hand, Chrissy, he knew, would pump him about Ellie, and he would also have to face Rhona, but yet he was tempted. If only to see if Rhona looked better than she had at the strategy meeting.

From that thought sprang another.

Despite Janice having given him tasks, ostensibly as part of the team, he most definitely wasn't in the driving seat. Something that was pissing him off. Still, if he wasn't essential, then they wouldn't miss him too much if he wasn't around, and he was free to knock off at normal times, rather than be on constant duty. That idea brought a faint smile to McNab's lips.

The late sunshine was having the 'taps aff' result Glasgow was known for. Three blokes with undeniably the physique for it had dispensed with their upper garments and were operating the 'sun's out, guns out' principle, much to the pleasure of the passing females, whose verbal responses and selfies were no doubt immediately destined for social media.

The feeling of being outside life, looking in, was one McNab was used to. If you were a detective, that was essentially your role. Watch everyone, trust no one, and most of all remember everybody, but everybody, had a secret – and more often than not, that secret could bring a brush with the law.

Even now, he was figuring out the backstory to everyone in the little tableau before him. He'd already checked out the faces of the three guys to see if he knew them. He wasn't a super recognizer like Ollie, but if he'd busted someone, he usually remembered.

McNab found himself almost disappointed when nothing about them seemed familiar, which made him, he acknowledged, a sad bastard.

He could imagine Ellie's reaction to that, if she'd been here.

The sudden thought of Ellie cut through him like a knife, and he checked his mobile again, just in case she'd got back to him, aware now that whatever message he left would likely go unanswered.

Did she just want him out of her life for good?

Maybe it was the detective in him that didn't believe that to be true. He'd seen enough lies told to believe he could recognize one, despite the Viking's lecture suggesting the contrary. Ellie was afraid of something. He'd seen that in her eyes at the speedway. And that something involved him, but McNab wasn't convinced that it *was* him.

Folk were nervous around the police, even if they hadn't done anything wrong. Ellie had been acting as though she had done something wrong.

Maybe she'd screwed someone else and it was just guilt he'd seen.

McNab shook his head. He didn't accept that. Ellie had been pretty straight with him up to now, almost painfully honest at times. They hadn't vowed to be exclusive, but she'd told him outright that if she was thinking of having sex with anyone else, she would tell him first, and that he should do the same for her.

That had been an interesting if uncomfortable conversation.

McNab had eventually agreed to the arrangement, although he didn't like to point out that offers like that didn't come his way too often.

As the idea took root, that it was something to do with his job which had so spooked Ellie, McNab thought again about the phone call she'd made the night of the tunnel discovery, which led then to the memory of those motor-bike tracks. Then her minder at the Harley shop, who seemed very keen that McNab should leave, and even keener when he discovered that the guy seeking Ellie, namely himself, was a cop.

Could it have been someone from the Harley gang who had called in the body?

That would make sense if they'd turned up there to race and discovered the remains. The operator who took the anonymous call had been unable to confirm the gender of the caller.

Might it have been a female, even Ellie?

If so, had that been enough to make her break off contact with him? McNab pondered such a scenario. If she had been down there, and they thought up to four bikes had, then they had been there illegally, but it wasn't exactly the crime of the century.

What if they'd seen something more than a dead body? What if they'd seen the perpetrator?

That train of thought spooked McNab.

Had Ellie gone into hiding from him or maybe because of who or what she'd seen in the tunnel? And what about her mates? Izzy hadn't seemed perturbed at all by meeting him at the speedway. In fact she'd seemed pleased, by the way she'd kept throwing Ellie encouraging looks.

Encouraging Ellie to do what? Find out what she could from him about the investigation?

McNab went for the car, aware that he was likely too late to meet Chrissy at the jazz club. He should head back to the station, catch DS Clark, who would, no doubt, still be there, and report what had happened at the Harley shop, plus his thoughts about it.

As he reached the car, just in time to thwart a parking attendant intent on giving him a ticket, his mobile rang. McNab flashed his ID at the surprised meter man, then answered the call.

It was Ollie.

'Come see what I've found on the two old guys at Marshall's.'

35

'So where d'you suggest we go?' Conor said as he manoeuvred the car into a parking space outside the building he said housed his own flat.

Getting her bearings, Rhona realized how close they were to the gated entrance at the eastern flank of Kelvingrove.

'You're right next to the park,' she said.

'I am, which makes the bike the sensible travel option. However, it's still being fixed, so I was lazy enough to take the car to work today. So,' he said, 'where do you normally go for a drink?'

'After work, usually Ashton Lane.' Rhona could have mentioned the jazz club and Sean at that point, but chose not to.

'Do you want to go there?' he offered.

'Let's find somewhere closer, then I just have to climb those,' Rhona indicated the steps that led up to Park Circus, 'and I'm home.'

Five minutes later they were seated in a bar on Sauchiehall Street with a welcome drink in front of them. Rhona had stuck to white wine, while Conor had taken his time choosing a craft beer.

'Skye Gold?' Rhona had said, a little surprised by his choice.

'I sampled the Red and the Black versions when I went walking there,' Conor had told her. 'Good stuff.'

'So,' Rhona said, 'you know my home island?'

'You're from Skye?' Now it was Conor's turn to be surprised.

'I wasn't born there, but my parents were.' Rhona told him about the cottage. 'With arguably the best view on the island.'

'D'you go back often?'

'Not as often as I'd like,' she said. 'I was briefly there last autumn, not since. But I do plan to go for Christmas.'

Although she'd contemplated this, Rhona hadn't been sure about it until this very moment. Probably because both Sean and Chrissy would expect her to be in Glasgow over the festive period.

'Tell me more about your work,' she said, changing the subject.

'You're sure? I might send you to sleep,' he joked.

'I'll take that chance.' Rhona smiled her encouragement.

'Sleep is, to my mind at least, the strangest and most amazing thing that we do every day,' Conor said eagerly. 'Did you know on average we will spend thirty-six per cent of our life asleep?'

Rhona pulled a face. 'I doubt I will.'

'Then you need to address that, and soon,' Conor told her, his tone immediately serious. 'If you only get six hours' sleep a night for six weeks straight, that's as destructive as getting none for forty-eight hours,' he warned.

'Why?' Rhona genuinely wanted to know.

'Because sleep flushes toxins out of the brain and it consolidates our knowledge, getting rid of all the stuff we don't have to remember.' He was watching her reaction. 'Added to that, during sleep, our imagination runs free and unhampered by the process of just being alive. We see and experience things we couldn't possibly imagine when awake.'

'Like Einstein and relativity?' she reminded him.

'Exactly. Einstein said imagination was more important than intelligence. If students only slept more and partied less . . .' Conor smiled. 'Seriously, though, how the brain works is the last great frontier. And understanding sleep is a big part of that.'

Rhona sipped her wine. For an evening that had started out so badly, it had definitely improved.

'Go on, this is interesting,' she urged him.

'Well,' he began again, 'your brain is relatively quiet throughout most sleep phases, but during REM sleep it definitely comes to life.'

'To sleep, perchance to dream?' Rhona offered.

Conor's expression darkened as he completed the famous quotation. 'To die, to sleep – to sleep, perchance to dream. Ay, there's the rub. For in this sleep of death what dreams may come . . .'

Rhona had forgotten the context of the quote and Hamlet's thoughts of his own death. Now it seemed almost too apt.

To cover the moment, she said, 'So REM sleep is essential?'

'It's absolutely critical. Without the slow-wave sleep which helps our bodies recover physically *and* the REM sleep phases –' he halted for a moment – 'then we literally start to die.'

He met her eye at this point, his own gaze troubled, and

Rhona realized he was thinking about Andrew Jackson again and what he hadn't done for him.

Conor put down his glass. 'I should really be getting back. I've some work to do before tomorrow,' he said.

Rhona nodded. 'Me too.'

They left their drinks unfinished and went silently to the door. When they reached the car, Conor offered to accompany Rhona to the top of the nearby steps and thus nearer home.

'They're not very well lit,' he warned her. 'And with the neighbouring undergrowth so close . . .'

'I'm not afraid of the dark or the undergrowth,' Rhona told him. 'Besides, running up those steps is how I keep fit,' she added.

Her attempt to lift the mood again was rewarded with a half-smile. 'Okay, but remember, don't stray from the path,' Conor said, quoting Tolkien.

'I won't,' she promised.

Stopping halfway up, Rhona turned with a wave, only to find Conor gone.

36

Ollie's call had been a godsend. No decision to make and yet somewhere to go.

The more info he took back to Janice the better, even better if none of it was gained through going off-grid. He was playing good cop at the moment and, if not exactly enjoying it, McNab recognized it as serving a purpose.

Ollie was in IT, his desk displaying the refuse of what he'd consumed since McNab had been there last. He looked up at McNab's approach, perhaps hopeful of more brain-stimulating fodder. McNab didn't usually disappoint, and didn't now, although his offering of a single caramel log from the dispensing machine, an Ollie favourite, didn't seem quite enough at this late hour.

'If this is good, I'll buy you that pizza at Marco's,' McNab said in a rare moment of generosity – or was it that even Ollie's company was better than eating at home alone?

Ollie didn't say yea or nay, just ushered McNab into a seat and urged him to take a look at the largest of his three current screens, on which there was a list.

Without taking time to read the contents, McNab immediately said, 'What is this?'

Ollie sighed in what McNab assumed was exasperation. 'Your two old dead guys were enrolled on this free MOOCs course,' he said.

McNab had heard that MOOCs word before, at Stanley Robertson's house.

'What the fuck does MOOCs mean?' he said in irritation.

Ollie looked taken aback that he didn't know. 'Massive open online course. Universities all over the world run them and they're free via the internet.'

'Okay,' McNab said, somewhat mollified. 'What course were they taking then?' he said, never expecting to hear the answer that followed.

'One on forensics,' Ollie told him.

'You're fucking kidding me?' McNab said with a little laugh.

Ollie shook his head. 'Nope. Very popular it is too. Run by Glasgow Uni. Even stars Dr MacLeod,' he added.

'What?' McNab's voice rose in accordance with his amazement.

'Some of the lectures are recorded from the diploma course that Dr MacLeod lectures on,' Ollie explained in a patient manner.

McNab didn't like that, but he wasn't exactly sure why.

'That's their only connection with each other?' he asked.

'I haven't found anything else, except of course the company that they chose to bury them,' Ollie said.

'One was cremated,' McNab corrected him.

'Dust to dust. Ashes to ashes,' Ollie said soulfully.

McNab stared at him. 'You do fucking realize there are no computers in the afterlife?'

'How do you know?' Ollie said, all wide-eyed. 'Maybe, just maybe, we're all in *The Matrix*.'

'Oh, fuck off,' McNab said, and meant it.

*

Ollie had declined his offer of a pizza, so now McNab had a decision to make. Eat alone at Marco's again or go home and order in. After Ollie, he'd checked if Janice was still about, only to discover that she had a life which she had gone home to. Unlike himself.

He wallowed for a moment, recalling other nights when he'd picked up Ellie and they'd eaten together and ended up at her flat or his.

That prompted his call, which was ringing out now. McNab didn't expect an answer, so was shocked when he got one.

'Michael?'

Her voice was sweet to his ears at first, then he registered something other than pleasure.

'Where are you?' McNab demanded.

There was a moment's silence, then in a shocked whisper, she said, 'He wasn't dead.'

37

She'd asked Sean not to come back tonight so that she might have the flat all to herself.

Beware of what you wish for sprang to mind as Rhona locked the door behind her, the turning of the key echoing in the silence.

In the kitchen, Tom's uneaten food was a sad reminder of what had just happened to her cat. Rhona lifted the dish and took a closer look at the contents, but there was nothing in there bar the dried pellets of food Tom always had.

Noting his escape route was still open, Rhona had the brief thought while closing the window that she could venture onto the flat roof and check if there was anything up there that might have caused the damage.

But definitely not tonight and in the dark.

In the sitting room her laptop lay open where she'd left it in the horror of the moment when she'd realized something was badly wrong with Tom. The sharp smell that had alerted her then still lingered.

It would have to be cleaned up, before she could settle down to work.

As Rhona went to fetch the means to do that, another thought occurred. If she retrieved a sample of the vomit, she might be able to identify what had provoked it. As she'd told Conor, they couldn't check for toxicity unless they had an idea what they were looking for, but something in the pungent mess might give her a clue. And if it was something present on the roof she would curtail Tom's visits up there.

Something he wouldn't be happy about.

Her sample collected, Rhona stored it in the fridge and returned to a more fragrant sitting room. She checked her mobile and found a missed call from Chrissy.

She briefly contemplated phoning back, but noting the time, decided not to. Chrissy might indulge in a quick drink after work, but she was always home to put her son, wee Michael, to bed, and her time with him then was sacrosanct.

The story of Tom's life being saved by 'the handsome' Dr Williams would have to wait until morning. Rhona could already picture Chrissy's eager delight in the retelling of that tale.

The heat of the day had dissipated and Rhona now felt a slight chill in the room. She rose and turned on the fire, then went to close the curtains. Below, the park was enveloped by darkness, the steps she'd climbed earlier merely a faintly lit path. Rhona thought of Conor returning home, his mind still troubled by what he thought he hadn't done for Andrew Jackson.

It wouldn't have been ethical for her to reveal that they were already considering the possibility that Andrew had taken his own life. It might well be revealed that he'd used the yew needles she'd discovered in the flat to achieve that.

Why he would have gone into the tunnel to die, she couldn't as yet fathom, but Conor's statement tomorrow about Jackson's state of mind would no doubt be welcomed by the investigation team.

At moments during their conversation in the pub, she'd wondered if Conor hadn't yet revealed everything he knew about the victim. Conor wasn't a medical doctor, so he didn't have to adhere to the code on doctor–patient confidentiality, but she didn't believe he'd voiced all his concerns in either of their conversations.

The thought occurred that maybe the best person to talk to Conor was Magnus, there being undoubted crossover between their academic areas. Magnus might perhaps reassure Conor that he wasn't to blame, even inadvertently, for Jackson's death.

Rhona made a mental note to suggest that to Bill in the morning.

Settling back on the couch, she checked through the list of recently delivered messages, aware that lab results, particularly regarding DNA, weren't particularly speedy. Had there been clear evidence that Jackson's death was a homicide, her impatience would have been even greater, although the discovery of forensic suit fibres on the body had rendered the picture even more complex, and she was keen to know if any DNA had been found on the fibre.

Registering that nothing new had arrived in her absence, Rhona shut the laptop. She should, of course, if following Conor's advice, head for bed and get more than six hours' sleep. She smiled a little at the memory of his intensity as he'd spoken of his work, something she could relate to herself.

He'd even gone so far as to offer her a sleeping aid. 'I use it with my patients and it has a good success rate,' he'd said, before adding, 'Andrew wouldn't use it, unfortunately. So the only sleep he got was at the clinic.' At that point Conor had fished out a USB drive from his pocket and offered it to her. 'Play this on your computer when you get into bed. You'll fall asleep faster, and sleep more soundly.'

'And my imagination will improve?' Rhona had joked.

'An added bonus,' he'd said.

Rising, Rhona decided a shower before bed was in order, if only to dispense with the lingering scent, imagined or otherwise, of Tom's dice with death. Crossing the hall, she double-checked the front door was locked before heading for the shower.

Stripping, she turned the regulator to a little hotter than usual and stepped under the spray. The pin needles of heat brought a blush to her skin and, more importantly, the beat on her head helped calm her thoughts.

She hadn't regarded herself as a poor sleeper, but a demanding work schedule had often resulted in fewer hours than Conor had recommended. Heading to bed earlier hadn't always helped, as her brain had then taken the opportunity to go into overdrive. Tonight, Rhona recognized as just such an occasion.

So maybe she would take his advice and use the sleep aid.

The shower on full power, she didn't hear the house phone ring out at first. More used now to the mobile, the main line was sometimes used by Sean when she didn't respond to her mobile.

Rhona stepped out of the shower and, wrapping a towel round her dripping body, went to answer it. If it was Sean returning her call, he might just have an inkling about what had made Tom so ill.

'Hello?'

It was either a poor line or the background noise of

music and chatter was simply drowning out the caller's response.

Rhona tried again. 'Hello? Sean?'

The background noise ceased as though someone had put their hand over the receiver.

Rhona waited.

The words now spoken were definitely not being said by Sean. In fact it was a voice Rhona didn't recognize, either its gender or its owner.

'Who is this?' Rhona demanded.

The voice repeated the words, leaving her in no doubt as to what was being said.

38

McNab tried the recall button, but this time there was no answer. Ellie's whispered words, 'He wasn't dead', made no sense, although if she was talking about the body in the tunnel, then that meant she had definitely been down there.

McNab's final demand, asking again where she was, hadn't been answered. He'd already left the station when he'd placed the call. He could turn round and head back there, and ask Ollie or whoever was on duty to put a trace on her mobile. Then he would at least know where Ellie was.

But something stopped him. If he did that, then Ellie became part of the investigation, and he wasn't at all sure she was. He definitely needed to speak to her face to face before he took this any further. But how was he to achieve that?

There had been background noise including loud music during the call, which suggested Ellie was in a bar or a club when she'd contacted him. McNab tried to recall where she and her friends hung out. Was it one of the places she'd taken him? In the excited blur of their early courtship, they'd visited lots of different bars, although rarely for long, the desire for sex having driven them to whichever of their flats was the nearest.

McNab recalled one place where the rock music had been turned up high, which was also a much-loved venue for bikers, judging by the Harleys and Triumphs that had been lined up outside. Ellie had seemed well known there, and there'd been food on offer. Something, McNab acknowledged, he would welcome.

Heading back into the town centre, he ditched the car as soon as possible and walked the rest of the way. He hadn't remembered the name of the pub, but a quick online search had brought up an image of the bar frontage, which, he recalled, had looked more like a fancy-dress outlet than a rock bar.

Outside it now, he ran his eye over the current row of motorbikes, hoping to find Ellie's among them, and was disappointed when he didn't. Still, if she was planning to consume alcohol, Ellie wouldn't have brought the bike. She was a stickler about that, and not just because she was dating a cop.

When he opened the door, the music hit him like a wall. McNab checked out the upstairs clientele, including those clustered round the pool table, but saw no one he recognized. Ellie had taken him downstairs on their visits, and he headed there now, the music accompanying him.

Despite the noise level, folk still seemed to be having conversations, which impressed McNab no end. He headed for the bar and, waving the offer of a menu away, ordered the pizza slices and curly chips he'd shared with Ellie.

The barman looked familiar, so McNab acted as though he too should be recognized.

'Ellie sold me on the curly chips,' he said, hoping for a positive response to the name drop.

The bartender took a second look, although it wasn't

clear he had recognized either Ellie's name or McNab's face by his stock response of 'How you doing?'

'Good,' McNab said with a wide smile. 'I'm supposed to meet Ellie Macmillan here. Have you seen her?' He attempted a searching look around the room.

'Nope, sorry,' the barman said, giving the impression he did at least know who Ellie was. 'Where you sitting?'

McNab gestured to an empty table with a view of the room.

'I'll send her over when she appears. Are you wanting a plate to share?'

McNab said yes to keep up the pretence that Ellie was expected. He was hungry enough for two anyway.

'What about a drink?'

McNab ordered a pint.

Seated at the table, the large plate of pizza slices and curly chips in front of him, McNab kept his eye on the room as he ate.

After he'd taken McNab's order, the barman had gone briefly through the back. Since he'd entered the order on the till screen, McNab suspected his disappearance had nothing to do with the food, plus he'd caught the quick glance sent in his own direction beforehand.

He began to wonder if this was just going to be a replay of what had happened to him earlier in the Harley shop.

If Ellie had made it plain to her friends that she didn't want to see him, whenever or wherever he might turn up . . .

The pretence that Ellie was going to appear being over, McNab set about finishing the food. At least by doing that, he was avoiding drinking the beer, which he now craved. An image of the rest of the night was panning out in front of him, and it definitely involved visiting the off-licence on his way home.

His head shot up as a female voice interrupted that line of thought.

'Michael?'

It wasn't Ellie, but it was near as dammit.

'Izzy.' McNab rose in delight and almost hugged her. 'Is Ellie with you?' He looked about.

She gave an abrupt shake of her head. 'Ellie's not here. I don't even think she's in Glasgow.'

McNab now registered how strained Izzy's face was.

'What's happened? What's wrong?' he said, his heart sinking.

It came out in a rush, as though Izzy was afraid she might stop herself before the end. 'Four of us were racing in the London tunnel. We saw the body. Ellie wanted to tell you.' Izzy hesitated. 'I stopped her.'

As McNab processed the startling confession, a lot of things suddenly started dropping into place, in particular Ellie's call that night when he was at the crime scene.

That's what she'd phoned about and he'd behaved like a prick in his response.

McNab took refuge in facts. 'Tell me exactly what happened.'

The words flowed, anxious as she was to be rid of them. 'We were racing. Ellie made it to the car a second before me. She spun her back wheel round to get there. I was blocked and pissed about it. She went through. I pulled up. Then Gemma and Mo came up behind and . . . we saw him.'

She halted there, a flash of relived horror crossing her face. 'Ellie went up close. She touched his neck. She said he was dead.' She halted and gathered herself. 'We sent the other two home. Then we argued. I told her not to report it. I was screwing the guy who gave us the key. He would get the sack if we told.'

She threw McNab a challenging look. 'I'm not giving you his name,' she said defiantly.

'I don't care about him,' McNab told her. 'When did you last see or hear from Ellie?'

'Not since the speedway last night. She's not answering her phone and she's not at the flat.'

'What about her dad? Could she be at home?'

Izzy shook her head adamantly. 'No way is she there. She hates his new wife, *Sylvie*.' She made a grimacing face. 'Ellie only sees her dad at the speedway because *Sylvie* doesn't go there. She doesn't like the smell of petrol,' Izzy added as a finale to her obvious disgust at the new wife.

'But could Ellie have told her father where she was going?'

'And not tell me? I don't think so,' Izzy said adamantly.

'She called me earlier.' McNab had wanted the whole story before he told Izzy that.

Izzy looked at him, open-eyed. 'Fuck. Is she okay?'

McNab couldn't answer that. 'She said something weird, but maybe now it makes sense.'

'What did she say?' Izzy demanded.

39

'Taxine is a collection of alkaloids which occur naturally in yew trees,' Rhona explained to Bill. 'Fifty to one hundred grammes of chopped leaves is sufficient to kill an adult. They can be brewed like tea for drinking or made into a potion and added to some other beverage.'

Bill looked thoughtful. 'Such as red wine,' he muttered. 'But I understood the wine at the locus tested okay?'

'It did,' Rhona agreed. 'But he may have already taken the potion, and the wine in the glass could have been purely symbolic. Like the bread,' she added, 'which he didn't consume.' Rhona explained the theory she and Chrissy had come up with regarding the bread and the presence of teeth marks, but absence of DNA.

'When will we know if it was taxine that killed him?'

'Now Toxicology know what to look for, quite quickly, I expect.'

Bill turned from her then and stared out of the window. Something was bothering him and Rhona didn't think it was her explanation about the taxine or even her story of what had happened with Conor.

She waited, knowing Bill was about to tell her, and hoping, whatever it was, it didn't involve McNab.

With a tensing of his shoulders, Bill seemed to make up

his mind. He turned abruptly from his view of the city and, going to his desk, handed Rhona a piece of paper.

Rhona examined it, aware that whatever it contained was what was worrying him.

Skimming the contents, she swiftly located her own name. The fact that it was there at all was enough to forewarn her. Still, she didn't buy what the report stated.

'It's possible, but unlikely,' she said.

'That's what I thought.'

'My DNA could have been on the scene, although most skin is covered by the PPE.'

Rhona thought back. Had she inadvertently scratched her cheek with her wrist? Or by leaning over the victim, allowed skin cells to drop in?

She replayed that night in the tunnel. She'd replaced her outer gloves regularly. She'd certainly been tired, especially towards morning. Even thinking about it now, the smell of the place returned, a mix of damp and disuse and the rank stink of diesel from the generator.

The ballast was sharp, it might have penetrated her suit, but surely she would have noticed? When Chrissy had identified the fibre as one coming from a PPE suit, neither of them had considered it might have been from hers. But it could have been. They weren't able to check now in any case, the suit having been already discarded.

Everyone who worked with forensic services had to provide a buccal swab for elimination purposes. The presence of her DNA on the fibre found in the nostril was unfortunate, but an explanation was possible. As to how the fibre got there in the first place . . .

But that wasn't the deposit Bill was really concerned about.

'I can't see how this second contamination could have happened,' she said, even surer now that she was right. 'The body remained clothed at the crime scene.'

'So you had no contact with any part of it under the clothing?'

'None,' she assured him. 'I saw the body naked for the first time at the autopsy.'

Rhona's brain raced round the problem, trying to be logical, questioning herself and her actions. Imagining ways that this could have happened and without her knowledge. She'd been in the tent alone for a long time. No one could vouch for her, except herself. Yet still her mind kept coming back to the one conclusion that made any sense.

'I believe there is a possibility that both DNA samples were planted on the body.'

Bill remained silent, but she knew his mind was analysing what she'd just said.

'That would be difficult to prove.'

'Exactly, and it throws doubt on how I processed the scene.' Rhona halted, remembering McNab's earlier remark that they were being played by the fucker who'd left the body in the tunnel. She repeated this for Bill.

'So the perpetrator has forensic knowledge?'

'A lot of people do,' Rhona said. 'They watch TV, read the books. Take courses in it. And you can buy a PPE suit online.'

She had happily taught those who wanted to know more about the subject, although McNab had voiced his opinion, more than once, that he didn't like giving ammunition to any fucker who might use it against them.

'Why your DNA? How could they know you would be the one to process the scene?'

'They're close enough to me to find that out,' Rhona said with a shiver of realization at how many people that could encompass. 'Or it didn't matter if it was me or not who attended the scene. My DNA would still be found, which was the point.' She paused. 'They must know our DNA is stored for elimination purposes.'

Bill was watching her intently, reading her expression, which said there was more. 'What is it?' he finally said.

Rhona told him. 'I had a call late last night on the house phone. An indistinguishable voice on a noisy line.'

Bill looked concerned. 'A nuisance call?'

'Maybe, although . . .' Rhona hesitated.

There had been no long silences. No heavy breathing. No sexual references. Just a repeated short sentence, which at the time made no sense.

Rhona had spent most of the night trying to work out what those words might refer to, if anything at all. Sleep, when it had come, had been punctured by bad dreams about remembered secrets that might just fit the accusation.

'What did this caller say?' Bill prompted her.

'They said, "I know what you did".'

40

Despite the bout of good weather, Magnus found the lecture theatre full. The chosen titles for their dissertations were due in by the end of the week and Magnus suspected today's topic would prove a popular choice for many. Hence the eager faces before him.

Everyone likes to imagine that they can look into the mind of a killer.

The popularity of forensic psychology, and criminal profiling in particular, was strong among the student body and the general public, but not necessarily among all serving police officers.

Magnus sent a swift glance to the current contingent's preferred location, to find the magnificent seven sitting as usual in a tight-knit group. He imagined he could almost smell their animosity flowing towards him. They always offered 'considered' criticism on his subject matter – the lecture on whether police officers were no better at spotting a lie than the general public being a particular source of disagreement.

But today's topic will be the one I take the most flak for, Magnus thought, reading the expressions on those faces.

On his entry, the class had moved swiftly from chatter to silence. Magnus was never required to call them to attention. It was, he acknowledged, gratifying to observe such an interest in his subject, even if the police personnel, the ones most likely to make use of it, seemed the least enamoured by it.

The slides he planned to show centred on the Stonewarrior case, probably the most famous of the cases he'd worked on with Dr MacLeod. Stonewarrior had been an artificial reality game, an ARG, its access restricted to the perpetrator's victims. The game had featured Neolithic stone circles and Druidic practices, and the story of its role had caught the public's imagination, especially when they themselves had been invited by the perpetrator to forecast the Neolithic circle where the next body might be found.

The image now on the screen was of the first locus in that case. Magnus was surprised by the sudden rush of emotion he experienced on viewing it again. A teenage boy, taking a walk on a Sunday morning with his dog in a park to the south of Glasgow, never to return home.

The stone circle stood on a grassy hilltop with a panoramic view of the city spread out before it. In its centre lay the body, face down, as though in supplication in this place of the ancients.

Gathering himself, Magnus began to describe the scene in fuller detail.

'The body had been laid out in a precise pose, the hands angled so as to point in specific directions. This was the case in subsequent loci, although the directions were different.'

He halted for a moment, remembering.

'In her examination of the scene, Dr MacLeod discovered a stone in the victim's mouth with a number etched on it. In the case of the first victim, that number was five.'

There was a studied hush in the room, as though everyone was holding their breath.

A hand went up and Magnus invited the questioner to speak.

'What did the hands point to?'

Magnus explained. 'Eventually, by lining up the various directions, we linked them to the sacred pentagram of Scotland, essentially five Neolithic stone circles, which,' Magnus added, 'subsequently became crime scenes.'

The enormity of the task faced by Police Scotland during this case had begun to filter into their consciousness. Many in the room would have heard some of the details via the news feed, but few would have viewed the locus and victim, except perhaps among the police officers.

Then the second question from someone three rows back.

'How did the signature help identify the killer?'

Before Magnus could attempt an answer, one of the female officers called out, 'It didn't.'

All faces now turned to her.

'It was a detective who engaged online with the Stonewarrior game and located the killer,' she announced.

Now that was something the audience didn't know.

Realizing she had their full attention, she continued. 'He did it against orders and subsequently faced a disciplinary committee and was demoted from Detective Inspector. Despite the fact that it was he who apprehended the killer.'

Magnus found himself holding his breath and unable to interrupt the flow of barely suppressed anger emanating from that area of the room, probably because he too had been distressed by the way McNab had been treated.

The officer wasn't finished yet.

'Is it not the case, Professor Pirie,' she said, 'that forensic psychology didn't solve the Stonewarrior case, but good policing?'

The atmosphere had been different after that. The eagerness that had met him on entry had dissipated. They'd listened to his talk on the signature and the profiling work he had done on the perpetrator and taken their notes religiously, but the officer's intervention on the real reason the killer had been caught had changed their perceptions.

Magnus wasn't against that. Profiling, he knew, wasn't the answer, but merely another piece of the jigsaw. That wasn't what had disturbed him as he'd drawn together his conclusions, one eye on the clock.

It had been the female officer's final comment, before he dismissed the class.

'Isn't it true that the detective in question was the real target for the perpetrator in the Stonewarrior case, and if that had been established earlier by profiling, then the other victims could have been saved?'

It was a question he'd had to answer with a 'yes'.

Rather than depart first, Magnus had taken his time in packing his briefcase and disengaging his presentation laptop, allowing the room to empty. Today, no one stayed behind, keen to ask questions, which he was both grateful for and a little saddened by.

Emerging from the lecture theatre, he found he was wrong. Someone did want to talk to him or perhaps just berate him further.

She held out her hand. 'Detective Constable Shona Fleming.'

Magnus took the hand, which he wasn't sure was offered in friendship.

'We get a lot of guff about stuff like yours,' she said. 'Sometimes we kick back.'

Magnus nodded, unwilling to do more than that.

'Can I talk to you about the body in the tunnel?'

She was tall, almost level with him. Her voice in the lecture theatre had been confident. Her stance was equally so. Magnus, registering all of this, was also taken aback by the question, having expected something more about Stone-warrior.

'I have a theory, Professor,' she said, 'which I'd like to run past you. Can we get a coffee?'

41

When she reached the lab, Rhona discovered a note from Chrissy explaining she'd had to go out, but would be back shortly.

The tone suggested that word on her DNA match to the body had already reached Chrissy's ears, despite Bill's attempts to prevent it becoming common knowledge.

Nothing travels faster than bad news.

A pot of coffee stood ready and waiting for her on the hotplate, a chocolate croissant on a plate alongside. Rhona said a silent thank you to her forensic assistant and poured herself a cup.

Drinking her coffee, Rhona found herself energized by her meeting with Bill rather than threatened by it. While they'd questioned whether they were dealing with a homicide or a suicide, the existence of a perpetrator had remained elusive. Now that there was some evidence they might be being played, everything had changed.

Rhona, boosted by that thought, lifted her mobile. It was time to talk to McNab instead of avoiding him. After all, their difficult relationship was as much her fault as his.

It had been after her father had died, and with his death, her last chance to reveal to him that she'd had a son had gone. She hadn't told her father that he was a granddad, even on his death bed. It was a cruelty Rhona couldn't forgive herself for, but one she'd had to learn to live with.

She'd drowned that feeling with sex, and the recipient she'd chosen had been a gullible partner in that coupling, expecting more of their relationship than Rhona had ever been willing to give. It had been a cruel misconception. When she'd broken things off badly with McNab after three months, he'd been devastated.

He'd hung around, if not exactly stalking her, then waiting and hoping for a rematch. Bill Wilson had finally saved the day by posting him to the Police College. Banished, McNab had returned weeks later, seemingly accepting now that their relationship was over.

But it wasn't, and Rhona doubted that it ever could be, particularly in view of what had happened during Stonewarrior.

The number rang out and Rhona wondered if McNab was staring at the screen, planning to decline her call, just as she had his on numerous occasions, then he answered.

Rhona knew immediately that something was badly wrong, even when met with his silence.

'What is it?' she said, expecting he'd already heard about the fibre.

McNab's voice cracked as he answered. 'They've found her.'

Rhona's mind was racing. 'Who?' she said.

Ending McNab's call, Rhona had gone swiftly to the lab window and, looking downwards, caught a glimpse of a couple of police vehicles through the green foliage, their bodies glinting in the sunlight.

So close, she thought as she exited the cloisters and made for the downward path she normally used to walk home by, busy now with folk exploiting it as a vantage point to check out the police presence in the park below.

As she drew nearer, she noted that two concentric cordons had already been set up, the outer one attracting attention from the sunbathers in the park.

It was, she registered, a challenging locus. The trees offered some shelter from prying eyes, although there were plenty of vantage points, like her own lab, where what was happening below could be recorded. The perimeter too was tricky. You couldn't man the full length of the police tape, and interested parties could find a way through.

Whatever precautions were taken, Rhona didn't doubt that photos from however distant would feature on the lunchtime news. Approaching the outer cordon, she found DS McConnachie awaiting her arrival.

'DS McNab said you were on your way.' Handing her a suit, his look was one Rhona couldn't begin to interpret.

If I question whether everyone I meet knows about the contamination . . .

Saying nothing, Rhona got kitted up, signed the sheet and ducked under the tape. A designated path snaked across a rough patch of grass and headed into the thick undergrowth that circled university hill. Twigs snatched at her as she walked, but Rhona was glad to see that no attempt had been made to cut back the bushes until the area had been fully examined.

Yards further on, the undergrowth grew thinner and ended in a small clearing, in the centre of which stood a horribly familiar tree. The tree of her nightmare. Rhona halted in surprise.

Had she been this way before and stored a memory of the tree's existence, her subconscious conjuring it up for her dreams?

Now in the flesh, Rhona recognized it as a mature yew tree – the peeling, reddish-brown bark with purple tones, the straight small needles with pointed tips, dark green above, green-grey below.

It certainly was a nightmarish image, and not just because of the thick, ribbed body and dark, heavy branches.

Rhona held her breath behind the mask, seeking to delay the impending assault on her senses, but the smell of heat and decomposition still hit her nostrils as the angry buzzing of flies, disturbed at their feasting, filled her ears.

The girl's body was seated against the trunk, her hair interwoven with yew twigs, one of which partially covered her face. Her hands were clasped together on her chest, her legs outstretched. She was wearing a floral dress and black pumps. On the ground nearby stood a stemmed glass filled with what Rhona assumed would be red wine. Nearby sat the token bread, partially eaten.

There were two suited figures next to the body, one hunkered down and taking a closer look. The other was definitely McNab, his stance instantly recognizable. He didn't turn on Rhona's approach, but kept his eyes fastened on the scene before him.

The yew twig partially obscured her face, but Rhona recognized the slim figure, the frame of hair. Gone was Claire Masters's bright smile. Gone too her shining eyes.

The other figure now beckoned her to join him, and Rhona noticed the sharp blue gaze of Dr Walker.

Once crouched beside him, the image before her became even more stark. The yew twig near her mouth, Rhona suspected, hadn't been the means of killing her. The ligature, a thin brown cord wound round her neck and attached to a lower branch, possibly had.

Rhona glanced at the stone statue that was McNab and knew he was working out how he had somehow brought the victim to this point. When they'd spoken on the phone, he'd already made up his mind it was Ellie's body that had been discovered, but was incoherent in his explanation as to why. Now relief that he'd been wrong was being subsumed by guilt regarding the actual victim.

'The Detective Sergeant says he knows her?' Dr Walker was saying.

'Her name is Claire Masters. She works . . . worked at the funeral parlour that had a break-in prior to the death in the tunnel. Claire believed that someone had eaten and drunk over two of her charges and alerted us to that.' Even as she said this, Rhona was questioning, like McNab, how that might have put the girl in such danger.

'A low-level suspension, at the level of the neck or below, is a classic suicide –' Walker hesitated – 'but we'll have to get her on the table to tell if it was.'

'And the yew mask?' Rhona said, aware that the pathologist knew nothing as yet about her discovery of the needles in the former victim's flat or whether they would prove to be instrumental in Andrew Jackson's death.

'The yew does have significance in death rituals,' he offered. 'How upset was the girl about what happened at the funeral parlour?'

'Very,' Rhona said, without elaborating further.

'In a suspected suicide, we would normally sever the cord, but preserve the knot for examination.'

'I don't think the cord should be cut,' Rhona said. 'Until I process the body.'

'Okay,' he said, reading her expression. 'What about securing the locus?' He glanced at the sky which had become increasingly grey. 'A downpour with wind is forecast.'

'There'll be plastic sheets in the forensic van,' Rhona said. 'But I may ask the Fire and Rescue servicc for support. They have experience in locations like this and generally their tarpaulins don't blow away.'

Dr Walker didn't interrogate her further. 'Can we settle on first names in the future? I'm Richard. Richie to friends,' he said.

'Rhona,' she offered.

'Then, Rhona, I'll see you at the post-mortem.'

42

Magnus sat across the coffee table from the woman of his recent dreams. She, of course, had no knowledge of the way his mind had played tricks with his sexual desire to conjure up the most unlikely of playmates.

DC Shona Fleming had, he read, no sexual interest in him whatsoever. What she was interested in was taking Magnus and his techniques down a 'peg or two', which unfortunately made her even more alluring.

As a psychologist, Magnus knew that he should make eye contact, but not too challengingly. He certainly shouldn't look away or, worse still, lower his eyes from her face to her chest, or more honestly, her breasts, which in truth he had imagined on occasion, although only in his dreams.

Fighting his sexual ego, Magnus analysed that the more DC Fleming challenged him professionally, the more his desire for her had grown. He felt at that moment an absurd need to tell her that, if only to clear the air between them.

That, of course, would be a disaster.

She was observing him now with a studied expression that only made things worse.

'Well?' she said.

In that moment Magnus realized he hadn't actually been listening, not properly anyway. He adopted a thoughtful expression. 'Okay, run that past me again, please?'

She regarded him like a recalcitrant child.

No wonder she thinks I'm a waste of space both professionally and, he suspected, personally.

'As I said, I'm doing the donkey work on the tunnel investigation, mostly CCTV stuff and routine questioning.'

Magnus nodded, remembering that at least.

'I didn't get to see the crime scene and I'm not invited to strategy meetings, whereas *you* are.'

Hence the bone of contention.

Magnus considered saying that her job was still a vital one, and inviting all officers involved in the case to the strategy meetings wouldn't be practical, but wisely he didn't.

'If you have a theory, you should tell your immediate superior,' he offered, but didn't add, 'rather than me'.

She made a sound in her throat that reminded him of McNab. As he contemplated whether he should suggest she divulge her theory to the detective sergeant, she came back in.

'I think you're all being played.'

'What?' Magnus said.

'There are sixty people in that lecture theatre. How many of them are police professionals?' When he didn't answer immediately, she added, 'Do you even know?'

Magnus didn't, because he was only a guest lecturer, but saying that wouldn't hold sway with DC Fleming. When he didn't immediately respond, she said, 'You and Dr MacLeod tell anyone who attends these lectures how we work, both psychologically and forensically. And I think someone with that knowledge is using it to fuck with us.'

'You think someone killed Andrew Jackson in order to test us?'

'You must have considered that a possibility,' she said sharply. 'Forensically it's complicated and we still aren't even certain if we're dealing with a homicide or a suicide, which is clever in itself. Then the wine and bread nonsense, which was bound to get *you* involved,' she said, her tone indicating exactly what she thought of Magnus's contribution.

Magnus tried to focus and block out her scent, which was growing stronger the angrier she became.

'It's a valid theory,' he said quietly, studying a space somewhere between them in order to avoid concentrating on her eyes, which were flashing in a mixture of excitement and outrage.

Most murders were unplanned and often messy. This one didn't tick either of those boxes. Organized killers liked to defy the police, seeing themselves cleverer and therefore able to get away with the crime undetected, which they sometimes achieved. Hence the existence of cold-case files. Magnus didn't want this to be one of those.

He said as much, before adding something DC Fleming didn't like.

'Of course, we can't dismiss the possibility that a perpetrator with that degree of knowledge may well be one of our own.'

43

'It's not your fault,' Rhona stressed.

'No?' McNab gave Rhona the hard stare. 'So is it yours? You went back for the shirt, remember? Maybe the perpetrator found out about that?' The nerve at the side of his face twitched his anger. 'We're being fucked with, and one death wasn't enough to prove the point.'

They were standing at the edge of the clearing as a team from Fire and Rescue completed their erection of a tarpaulin. Already the wind was up and tossing the branches as the first heavy drops of rain pattered the leaves.

McNab kept his eyes on hers, demanding a reply, so Rhona gave him one.

'I think you may be right.' She glanced over at the sheeting now enclosing the body of Claire Masters.

When McNab looked surprised by her response, Rhona told him about her earlier conversation with Bill.

'Someone planted your DNA on the victim's groin?' he said in disbelief.

'The scrotum, to be exact,' Rhona said. 'The sample on the PPE fibre in the nostril might just have got there by accident.'

'But you don't think so?'

'Not when my DNA was found on a fragment of fibre in

the turbinates further up the nasal passages, suggesting that the victim had breathed it in while still alive.'

Rhona changed the subject, more interested now in finding out why McNab had believed the victim could be Ellie.

'She found the body in the tunnel,' he told her. 'They were racing their bikes down there, Ellie and three others.' McNab's look darkened. 'She called me that night when I was with you.'

'In the pub?' Rhona interrupted him.

McNab shook his head. 'No, later, when we were in the tent.'

Rhona remembered the call now and McNab's reluctance to answer.

'I answered once I was outside.' He pulled a face. 'Blew her off before she could tell me what was worrying her.'

'But that doesn't mean she's in danger,' Rhona countered.

McNab stared towards the newly erected tarpaulin. 'She finally answered my call last night. She sounded shit scared. Said the guy in the tunnel wasn't dead.'

'She checked for life?'

'It seems so.'

Rhona recalled the partial print she'd lifted from the neck. *Had Ellie felt for a pulse?*

'What else did she say?'

'He wasn't dead. That was all.' McNab rushed on like a worried dam breaking. 'And now she's disappeared. She's not been to work. There's no answer at her flat. Izzy, her pal, says she's not at her dad's.'

'What about her bike?' Rhona said.

'Gone – or at least I can't locate it.'

'You've put a trace on her mobile?'

'I asked Ollie to do that after the phone call,' McNab confirmed.

Rhona understood McNab's concern at Ellie's disappearance, but if she was upset at not informing the police, and worried about the implications of that, she might just have made herself scarce. She could simply have taken off on her motorbike. Headed north or west or even to the islands, like the legion of bikers who roamed the Highlands during the summer months.

'There's no reason to suggest the perpetrator even knew she was down there,' she said.

McNab threw Rhona a look that suggested he didn't buy that, and despite her encouraging words, Rhona felt the same. If the victim was still alive when Ellie found him, there was a chance the perpetrator hadn't been too far away.

DS McConnachie was signalling that the locus was now secure from wind and weather if Dr MacLeod wanted to start her examination of the body.

'You okay to do this?' McNab said.

'They haven't taken me off the case . . . yet,' Rhona told him, although if her DNA on both the body and the fibre couldn't be explained, then she would be. 'Go find Ellie,' were her parting words to McNab.

Chrissy took in the sitting body, the display of yew branches and the ligature. 'And this is the girl from the undertaker's?'

Rhona nodded.

'Jeez,' Chrissy said, obviously shocked. 'Why kill her? Nothing she said or did gave us any forensic evidence on the perpetrator.'

Chrissy halted, studying Rhona's expression. 'I take it we're not considering this as a possible suicide?'

'We haven't cut the rope.' Rhona indicated the thin cord against the trunk.

'Good,' Chrissy said. 'Okay, shall we get going?'

The rain beat at the overhead tarpaulin, the wind flapping the side walls. Rhona had no fear that her temporary shelter might be swept away, but the sun's warmth had been obliterated.

Chrissy had been verging on apoplectic on hearing the full story of the DNA contamination. 'There's no way you would have let that happen,' she'd protested, taking the insult as personal, even though she hadn't been present in the tunnel to substantiate the point.

Rhona appreciated her support but still insisted that it was Chrissy who would perform the tasks which she normally did.

To Chrissy's worried question about what would happen next, Rhona had confirmed what her assistant already knew.

'They'll test again, then get another independent lab to do a secondary test. If the fibre matches the make of suits we use, and they confirm the DNA match, then I won't be allowed to work on the case until they decide how my DNA could have arrived there by secondary or tertiary transfer. As for the DNA retrieved from the testicles . . .'

Chrissy mouthed an expletive. 'Could that have happened at the PM?'

Rhona couldn't see how, and told her so.

Chrissy moved back to the fibres. 'Do you describe the materials used in forensic suits in the course? Tyvek might make us sweat but it doesn't easily shed fibres, except maybe round the cuffs.' She paused. 'Did anyone ask about control samples from the suit batches for comparison purposes? Did you mention the ones you favour?'

It wasn't part of the course, but if asked the question, Rhona knew she would have answered honestly.

'Did anyone ask?' Chrissy demanded.

Rhona had no idea. 'I can't remember,' she admitted.

'You'd better try,' Chrissy warned her. 'McNab says the two dead guys at the undertaker's were doing your online course. That's the only thing they found that connected them.'

Now that was interesting.

'McNab never mentioned that,' Rhona said.

'Probably too busy worrying about Ellie,' Chrissy told her.

44

Magnus halted for a moment, finding the deluge of scents momentarily overwhelming. Woods still affected him like this. Coming from Orkney, where a tree was a rare occurrence, the olfactory power of closely packed foliage always took him by surprise.

As a child he'd been troubled by the intensity of his sense of smell but had gradually developed mechanisms to control his hyperosmia. It was, Magnus knew, genetic, inherited from his mother's side. Although she herself hadn't been subject to it, she'd seen it in her own father who'd been known to smell sickness in his cattle before an illness presented itself. Much like the woman recently in the news who could detect early Parkinson's by scent alone.

The sun had come out again and was beating down on the rain-soaked leaves, creating spirals of evaporation. He could distinguish a variety of woody smells, but as he approached the glade that was the locus, Magnus knew at once that he was in the presence of a yew tree.

The sacred tree's rich scent emerged immediately – crisp, clean, but also thick and sweet. Magnus felt like he'd just parachuted into a forest and been hit by every tree on the way down.

Yet, despite the yew tree's power, he could still smell death.

A myriad of thoughts swept over him at that moment, the most powerful being, why here? And why involve a yew tree?

The Druids, Magnus knew, considered the yew to be the most potent tree for protection against evil, a means of connecting to their ancestors, a bringer of dreams and otherworld journeys, and a symbol of the old magic. In hot weather like today, it gave off a resinous vapour, which shamans had inhaled to gain visions.

Magnus only wished it would do that for him now. If only to better understand what they were dealing with here.

McNab's call about the body had surprised Magnus. Not to discover, sadly, that he had been right about the likelihood of another victim, but that McNab had been the one to ask him to come to the locus. The detective sergeant had been brief, his voice angry as he'd revealed the identity of the victim.

Despite his concern that another death might follow Jackson's, Magnus hadn't considered the young woman working in the undertaker's to be a likely target. In the attack on Claire's clients, the perpetrator had appeared to be practising the use of his signature, perhaps even advertising what was to come.

Most folk in Claire's situation would have cleared up the mess and said nothing, wishing to avoid any bad press for her employer. Had that been the case, the police would never have known about the break-ins.

Did Claire die because she told the police? Or perhaps

because she'd engaged with the perpetrator without realizing it?

Magnus pressed his face to the ancient trunk and breathed in the powerful resin before securing his mask and entering the tarpaulin structure.

'This is the first time I've heard about the possibility that Andrew Jackson may have died by means of yew needles,' Magnus said. 'Have you proof of that?'

'We're awaiting the results for the presence of taxine from Toxicology before announcing it,' Rhona told him.

Magnus looks stressed, she thought. Not unusual in the circumstances, but unusual for Magnus, whose outward air of calm was the norm.

They'd taken themselves outside the tent and moved to sit on a fallen log on the perimeter of the circle. Someone had brought them coffee from a vendor who'd taken advantage of the police presence in the park and the associated interest from the general public.

'If so, how was it administered?' Magnus asked. 'Via the wine?'

'He hadn't consumed either the wine or bread at the scene,' Rhona told him. 'That has been established.'

'But that doesn't mean a doctored drink hadn't been used,' Magnus mused out loud.

'We found a needle mark in a black band tattooed on his leg. So he could have consumed it or had it injected.'

'And a victim of taxine may display no other symptoms before the heart stops,' Magnus said. 'So he could have gone down there, administered it and awaited his own death.'

Rhona was puzzled as to how Magnus knew so much about the drug.

'The yew plays a big role in the whole Druidic/Celtic mythology and I had to do a lot of reading up on that during the Stonewarrior case, do you remember?'

Rhona only wished she could forget.

'Is there any reason you've uncovered that would explain why Jackson, as far as we know a young and successful professional model, would choose to kill himself?' Magnus asked.

As Rhona explained about her visit to Dr Williams and the sleep clinic, Magnus's expression grew grim.

'Perpetually having to deny himself sleep because of fear of sleep paralysis must have been torture,' Magnus said. 'If true, then we have a motive for suicide in Jackson's case, but,' he glanced towards the tent, 'not, I think, for Claire Masters?'

'She was certainly distressed by what happened while the victims were in her care.' Rhona recalled the open and friendly girl she'd met at the funeral parlour. 'But I don't believe Claire was suicidal because of it.'

'Despite being linked with the Jackson killing and the press hounding her about the wine and bread?' Magnus countered.

'Claire was, in my opinion, a very level-headed young woman,' Rhona said. 'She was angry at the treatment of her charges, but was well aware she'd done nothing wrong.'

'So this little tableau was manufactured for our benefit?' Magnus said. 'Matching a theory that was presented to me at the lecture this morning.'

'And that was?'

'Just as in Stonewarrior, criminal profiling is failing in

the current case. In fact, DC Shona Fleming is convinced, as are her comrades in arms, that we were being played by the perpetrator, who has sufficient knowledge from courses such as ours to fool us as required.'

'McNab thinks exactly the same,' Rhona told him, aware she hadn't yet revealed her own DNA part in the existing drama.

'The sergeant's name came up during the discussion,' Magnus said. 'Detective Sergeant McNab, DC Fleming reminded me, was the serving policeman who actually apprehended the Stonewarrior perpetrator, and for that he was demoted.'

Anger bubbled up in Rhona. 'That's ridiculous,' she told him.

'But essentially true,' Magnus countered.

'McNab was demoted because he acted like a prick and went AWOL. He knew what would happen and, in my opinion, courted it.' Rhona barely paused for breath. 'He never wanted or intended being a detective inspector, because that would require not doing whatever he fancied.' She halted there, aware that she may have overstepped the mark.

The barely supressed anger in her words had surprised Magnus and he was now observing her with a psychologist's eye. Something Rhona didn't desire or welcome. Magnus had probably been aware that things hadn't been great between her and McNab since the case under discussion, but he had no idea why. No one did.

And I have no intention of telling him.

She gathered herself up and, finishing her coffee, dispensed with the cup and proceeded to put on gloves again, making clear by such movements that she didn't want to discuss the matter any further, although there was something else she did want to say.

'Dr Williams at the sleep clinic is keen to talk to you about Jackson. I'll give you his number.'

45

Dusk was fast approaching, the long summer days they'd become accustomed to growing rapidly shorter. The team had set up a generator and arc lights but the chances were she wouldn't require them for long. With Chrissy on hand and a couple of SOCOs helping, their work on the body had been swift and, Rhona believed, thorough.

Homicidal hanging was extremely rare. It was difficult for a single assailant to carry it out unless the victim was unconscious either by injury or a drug. Claire was certainly small and light, but she wasn't the size of a child and there was no evidence of a struggle.

Nothing under her fingernails, no obvious bruising. There were no marks to suggest she'd been dragged to the place of her suspension. In a true suicidal hanging, the rope was pulled downwards. In this case, the marks on the branch suggested the opposite.

There were no fibres on Claire's hands from the ligature, although in a suicidal hanging there would have been, unless the girl had used gloves, which she could hardly have removed from her hands after death. Sometimes a suicide victim could arrange their death to look like a homicide, implicating someone for motives of revenge, but . . .

Left alone at her request in the tent, Rhona had been writing up her report on what she'd discovered here. The wind had dropped, making the throb of the generator more discernible. At times like this the tent seemed to Rhona like the beating heart of the investigation. Once the body was removed, that heart stopped, but the dignity of the deceased would still be preserved, as it should be.

Rhona flipped back to the Gladstone quote she always started a new notebook with.

> Show me the manner in which a nation cares for its dead and I will measure with mathematical exactness the tender mercies of its people, their respect for the laws of the land, and their loyalty to high ideals.

And with that thought in mind, Rhona said her personal goodbye to Claire Masters and exited the tent. Dusk had penetrated the surrounding woods, casting dark shadows, reminding her of Conor's shadow men, who threatened and terrified their victims.

Just like Claire.

The post-mortem would reveal more, as would a forensic study of the type and chirality of the knot used in the ligature, which should tell them if the person who'd tied it was right- or left-handed.

Rhona halted for a moment, her eyes only on the yew tree and its ancient bloated trunk.

She'd had no idea such a tree existed in the park, let alone so close to her place of work. Glancing up at the frontage of the Gothic building that dominated the skyline, she wondered if, when back in her lab, she might even be able to discern it from the window.

If I didn't know of its existence, how then could I have dreamt of it?

For there was no doubt in her mind that this particular tree was the one in her dream, or rather, nightmare. She acknowledged that on entering this clearing, had she spotted disturbed earth beneath its branches, she wouldn't have been surprised.

Rhona thought then of Conor's words on how in dreams the imagination was given free rein. And, via their darker side, how dreams might paralyse us with our buried guilt.

My buried guilt.

Chrissy had tried to persuade her to come for a drink at the jazz club after they'd finished on site, but Rhona had had no heart for that. She'd slept badly the previous night after the weird phone call and now made up her mind to head for home, eat what was left of Sean's casserole and go to bed, maybe this time make use of Conor's sleep aid, if there was a chance that by listening to it she would get at least eight hours' uninterrupted slumber.

The recurring headache had returned and with it a dull pain low down in her groin. Rhona had long ago stopped blaming the red wine and was now convinced that a vague virus was the likely culprit, irritating but inconsequential, which would disappear once she had a proper rest.

She put in a call to the vet as she made her way home. Tom, it seemed, was recovering, but they would prefer to keep him another night.

'Any idea what he might have eaten?' the vet asked.

'I've collected some of his vomit,' Rhona told him, 'but nothing distinguishable in there. If I find time at work, I might take a closer look.'

The vet, aware of her profession, said, 'If you do find the culprit, please let us know, in case another victim appears.'

Rhona agreed to do that, then rang off. Missing Tom's company as she was, the only patient she wanted to tend to tonight was herself.

Reaching home, she found the flat stuffy and too warm, the south-facing sitting room in particular, where the sun had been beating on the windows for a large part of the day. Passing the spare room, Rhona realized that Sean must have come back for some reason, the formerly tidy bed now strewn with clothes.

She contemplated giving him a call, but decided she didn't have the energy for even a brief conversation. The kitchen, *thank goodness,* was cooler, Tom's escape window to the roof still open. Rhona dumped her bag and tried to decide what she should do first, eat or shower.

Checking the slow cooker, she found to her dismay that it was empty. *Had Sean finished the remains of the stew?* The rest of the red wine had gone too. Disappointment swept over her as she realized she'd have to phone out for pizza instead.

Opening the fridge door in the forlorn hope that she might find something edible inside, Rhona gave a little whoop of joy at what she found there. It seemed Sean had transferred the remains of the casserole from the slow cooker to the fridge. Something she should have done last night.

Even better, there was a bottle of chilled white wine alongside it.

Had Sean been there at that moment, Rhona would have more than kissed him.

Slipping her meal into the microwave, she set the timer, then headed for the shower. Ten minutes later she was sitting, feet up, with a plate of stew and a large chunk of the remaining Henrietta's bread, a glass of wine on hand.

The stew tasted richer and even more aromatic than it had the previous night. Rhona wondered if Sean had added anything in the interim, maybe the remains of the red wine.

Mopping up the juice with the bread, she literally cleaned her plate and, with a satisfied sigh, went to refill her glass. The wine plus the food was definitely having the desired effect, Rhona thought, as she smothered a yawn. Maybe she wouldn't require Conor's sleep hypnosis recording after all.

As she stood in the hall contemplating whether she should just head for bed, the phone rang. Her initial response was to answer, but after the last time, she thought twice about doing that.

If it was a robotic caller, it normally gave three rings, then stopped. If it went to voicemail instead and it was someone she wanted to speak to, she would pick up, she decided.

At that moment there was a loud thump from the kitchen. Her immediate thought was that it was Tom jumping down from the window seat, but it couldn't be the cat because Tom wasn't here.

Rhona headed for the kitchen to investigate, just as a voice started recording.

'Rhona. Are you there?'

Rhona halted midway to the kitchen and went for the phone instead, surprised at how pleased she was to hear Sean's voice.

'You okay?' he said. 'Chrissy told me about Tom.'

'He's fine,' Rhona said. 'He'll be home tomorrow.'

'Good. Was there enough stew left for tonight?'

'There was. Thanks. It was delicious. And the wine,' she added.

'Chrissy said the red wine gave you a headache.' Sean sounded puzzled.

'The bottle of white in the fridge,' Rhona corrected him.

A female voice on the other end abruptly interrupted Sean's response to that, and after listening to whatever issue he was required to address, he came back with, 'Sorry, a problem with the sound system. Can I call you back?'

'Don't bother,' Rhona said. 'I'm headed for bed shortly.'

Sean gave her a brief 'okay' and rang off.

Calls to and from the jazz club were often interrupted like that, Rhona acknowledged. Just like calls to the lab were for her. Determined not to be pissed off by the female voice which she'd recognized as the lovely *Imogen, the post-graduate student of archaeology,* in Sean's words, *working nights to help pay the rent,* Rhona consoled herself by heading for the kitchen to top up the wine Sean had bought for her.

Momentarily forgetting the thudding sound earlier, she now discovered its origins and possibly the reason for Tom's emergency visit to the vet.

The head lay askew, almost severed from the neck, the glassy eye staring blindly up at her. Its patchy feathers suggested a disease of some kind which had weakened its power and perhaps sense of direction. Rhona imagined the gull missing the landing space above and hitting the partially open window, breaking its neck in the collision, to fall through and land with that thump on the floor.

Rhona went for the rubber gloves, her intention being

to bag the dead bird and take it down to the refuse bin. Realizing that a diseased gull like this might have been Tom's downfall, Rhona squatted next to the body and took a closer look.

Her touch, even through the gloves, told her that her initial analysis of what had happened couldn't be right.

Death came in many forms, but a bird that had recently flown would still be warm, unlike the stiffened body she now saw this was.

Had it died on the roof and, with a little help from the wind, fallen off and been blown in at the open window? Even as she considered the scientific possibility of this, Rhona didn't believe that could happen.

Then how had it got here?

It was possible to gain access to the roof from the open kitchen window, but you had to be a cat or unafraid of heights and a little mad to try it. Coming back down would be equally fraught for anything other than a feline or a mountain climber.

The only person she knew daft enough to gain entry via the roof had been Sean, and only then after a few whiskies, which had either increased his chance of success or failure. They'd fallen out spectacularly over that escapade, which he'd used to show her why she shouldn't leave the window lying open, in particular at night.

Rhona had responded with a characteristic rejection of being told what to do, believing his trip to the roof was more about Sean proving a point, rather than for her protection.

Rhona abandoned the bird and, going to the window, opened it wider. Sticking her head out, she attempted to look upwards. Despite watching Sean achieve the roof from here, she was still unconvinced it was possible.

A quick and scary look down four storeys to the convent garden below suggested that anyone who would choose this method of accessing the roof, instead of the pull-down ladder on her landing, must have a death wish.

One that she didn't share.

At that moment something brushed her face and, reaching out, she caught the offending article. It wasn't, as she'd suspected, a floating feather, but a fine wire noose dangling from the roof. Immediately going back inside, Rhona went over to the bird.

No wonder the neck was almost severed from the head.

There had been much talk earlier in the year of dissuading the gulls from nesting on the roof and by a variety of means. Had wiring their nesting area been one of them?

Even as her rational mind considered how the bird might have come to rest on her kitchen floor, another creeping thought entertained an altogether different scenario.

What if Sean had been right when he'd suggested that she was vulnerable to nutcases who knew what she did for a living, and might take an unhealthy interest in her because of it?

And what about McNab's belief that they were being played, her in particular?

I know what you did. The muffled words uttered on the phone the previous night returned now with a vengeance.

Rhona bagged the bird and put it in the bin. She would dispense with it tomorrow. Crossing to the window, she banged it shut and secured the brass lock, telling herself as an excuse that Tom wouldn't need to go out tonight.

46

McNab stood by the window watching night descend. In the city it was never truly dark, even in the wooded confines of Kelvingrove Park. He didn't like countryside dark at all. In fact he felt positively smothered in open spaces and under open skies. At least here in the city you knew as a human being you meant something, had done something, such as erected these buildings, laid these roads and produced the electricity that lit them.

In the countryside, you were nothing more than every other creature that inhabited that space, with nothing to prove your superiority as a species. Nothing to show for centuries of progression.

As for woods, they were the worst, even the small ones, where they'd been today.

McNab went over to the sink and ran the cold water, ostensibly to splash his face, but in reality to wash away the tears that had sprung up in his eyes at the memory of Claire Masters *sitting against that fucking tree. When he found the bastard . . .*

McNab imagined all the things he might do to the perpetrator, knowing he would in fact do none of them.

If caught, he would simply arrest him. He would be brought to court and given a 'fair' trial, the outcome of which might be a dozen years or a place in a secure hospital, perhaps freed in the future to perpetrate such vile acts again.

You stopped that happening once before, an inner voice reminded him. *And Josh Kearney deserved to die, whatever Rhona said.*

McNab glanced at the whisky bottle on the table, glass by its side. He'd made a point of eating a fish supper on his way home, consuming it to line his stomach for the onslaught of whisky he had planned.

Turning off the tap, he forced his anger to dissipate with the draining water, then dried his face. He couldn't save Claire, but he might manage to help Ellie, who surely had an even greater call on him.

You have no proof that she's in danger, he told himself again.

In fact Mannie at the Ink Parlour hadn't voiced any concern. 'Ellie sometimes takes off on her bike. Needs the open road,' he'd said. 'Have you two fallen out?'

McNab had said no, although he wasn't sure it was the truth.

'Try the Dunedin Chapter Facebook page. Check if there are any ride-outs on the go. She may have joined one.'

McNab had felt a little better after that, although it had been obvious that Mannie knew nothing of what had happened in the tunnel, nor Izzy's fear for her friend. So he'd called Izzy and told her Mannie's thoughts and, after a pause, she'd agreed that that was what Ellie sometimes did, and yes, that might be the answer.

McNab suspected when Izzy rang off that his call had merely served to put *her* at ease, not him.

Then had come the other call, to him this time, and unexpected, out of the blue.

Mary's voice had sounded throaty, as though she was back on the smokes or hitting the bottle. McNab recognized the syndrome because he'd experienced it himself often enough.

They exchanged what might be regarded as pleasantries, but in reality the back and forth between them was more of a disguised interrogation, on both sides. What McNab remembered most about Mary Grant was the way power had always shifted between them. When the power had been with him, he'd felt sorry for her. When it lay with her, she'd often taken pity on him.

That power could never be evenly distributed. McNab doubted if it could in any relationship, recognizing that what had been between him and Mary wasn't that different from what currently existed between Rhona and himself.

He also acknowledged that he and Ellie had not reached that point, as yet, probably because it signified commitment of some sort, or at least the beginning of the next stage of a relationship.

'How are you, Mary?' he managed.

'Mending.' As she coughed, McNab recalled her figure in the hospital bed, broken and battered, and how badly he'd felt about that. Then an image of Davey, her husband, and his old mate, came to mind. And with that, the memory of what Davey had done, and hate reappeared like a bright hot flame in his chest.

'What can I do for you?' McNab said, his voice now officious rather than friendly, a change that didn't go unnoticed.

'For a start, you can stop talking to me like an arse.'

He could make out her breathing as she waited, expecting an apology.

And there it was, the shift in power.

'Sorry,' he said.

'Accepted.' She sucked in a breath and McNab wondered what was yet to come. 'After you visited us that night with Ellie, Davey went and bought a fucking Harley.'

'What?' McNab said in disbelief. *Bloody Davey with money to burn.*

'I want you to take it away,' Mary said.

'Take it where?' McNab struggled for her meaning.

'I want you to have the bike. You caught the bastard. You found out what he was doing. I want you to have the Harley.'

'Davey wouldn't like that.'

'I don't give a damn what Davey would like,' Mary said. 'Can you come and get it tonight?'

'Mary, that's not a good idea,' McNab said, glancing at the whisky again.

'We need to talk. In the hospital, you promised me we would talk.'

He had promised to keep in touch, and he hadn't kept his promise, even when Ellie had reminded him of it.

'Are you on duty?' she asked.

'Nope,' McNab admitted.

'Then come round and get the bike.'

McNab glanced over at the waiting bottle. What would be the more dangerous route to take – the whisky or Mary?

He'd been wrong about the drink and the fags. Mary was deep-throated all right, but McNab now believed it was because she'd been crying. If he was right, then she'd made a decent job of tidying up the evidence of it before his arrival. The make-up looked perfect, as did the hair.

McNab had questioned himself all the way here as to

why he'd come. The fact that he'd grabbed a taxi also suggested that a) he was likely to drink or b) he did plan to ride the bike back.

She'd taken a few moments to answer the door to him. As he'd waited, McNab had imagined her standing in that big hall with its polished wood panelling, wishing to God she hadn't phoned him in the first place. Then the door opened and there she was. The Mary he remembered, but without the husband.

'Mikey.' She gave him a tentative smile. 'Come on in.'

She didn't ask for his jacket, just marched off towards the kitchen expecting him to follow, which McNab did. The rest of the house lay in darkness, unlike the evening of the dinner party when it had been lit up like a beacon to affluence and success. Davey had wanted to show off to his teenage mate just how good life had been to him.

And I played the same game. Taking my biker chick girlfriend. Arriving on her Harley. What a pair of sad, lying, competitive bastards we were.

Entering the kitchen, McNab was immediately struck by how different the room appeared from the last time he'd been here. Now it looked lived in, as though Mary had moved in here and abandoned the rest of the house. Glancing back at the doorway, he suddenly remembered Ellie walking in on Mary and him, and guessing there was more to their conversation than just making the after-dinner coffee.

God, Ellie was pissed off, and rightly so. They'd had their first argument over it.

'How's Ellie?' Mary said, as though reading his mind.

McNab was about to give the statutory *fine*, then said instead, 'Off on a motorbike jaunt. The Highlands, I think.'

Mary gave him a studied look. 'She's a lovely girl.'

McNab immediately interpreted Mary's rendition of the word *girl* to indicate she thought him too old for Ellie. He was about to protest this, although he thought it himself at times, but managed to stop himself.

Then came the hundred-dollar question. 'Join me in a drink? I've a nice malt here you'd like.'

'If I'm taking the bike back . . .' McNab trailed.

'Sorry, I called my lawyer. Seems we have to sign some papers first.' She flourished them as evidence. 'Once the lawyer okays them, I'll have the bike delivered to you, or you can come back for it yourself.'

McNab still wasn't sure if such a transaction would work on his end. A serving policeman being given an expensive Harley by the wife of a convicted felon.

But if a lawyer okayed it, who was he to argue?

A fleeting image of his boss's expression at such a development came to mind and it didn't look happy.

Mary was flourishing the bottle, awaiting an answer to the proffered drink.

Fuck it, McNab thought. *It's been a shitty day.*

'I'll get a taxi back,' he said.

'Good.' She smiled at him in a way he remembered.

They hadn't drunk much up to now, but talked plenty. McNab realized that though he'd promised Mary this chance in the hospital, he hadn't kept his word, so eventually she'd had to approach him. And the bike had been the way to do it.

Mary hated motorbikes. Davey had admitted if he was brave enough to go against her wishes and buy one, he'd have to ride it behind her back.

That wasn't the only fucking thing he was riding behind her back.

McNab realized Mary was about to give him a refill. He'd counted three up to now, although not really singles. McNab reached out as though to prevent her pouring, but somewhere in between his hand let him down.

'It's okay,' she said. 'I'm counting.'

McNab took a mouthful. Mary was right. It was a very nice whisky. He glanced at the label and suddenly realized what he'd been drinking.

'Jesus, fuck.' His eyes widened in astonishment. 'This is a Fifty-Year-Old Speyside Glen Grant. It must have cost—'

'Just over four and a half grand,' she told him. 'Davey was into buying expensive whiskies. A good investment, he said. I've decided it's better to drink them.'

They toasted to that.

McNab decided that he was comfortable in this kitchen, more so than the last time he'd visited when it had seemed so shiny and ordered. Mary had moved in a big couch and there were books and other items scattered about that suggested she was using it as her living room. McNab thought of all the other spacious rooms in the mansion overlooking the park, of the big garden and the triple garage and the fancy cars.

'How's the business?' he said.

'Beauty business didn't take a hit at all. In fact the trial just brought more punters in. After all, I was the innocent one. I just had a creep for a husband. There are lots of women who can relate to that.' She gave McNab a knowing look. 'Davey's side is still ticking over. The men who gamble don't care who makes that possible.' She paused for a moment. 'Although the proceeds of crime boys are on to his assets, even as we speak.'

McNab wondered if that was what had prompted the call about the Harley.

Reading his thoughts again, she said, 'Fortunately we kept our assets separate. I'm selling the house. I've bought a penthouse flat down by the river with a view to die for.' She smiled. 'I move there in three weeks.'

McNab was pleased for her and told her so.

'And you don't have to worry about the Harley. That's definitely mine to dispose of as I wish. The stupid bastard registered it in my name. The insurance was cheaper that way.'

Good old Davey. Always guarding the money.

'I married the wrong guy,' Mary said with a challenging look. 'I should have stayed with you.'

'I was a prick back then. And let's face it, I still am.'

'But you were – *are* – the better man.'

McNab looked around the room to avoid meeting Mary's eye. 'You wouldn't have had all this if you'd stayed with me.'

'No,' she nodded. 'And, if I'm honest, I needed all this. Still do.'

She topped up his drink. They were easily halfway down that expensive bottle, but McNab felt okay – no, he felt good. The shitty day seemed to belong to someone else now.

'There's something I never told you . . . about us,' Mary said. 'Something Davey doesn't know about either.'

McNab waited, aware by her expression that what she was going to say he probably didn't want to hear.

And he was right.

'I was pregnant when I broke it off with you.'

McNab wasn't sure he'd heard right. 'You were pregnant?' he repeated.

'I knew you'd freak at that, so I never told you. I didn't tell Davey either.' She shrugged and took another mouthful of whisky. 'I had an abortion.'

McNab was still processing the 'I was pregnant' bit.

'It was mine?' he asked in amazement.

'I didn't sleep with Davey until after I left you.'

'But you were seeing him,' McNab heard his accusing voice say.

'But we weren't having sex,' she insisted. 'Davey didn't like that, but I wasn't sure back then if it was him I really wanted.'

This was all too much to take in for McNab. His head was buzzing with fine whisky and the amazing revelation that he might have been a father.

'So the baby was definitely mine?' he checked.

'Yes.' Mary looked offended that he should think otherwise.

'And you never told me . . .' That wasn't a question for Mary, just a statement of fact to himself.

Christ, he might have been a father. Had a son or a daughter. What age would they be now, a teenager? Jesus. McNab felt suddenly bereft at the absence of that possibility.

What if Mary had stayed with him and they'd had the kid together?

She was reading his face. 'You were a prick back then, remember? You would have shat yourself if I'd told you I was pregnant.'

McNab gave a small laugh, because she was right. That's exactly what he would have done. Either that or run a mile.

'Davey wanted kids, but I don't think he would have wanted yours. Anyway, we tried, but I didn't get pregnant again. Maybe that was my only chance. So my businesses became my babies.' She swallowed the remains of her whisky and reached for the bottle again.

'Why tell me now?' McNab wondered.

Mary shrugged. 'Who knows? Too much whisky. Or nostalgia for what might have been. Anyway, as I said, I married the wrong man.'

McNab wondered how many times over the years he would have loved to have heard her say those words. Too many. So why didn't it matter now? Even as he looked over at Mary, it was Ellie he was seeing in his mind's eye.

McNab knew if he stayed any longer, drank any more, where it – they – would end up.

Maybe he might think of it as a long-awaited farewell fuck, but he had a feeling Mary wouldn't.

And so the power shifts, yet again.

McNab pushed his glass away and stood up. 'I have to go.' Before she could answer, he brought up the taxi call button and pressed it. Mary remained silent as he told the operator where he was and where he wanted to go to.

If only directions for life were that simple, McNab thought as he pulled the heavy front door shut behind him and walked to the waiting cab.

47

Rhona was surprised at how quickly she'd fallen asleep after the events of the previous night. Perhaps the meal and the wine had helped or the reassuring words she'd exchanged with Sean or, indeed, the sleep aid Conor had given her, although she had no recollection of what the recording had said, past the opening musical cadence.

Whatever the reason for the deep sleep, or drop into unconsciousness, she was grateful for it.

Last night, if not frightened by the arrival of the gull, she'd certainly been disturbed by it. Still unsure if the dead bird had accidentally been deposited in her kitchen or had arrived there on purpose, the incident had reminded her of another dead offering she'd found in her flat, deliberate that time.

Tom's predecessor had been called Chance. And Chance had been killed in retaliation when she'd crossed psychopath Joe Maley. Chrissy had been the one to discover Rhona's former pet lying behind the sofa in the sitting room, his head severed from his body.

I didn't let Maley's threat stop me from doing my job then, and whatever's going on, it won't stop me now.

With that determined thought, Rhona had headed for bed, plugged the pen drive into her laptop and set it to play.

It was like the music of the heavens, she remembered. *I closed my eyes and let it wash over me. After that, nothing.*

Swinging her legs out of bed, she rose and headed for the kitchen. As she spooned coffee into the cafetière, the smell of it hit her nostrils and she felt that all too familiar queasiness come over her again.

This is getting ridiculous, she told herself as she headed swiftly for the bathroom to lean over the toilet bowl.

Beads of sweat popped out on her brow and she felt a wave of heat encompass her.

The last time I felt like this was when I gave blood and got to my feet too quickly afterwards.

Rhona, surer now that she wasn't going to be sick, slowly rose to her feet and splashed her face with cold water.

Viruses, she reminded herself, were usually over within a week. She would just have to put up with it until it ran its course. Even as she thought this, Rhona wished that she had done something about the slow puncture, because driving to work seemed preferable to walking through the park on what were definitely wobbly legs.

The air will do you good.

Opening the main door twenty minutes later, she found her prediction to be true. Last night's rain had freshened the air, and Rhona took a deep breath of it. Heading down the steps towards the park, she noted the continued police presence among the trees, signalling that teams of SOCOs were still combing the undergrowth. The sight of this spurred her on. The post-mortem on Claire would likely be scheduled for today sometime and she wanted to be there, nausea or not.

As she entered the park, her mobile rang.

'How are you?' Bill asked in a concerned voice. 'Chrissy said you were under the weather.'

'I'm fine,' Rhona assured him. 'Just heading into work now. What time's the PM on Claire?'

Rhona guessed by the pregnant silence that followed her question what was about to come.

'I've been taken off the case,' she said, before Bill could tell her so.

'Just until they work out how your DNA was on the body.' Bill was trying to sound reassuring. It wasn't working.

'Shit.'

'I agree, but I'd use even stronger language than that.' Bill paused. 'You could take a couple of days off, get over the virus Chrissy says you have?'

'I'm fine,' Rhona repeated, as much to convince herself as Bill, 'and I have plenty of other work to be getting on with.'

She was pissed off, but she wasn't defeated, and sitting at home definitely wasn't an option. She told Bill so. 'Chrissy processed Claire. I supervised. There's no way my DNA is on her body.'

'Good,' Bill said, sounding relieved.

'On that subject, when's the next strategy meeting?' Her testing question resulted in an uncomfortable silence on the other end of the phone.

Fuck it, she thought. 'You don't want me there?'

'I do want you there,' Bill countered. 'But orders are for you to stand aside from all aspects of the investigation pending an explanation for the presence of your DNA.'

'My DNA was planted. That's the explanation.'

'We'll focus on that. Until then, send Chrissy in your place. That way you stay in the loop. Just play it by the book and we'll sort it out.'

'Now I know why McNab goes AWOL at times,' Rhona said, exasperated.

'But you're not McNab,' Bill reminded her.

'You look like shite,' a waiting Chrissy told her on entry.

'Always the kind word,' Rhona retorted.

'Seriously, though, you should probably see a doctor.'

'And be told I have a virus?'

Chrissy examined her with an eagle eye. 'What are the symptoms exactly?' she demanded.

'Intermittent headache, nausea, occasionally light-headed . . .'

A look came over Chrissy's face which Rhona failed to interpret.

'What?' she demanded.

Chrissy shook her head as though dismissing whatever possibility had come into her mind.

'Tell me,' Rhona insisted.

Chrissy shrugged and raised an eyebrow. 'I don't suppose there's a remote chance you could be pregnant?'

Rhona's immediate response to such a shocking suggestion was a firm 'no'. She shook her head to emphasize the fact. 'That's not possible.'

'You and Sean *are* doing it?' Chrissy checked, with a worried expression.

Rhona threw her a look that would have curdled milk. 'I'm on the pill.'

'You haven't missed one?' Chrissy said. 'Late-night working can screw the timetable up.'

Rhona was about to insist that she hadn't, then the horrible thought that she might have lodged itself in her brain.

Chrissy was watching her closely. 'Did you take it this morning?'

Rhona remembered the rush to the toilet. The relief when the nausea lessened, in the aftermath of which she hadn't taken the pill. Now thoughts came tumbling back of switches in her timing, when she'd taken it in the early hours of the morning after returning from the tunnel or next day when she remembered.

But had she missed one?

She simply couldn't answer that without checking the box, and it would be at home in the bathroom.

'There's one way to find out,' Chrissy declared. 'I'll go get us some breakfast and visit a pharmacy.'

Rhona realized as the door shut behind her assistant that because of their preceding conversation, she'd failed to mention that she'd been removed from the tunnel case.

God, she'll be pissed about that.

Not as pissed as you'll be if Chrissy's suggestion turns out to be true.

Fear swept through her, accompanied by the memory of a previous occasion when she'd experienced similar symptoms to what had been happening recently.

'No,' she said again, even as she imagined what she would do if it were true.

Rhona muttered a prayer to whatever God might be listening that she wouldn't be faced with such a decision a second time.

48

McNab felt a surge of pity for the young bloke sitting in front of him.

The elderly Mr Marshall had been sorely distressed, finding ways of blaming himself for not protecting Claire, but Claire's boyfriend was way beyond shattered. McNab had seen the result of violent death on the bereaved before. It never got any better.

It had been revealed that Claire's parents had retired to Spain, and she and Taylor had been living together for two years.

'We were going to get married,' he said to an empty space just left of McNab. 'Just a registry office ceremony, nothing expensive, then have a honeymoon in Spain, not far from her parents. God, do they know?' he added, a look of horror on his face. 'I don't have to . . . '

'A family liaison officer will have done that,' McNab told him.

The FLO would take care of Taylor too, keeping him abreast of developments, finding out anything he knew that would help find Claire's killer. They couldn't make things better for those left behind, but their aim was that things wouldn't be worse.

It was a job McNab wouldn't relish for himself, though.

'This is all my fault,' Taylor was saying. 'If I hadn't told her to go to the police about the break-in . . .' He tailed off, his voice cracking.

McNab wanted to say it was more likely his fault. He hadn't taken the break-in seriously enough. As soon as he'd thought there might be a link to the tunnel case, he should have considered Claire's safety. He hadn't. Instead all he could think of was how it might help him get back on the major investigation.

'You did nothing wrong,' he said instead. 'Now, what we have to concentrate on is catching the person who did this.'

Taylor nodded at this suggestion like a drowning man being offered a lifebelt.

'Tell me exactly what Claire said about the break-ins, after I'd spoken to her about them.'

'Well, she was upset about the shirt, and the forensic woman turning up.'

'Dr MacLeod?'

He nodded. 'She'd tried to wash out the stain, but told you she hadn't. She felt terrible about that.' By the look on his face, the lifebelt was no longer holding his head above water.

McNab drove on. 'The two men were doing the same online course in forensics. Did Claire mention anything else that might connect them?'

Taylor shook his head dismissively. 'They didn't know one another. One had family, the other no mourners at all. Claire felt sorry for him.'

'Harry Martin?'

He nodded. 'She said he was awkward.' He looked at McNab. 'How can the dead be awkward?' He gave a half-smile. 'When no one came for him, she felt sad. Said she should have been kinder, because he was lonely.'

God, the guy would cry soon. McNab couldn't cope with that.

But the tears didn't come. The glint in Taylor's eye turned out to herald a memory.

'Someone did come in to view him.'

McNab's ears pricked up.

'Claire said she was really pleased, but then it turned out they'd got the wrong man.'

McNab's hopes fell along with Taylor's expression, but he pursued it anyway.

'Man or woman?'

'A man. Took a look at the body and said he'd made a mistake. It wasn't who he thought it was.'

McNab felt his heart quicken. 'Did Claire describe this guy?'

Taylor threw him a quick glance. 'Is it important?'

McNab tried to look calm. It could be nothing and he didn't want Taylor to suddenly make things up to try and be helpful.

'Everything you can tell us is important,' he said.

Taylor concentrated for a moment. 'It was before the break-in when she was sad about Mr Martin having no one. Just some son in Hong Kong who Mr Marshall said was paying the bill. Claire couldn't believe it when she was told he wouldn't even come over for the funeral.' He glanced at McNab. 'Claire went to that, you know? She was the only one there except for a Polish nurse from the retirement home.'

McNab nodded. 'Did Claire describe this visitor?' he repeated.

'Not really, although she didn't like him. Said he wasn't kind. Kindness was her motto.'

'Why did she think he wasn't kind?' McNab said.

'It was because of what he said.'

49

Despite my detailed planning, I have made mistakes.

I was too ambitious with the DNA at the first locus. Although, had I left only the impregnated fibre, it may have been explained away too easily, and I wasn't to know she would leave the body clothed.

I should not have engaged with the girl in the funeral parlour. I did need to see more of the premises, but the girl took too much interest in her 'charges' as she described them, and she was inquisitive.

However, I did want to trial the Sins of the Dead scenario and where better than at a funeral parlour? The fact that two of the old folk taking the online forensic course died within days of one another was an added bonus. I fully expected the girl not to report the incidents to the police, because they reflected badly on her and the company. I was therefore quite impressed by her tenacity, although had she been less caring, she might well still be alive.

The lectures are over now. In the final one the professor was openly challenged by the police officers, in particular the tall female, DC Fleming. I've seen the professor look at her before, when he imagines no one can see. She doesn't return his interest.

Or does she?

And she brought up Stonewarrior. How Pirie had failed on that one. How the detective, McNab, had got it right. But she doesn't know that McNab's biker girlfriend was down there that night.

I wonder if the detective even knows that?

Yes, I may have got some things wrong, but playing the role of sin-eater was right because everyone has sinned and if they're going to die suddenly, someone has to remove their sins for them. Plus, it drew in Professor Pirie.

I will miss the course. However, I do plan to submit a topic for my final paper. I have chosen 'Buried and Hidden Bodies'. I have a month in which to research and write it. I don't think it will take that long.

Also, I have decided what my next move will be.

It will be unexpected, that's for certain, but unfortunately people are unpredictable. You can never tell exactly what they will do, and I do have a sense that someone has caught my scent, however well I have covered my tracks.

Still, everything happens in threes in stories, so I don't see why it shouldn't in mine.

50

'Where's Rhona?' McNab said, looking around the room.

'She's not coming. I'm here in her stead.'

'Why? What's wrong?' McNab's previous fears over Rhona's demeanour resurfaced.

Chrissy threw him a 'you don't know?' look, which didn't help.

'What?' he demanded.

'Rhona's been taken off the case.'

McNab floundered at this. 'What the fuck!'

The room was swiftly filling up. McNab was suddenly conscious of all eyes taking in their little tableau as the officers filed in.

'No one told me,' he hissed.

'Rhona only found out from Bill this morning.'

'Looks like the whole fucking force knows now,' McNab muttered under his breath at the disguised looks of both sympathy and anger from his fellow officers. 'They must know it was a set-up?'

'Bill thinks so, but it'll be hard to prove. He told her to lie low. I'll deliver her material and keep her informed. They can't stop her having an opinion,' Chrissy finished.

Nor me, McNab thought.

At that point, DI Wilson entered with the Viking. The

look on the boss's face said it all, McNab decided, although in the past that look had tended to be about him.

'Come on,' Chrissy urged McNab to follow her to the front, which he did with alacrity, having something himself to contribute to the proceedings.

McNab had never seen Chrissy nervous before, or perhaps she'd just covered it well with her in-your-face patter. She was using notes, probably prepared by Rhona, but she barely glanced at them. Her anger at having to be here in Rhona's place showed in the steely determination and in the manner in which Rhona's findings were delivered.

'Cardiac disturbances after intoxication by yew are ascribed mainly to the alkaloids paclitaxel and taxine B. The taxine alkaloid is absorbed through the digestive tract very rapidly, and the signs of poisoning manifest themselves after thirty to ninety minutes. An infusion made from fifty to one hundred grammes of needles is considered to be fatal as no antidote is known.'

She continued. 'Yew needles were discovered by *Dr MacLeod,*' she stressed the name, 'between the floorboards in Jackson's flat. This alerted her to the possibility that taxine might be involved in his death. Up to that point Toxicology had had no idea what to look for.'

Chrissy paused for the importance of Rhona's role to sink in, before carrying on.

'How the poison was administered is still not clear. Neither the wine nor the bread at the scene contained taxine. However, he may well have consumed it in a drink earlier and the symptoms of poisoning appeared within the time stated, resulting in death.'

As the pictures of Jackson were now replaced by those

of Claire, there was a murmur from the assembled officers, many of who would not yet have seen yesterday's recordings of the crime scene.

For McNab, the image on the screen only reinforced the one that seemed to have taken up permanent residence in his brain. He forced himself to examine it again, none the less, Chrissy's voice the soundtrack to that terrible moment when he'd thought to find Ellie and had found Claire instead.

'Claire Masters, who worked at Marshall's Funeral Home, was discovered sitting against a yew tree in Kelvingrove Park, a branch of yew covering her face, apparently having hanged herself. However, on closer inspection, the context of the locus suggests she did not commit suicide, although an attempt has been made to suggest this.' Chrissy ended with, 'As you can see from these pictures of the marks made by the cord on the branch, the body was pulled upwards, not downwards.'

As Chrissy stepped aside, McNab's focus moved to the boss. *Surely he would say something about Rhona's situation now?*

Instead, Bill indicated that DS McNab himself would be next up to speak.

Suddenly in the spotlight and definitely not expecting it, McNab nevertheless knew exactly what he had to say.

The question was would he be permitted to say it?

The place fell silent as he approached the front. Avoiding the boss's eye, McNab faced the team.

First up, Claire's visitor.

McNab related Taylor's story. How Claire's visitor to the funeral parlour had claimed to know Harry Martin, then said it was a mistake. 'Claire thought him unkind, because he'd commented on Mr Martin's girth, suggesting he'd been too fond of food. Subsequently, the remnants of the bread were found on Mr Martin's body.'

He paused for a moment to let the significance of that sink in.

'I admit that I didn't take the break-in at Marshall's seriously enough. If the perpetrator believed Claire might identify him, that would have put her in danger, especially if Dr MacLeod was viewed making a visit to Claire three days ago.' He paused again, albeit briefly. 'I believe I failed to protect Claire Masters.

'As for Dr MacLeod,' McNab continued, 'we all know her work. There is no way she would contaminate a crime scene. We are being played by the perpetrator, and providing a reason to have Dr MacLeod removed from the investigation is part of that.'

The ripples of disquiet in the room had shifted to angry muttering. McNab rushed on for fear the boss would order him to stop.

'Harry Martin and Stanley Robertson were connected by more than just their chosen undertaker's. Both men were taking an online course as part of the Diploma in Forensic Medical Science, the exact course Dr MacLeod and Professor Pirie lecture on.'

At this revelation the shit hit the fan. Even as the noise rose in the room, McNab spoke above it.

'So, instead of persecuting Dr MacLeod, we should be questioning the officers and members of the public taking this course. We should be asking who was party to the brand of forensic suit Rhona favours. Who could have got close enough to Rhona to sample her DNA and use it. That person is playing with us, using the forensic knowledge we probably provided them with. That person killed Andrew Jackson and Claire Masters. That person will likely kill again.'

51

The package sat on the counter where Chrissy had left it when she'd set off for the strategy meeting. Still in its Boots paper bag, it stared back at Rhona, defying her to open it and make use of the contents.

But she wasn't ready to do that yet.

What she should be doing, in normal circumstances, was conducting an examination of the ligature they'd removed from Claire Masters, but frustratingly that would have to wait until Chrissy returned from the strategy meeting.

Instead, Rhona decided, she would study the sample she'd brought from home, in an effort to discover what Tom had eaten that had made the cat so ill.

As she fetched it from the fridge, Rhona wondered how Chrissy was getting on. They'd gone over the notes she'd made and Chrissy understood perfectly what must be said. The main problem would lie in controlling her righteous indignation at having to appear in Rhona's stead. Chrissy wasn't known for mincing her words, but she would have to do so today. The room would be sympathetic, but Chrissy's fury at what had transpired to bring her there might be difficult to disguise.

With a dismissive and, she vowed, last glance at the Boots bag, Rhona turned her attention to the cat's vomit. When she'd first spotted it, she'd been more concerned with Tom's comatose condition and weak pulse. When cleaning it up, she'd paid little attention to the substance, more concerned at the time with getting rid of the smell.

The acidic scent still lingered but not as strongly as before and through the mask it was barely noticeable. Despite this, Rhona experienced again that faint feeling of nausea that appeared to be haunting her.

How could she work like this? She couldn't even test the cat's vomit.

Maybe she should go home, like Bill suggested. Have a few days off. The virus would have played out by then, and maybe, just maybe, the powers that be would decide to allow her back to work.

Then again, a small voice said, *if it isn't a virus that's causing the nausea . . .*

Rhona swore under her breath and determinedly put her eye to the microscope.

As the deposit came into focus, she could discern some of the contents. A wisp of a feather, possibly from the dead seagull, suggesting Tom may have tried eating it. Some part-digested dried food pellets. What looked like an insect, maybe a spider, and something else. Green, but bleached pale by stomach acid.

Her first thought was a blade of grass, but the shape was wrong, being more needle-like in form. Besides which, where would Tom find grass on the roof?

Spreading the mixture a little to get a better view, Rhona noted a darker, redder mass behind, *like the outer casing of a berry*?

In any other circumstances, her first thought would not have been that the berry might be that of *Taxus baccata*.

In this instance, however . . .

Though the flesh of the berries was free of taxine, the seed within was highly toxic. Unbroken, it could pass through the body without being digested and thus cause no harm, but if the seed were chewed or broken, poisoning would occur.

Rhona abandoned the microscope and religiously filled the coffee machine and switched it on, using that methodical task in order to focus her thoughts.

Was it possible that Tom had been poisoned by the seed of a yew?

If so, how could that have happened? Had he been an outdoor cat, it was perfectly possible. Even dead branches trimmed from a yew still held their toxins. Cows had been known to die through ingesting their remains while grazing.

But Tom hadn't been outside, except for his trips to the roof. And the dead gull had been up there. Could he have ingested something toxic from it?

Rhona glanced at the clock. How long before Chrissy came back? She badly needed to talk to her about this.

She poured a coffee and then found herself unable to drink it. Not nausea this time but a powerful sense that this, if true, was significant in more ways than she could imagine.

Okay. She would go back to the flat and check out the roof, though, of course, without testing Tom's vomit for taxine she could not be sure of any of this.

Should she request such a test? Or was she simply being paranoid?

Rhona checked the clock again, then contemplated calling Chrissy's mobile. If she did, then she knew Chrissy would immediately ask if she'd used the pregnancy test.

I will have to admit I haven't or else lie and say I did and all is well.

As yet, Rhona wasn't ready to do either of those two things.

Her best bet, she now acknowledged, was to go home immediately. Check the roof. Even as she decided this, she cursed herself for having disposed of the dead seagull. She'd taken the bag down to the bin on her way out this morning. *No matter.* She could still retrieve it. It wouldn't be the first time she'd raked around in bins for forensic evidence.

After which I will use the pregnancy test.

52

When the boss summoned McNab into his office after the meeting, McNab fully expected a dressing-down for his outburst, especially since he'd spotted DCI Sutherland at the back of the room, even as he'd been asked to address the team.

Anticipating a rollicking, McNab found himself in receipt of a nod and a half-smile instead.

'Well done, Detective Sergeant. I believe DCI Sutherland will have to take what you said on board now.'

McNab suddenly understood why he'd been called to the front.

'You set me up, sir?'

'I wouldn't say that exactly, but I was relying on your honesty. And that's what I got. Officially I couldn't have said those things quite as freely.'

'But will it get Rhona back on the case?'

'They'll wait an appropriate time to save face, but yes, I believe it will.' The boss settled into his chair. 'It appears Jackson was a Cosworth fan, which might account for his visit to the tunnel. IT just located him on a Facebook page for enthusiasts.'

'Is the wreck in the London tunnel listed on there?' McNab said.

'No.'

'Then the perpetrator may have contacted Jackson via the page to tell him of its existence?'

'A valid theory and the only one we have up to now as to why he was down there.'

'Rhona suspected he had walked in there, by the soil deposits on his shoes,' McNab reminded him.

The boss nodded in a manner that indicated something else was about to be added to the mix. Something, McNab suspected, that concerned him.

'The footprint near the body was of a biker boot size six.' The boss waited as though expecting McNab to respond to this. McNab swallowed with difficulty, his throat suddenly dry.

'Sir,' he began, but was interrupted.

'The partial print on the neck threw up a match on the database. Ellie Macmillan's.'

Fuck. Why was Ellie on the police database?

As though reading McNab's expression, DI Wilson continued. 'Her fingerprints were taken because of a break-in at the Harley-Davidson shop late last year, to eliminate the staff from the enquiry. The case hasn't reached court yet so they're still on there.'

McNab's initial relief that Ellie hadn't been lying to him when she'd said she hadn't been in trouble with the police was now replaced by the reality of what this was leading to.

'Did you know that your biker girlfriend had been in that tunnel, Detective Sergeant?'

No point in denying it now.

McNab launched into his story. 'I spoke to DS Clark two days ago about the bike tracks and asked permission to check with Ellie at the Harley shop if she knew of anyone using the tunnel. She wasn't there nor at her flat and wasn't answering my calls. Then she called me late at night. All she said was, "He wasn't dead," and rang off. Then her friend Izzy revealed four of them had been down there and seen the body. Ellie looked for a pulse and told them he was dead. They'd freaked out at that and decided not to report it. Then realized someone else had. Since then Ellie's gone off-grid, sir. Her friend Izzy thinks she's gone off on the bike somewhere.'

The boss had listened in silence to all of this, his expression inscrutable. Now he spoke.

'I want her found and brought back here, Detective Sergeant. And let's get this Izzy in here and whoever else was in that tunnel.'

McNab knew that was something he should have done himself and sooner than this. The look on the boss's face only reinforced that.

'How much of this was DS Clark made aware of?' the boss now demanded.

'I asked her permission to contact Ellie about the bike tracks in case she might know who'd been racing down there. That's all.' McNab hoped his explanation would be enough to cover Janice's back.

At that, he was summarily dismissed, his move from hero to idiot accomplished inside ten minutes.

McNab headed for the coffee machine, although something stronger would have been more welcome.

Christ, he hoped he hadn't landed Janice in it. She'd taken enough shit in the past on his behalf.

His dressing-down by the boss had been well deserved, but McNab still wasn't sure what he could have done differently.

You should have reported what Ellie said to the boss, just as you did with Rhona. You should have told him you thought Ellie might be the victim yesterday morning. Not Claire.

McNab downed the double espresso but it did little to take the edge off his agitation. Revealing Ellie's story had only served to remind him of his fear for her well-being. If the perpetrator had seen the girls down there . . . If Ellie had seen him and hadn't told the others, just like she'd lied about Jackson being dead . . .

The boss had ordered him to find Ellie. McNab desperately wanted to do that, but he didn't see how it was possible.

Ollie had run a trace on her mobile and got nothing. If she'd gone AWOL then the likelihood was she'd switched the mobile off so he couldn't locate her. Alternatively, she'd truly gone off-grid where there was little possibility of a signal.

And there was plenty of opportunity for that in the more remote parts of Scotland.

Then again, a single biker was more noticeable than one in a group. Maybe Ellie was hiding in a crowd? Every biker looked the same in the waterproof gear and helmet.

McNab remembered Mannie's advice and, taking out his mobile, he pulled up the Dunedin Chapter Facebook page.

53

On re-entry, Rhona secured the door by putting on the heavy old-fashioned door chain, something she rarely did, even at night. Sean had remonstrated with her more than once about that, but Rhona had always felt safe here.

So why was she doing it now?

Refusing to answer that question, even to herself, she dumped the bag containing the dead seagull next to the kitchen sink. It had taken some ingenuity to retrieve it from the large bin, and had involved taking down a chair to stand on and a means of propping the lid open. Designed to be lifted by the refuse lorry, and tipped and emptied automatically, the lid required a foot on a metal bar to aid opening.

Having initially failed to hold it open long enough to locate her bag, it had come down heavily on her in the process.

As she'd turned the lock, Rhona had winced at what would no doubt prove to be heavy bruising on her upper right arm. Still, she smiled grimly to herself, she had got what she wanted.

But there was still the roof to check.

Rhona baulked a little at that. No fan of heights, the roof wasn't somewhere she would choose to go. She contemplated whether it was really necessary to go up there at all, since she had retrieved the dead gull.

Dismissing that as a lame excuse, she double-bagged the bird and put it in the fridge, then went to change into clothes more suitable for clambering about on the roof.

Retrieving the pole hook for the trapdoor, she exited, checked for her keys, then pulled the door shut behind her.

The metal steps extended, Rhona cautiously climbed up, unbolted the trapdoor and emerged onto the flat roof, which was surrounded by a low stone balustrade. Sean had managed to persuade her on one occasion to take in the delights of Glasgow from this commanding viewpoint. A year or so ago, at Hogmanay, they had watched the city fireworks celebration. Despite it being spectacular, Rhona would still have preferred to watch it from the bay window in the sitting room or even from the park below.

Steeling herself against what was definitely a stronger breeze up here on the rooftop, she took a look around. The gull had swung in at the kitchen window. *Where exactly was that in relation to her position now?* Getting her bearings, Rhona left the trapdoor open and moved in that direction.

On her way, she could see no evidence that wiring had been used to dissuade gulls from landing on the roof. Also she'd had no notification as a resident that there had been any such plan, so it seemed unlikely.

Picking her way through puddles from the last heavy shower, Rhona now stood above her own kitchen window. Far below, the convent garden was bathed in sunshine, although heavy dark clouds were massing on the horizon, suggesting the rain was destined to return and soon.

Cautious about approaching the knee-high balustrade, the only barrier between herself and an attack of vertigo, Rhona crouched to take a closer look at the carved stone barrier, checking it for the wire that had descended to her window.

It didn't take long to spot it. Wound round the upper section of one of the pillars, it hung loose below, waving in the strong breeze. Might the wire have been originally attached to the seagull? Taking out her mobile, Rhona took a video of its position and of the knot that held it in place, before carefully untying it with gloved hands.

A few feathers had stuck to the balustrade, glued there by what she assumed was dried blood. Nearby, she spotted more remains, clotted blood and what might be evidence that Tom had encountered the bird up here, as suggested by his vomit.

There was, after careful inspection, no sign of yew needles or berries, either partially consumed or not.

If Tom had eaten yew in whatever form, it looked as though he had done it via the bird's carcass.

Winding the wire into a neat bundle, Rhona slipped it into an evidence bag. The scene on the roof and the associated earlier incident with the bird made no sense to her even now, but she couldn't dismiss the possibility that someone had deliberately set out to either frighten her with a dead bird or to injure her cat by offering it poisoned food.

As she rose, a gust of wind caught her and Rhona grabbed the balustrade to steady herself as a loud bang signalled the trapdoor being blown shut behind her. Unnerved by the thought that she might not escape the roof, Rhona immediately headed in that direction.

The rain came on in earnest as she felt around the door for the embedded ring which would allow her to lift it. The earlier arm injury screamed out at her as she struggled against the wind to open it enough to let her drop down onto the top of the metal steps.

Inside now, her hair and face soaked, she paused to pull the hatch closed behind her, just as the sound of footsteps signalled someone coming up the stairwell.

As Rhona slid the bolt into place, a figure appeared on the landing.

Conor's expression was, Rhona thought, as startled as her own when he spotted her above him on the ladder.

'I was checking the roof for dead birds.' Rhona indicated her gloves. 'In case that's what made Tom ill.'

'And did you find anything?'

She could have told Conor then about the dead seagull incident but for some reason chose not to. Just indicated instead that she'd found nothing of significance.

'How is Tom?' Conor asked.

'On the mend. I have to pick him up later.' Rhona suddenly remembered the flat tyre and cursed herself that she had done nothing about it.

Conor seemed to be reading her mind. 'I was passing on the bike and noticed your tyre was still flat. I could put the spare on if you like?'

It was a generous offer. One that Rhona decided she would accept.

'Would you? That would be great.'

'If you let me have your car keys.'

'Of course.' Rhona roused herself and, stepping off the ladder, pushed it back into place and fished out her door keys. 'Come on in. I'll get them for you.'

As Conor made to follow her into the kitchen, Rhona suddenly remembered she'd left the pregnancy test, now out of its bag, sitting in full view on the table. Something she had no wish to advertise.

'If you wait here,' she said, halting Conor in the hall while she fetched the keys from her handbag.

Reappearing, she found him standing outside the open door of Sean's room. From the look on his face, she was pretty sure he'd sussed the debris in there as belonging to a male.

Mustering himself, he said, 'Should take fifteen minutes or so, if all goes well.'

'I'll put some coffee on.' Rhona matched his matter-of-fact manner, while inwardly castigating herself. *For what?*

Leaving the door off the latch for his return, Rhona scooped up the pregnancy test and headed for the bathroom.

She had put this off long enough.

While rifling through her bag for the keys, she'd unearthed her pill strip, and just as Chrissy had suggested, she'd missed one, over and above this morning's.

There was a small but not insignificant chance of a pregnancy. Rhona didn't need to be a scientist to know that. Even now as she broke open the package, she was aligning dates with when she'd last had sex and when her next period was due.

The nausea she was experiencing now, Rhona recognized as fear.

54

Chrissy had assured him that Rhona had gone home, but she'd seemed pretty cagey about why exactly. Which was unusual for Chrissy. McNab had always counted on her to be straight with him. Even when he didn't like what she had to say.

When he'd demanded to know if Rhona was ill, Chrissy had looked as though she might reveal something, then had quickly changed her mind.

'Bill told her to take a couple of days off till all this blows over, and she decided she would.'

McNab didn't buy that, mainly because, although Chrissy was a better liar than Rhona, she wasn't that good.

After they'd parted, McNab had tried Rhona's mobile, which had rung out unanswered. She could of course be ignoring his call. At that point he'd decided he'd prefer to speak to her face to face.

McNab found a parking space just off Sauchiehall Street and, walking through the park, made for the steps leading up to the Circus. En route he noted that the yew tree locus was still cordoned off, the whole area being examined, they'd been informed at the meeting, by the soil scientist who'd aided Rhona in the Sanday case.

The heavy shower he'd driven through from the station had dissipated and already the surface water was evaporating in the heat of the sun. McNab headed up the steps two at a time. Reaching the top, he spotted Rhona's car parked a few yards from the main door of her block.

Mustering himself, he approached the entrance, aware that there was every chance Rhona would deny him entry when he rang her buzzer. But it seemed his luck was in. Finding the latch off, McNab ignored the intercom and headed up the stairs, keen now to get this over with.

As he reached the third landing, McNab heard voices in conversation from above, one undoubtedly Rhona, the other a man, whose voice he didn't recognize. McNab stopped in his ascent and waited, not sure whether he should appear right at this minute. Then again, if Rhona's door was already open, she was unlikely to shut it in his face.

As McNab reached Rhona's landing, the tall figure turned to face him. McNab did a quick reconnoitre, just like he'd done with the guys in George Square, and decided he'd never seen this bloke before, in any capacity.

Checking Rhona's face when she caught sight of him, McNab saw a mixture of what he read as guilt and annoyance.

'Detective Sergeant McNab,' she announced. 'This is a surprise.'

One she obviously didn't relish.

Her companion, on the other hand, appeared quite pleased to hear who had just arrived.

'Dr Conor Williams, Glasgow University Sleep Clinic,' he introduced himself.

'Conor kindly offered to change my flat tyre for me,' Rhona added, somewhat unnecessarily, McNab thought.

McNab gave the man a cursory nod then, taking his chance at the open door said, 'I'll wait for you inside.'

'I'll be on my way then,' McNab heard Williams say as he headed for the kitchen.

Jeez. Who the hell studies sleep? McNab thought as he marched in to discover a coffee pot on the table, a mug on either side. McNab pondered what the cosy tête-à-tête had been about. Certainly Conor had looked pretty at home in Dr MacLeod's company.

McNab countered a feeling of jealousy with a reminder that he'd just passed what was obviously the Irishman's room, indicating that Sean Maguire was still in the picture and had not been replaced by Dr Conor Williams.

Hearing the front door being closed, McNab fetched himself a fresh mug and poured out the remainder of the coffee.

When Rhona entered, the look on her face was hardly welcoming.

'Why are you here?' she said.

'I could say the same to you,' McNab countered.

'I'm off the case.'

'But not the job. Never off the job.'

Her expression at this suggested his words had hit home. Regardless of the current circumstances, the Rhona MacLeod he knew would still be at the lab. There were numerous tasks she could have been working on outwith the Jackson case. He knew that and so did she. So why wasn't she?

Rhona turned from him but not before McNab had registered what he could only describe as a look of panic. He watched as she went to the fridge, opened it, only to swiftly close it again, as though unsure why she was there at all. Then apparently mustering herself, she proceeded to fill the kettle and switch it on. As she did this, McNab was taken aback to note that those normally steady hands of hers were undoubtedly trembling.

What the fuck was wrong with Rhona?

McNab's first instinct was to get in there, while her defences were down, and demand to be told what was going on, but something stopped him.

'Can you make the coffee stronger this time?' McNab said as he exited, pretending to go to the toilet when in fact he just needed out of the room for a moment.

Nothing was right about this. Nothing at all. Not Chrissy. Not Rhona. Plus, despite what Professor Pirie had said in his lecture, McNab did know when folk were lying, even if the lies were being left unsaid.

They'd been through a lot together, he and Rhona MacLeod. Some bad – *very bad* – as well as good. McNab regretted it had come to this and knew exactly where the rot had set in.

But that couldn't be changed now. Or ever.

But it isn't about that – or at least he didn't think so.

McNab stood, hands on the sink, staring at his own reflection in the mirrored cabinet. He was at a loss, he had to admit it. But, he decided, he would outline his fears that she might be a target, for at least the perpetrator's desire to challenge the investigation, and in particular the forensic side of it. He would question Rhona about the students in her lectures. About who might have access to her DNA. About everything he'd mentioned in that meeting.

Having made that decision, McNab ran the cold water, splashed his face and reached for the towel. As he did so, he caught sight of something he recognized, because it wasn't the first time he'd encountered such an item discarded in a wastepaper bin.

McNab reached in and took it out.

55

'It's none of your business.'

Rhona had initially remained silent and stony-faced when asked for an explanation for what he'd found in the bathroom. McNab couldn't blame her. His language had been out of order. His obvious anger even more so.

He sat down, wanting her to do the same, but still she stood there, defying him. A lesser woman, he realized, would have walked out on him by now, or ordered him to.

'What are you going to do?' McNab tried again.

Her shoulders sagged a little. 'I haven't decided yet.'

McNab thought, by the way Rhona said it, she already had.

'You'll tell him first?'

'I haven't decided that either.'

Her face was set now, like it had been on that hill above Glasgow after he'd done what she'd forbidden him to. McNab suddenly didn't want them to harbour any more secrets.

'Does Chrissy know?'

She glanced at him then, her eyes determined. 'No.'

That floored him.

'Then why was she so cagey about you being ill?'

'I was having bouts of nausea. Vomiting. I thought I had a virus . . .' She tailed off.

McNab latched on to that explanation. 'Maybe you do? It's not a hundred per cent. Is it?'

The old Rhona reappeared, albeit briefly, and gave him a wry smile. 'You want the scientific answer to that?'

'Fuck, Rhona. I'm sorry.'

She shrugged her shoulders. 'Why? It doesn't affect you either way.'

McNab wanted to say he wished it did, but never would.

They were stuck there in that moment, somewhere in no man's land. How could he speak to her now about the reason for his visit? And yet, maybe that's exactly what he should do. As McNab cleared his throat, they both heard the front door open and someone come in.

'Sean,' Rhona said under her breath and shot McNab a pleading look, the words *don't say anything* left unspoken.

The Irishman paused in the kitchen doorway, a bag of groceries in his hand, a surprised look on his face.

'I thought you'd be at work, Rhona,' he said.

'I came home to write reports. Fewer interruptions.' Rhona attempted what might have been a laugh. 'Then DS McNab turned up.'

'So I see.' Sean looked to McNab, as though awaiting an explanation for his presence there.

Now would be the time to make himself scarce, but McNab wasn't willing to go, just yet.

'Rhona's got something to tell you,' he said firmly.

If a look from Rhona could kill, McNab acknowledged he would now be stone dead.

Sean's eyes moved between them. McNab watched as fear flickered there.

Fuck. He thinks we're screwing.

'About what?' Sean finally ventured.

As Rhona attempted to form a response, McNab jumped right in.

'She's at home because she's been taken off the tunnel case. Her DNA was found on the body, somewhere it couldn't have been.' He continued before Rhona could stop him. 'We believe it was planted. We also believe the perpetrator may be targeting Rhona directly.'

The impact of his statement was twofold. McNab heard an escape of breath from Rhona as relief flooded her, and Sean's expression moved from fear he was about to be dumped to concern for Rhona's well-being.

He turned to her. 'Is this true?'

McNab watched as she gathered herself. 'It's possible,' she admitted.

'I'd put it more strongly than that and so would the boss,' McNab said. 'That's what I came here to tell her.'

Rhona walked McNab to the door, desperate to have him leave, aware that getting Sean to do the same might be more difficult. She needed to eat something, but worried that if she did, her stomach would give her away again. Something she didn't want either men to see or comment on.

Stepping onto the landing with McNab, Rhona drew the door half closed behind her, then said what had to be said.

'Thank you.'

McNab, looking surprised, gave a small nod and a half-smile.

He looks as rough as me, she thought.

'Will you tell Chrissy?' he said in return.

Rhona wasn't sure she would and told him so. 'I don't want to be persuaded by anyone either way. This is my decision.'

He looked pained by that. Rhona thought he was about to lecture her again, but that's not what happened.

'I went to see Mary Grant last night,' he began. 'She told me she was pregnant when she left me for Davey. It was mine or so she says. She got rid of it. Never told me or Davey.' McNab halted, a catch in his throat. 'I guess she thought the same way as you.' He gave a little laugh. 'I'd have been a shite father back then. Maybe even now. Mary knew that.'

Rhona almost said *she should still have told you,* but stopped herself in time.

'So. It's to be our little secret, Dr MacLeod?'

'For now, at least.'

'Okay, Rhona. Whatever you say.'

As he turned to go, Rhona suddenly remembered.

'What about Ellie?' she said.

'Her pal Izzy and Mannie at the Ink Parlour think she's gone AWOL on the bike. Seems she does that sometimes.'

'Any idea where?'

'There's apparently a big Harley rally this weekend called Thunder in the Glens. They say up to four thousand bikes on the Facebook page.'

Rhona knew the name. 'That takes place every year in Aviemore,' she said. 'Sean played a gig at it once. Can you check if Ellie's a registered attendee?'

'Probably.'

'Even if she's not, that doesn't mean she won't be there,' Rhona urged him.

'So what are you suggesting? I go looking for her in Aviemore among four thousand old guys with beards and tattoos?'

'If that's the contingent, then Ellie'll be easy to spot. You could forward a photo to the Aviemore police. Ask them to look out for her.' Rhona thought of something else. 'The Harley-Davidson shop will have a presence. If Ellie goes, she may turn up at their tent.'

McNab nodded at that, although his thoughts seemed elsewhere. He turned to go, then suddenly reached out and touched her arm.

'You can call me, you know? Any time. And be careful. I meant what I said about you being targeted.'

As Rhona watched his tall figure descend the stairs, she knew the Mary story, if true, had been McNab's attempt at persuading her to tell Sean the truth.

56

'Do you want me to pick up Tom?' Sean said when she re-entered the kitchen.

'That would be good.' Rhona realized she was missing the cat. Missing its warmth and affection.

She'd not revealed the possibility that the cat had been deliberately poisoned during McNab's explanation of why they thought she may have been targeted, wanting to be sure of her facts first. The strange phone call had come up, because it seemed Bill had already told McNab about that.

'*I know what you did,*' Sean had repeated. 'What does that mean?'

Avoiding McNab's eye, Rhona had explained, 'We think it probably referred to the DNA contamination.'

'So who would know about that?' he'd queried.

'The whole fucking force,' McNab had said.

'You think it might have been a colleague who made the threatening call?' Sean had been obviously perturbed by such an idea.

Having had no desire to see Sean any more concerned than he already was, Rhona had intervened at this point.

'Can I chat to McNab alone?' she'd said.

Albeit grudgingly, Sean had left them to it then, while McNab doggedly brought up the subject of who might have known her preferred PPE suits and had access to her DNA.

'That's a long list,' she'd told him.

'One we have to make. Plus the folk on the course. You and Pirie supplied them with enough knowledge to do all of this.'

McNab had had a point, but it'd seemed to Rhona that the knowledge needed had been more extensive than what had been covered in her lectures. Something she wasn't prepared to say as yet.

Sean's voice suddenly brought her back from such thoughts.

'I put a gammon in the slow cooker. It'll be ready around five,' he was saying. 'I'll do the vegetables when I get back.'

'You don't need to stay,' Rhona said firmly. 'I'm fine. And I have reports to write, remember?'

'McNab seemed keen you have company.'

'I like my own company.'

Rhona knew as she said this that it was cruel, particularly in the circumstances, but she didn't think she could spend any more time with Sean and not say something.

And she wasn't ready for that yet.

'I think better when I'm alone,' she softened the blow. 'When's your night off?'

'Tomorrow.' A shadow crossed his face. 'But I've got something planned. Sorry.'

Rhona was about to ask if that something involved Imogen, the archaeology post-grad, but managed to stop herself. She had set up the boundaries of their relationship. Sean was playing along with them. She could hardly criticize him for that.

Especially now.

Despite her best efforts, Rhona realized she was sizing Sean up as a potential father. As for herself as a possible mother, Rhona didn't want to go there. She'd failed once spectacularly.

But you never considered abortion back then . . .

'Rhona? Are you okay?'

Her thoughts in turmoil, she had no idea what Sean had been saying, if anything.

She nodded. 'I'm fine. I just need to write up my report on Claire Masters.'

Sean appeared to accept this. 'I'll get the cat, then leave you be.'

God, he was being so reasonable. With every kind word Sean uttered, Rhona imagined herself stabbing him in the back.

If I don't tell him, the secret will lie between us forever. She thought of Mary Grant suddenly revealing the fact that McNab might have been a father, *had* been a father, for a brief time at least.

When the door shut behind Sean, Rhona felt a surge of relief. It was obvious that should she not tell him and have the abortion, their relationship would have to end. How could she continue to be with a man she'd done that to?

And if you have the child, does that mean you have to stay with Sean?

Rhona heard the ping of an incoming text and knew it would be Chrissy. She'd already decided what her response would be and promptly texted back, 'All okay', even though nothing could be further from the truth.

57

Magnus watched as McNab examined the list of dissertation titles, grouped by profession. Magnus was aware that most participants had, not unsurprisingly, chosen topics closely linked to their own work.

A favourite with the law fraternity was the manner in which forensic evidence was examined in court. Those working in pathology largely concentrated on the autopsy and how injuries might be interpreted.

Rhona's lectures had resulted in the majority of topics submitted, most focusing on the scene of crime and the importance of context and examination. A few had decided to look more closely at DNA and what it offered now and for the future. Toxicology had made an appearance via recreational drugs and poisons, as had the importance of forensic soil science in tracing a perpetrator.

'What about your area of expertise?' McNab said with a raised eyebrow.

'Just three,' Magnus told him, 'on the next page. All from serving police officers.'

McNab ran his eye over the titles, a smile playing the corner of his mouth. *'Does Profiling Work,'* he quoted, *'a discussion from the police perspective by Detective Constable Shona Fleming*. Do I know her?'

'Tall, mid-twenties, long dark hair.'

Despite trying to sound bland about Shona Fleming, Magnus knew immediately that McNab sensed otherwise.

Jeez, the guy's ability to intuit was ridiculous.

'She's doing groundwork on the case, CCTV et cetera,' Magnus hurried on. 'It was DC Fleming who told me she believed the perpetrator was using their forensic knowledge, perhaps gained from a course like ours, to control the investigation.'

'So not a fan of letting the general public know all our secrets?'

'No.'

'I'm beginning to like DC Fleming.' McNab returned to the remainder of the titles.

'Who submitted the ones at the end?'

'Participants from the general public.'

'Three went for buried or hidden bodies,' McNab said with interest.

'It's Rhona's area of expertise,' Magnus reminded him. 'What about the MOOCs participants?'

'There were a hundred signed up for the short free course, but the full diploma course is also online, you can take it part-time over anything up to three years.'

'A lot of people to check out,' Magnus said worriedly.

'You're the one who claims to be able to profile the killer,' McNab said. 'Tell me who to look for amongst that lot.'

McNab was right. He should be able to give a profile, yet it seemed to Magnus that his image of the perpetrator was made of constantly shifting sand.

'The signature of the bread and wine, the image it conjured of a sin-eater, was powerful and initially pointed to someone with such an agenda,' he began.

'A religious nutter?'

'Maybe, then again it may have been staged in order to draw in the services of a forensic psychologist.'

'Like yourself?'

Magnus nodded. 'Jackson was actively gay and that could be construed as a sin by some religions. As for Claire, I've heard nothing to atone for there . . . unless he didn't like the interest she showed in her charges.'

McNab's forehead creased in thought. 'Bastard. I bet that's exactly why she had to die. She saw him.'

Magnus continued. 'Jackson was prone to sleep paralysis according to Dr Williams at the sleep clinic. If that was known to the perpetrator, it was a useful way to fake his suicide and confuse the issue. Putting us to the test even further.'

'I ran into Williams at Rhona's earlier today.' McNab looked thoughtful. 'I understand he came in and gave a statement about treating Jackson for sleep paralysis.' He paused. 'Any idea how he knows Rhona?'

'They work at the same university?' Magnus suggested.

McNab returned to his previous line of thought. 'Why would the perpetrator portray Claire's death as suicide, when it could easily be proved not to be?'

'Maybe he overreached his knowledge? Or he's just playing dumb this time round?'

'So what next?' McNab said. 'For there will be a next,' he added grimly.

Magnus nodded. 'I fear so.'

'He's played the DNA card, the fake suicide, and tidied up loose ends with Claire, so?' McNab prompted.

Magnus glanced at the topics list again. 'If he did do the course, it could be anything on there. What's perhaps more significant and useful to know is how he got his victims to go to the loci.'

'Turns out Jackson was a Cosworth enthusiast. There's a Facebook page,' McNab said. 'That would have proved an attraction.'

'Which only adds to your list of potential suspects if he met the killer on there. But what about Claire? What drew her to the yew tree in the park, within sight of the university and Rhona's lab?'

A sudden thought openly crossed McNab's face. 'Might she have been going to see Rhona?'

'D'you have Claire's mobile?' Magnus said.

'No. Nor Jackson's.'

'Which probably means they'd both provide evidence.'

McNab ran his hand through his dark auburn hair. *He looks rough,* Magnus thought, *but not hungover*.

'Coffee? Strong?'

McNab nodded.

As Magnus set the espresso machine in action, he said, 'As you know, organized killers often seek to be in control of the proceedings of an investigation, even being seen to take a helpful part in it. Does anyone strike you as doing that?'

McNab gave a ghost of a smile. 'DS Fleming and most of her consort who did the course would fit that bill.'

Having turned off the sound on his mobile so as not to be interrupted, Magnus now watched it skitter across the desk, indicating an incoming call. Glancing at the screen, he found a name he hadn't expected.

After their discussion post-lecture, DC Fleming had surprised Magnus by requesting his contact details.

'The switchboard will put you through to my office or

my email is on your course notes,' had been Magnus's stock reply.

When she'd asked if she might also have his mobile number, Magnus had been taken aback.

It obviously showed, because she'd come back with, 'It's quicker sometimes to speak to someone directly.'

'Might this be about the course or the tunnel case?' he'd asked.

'The course is over, Professor, so I'm not your student any longer,' she'd reminded him with a smile. 'I might, however, want to talk to you further about the case.'

Magnus had hoped his disappointment that the reason wasn't personal hadn't shown on his face.

The mobile still vibrating, he collected himself and answered it, aware that McNab was watching.

'DC Fleming,' he said for McNab's benefit.

'Are you free later? I'd like to run an idea past you. We could meet for a drink to discuss?'

'Okay,' Magnus managed. 'Where suits you?'

She named a bar not far from his flat. *Did she know where he lived?*

'Fine,' he said. 'What time?'

Ringing off, Magnus faced McNab. 'DC Fleming wants to meet for a drink to discuss the case.'

'I didn't know you were that close.'

'We're not,' Magnus stressed. 'She wants to run an idea past me.'

'Why not her superior?'

'She agreed with you before anyone else did,' Magnus found himself defending her.

'And she wants to get closer to the investigation than she is at present,' McNab said.

Maybe that was it, Magnus thought. Maybe he was being used to get closer to the investigation. To perhaps discover his take on it. Maybe even to use it in her dissertation?

'Go for it, Professor,' McNab urged. 'I'll expect a full report after the event.'

58

It had been so different the last time.

If she'd known as early as this, would she have made the decision as quickly as she was doing now?

There had been no helpful online services back then. No little videos with a kind voice narrating about the difference between a medical and a surgical procedure.

No message that it was *her body, her choice*.

Rhona felt uncomfortable with that message. Not because she didn't believe it, but because each time she heard it, she thought of Sean's look of concern when he'd departed after bringing back the cat. His kiss and promise to check in with her tomorrow. His final request that she 'be careful'.

As for McNab's tone and expression as he'd told his own story of lost fatherhood . . .

Now would be the time, Rhona thought, to look back at snaps of Liam as a baby. His birthday parties, Christmases. Remind herself of what it meant to be a mother. But that wasn't possible. Only his adoptive mother had been around for any of that.

All she had was that first glance at her newly born son, the scent of him, the tiny face, the puckered lips, his cry that even now, when remembered, tore at her heart.

Rhona forbade herself such thoughts and, steeling herself,

dialled the number presented on the screen. Almost immediately a female voice answered. Rhona took a deep breath and explained her situation.

'When would suit you to come in?'

'As soon as possible,' Rhona said.

Minutes later, with a date and time agreed, she rang off.

It had been as easy as that.

With the decision made, the nausea seemed already in retreat, suggesting anxiety had played a major part in its presence.

And she actually felt hungry.

Rhona fetched the new loaf Sean had bought and contemplated frying some bacon to go with it. The fact she could now think of fried bacon without feeling sick felt like freedom.

She put on the pan and fetched the bacon and eggs from the fridge.

Tom in the meantime had taken to mewing at the kitchen window, annoyed that his route to the roof was being denied. Rhona spoke softly to him, rubbing his ears as he liked, explaining why he couldn't go up there.

Yet why not?

The seagull carcass was wrapped up safely in the fridge. There was nothing now to do Tom any harm. He could have his freedom back, just like her.

Rhona unlocked the window and opened it, and with a rich purr of delight, Tom was out and darting upwards.

Breathing in the scent of frying bacon, Rhona buttered two thick slices of bread in anticipation, then added an egg to the frying pan.

For the first time in days, she began to feel human. Not exactly well, but not, as McNab would term it, 'like shite'.

But you got to this point by lying, a small voice reminded her. *By omission at least.*

Added to that, she'd included McNab in her secret. That, if anything, was a betrayal of Sean. The feeling of freedom was beginning to dissipate. She knew her secret would be safe with McNab, but it would bind them together, just like the last one had.

And secrets had power.

McNab was right. She would have to tell Sean. The question was when. Before or after she had the termination?

Rhona pushed the plate away.

Somehow bacon and eggs didn't seem as enticing after all.

In times like this she had always sought refuge in her work. McNab had been right about that too. She might be off the case, but that didn't mean she shouldn't work. The plan had been that Chrissy would keep her informed of developments. Rhona was in little doubt that she would keep her word.

Abandoning her meal, Rhona retreated to the sitting room with her laptop. From the window, she was no longer certain if there was still a police presence near the yew tree, although she suspected there would be. Soil expert and colleague Dr Jen Mackie, who'd helped her on the Sanday case, had been drafted in, initially on the identification of the soil found on Andrew Jackson's shoes, and now to try and decipher the path Claire Masters had taken to her death, and who, if anyone, might have accompanied her there.

Settling down on the sofa, feet up, Rhona first scanned for Chrissy's emails, of which there were a number. Reading them in chronological order, she found the first to be a detailed report on the strategy meeting, with a full account of McNab's contribution, which appeared to have been dominated by his angry response to her situation and his theory that she'd been set up by the perpetrator.

'God, he was great. I couldn't have said it better myself,' was Chrissy's response.

In contrast, Rhona remembered her own reaction when she'd seen McNab's auburn head appear on the stairs. How irritated she'd been at his sudden arrival, and the fear that he'd caught her at a particularly bad moment.

Up to that point she'd managed to put on a suitable front with Conor until she could bid him goodbye. McNab, she'd known immediately, wouldn't be so easily fooled.

And he hadn't been.

McNab read her better than anyone, even Chrissy, and definitely Sean. Something she resented, yet at times welcomed, because with McNab she didn't have to pretend.

And in the kitchen, knowing how distressed she'd been, he'd made himself scarce to give her time to recover. If he hadn't done that, gone to the bathroom, then he would never have discovered the tester, buried in the waste bin.

Rhona read again Chrissy's glowing report of exactly what McNab had said on her behalf.

> DCI Sutherland was in the room, but it didn't stop McNab. I think Bill was pleased, although he obviously couldn't show it. With what McNab said, they'll have to let you come back and soon.

She'd been giving McNab constant grief since the Stonewarrior incident, yet here he was championing her, even if it meant he might be disciplined himself.

Rhona moved to the next message whose attachment was a report from Jen Mackie on the soil found on Jackson's shoes. There appeared little doubt from her analysis that it matched the samples taken from the tunnel and the likelihood was that he had probably entered via the former Bridgeton station, Jen having also identified tiny fragments of the old mosaic flooring from there stuck to his shoes.

So Jackson had walked in, possibly to check out the car, but had someone accompanied him or been waiting there for him?

On her return from the meeting, Chrissy – following Rhona's instructions – had taken a closer look at the ligature. Rhona brought up the images she'd taken herself at the locus and compared them now to the ones Chrissy had sent through, with her resultant conclusion.

Claire Masters had definitely been right-handed, according to her partner, Taylor, yet the scene, the way the ligature had been placed, the knot used to tie it, had suggested otherwise.

The placing of the bread and wine in both the tunnel and park loci matched, with the wine glass on the left and the bread on the right, indicating a left-handed setting, yet Andrew Jackson, Rhona knew, had also been right-handed.

Rhona thought back to the first time her son, Liam, had eaten with her here at the flat. A fraught situation only rendered a success by Sean's good humour. It was only then she'd learned that her son was left-handed, as he'd covertly shifted his meal setting to suit.

If Andrew Jackson had been responsible for his last supper, why would he have done otherwise?

Rhona moved on now to an email from Magnus to McNab with herself copied in, entitled 'Dissertation Topics'.

Rhona read through the names, trying to conjure up a face to match each of them, without much success. The most vocal of the participants had tended to be the serving officers. They hadn't given her a particularly difficult time. Forensics was well established now, although it had taken years to convince some of the diehards of its growing importance in investigations. Those in the room hadn't been as accepting of the opportunities of forensic psychology, however, and she knew Magnus had been the recipient of a decided antipathy.

Checking the essay titles against his lecture topics, she immediately spotted DC Fleming's submission. So DC Fleming had decided to go for the jugular. Magnus, Rhona knew, wouldn't take offence at that. In fact he would likely welcome her submission.

It appeared from the timeline that Magnus's email had been in direct response to one from McNab asking him to look specifically at proposed titles relating to her own lectures.

He definitely believes someone's fixated on me.

Rhona ran her eye down the subjects chosen, the majority of which were standard topics lifted from each of her lectures. The investigation of the scene of crime had proved to be the most popular, the more heavily scientific topics such as analysis of fibres, DNA and toxicology less so.

Nothing in that list suggested any link with the two most recent crimes. Nothing about poison, natural or otherwise, or distinguishing suicide from homicide. Only one of Magnus's group had chosen a topic which echoed an aspect of the current investigation and that was the signature and modus operandi of a killer, a standard topic.

Her own lectures had covered, albeit broadly, the subject

of buried or hidden bodies and three people had submitted a title that might be in that area, but without reading the completed work, it was hard to single any of them out.

The only submission that clearly challenged the content of the course was DC Fleming's on criminal profiling.

Yet McNab's gut instinct shouldn't be discarded. He had a habit of being right. Not always, but often enough to pay attention to. Bill thought so too, if he'd given McNab a chance to speak out at the meeting.

The forensic material collected at the second crime scene had yet to be fully examined, but if her own DNA turned up there despite her not having processed the body, it would offer some proof that McNab had a point.

During their kitchen discussion, he'd asked her outright if anything else suspicious had happened to her. Rhona had said no, despite Tom's sickness being caused by poisoning. Her own nausea had turned out to be a symptom of pregnancy, so no poisoning there. Besides, she'd only eaten and drunk what Sean had provided for her. Except for the red wine mysteriously delivered to her front door.

Rhona recalled the nightmarish sleep that had followed. Had the red wine been drugged in some way? But she thought Sean had tasted the red wine too, or maybe used it in the casserole.

Rhona considered whether Conor had been responsible for the wine. *Surely he would have mentioned it?* Or maybe the new guy, Craig, she'd met on the stairs a couple of times, who seemed pretty friendly and had asked her name.

But I have no proof there was anything wrong with the wine, Rhona reminded herself. *Apart from the troubled sleep and hellish nightmare that had followed.*

The only thing she couldn't explain was the possible yew berry in the dead seagull, and why the carcass had been fastened by a wire to the balustrade above her flat.

And that, she could do something about, if she went back to work.

As she made her decision to do just that, the report from Toxicology appeared in her in-box.

Rhona clicked it open and began to read.

59

I have a decision to make.

I could, of course, break the pattern of three, but am not inclined to do so. I've foreshadowed my actions up to now and will do so again.

It's just the way in which I choose to do this that's important and significant.

I've also submitted my dissertation title.

The detective who takes such a personal interest in Dr MacLeod might pick up on that, if he reads the submissions. Surely, by now, someone in the investigation team will have had the wit to pick up on my clues?

I hadn't anticipated the arrival of the female bikers in the tunnel, although it has in many ways added to the enjoyment.

Hence, my indecision.

The girl who checked the body and is apparently having sex with the detective sergeant went AWOL after my phone call. I suspect I know exactly where she's gone.

60

The three girls had come in together, the sound of their bikes roaring up apparently reminding Sergeant McIvor of his long-lost youth.

'Girls didn't ride back then, except on pillion,' he informed McNab, a little regretfully.

'Where are they?' McNab interrupted his reminiscing.

'Together in room three.'

McNab had every intention of separating them, but he was interested in observing how they operated as a group first.

'Does DS Clark know they're here?' he said, wondering how long he might have before Janice arrived.

'I'm trying to locate her, sir.'

McNab stopped at the coffee machine on his way and had a couple of caffeine shots. He'd already informed Janice of the previous conversations he'd had with Izzy, by phone, at the speedway and the most recent at the Rock Cafe. McNab ran these over again in his mind as he approached the interview room.

Having been told that they'd arrived by bike, McNab wasn't sure why he was surprised by the leathers. All three outfits were distinctively different. Izzy's had a blood-red splash. As for the other two, one sported a white skull which reminded him of his own inked back, the other a pink stripe.

All three stood up on his entrance, the chairs scraping back on the tiled floor. McNab silently studied the faces before introducing himself, thanking them for coming in and suggesting they sit back down.

As they did so, the other two shot a quick glance at Izzy, perhaps looking for guidance.

The paper Sergeant McIvor had given him had their three names and addresses on it. McNab studied it now and tried to match the other two to their names. Mona Ritchie he thought might be the pink stripe, with Gemma Johnstone the skull, but that proved to be wrong.

'That's Mo,' Izzy told him, pointing to the skull, when McNab tried out his theory. The contrast between the frightened face and the defiant skull couldn't have been greater. Pretty in pink turned out to be Gemma, who, McNab decided, almost matched Izzy in her defiant attitude.

Recalling the scene with Ellie and Izzy at the speedway, McNab figured Ellie as the leader with Izzy close behind and Mo never likely to be.

'Why are we here?' Izzy asked.

'Because you were in the tunnel the night Andrew Jackson was murdered.'

'He was murdered?' Mo's eyes grew wide with fear.

At that, the door opened and Janice appeared. She darted McNab a swift glance, which he interpreted as *I hope you haven't started without me*. In response McNab handed her the paper and told her that Sergeant McIvor had shown the girls in here to await her arrival.

Janice swiftly introduced herself and explained that they

would be interviewed in turn by herself and DS McNab, with respect to the Andrew Jackson case, whereupon Mo was asked to stay where she was and the others were shown out.

Janice's choice of Mo to start the proceedings was, in McNab's view, an astute one. By far the most intimidated by the surroundings, she also looked keen to get everything off her chest.

McNab left Janice to do the questioning while he observed and listened. Mo's delivery was a little breathless, but it sounded truthful. And it matched what Izzy had told him earlier. Although it did omit the fact that Izzy had persuaded Ellie not to call the police. According to Mo, they had left that decision to Ellie and Izzy.

Seemingly satisfied, Janice halted the recording and indicated Mo should leave the room, but not the station. Once she'd gone, Janice turned to McNab.

'Well?'

'It matches what Ellie told me, and Izzy, when I spoke to her at the Rock Cafe,' McNab confirmed.

'Let's have Izzy in next then and see if her story's changed in any way,' Janice said.

Izzy reminds me of Ellie, McNab thought as the girl strode in, head held high. *Even when she's obviously frightened.*

'I've told Michael everything I know,' Izzy said, when asked by Janice to review that fateful night in the tunnel.

At Izzy's usage of his first name he saw Janice start, and he fervently hoped she wouldn't pull Izzy up on it. She didn't.

Instead she said, 'I'd like to hear everything you told my colleague, Detective Sergeant McNab.'

Izzy nodded and did as requested. To McNab's mind, it

was all there, every conversation they'd had. He nodded to Janice, who then indicated he should take over.

It was time to put Izzy on the spot.

'Did Ellie say at any time that she might have detected a pulse in Andrew Jackson's neck?'

'A pulse?' Izzy looked horrified. 'You think the guy was alive when we left him?'

'What did Ellie say exactly, when she felt his neck?'

'I told you, she only touched him for a second, then she said he was dead.' Izzy glared at McNab. 'Did she tell you something different?'

'In the one call I got from Ellie since her disappearance, she said, "He wasn't dead".'

A torrent of emotions crossed Izzy's face at this. 'Jesus, there was a chance he was alive and we left him there?'

'We can't know for certain he was,' McNab said, 'just that he may have been.'

'Ellie thought, we all thought, the guy had committed suicide. The weird way he was lying next to the car. No blood, no weapon, and the creepy wine and bread thing. Jesus, why didn't Ellie tell us if she felt a pulse?' Izzy halted suddenly, staring into some memory. 'Oh, fuck!'

'What?' McNab prompted, sensing an explanation of Ellie's reaction might be forthcoming.

Izzy stared at McNab, her eyes bright with tears.

'Danny, Ellie's wee brother, committed suicide three years ago. It was Ellie who found him.'

Janice, hearing McNab's intake of breath, turned, her look questioning. McNab gave a brief shake of his head indicating he hadn't known anything about that.

Jesus, no wonder Ellie had freaked.

'She still blames herself. Thinks she should have spotted something sooner.'

McNab recognized the classic response of every family member and friend who had found themselves in that position.

'How did her brother die?' Janice said.

'An overdose,' Izzy said.

McNab knew the figures. Male suicides numbering more than twice the number of females and growing. Most of them aged under thirty-five.

No wonder Ellie had called him that night, McNab thought. *And he'd let her down.*

McNab took himself outside. He needed some air and he needed to be alone to process everything that had happened in that interview room.

After Izzy's revelation about Ellie's brother being the possible reason for her reaction to finding the body, they had brought in Gemma, whose recall of that night had matched the others. Her response to the possibility that Jackson might have been alive was one of dismay that they hadn't called for help immediately.

'We were scared of getting into trouble.' She'd shaken her head at that. 'We should have been braver.'

The sessions complete, they now had the number for Dougie, the supplier of the entry keys and password. All three interviews had rung true to both himself and Janice, whose main concern had shifted to Ellie's state of mind and the necessity to know her whereabouts.

'Keep trying her,' she'd told him, 'and check with IT. Maybe they've picked up her mobile signal by now.'

McNab listened as his call rang out. *If he could only tell*

Ellie that everything was out in the open and that there was no reason for her to hide any more. When it disappointingly switched to voicemail again, McNab said exactly that, ending with a plea for Ellie to return and a heartfelt apology for screwing things up between them.

After which he contacted Ollie, who answered immediately.

'I've been trying you for the past half-hour.' He sounded peevish.

'And now you've got me,' McNab said.

'Your girlfriend's just used her mobile. She called the Glasgow Harley shop. She's in or near Aviemore.'

'Thank you,' McNab said.

61

The grassed area to the east of the sprawl of Aviemore Centre buildings had been designated a campsite. Ellie, with no idea where she would end up when she'd hit the road, had come prepared. Her solo tent was now safely sandwiched between two large motorhomes with friendly occupants.

It had been the right decision to come north, she decided, although she'd taken a circular route to get here, having initially headed west along the Clyde, catching the ferry to Bute.

That's when she'd met Garthe.

Ellie had found herself a seat in the main cabin, next to the window, and plumped her saddlebags down beside her. The ferry had quickly filled up, most folk trundling suitcases, either headed to the island on holiday or returning home from vacation elsewhere.

She'd spotted a small posse of motorbikers as she'd boarded, recognizing their voices as being from the north of England. Just before the door had closed, another biker had come aboard, not, she suspected, with the bigger party, but solo like herself.

Luckily none of her fellow riders had chosen this part of the lounge to pass the forty-minute journey, which Ellie had been glad about. Bikers were known to be a garrulous bunch and she hadn't fancied being questioned, however friendly the enquiry.

She'd already decided that answering the call from Michael had been a mistake. As soon as she'd ended the conversation, she'd switched off her mobile, hoping to prevent Michael from tracing her movements and, even more importantly, preventing the creep who'd seen her in the tunnel from calling her again.

That's when a voice had interrupted her thoughts with a 'Is this seat taken?'

Ellie had looked up to find the single biker, helmet in hand, wearing a wide smile and awaiting permission to sit alongside her.

Her first thought had been to lie and say yes, since there were plenty of other empty seats available. But something had stopped her. His accent for one, which she recognized as coming from way further north than this, and certainly not from Glasgow.

'Go ahead,' she'd offered, moving her saddlebags onto the floor.

'Nice bike you're riding,' he'd said as he'd settled himself down.

'I like it,' Ellie had said.

'Harley dominates the female market share,' he'd smiled at that. 'And women are the fastest-growing segment of new riders.'

'I take it you work for Harley-Davidson?' Ellie had responded with a laugh.

'Nope, I just write stuff for a motorbike lovers' website in my spare time.' He'd held out his hand at this point. 'Garthe Tulloch, from Shetland originally, currently based in Newcastle.'

'Ellie Macmillan, from around here,' Ellie had said cautiously.

'Like from Bute, where we're headed?' His eyes had lit up at this.

Ellie had shaken her head. 'No, but I had holidays there when I was a wee girl.'

'Are you on holiday now?' He appeared to like that idea.

Ellie knew she was painting herself into a corner, but once you started lying . . .

'I decided to take to the road for a few days. Saw the ferry . . . and got on. Not sure where next.'

Garthe nodded. 'I like solo rides. Don't have to agree where to go next, although I am aiming for Thunder in the Glens by the weekend.'

'Thunder in the Glens,' Ellie said, aghast. 'I've forgotten it was this weekend.'

God, Roddie would be mad at her. She'd promised to help out in the shop in Aviemore over the Thunder weekend.

'You been before?'

'I have. I work part-time at West Coast Harley in Glasgow. They usually have a stall there.'

'My first visit,' Garthe had said. 'Looking forward to it. I take it you're not on the stall this year?'

She should be. Or maybe she wouldn't have a job at West Coast to go back to.

Ellie had made a non-committal sound at that point, already wondering if that's where she should go.

In the end she had, but not with Garthe. Chances were they might bump into one another here, although with around four thousand bikers, that wasn't a certainty.

Ellie shut up the tent and, grabbing her bag, headed for the path that took her past the supermarket car park and into the village centre. The annual HD pilgrimage to Aviemore was in its twentieth year. According to her neighbours in the motorhomes who'd driven here from Germany and Italy respectfully, it was now the largest Harley-Davidson rally in Europe.

Ellie could well believe it as she joined the crowds and roaring bikes heading onto the one and only main street where various venues offered food, drink and music from open stages.

Her heart lifted at the sight of so many kindred spirits and, for the first time since that night in the tunnel, Ellie felt safe. Safety in numbers. Safety among her own kind.

She'd already called Roddie, apologized for pissing him around, swore all was well now and that she'd be in Aviemore as promised. His response had been decidedly cool. He'd also revealed that McNab had been to the shop, 'throwing his weight about', but he'd told him nothing, as requested.

'I take it it's over between you two?' he'd said hopefully.

Ellie had muttered a 'yes' and hung up, feeling she'd now betrayed McNab yet again.

The truth was, she thought, as she bought a drink at one of the open-air bars, there was no way she and McNab could be together. Not after what had happened.

Not after what she'd done.

She carried her wine out to a vacant place near the perimeter wall and perched there, glad to be back among friendly faces. She realized she was even open to someone striking up a conversation, something she'd been studiously avoiding since she'd left Glasgow. Camping wild, buying just enough food to get by, with no pub visits, she'd been avoiding company and news.

Tomorrow she would have to report to the shop and face

Roddie, who would no doubt try to get to the bottom of her disappearance and what that had had to do with the law. Until then, Ellie decided, she would relax, maybe even get a little drunk.

She supped some more of the pink liquid that was masquerading as rosé wine and contemplated switching to a local beer instead. Swallowing the remainder, she binned the plastic glass and headed inside to the main bar.

A solitary TV was playing silently on one wall, the statutory line of news running along the bottom. Ellie instantly recognized the image on the screen as Glasgow University with Kelvingrove Park below. Turning away, Ellie gave her order to the barman.

'Which one?' he said with a bemused look, pointing to a row of local beers.

'Choose for me,' she suggested.

'Okay.' He rose to the challenge with a smile. 'Let's see, what bike do you ride?'

'A Fat Bob.' She met his smile with one of her own.

He widened his eyes in appreciation. 'Cool. Then I think it's a Wildcat for you.'

Ellie didn't bother asking why, but she appreciated his patter. 'Okay, I'll try a pint of that.' While he poured, she glanced back at the screen where the image had changed to police activity among the trees. Along the bottom ran the words: *Body found in the park identified as twenty-three-year-old Claire Masters. Police suspect a link to the London Road tunnel murder of Andrew Jackson, a male model.*

Ellie gripped the counter, her legs no longer capable of holding her up.

'You okay?' The barman, spotting this, came swiftly out,

and without fuss steered her to a nearby seat. Ellie sank down gratefully.

'I'll fetch your pint.'

Setting it down, he appeared to be awaiting an explanation.

'I've been on the road for days,' Ellie said. 'I probably just need some food.'

'I ordered a fish and chips too many on the last order. Would that do?'

'Please,' she said gratefully.

'Coming right up.'

Ellie took a long draught of the pint and, despite her best efforts, found her eyes drawn again to the screen, but the image and message had changed and she began to wonder or maybe hope that she'd only imagined what she'd read there.

When the barman returned with her meal, Ellie thanked him and assured him she was fine. Then offered to pay.

'On me,' he said. 'If you let me admire the Fat Bob sometime over the weekend?'

It was a come-on, but in the nicest possible way. 'Visit the West Coast Harley tent and you shall meet Fat Bob in person,' Ellie said.

'Great.' He held out his hand. 'I'm Kenny West by the way.'

'Ellie Macmillan.'

'See you later then.' He gave her a big smile before heading off.

Turning away from the TV, Ellie concentrated solely on her meal. It worked for a while, at least until, from the corner of her eye, she realized the piece on the Glasgow murder was being repeated.

The guy they'd found in the tunnel had been murdered.

Pushing her half-eaten food away, Ellie reached for the beer glass, her hand trembling.

Despite everything that had happened down there, she'd thought or convinced herself that it had been a suicide, however much that had upset her because of Danny.

But murder?

A sudden memory of that night swept over her. She could smell again the damp tunnel, see the others grouped together, their shocked faces caught in her headlight.

Ellie withdrew her hand from the glass, suddenly recalling the touch of skin under her fingers, the faintness of a pulse. Fear consumed her and somewhere in that fear the bright searching light of a distant torch found her face.

He saw me. He knows what I look like.

And, a little voice reminded her . . . he has your mobile number.

How was that even possible?

She hadn't recognized the muffled voice, but then again she'd been too stunned and frightened to even think. Could she have known the person down there? How would they have her number?

But, Ellie acknowledged, she'd given her number out freely. It was on her card for the Ink Parlour. It was on her card for the Harley shop. Anyone could get hold of her number, but they would have to know who she was first and what she did, and the Harley link was pretty obvious.

Maybe it was someone who knew we were down there racing that night. Someone like Dougie?

Ellie had no idea how much Izzy confided in Dougie. How often she even saw him. She suddenly realized that Izzy had every right to be angry with her. When Izzy had met Dougie at the Rock Cafe and learned from him about the tunnel and its possibility as a racing venue, Ellie had encouraged Izzy to work on him. Persuade him to give them access.

Had Izzy broken up with Dougie in the wake of the incident and given him back the keys? Could that have provoked the call to her out of spite? Dougie would have known about the body from the news, but how could he have known there might have been a pulse?

Only the killer would know that.

And it looked like the killer had struck again.

62

Rhona had contemplated using the car now that Conor had switched tyres, but it was such a fine evening that she'd decided to walk to the lab instead. That way she could also check out the continuing police presence near the locus.

She might not be permitted to work on the case, but that didn't mean she couldn't keep abreast of developments, and if Jen was still there, that would be possible.

Jen's profile of the deposits found on Jackson's clothing and footwear, as well as identifying the geological make-up of the tunnel floor, had also indicated traces of decomposing moss, urine, faeces, wild grasses and man-made hydrocarbons. All these combined to identify the victim's entry point as via the wasteland at the old Bridgeton station. Similar deposits would exist on anyone who'd accompanied him on his route.

Useful, but only if they identified a suspect and obtained their clothing and footwear to examine.

As Rhona approached the outer cordon, she registered how different this locus was to the London Street tunnel. With a mix of high and low trees, shrubs and understorey vegetation, Jen would be sampling around any area where someone had likely stood. The yew needles and seeds would be in abundance and easily picked up underfoot or on clothing.

Spotting the officer on duty at the cordon, Rhona introduced herself. 'I wondered if Dr Mackie was still on site?' she enquired.

'She is.' He hesitated and Rhona knew he was pondering whether he should allow her to cross the boundary.

Rhona saved him the bother.

'If you could say I'm here and there's no rush. I'll wait here for a bit.'

'Okay, Dr MacLeod,' he said, relieved. 'Be right back.'

Her view of the undergrowth signalled perhaps up to four people working the area, indicating Jen had likely brought some of her technicians with her.

Five minutes later, Jen appeared, although well disguised in the PPE suit, her identity only truly confirmed when the protective cap came off and her glorious mop of chestnut hair was revealed. With a characteristic grin, she waved across at Rhona.

'I don't want to interrupt,' Rhona said as she approached.

'You haven't. We're just finishing up.' She gestured to her vehicle parked up behind the police contingent. 'I have a flask of very good coffee. Want to share it with me?'

Rhona wondered if coffee was a wise move on her part, but smiled her acceptance anyway.

Once outside the confines of the forensic suit and seated in the car, Jen gave Rhona the once-over.

'What the hell are they thinking about taking you off the case?'

'It's the procedure in such circumstances,' Rhona countered.

'I could say fuck procedure, but since we both know

how important it is for us to cover all our bases, I won't.' She sighed and handed Rhona her share of the coffee.

It smelt hot and delicious, just as promised. Rhona took a cautious sip and made an appreciative face.

'I heard DS McNab was your champion at the strategy meeting and told Sutherland exactly what was going on.' By her expression, Jen obviously approved.

Rhona gave a wry smile. 'So Chrissy tells me,' she said, before swiftly steering the conversation away from herself to the locus.

'Well,' Jen began. 'We've sampled all the contact points – surface vegetation, soil west of the footfall of people who visited the scene. I have soil traces from the victim's feet. At first inspection I'd say she walked to the site from the south end, rather than was carried. Further prints suggest someone joined her there, coming from the direction of the university.'

'The university?' Rhona said, startled by this news.

Jen gave a little nod. 'Whoever it was left the tarred path about halfway down and cut through the undergrowth to the clearing.'

The path she referred to was the one Rhona used regularly to gain access to the park and to walk home. The path she'd hurried down when she'd received McNab's frantic phone call.

Jen came back in then. 'Have we any idea why she came to the yew tree?'

'Not as far as I'm aware,' Rhona said. 'Unless it was to meet someone.'

'And the post-mortem?'

'I wasn't in attendance,' Rhona said, 'but Dr Walker

dismissed suicidal hanging as the cause of death. Toxicology is checking for taxine.'

'If it worked for him the last time . . .' Jen said, looking to Rhona.

'It did. The report from Toxicology just came in.'

Jen glanced towards the trees, her expression both serious and sorrowful. 'Yew poisoning appears to be his thing. And a preoccupation with the sins of the departed, according to Professor Pirie.'

Rhona's eyes followed Jen's towards the trees as she contemplated her words. Bread, wine, poison and death, because of a perceived sin? Or was the presence of the last supper just a ruse to confuse those who sought to understand the motive behind the killings?

Rhona didn't know the answer to that question, but the manner in which her own life had recently played out reflected a not-dissimilar pattern, especially once you added in the weird phone call and the poisoned gull on her kitchen floor and Tom's possible poisoning.

'You okay?' Jen said. 'You look a little washed out.'

Rhona assured her she was fine, swallowing down the remainder of the coffee as evidence. 'I'm just heading to the lab.'

'It's a bit late for work . . .' Jen said.

'I like the lab when it's quiet. I'm better able to think.'

Jen indicated she understood such a sentiment. 'I'll be in touch then,' she promised, gesturing to the yellow crime scene tape. 'About this.'

'I'm not officially on the case,' Rhona reminded her.

'Then we'll meet for a drink and a gossip as usual,' Jen said with a conspiratorial smile.

Rhona opened the car door and, lifting out the bag containing the dead seagull, said her goodbyes.

Night was falling when Rhona finally departed the lab building, minus the gull carcass, which was now safely stored in the fridge, a sample taken from it and dispatched to Toxicology.

Exiting the university via the cloisters, she headed for the path she and Jen had discussed earlier, stopping for a moment at the flagpole to admire one of the plethora of views possible from the long frontage of the Gothic structure.

The night air was full of fragrance from a nearby bed of yellow dwarf roses and Rhona breathed in their scent. A setting sun had found the russet sandstone of the distant Art Gallery, setting it ablaze.

Drawing her eyes back, Rhona found herself focusing on the dark mass of trees that had hidden Claire Masters, reminding herself that Claire wasn't the first murder victim she'd processed within the park.

She stood for a moment, remembering. The trees hadn't been as mature back then, the undergrowth less dense, the view to the wide green expanse of the park more open.

And it had been a young male, a teenager, whose body they'd discovered there, a brutal sexually motivated death, and not the last before they'd finally identified his killer.

The case had coincided with her own search for Liam. No, she corrected herself, it had been the discovery of the perpetrator's second victim that had prompted her search.

A young university student, he'd looked so like her she'd initially thought he might be the son she'd given up for adoption seventeen years before.

Guilt had prompted her search. Guilt because it might have been Liam who'd died that terrible death in that hideous little room.

Even now after all this time, after making contact with Liam, who was alive and well, Rhona could still revisit the scene of that terrible night in her mind when she'd looked down on a face that so closely resembled her own.

'Rhona?' a voice called her from behind.

Startled, Rhona turned to discover Conor Williams approaching, wheeling his bike. 'I thought it was you. My, you've been working late.'

'As have you,' Rhona deflected his question, then remembered, 'But your work happens at night.'

'Not tonight,' he said. 'I've settled them down and left Ray in charge. Ray's the guy who's on your course?'

Rhona tried the name, but it didn't ring a bell. 'Sorry, but there are a lot of them. So what does Ray do while your patients are getting a good night's sleep?'

'He stays awake, I hope. Checks on their monitoring and I believe he watches stuff on Amazon Prime, plays games and listens to music. Or so he says and I have to believe him.' He paused. 'I take it you're heading home?'

'I am.'

'May I walk with you?'

'But you have your bike,' Rhona pointed out.

'A bike is poor company. No conversation.'

Rhona accepted Conor's offer, realizing she would actually be quite pleased to have a companion, through the park at least.

As they descended the path, Conor glanced towards the locus. 'Terrible thing, the death of that young girl. And they said on the news it was linked to Andrew's death, which they're now calling murder.'

When Rhona didn't respond, Conor apologized. 'You can't discuss it, I know.'

'The police have announced the two are linked, yes, but I'm not working the case any longer,' Rhona said, deciding to be forthright with him.

'Oh.' He appeared taken aback by that. 'Should I ask why?'

'You can, but I'm not at liberty to say.'

They walked on in silence for a bit, the whirr of his bike wheels a comforting background sound. The park was by no means deserted. In fact people were taking advantage of the warm evening and clear sky. Rhona wondered how many people had been about when Claire had come here. How many had contacted the police with sightings.

As if guessing her thoughts, Conor said, 'I walk past here most days. I didn't see anyone matching Claire's description.' He sounded as though he wished he had.

'Hopefully, someone will have,' Rhona said.

A burst of laughter from a nearby group gathered round the glow of a disposable barbecue and the distant sound of a musical concert at the open-air Kelvingrove bandstand seemed to belie the horror that had happened here.

'They're still working the scene, I see?' Conor said, thoughtfully.

'Forensic soil expert is on the job now,' Rhona told him.

'Gosh, that thorough?'

'That thorough,' Rhona assured him. 'Perpetrators forget that wherever they go they gather evidence about that place on them. Microscopic, but there none the less. And there's a soil map of the whole of Scotland.'

Conor looked impressed, but even as she said this, a feeling of doom crept over Rhona. A sense that however hard they might strive to find the killer, somehow he would outmatch them. Using the tools they, or perhaps she, had given him.

Yet she didn't think McNab and many of his fellow officers like DC Fleming were right in their desire to keep the general populace ignorant of the developments in detection.

Ordinary men and women would be called to jury duty when they did catch the perpetrator. They would be presented with the type of forensic and psychological material delivered in the course. And they would have to try and understand it, and come to a verdict.

The more educated the general population was, the better the courts could do their job.

'Penny for them,' Conor said after her long silence.

'Just work,' she said. 'It does become all-consuming.'

'How's the sleep pattern? Did you make use of my aid?'

'I did,' Rhona said, 'and it seemed to work. Either that or a big meal and half a bottle of wine were responsible.' She thought back. 'I went out like a light. Only heard the opening bit, then nothing until the morning.'

'Good,' Conor said. 'Any more night paralysis?'

Rhona shook her head. 'Thankfully, no.' Although who knew what would happen tonight after the day's events?

They had already crossed University Avenue and were on one of the bridges that spanned the River Kelvin, the banks of which were cast in deep shadow, although you could hear the rush of the river below.

In maybe ten minutes, they would reach the point of departure, where Conor would set off on his bike to his own flat and she would climb the steps to hers. Rhona could read the situation well enough to know that at that moment Conor would say something.

Ask her if she was in a relationship. Ask her out to dinner. Something.

At another time, she could well have said yes. Even now, in the strange hiatus in her relationship with Sean and the predicament she found herself in. Conor was a nice guy. She liked him. It was obvious he liked her. He hadn't been easily put off, and yet he hadn't come on too strong. A rare combination. Rhona decided to clear one thing up at least.

'Did you perchance leave a bottle of very good red wine at my front door after we met in the park?'

Conor looked startled by her sudden question, and mildly embarrassed. 'No. Should I have?'

Rhona laughed. 'No. It's just someone did. I drank it, even though I'm not a fan of red.'

'I take it there was nothing else available at the time?' he said with a smile.

'It was a bit like that,' Rhona admitted.

'Was that the one that helped with the night's sleep?' Conor said.

'No. That was a different one. White. Good quality too.'

'Your secret admirer left a second bottle?' Conor sounded as though he thought himself already out of the running, by omission at least.

'No.' Rhona almost said it was Sean, then changed it to, 'That one was bought.'

'Well, I suppose I should countenance against too much wine as, although it can send you to sleep quickly, the sleep it induces is not favourable to your well-being.'

'Sound advice,' Rhona said. 'And besides, your sleep aid is free,' she joked.

They had reached the steps.

'I was wondering . . .' Conor began.

63

It was late and she should go to bed, if she was to achieve the hours Conor said were required. Rhona smiled, remembering his intensity whenever he spoke of sleep and its absolute necessity for human health.

She should go to bed, but found herself unable to do so, aware that the likelihood was she would simply lie there, her brain torturing itself with the thought of what would happen tomorrow.

And I haven't spoken to Sean yet.

Rhona glanced at her mobile. If she called him, he would come over. She could tell him and explain her decision.

That made it all sound so easy, as though he were merely a bystander in the predicament she found herself in. Someone like the woman she'd spoken to on the phone. A neutral voice, kind and non-judgemental.

My body. My decision.

But there was something about Sean she was choosing not to remember. That he had a wife, Kitty Maguire. According to Sean, they'd married at seventeen, 'because she thought she was pregnant. So, like a good Catholic boy, I married her. Only there wasn't a baby, only a ring and a priest.' Sean had sounded sad about that.

When Rhona had suggested Kitty had tried to trap him,

Sean had been vociferous in his denial. 'I trapped her,' he'd said. 'I fucked her when I should have kept my cock in my pants, like my granny told me. Twenty years ago, where I come from, *that* was the crime.'

Rhona laid a hand on her abdomen, knowing there wouldn't be, couldn't be any response, although she didn't doubt the fact that she was pregnant.

You didn't have to be a scientist to know that with the type of pill she was on, she should have been more careful about taking it at the same time every day. Being late with a dose or skipping one altogether meant her hormone levels could quickly drop, which in turn would cause her to ovulate and greatly increase her chances of getting pregnant. On missing a dose, she should have used a condom or simply avoided sex for the next month.

Had she forgotten that or had she simply grown reckless?

Rhona roused herself from her bout of introspection and went to lock the door. Catching the scent of the slow-cooked ham emanating from the kitchen, she suddenly felt hungry. Tom had smelt it too and, having had enough of the freedom of the roof, wound himself round her legs, mewing in supplication.

As she lifted the gammon onto a plate, Rhona noticed that the slow cooker was set at *off*, which was odd. Had Sean come back, even though she'd told him not to? Barely warm to the touch, it had obviously been off for a while.

Sean, she reasoned, must have returned perhaps to see how she was, only to discover she'd gone out. Rhona checked her mobile which had been turned to silent, but there was no message from him via text or voicemail.

Whatever guilt she'd been experiencing regarding Sean had just been magnified. Swearing under her breath, Rhona went to the fridge, fetched the remains of the white wine and poured herself a glass.

Times had changed since she was first pregnant, she reminded herself. Now, there was even conflicting advice being given out on the need for complete abstinence during pregnancy.

But she didn't intend to get past three weeks, anyway.

Fifteen minutes later, having eaten her fill of both bread and ham to no ill effect, Rhona rose from the table only to find that, although her stomach was okay, she was definitely light-headed.

Sitting down again to regain her composure, she watched as the world of the kitchen began to rotate about her like some slow-moving fairground ride.

'This isn't funny,' she said sharply, although the words to her ears sounded long drawn out and hardly recognizable.

Fear entered now, wriggling snake-like into her thoughts. Pregnancy might make you light-headed, but it didn't slur your speech or distort your vision.

Yet still a small area of her brain clung on to rationality and that bit knew she would have to lie down, just not on the moving deck that her kitchen floor had become. Her bedroom was the goal, but could she make her legs take her there? And how to stop the room from spinning in the interim?

As Rhona forced herself to her feet again, she suddenly understood why this was happening. Somehow her brain, even in its confused state, had accumulated all the symptoms – the difficulty speaking, the loss of balance, the disturbed vision – and presented her with a diagnosis.

She'd ingested a drug, probably via the wine. Immediately, possible names presented themselves like a roll call:

Gamma-hydroxybutyrate, ketamine, rohypnol. Date-rape drugs commonly given with alcohol to multiply and accelerate their effects.

Knowing unconsciousness would swiftly follow, Rhona made a desperate grab for her mobile and met the wine bottle, sending it rolling across the table, propelling the phone with it.

Fuck! Fuck! Fuck!

The bottle met the floor with a resounding crash, its fragments scattering across the surface like tiny jewels to her drug-fuelled eyes.

Rhona sought and found the mobile among the debris.

Summoning what little control of her body she had left, Rhona slid to the undulating floor like a rag doll, her limp arms outstretched, desperate to make that emergency call before her inevitable drop into unconsciousness.

In that moment, somewhere between hallucination and rationality, Rhona saw it.

Hunch-backed, dark and brooding, it squatted in the corner of the room, watching and waiting. The demon in the Fuseli painting had come, and this time it was for her.

64

McNab stood in silence, waiting.

It would have been easier not to ask, but he'd given the boss his word not to go AWOL this time round. Instead, he'd come and told him where Ollie believed Ellie was.

Finally, the tall, spare figure turned from the window.

'Has she been in touch with anyone since the call to you?'

McNab indicated she hadn't. 'I checked with her supervisor at the shop, Roddie Symes. He maintains she hasn't made contact.' McNab paused there. Izzy he'd believed when she'd said the same, but he hadn't liked Symes's attitude and thought he was probably lying. 'Having said that, sir,' McNab continued, 'he may be covering for Ellie. She's asked him to do that before now.'

'Will Symes be at the rally in Aviemore?'

'West Coast Harley always have a stall at it.'

'And Ellie might go there?'

McNab nodded. 'I assume so.'

'What about the guy who supplied them with the keys for the tunnel?' DI Wilson asked.

'DS Clark checked him out. He's not a threat, she says, and his story matches Ellie's.' McNab cautiously returned to his subject. 'About Ellie, sir?'

DI Wilson turned again to his view of Glasgow. Beyond

him, McNab could make out the familiar morning skyline. McNab knew the boss was aware he was angling to go north, alone, to try and locate Ellie.

Even though I fucking hate the countryside.

McNab took a deep breath, knowing the response was about to come.

'Tell the Aviemore police you're on your way and give them a description of Ellie. Don't inform West Coast Harley. If Ellie knows more than she's said already, she may be in danger.' He didn't add 'like Claire Masters', but McNab knew that's who he meant. 'I want her back here and under our watchful eye.'

McNab let go his breath.

'Thank you, sir.' He hesitated, knowing he could screw the whole thing up with his next enquiry. 'There's one other thing, sir?'

McNab handed him the papers that had been delivered from Mary along with the bike. After casting his eye over them, the boss shot him a perplexed look, though not, McNab noted, without humour.

'We're talking about the wife of Davey Grant here?' He raised an eyebrow.

McNab nodded. 'The bike's hers to give, sir.'

'Are you playing this woman, Sergeant?'

'No, sir,' McNab said truthfully.

'Then I have nothing to say on the matter.'

'If I go by bike—' McNab began.

'You'll blend in,' the boss finished for him. 'Think you can ride that distance? It's been a long time since you were on the bikes.'

'I'll find that out, sir,' McNab said. 'And, sir, if she's moved on, it'll be easier to follow her.'

Emerging minutes later, McNab had a smile on his face. He'd taken a chance mentioning the bike along with the trip north, but after the boss had indicated DCI Sutherland's displeasure at his performance in the strategy meeting, and the DCI's order that the detective sergeant take a much lower profile in the current case, McNab had decided it was worth a try.

And it seemed the boss had been on his side. Keeping him on the case, but giving him a role well below the DCI's radar, and having a stab at locating Ellie and bringing her in at the same time.

For once it seemed things were going his way.

McIvor had deserted his post at the desk and was hanging about the entrance, savouring the said bike through the glass doors, envy written all over his face. He wasn't the only one, McNab noted as he went outside, fully kitted up via Mary, and glanced up at the windows.

McIvor had followed him, keen to get nearer the object of interest and envy.

'You do know what you have there?' he said.

'No. You tell me,' McNab said, although he'd already gained his knowledge on the bike via Mr Google.

'A top of the range CVO Street Glide.' McIvor's eyes popped as he said this. 'Limited edition. See that badge? That means it's one of only two hundred of these beauties. You know how much these cost?' McIvor was waiting for an answer.

'It was a gift,' McNab said, as though he didn't wish to discuss money.

'Jeez, some friends you've got.'

The word would get out soon enough where it had come from and he would be punished for it by his colleagues. But

McNab didn't care. The boss had okayed it. *Anyone else could go fuck themselves.*

Even as he climbed aboard, he knew there would be a price to pay, and most likely the demand would come from Mary. But for the moment he would pretend it was a gift, freely given and accepted, with no strings attached.

As he roared away for the benefit of his colleagues in the upper windows, McNab remembered he hadn't checked on Rhona this morning. He knew she wouldn't tell him what she'd decided, but he could at least have gauged from her voice if she was okay about it.

Rhona's not your responsibility, McNab reminded himself. *And she would be the first to tell you that.*

Besides, he had his own woman to find.

65

When he tried McNab's mobile after the morning lecture, it went to voicemail again. Frustrated, Magnus considered leaving a message explaining why he needed to see the detective sergeant, but in the end he just said, 'Call me.'

He could of course try via the police station. If McNab was in a meeting, they would at least give him a message when he came out.

Magnus dispensed with that idea. McNab was wedded to his mobile. If he wasn't responding it was because he couldn't.

After McNab had departed the previous evening, Magnus had headed home with the dissertation list, his aim being to study it in more detail and compare the titles with the background details of the participants on the taught course.

Which had proved to be sufficiently interesting to make him want to run it past McNab.

They could, Magnus acknowledged, be spending too much time and energy on that particular line of enquiry, but the investigating team, he knew, were covering a much wider remit. Although, according to DC Fleming, they'd come up with nothing as yet to give them a lead on the perpetrator.

Magnus checked his watch, establishing he had just twenty minutes before he was due at a faculty meeting about next session's intake. His hope of making contact with

DS McNab fading, he helped himself to the newly brewed coffee and contemplated the previous evening's meeting with DC Fleming.

From the onset it had become clear, to his psychologist persona anyway, that DC Fleming had no interest in him personally. The suggestion that they have a drink together had been for the relay of information only.

Magnus suspected that he'd proved a disappointment on that front, providing less than she'd hoped for. As for DC Fleming, she'd given her information freely, but it was, Magnus suspected, already available to him through the usual channels.

One thing she'd wanted to know more about was the soil and vegetation analysis of both loci, which had struck Magnus as interesting. The detail of such scientific data wasn't normally discussed at the strategy meetings. When he'd told her so, she'd seemed disappointed, mentioning that the topic had featured in a lecture in the course given by a Dr Mackie, a colleague of Dr MacLeod's.

Once Magnus had pleaded ignorance on this, she'd seemed to lose interest and had swiftly finished her drink and indicated she had to leave.

They had parted on friendly terms, Magnus did acknowledge that, with even a suggestion that they could try this again, *maybe after we've caught the bastard*.

Magnus didn't hold out much hope of a developing relationship, having decided he was a necessity in DC Fleming's world only as far as passing her diploma and helping in her attempt to move up the ladder.

Still, Magnus smiled in memory, he did admire her tenacity and grasp of the psychology of interview techniques. DC Fleming, he decided, was definite promotional material.

His interest piqued by her focus on the forensic soil aspects, Magnus took a quick look down the list again, recalling at least one that had referenced soil science. It had been submitted by a Ray Howden, who was a volunteer with Dr Conor Williams at the sleep clinic. Reading that reminded Magnus that he had, at Rhona's request, been asked to contact Dr Williams about his response to Andrew Jackson's death and had failed to do so.

Although, Magnus reasoned, Dr Williams could hardly blame himself now that Jackson's death was no longer considered a suicide. Still, it might be useful to talk it over with him.

With a quick glance at his watch, Magnus took a last look at the titles he'd singled out, together with his noted reasons alongside.

Having only this morning received notification that Jackson had died from taxine poisoning and that Claire's death hadn't been suicidal, he'd listed the small group of three who'd focused their attention in the area of drugs and poisons. According to the data file, one of them, Nick Gallagher, had only recently taken up a post as APT with the forensic pathologist Dr Sissons.

As Magnus had reminded McNab the previous evening, organized killers were known to engage in some way with the investigation if possible. That might mean they simply read and watched everything they could about it or they went as far as involving themselves directly with the police by offering insight or information.

In the case of missing persons, abductors had been known to join the search teams. Ted Bundy, the notorious American serial rapist and killer, had even served as a volunteer on a help line, offering advice to young women on how to stay safe from the predator stalking the college campuses – himself.

That's what he'd wanted to discuss with McNab. Everyone on that list had been engaged with the police throughout the course, and some, like the APT, worked closely enough to perhaps gain access to Rhona's DNA, but who among them had taken things just that bit further?

Like DC Fleming.

66

He was no lover of open country but McNab had to admit that it had its advantages, especially on the back of a bike. The A9 wasn't yet all dual carriageway, but even on the single stretches it was easy enough to by-pass the holiday traffic and lorries without exceeding the speed limit.

By the time he'd reached Drumochter Pass, he was at ease with the aptly named Street Glide and could understand why the other HD riders sharing the road with him liked having their annual rally in the Highlands. Miles of open road to explore as soon as you left the only major highway, with little traffic to worry about, offered a biker's dream.

McNab had made contact with the Aviemore police before his departure, only to have PC Ruaridh Mitchell greet him like a long-lost friend. The explanation for that seemed to be Rhona and her trip north during the recent joint investigation with Norway.

'I was with the CMR team that took Dr MacLeod up Cairngorm,' Mitchell had told him. 'And I worked with Police Inspector Olsen and Rhona at the airstrip. She mentioned you, Detective Sergeant.'

McNab had accepted Mitchell's friendly overtures, while wondering exactly what Rhona had said about him.

When McNab had gone on to explain the reason for his visit and to stress that the Aviemore constabulary were not to alert the young woman in the photo he'd sent, should they spot her, but await his arrival, PC Mitchell had been quick to reassure McNab they understood.

'We're expecting up to four thousand riders over the weekend and the truth is they all dress alike. Finding one rider, without word circulating, won't be easy.'

McNab was well aware of all that, but he also knew if Ellie got a whiff of his presence she would likely bolt. Her mobile was still being monitored, but Ollie suspected it had been turned off again, because Aviemore, unlike the West Highlands, did have coverage. He'd also pointed out that she might have moved to pay-as-you-go to avoid detection, especially knowing that McNab could have her traced.

It was a possibility, of course, but McNab was pretty sure Izzy would have let him know if Ellie had been in contact.

'Is she a member of the Dunedin Chapter who organize the rally?' Mitchell had asked at this point.

McNab realized that he had no idea.

Sensing this by McNab's silence, Mitchell had added, 'She would have the patch on her jacket?'

He described it as circular with a saltire background, a set of bagpipes on the right, lion rampant on the left, which didn't help McNab one iota. He realized that any remembered image he had of Ellie dressed in her leathers didn't focus on jacket designs.

'Okay, we could find out another way. When you arrive I suggest I introduce you to two locals who are in the chapter. They'll give you all the help and information you need and they can be trusted to keep quiet.'

The fewer people who knew about this the better. However, McNab knew he couldn't find Ellie on his own, so he agreed.

'Are you coming up by car or train?'

'By motorbike.'

'I didn't realize you were a biker,' Mitchell had said, sounding impressed.

McNab had ended that aspect of the conversation by admitting to having only recently reacquired a Harley after many years' abstinence.

'Well, it'll help,' Mitchell had said.

The long patch of new dual carriageway now allowed him to speed up and McNab swiftly passed the trundling lorries and even the faster-moving cars. The weather had stayed dry, for which he was grateful, although dark clouds were amassing over what he assumed was Cairngorm. God knows what it must have been like up there at Hogmanay in a blizzard, he thought.

Exiting Drumochter Pass, or Bealach Druim Uachdair as the sign named it, the blush of purple heather on the neighbouring hillsides became even more luscious. Checking out his route via Wikipedia before he'd set out, McNab now knew that Drumochter was the highest road and railway pass in the UK, and he'd also discovered that heather only came into bloom in August.

God help all those tourists who'd arrived in the Highlands of Scotland expecting 'the purple of the heather' at any other time of the year.

An RAF Tornado jet, set on using the pass for low-level practice, suddenly appeared to thunder above him, so close it seemed his head buzzed inside his helmet.

McNab saluted them with a press on his own accelerator and a whoop of encouragement. He was, he realized, actively enjoying this. Riding out here was way better than in Glasgow. Taking the turn-off for Aviemore, he met a mini roundabout, on the north side of which sat an Italian eatery called La Taverna. McNab made a mental note of that, his stomach already growling its hunger.

But first he needed to get the lie of the land and locate the police station.

Having shared the road with numerous bikers, it was now obvious where they had all been headed. The main street was literally humming with engine sound, the pavements thronged with bikers on foot, obvious by the outfits.

PC Mitchell had pointed out that his biggest problem would be in finding anywhere to sleep. McNab could see now what he meant, although he'd made small of it at the time.

'You could bed down at the station, unless you've brought a tent with you?' Mitchell had offered.

McNab had almost choked at the question. Why the hell would he possess a tent, a man who never left Glasgow unless forced to?

He could tell now why Mitchell had made that point as he took a left turn at the small roundabout to check out the camping area from outside the security cordon. It appeared pretty full already. McNab noted some of the number plates which confirmed what Mitchell had told him about the European spread of the visitors.

Having completed a full circuit of the village, McNab made for the police station and managed to find a space in the nearby car park, just big enough for the bike.

The long single-level concrete-block building that fronted the main street sported an 'opening hours' notice on the front door. From PC Mitchell he'd already learned that the opening times had been reduced to daytime only, with usually just a receptionist on hand. The station did possess a cell, although custodies weren't kept there any more but sent to Inverness instead.

'We can supply you with bedding,' he'd added as if McNab sleeping there had become a foregone conclusion.

And he was right, McNab thought, looking back at the sea of folk that had flooded the small Highland village.

Entering, McNab approached the glass-panelled reception desk. From there he could hear a muted interchange but couldn't see the participants. When the male and female voices erupted in laughter, McNab had the sudden paranoid feeling that it might be about his imminent arrival.

Clearing his throat loudly resulted in the immediate appearance of the male in question, whose resultant expression indicated that he knew exactly who McNab was.

'Detective Sergeant McNab.' He opened the intervening door and held out his hand. 'PC Mitchell. You made good time.'

McNab nodded, having no wish to indulge in small talk.

PC Mitchell called the woman over and introduced her as Irene Watson, the receptionist. 'Irene'll supply you with a set of keys and you can come and go as you please. We had hoped to give you a bed in the flat we keep for new recruits, but it's fully occupied, I'm afraid. If you want to follow me, I'll show you the cell.'

An effort had been made, McNab gave them that. He had a bed, the bedding he suspected having been brought in from elsewhere by the patterned quilt and pillowcase.

'Not much, but there's a toilet and shower as well. I've spent an odd night here myself when a blizzard's hit and I can't get home. Unlikely in August, although Dr MacLeod will vouch for how bad it can get at times.' Mitchell, noting McNab's expression, hurried on. 'The couple I was talking about will be in the Winking Owl for the next hour. It's over the road and to the right.'

'I saw it when I rode through the village,' McNab said.

PC Mitchell nodded. 'Jim and Fran Anderson. They'll be in the upstairs bar. I'll text them and say you're on your way. Not much point trying to describe what they're wearing, since . . .' He tailed off with a smile. 'You have my number. Just let me know if you need anything.'

'I take it you've had no luck with the photo I sent up?' McNab said.

'I thought it better not to circulate it until you decided how you wanted to play this. If I showed any of the barmen, word would be out big time.' He said that as though McNab had set them an impossible task.

McNab indicated he knew it was a catch-22 situation. 'Thanks for your help, so far,' he said and meant it.

'You're welcome. And good luck. I hope you find her.'

67

McNab crossed the road and, threading his way through the milling crowds, entered the car-park area of the Winking Owl, where he spotted that one of the tented shops was wearing the West Coast Harley sign.

He had a moment's elation at the prospect of walking in and finding Ellie, then realized there was no way he could go in there without raising the alarm, especially if Roddie was about.

Walking swiftly past, and forcing himself not to scan what area was visible through the wide opening, he made his way towards the rear of the car park. The crowds gathered reminded McNab of the speedway audience with mixed ages, plenty of women and loads of kids. It looked like the folk of Aviemore were mixing happily with their annual visitors.

The two open-air bars set up next to the main building were doing a roaring trade, as was the stall serving Orkney beef burgers and chips. McNab promised his complaining stomach he would be back, after he'd spoken with the Andersons.

Climbing the wooden staircase that led to the main bar, McNab entered the open double doors and was surprised to discover it wasn't busy inside, the punters obviously preferring to gather below, the weather being fine.

Glancing around, he spotted at least two tables that might be sporting the couple he sought, but before he could decide which to approach, a hand touched his arm from behind. McNab turned to find a woman who immediately introduced herself as Fran and ushered him towards a table tucked partially out of sight.

The man already sitting there rose and offered his hand in welcome. McNab thanked both for meeting him and they all took a seat. Even though used to awkward moments, McNab wasn't quite sure how to play this, but it seemed PC Mitchell had got there before him and it was Jim that led the way.

'Ruaridh said this girl you're looking for isn't in trouble . . .' The man paused, obviously not sure how to address a visiting detective sergeant from Glasgow.

'Michael will do,' McNab offered. 'And that's correct,' he said. 'Although,' he found himself saying, 'she just might be in danger.'

Jim's face hardened at that. 'Then we want to help.'

McNab wasn't even sure if what he'd said was true, but every time he recalled Ellie's voice the last time he'd spoken to her, he saw Claire Masters sitting slumped against that tree trunk.

He produced the photograph. 'This is Ellie.'

Fran studied it with interest. 'I don't recognize her. Is she a member of the Dunedin Chapter?'

McNab shook his head, indicating he didn't know the answer to that.

'Well, we can find out,' Fran said. 'I can also check if she's registered for the rally. If she is, she'll have been given a tag for herself and a matching one for her bike, for security purposes.' She went on, 'The tags get her free camping and entry to the three inside venues. We could ask security to look out for her tag?'

That was a definite possibility, but only if Ellie had registered. 'It's worth a try,' McNab said. 'She works part-time at the Glasgow Harley shop,' he added with a nod in the direction of the tent outside.

'So she might turn up at this one?' Jim said.

McNab explained the situation with Roddie Symes.

Fran nodded. 'Okay, so you can't hang about there.' She thought for a moment. 'I can ask some of the Harley Ladies? We could arrange shifts. That way you're free to look elsewhere.'

When McNab flinched a little at the thought of involving others, Jim came back in. 'We're all part of the Harley family,' he said. 'We look after our own. No one needs to know why we're doing it.'

McNab's eye was caught by the TV screen playing silently on the opposite wall. It was a report on Claire's death and its link with the Jackson murder. He imagined Ellie watching this and discovering, maybe for the first time, that the guy in the tunnel had been murdered and the killer had struck again.

McNab turned to find Jim's eyes on him, his face filling with anger.

'Is that what the lassie's running from?'

68

Leaving the bar, McNab went to check on the bike, realizing that Fran had been right. He should register, if only to have the Street Glide tagged for security purposes. Unused to owning anything that someone might like to steal, he was suddenly aware how worrisome that could be.

Blocked by a van that had arrived since he'd parked, McNab endured a moment's panic when he couldn't see the Street Glide, and was already imagining some bastard heading south with his new prize possession.

When its tail-end became visible, his sigh of relief was audible to more than just him. The guy sitting in the van with the window open gave him the thumbs-up when he realized McNab was the owner of the magnificent bike he'd just been admiring.

'A beauty,' he began, but was cut short in the inevitable string of questions by McNab's mobile ringing out.

Ollie, obviously hearing the background noise from the street, asked if he could talk, while McNab headed for the police station and stepped inside the outer door, shutting it behind him.

'Fire away,' he said once silence fell.

'I'm picking up Ellie's mobile again. She's definitely in the vicinity and she's had a couple of calls within the last hour.'

'Do you know who from?'

'One from a mobile registered to Roddie Symes, her supervisor at the shop. The other I haven't traced yet.' Ollie's voice rose a little in excitement. 'There's something else. I've been doing a background check on course participants like you asked. Turns out there's an R. Symes on the MOOCs course.'

Now that was a surprise. 'Is it the same guy?' McNab said.

'Unconfirmed as yet. Anybody can sign up for the free course and since it doesn't earn you university credits your details aren't checked.'

'So you can call yourself anything you like?'

'Basically, yes. But that doesn't mean I can't find out if it's true.'

McNab thought back to the altercation in the shop. Symes was a pain in the arse and thought he owned Ellie, and there was every chance he'd known about the tunnel races. Maybe even been down there watching. But might he be more involved than that?

'Anything else?' McNab demanded.

'Symes is in the Spey Valley now. Looking at my screen, I'd say he's bouncing off the same mast as you.'

As McNab rang off, an incoming text from Chrissy appeared at the top of his screen.

Can't locate Rhona. Call me, now.

69

As she struggled back to consciousness, it was the smell that hit her first.

A cloying scent such as she'd experienced in the London Street tunnel, dampness and earth, decomposition and hydrocarbons. Blinded by the dark, she might have imagined herself dead, had it not been for the beat of her heart in her ear and the sound of trickling water.

Her hands were tied, the tags cutting deeply into her wrists. Rhona shifted her body weight a little to one side in an attempt to reposition her arms behind her back and ease the cramp that had seized them.

She'd avoided doing this until now, afraid that the nausea she had under rigid control might gain strength by any movement.

She mustn't be sick. Not with the gag.

Rhona had seen enough overdoses to know that choking on vomit was the cause of death more often than the drugs the victim had ingested. Waiting for the moment to pass, she concentrated on analysing the effects of the drug she'd obviously been given before she'd lost consciousness and been brought here.

Her last semi-clear memory had been of the sound of breaking glass. But where had she been when that had happened? An image suddenly presented itself. A kitchen, *her* kitchen, with the window seat and the cat . . .

Tom . . . Tom had been there, mewing at her. Licking her mouth because she'd eaten something he savoured. Rhona shifted a little, feeling again the sharpness of broken glass beneath her, catching the metallic scent of blood. Her blood.

Was she injured? Was the blood still flowing, seeping into the soil she lay on, unhindered, edging her closer to death?

Panic at this swept in, pushing all reason away . . . but not completely.

Analyse, she told herself. *Think. You're a scientist.*

She wasn't bleeding to death. She was no weaker than when she had first come to. If she was bleeding at all, the flow wasn't serious. Rhona forced her mind back to that first memory and relived it, trying to urge it on to the next stage.

I was lying on the floor amid the broken glass and then what?

It came like a rush from the darkness, sweeping all rational thought before it. The thing in the corner of the room. Conor's shadow man. The demon from the painting.

Rhona choked on the memory, stomach acid rising in her throat as she relived the terror of that moment.

I was hallucinating from the drugged wine, her rational voice told her as it strove to take back control. Common with date-rape drugs.

That thought brought another. *Had she been raped while unconscious?*

Rhona drew her focus from trying to remember the sequence of events to attempting to interpret her injuries.

Working her way downwards, she established each pain point that signified bruising or cuts. Her feet were fastened together, her ankles, like her wrists, bitterly complaining at the cutting tightness of their bonds, but, as far as she could tell, her clothes were intact and she was experiencing neither vaginal nor anal discomfort.

Besides, if the intention had been only to drug and sexually assault her, then why go to the bother of bringing her here?

Because once wasn't enough?

Which prompted another thought as her head began to clear. When and how had the white wine been doctored? The first time she'd had a glass from it, she'd been fine.

She'd assumed Sean had bought it for her, after the incident with the bottle of red, but she recalled the interrupted phone call – *I didn't get to ask him.* Whatever way the bottle had got into the fridge, it had definitely been doctored between then and last night, which meant someone had entered her flat.

Maybe even been there waiting for her when she'd returned from the lab.

Just as she couldn't remember how she'd got here, neither could she remember who had brought her. No spoken words, no distinctive scent of her captor had imprinted on her memory. None of her senses had registered anything after the shadow man.

It was that image, Rhona realized, that had caused her descent into darkness.

Manoeuvring herself into a sitting position, she tried to work out where she might be. As her eyes became accustomed, might she be able to at least make out the walls of her prison?

Staring pointedly ahead, she imagined she did see a light. A pinpoint only, but growing brighter. Surely it was coming her way?

Rhona attempted a shout, only to have the gag swallow the sound. She tried again, and this time some of it did escape. At a third attempt, the remnants of her cry escaped to echo against – what? Rock, concrete?

The light had become a round beam, still small but piercingly so, with the power of her forensic torch. Someone was coming.

Rhona went from elation to dismay in seconds. There was no reason to assume it would be anyone other than her captor. The need to do something made her scramble backwards, but it only took moments for that passage to end. Throwing her head back for traction, it hit an obstacle with a crunch that brought tears to her eyes.

In the meantime the torch beam had grown bigger and rounder, approaching more swiftly than before. Footsteps began to echo from the walls. Her own breath rasping, and with no chance of retreat, Rhona took a chance and rolled her body, first right to swiftly meet another obstacle, then left.

Expecting a third wall, she was suddenly met with air. The floor fell here, she realized, into what, she had no idea. Had she been free to do so she would have dropped a stone and listened for its fall.

But if this was a constructed tunnel, why would there be a sheer drop?

The footsteps were nearly on her now. She had to make up her mind. Face her attacker or disappear.

Rhona rolled once, twice, feeling the crumbling edge give way under the pressure of her body. Then she was slithering downwards in a rush of soil and stones and running water, as the torch beam played the darkness.

70

'She hasn't responded to any of my emails or answered my calls.'

McNab could hear the growing alarm in Chrissy's voice and wanted to reassure her. He thought he knew where Rhona might be, but having been sworn to secrecy, he could hardly tell Chrissy where that was.

'I was at Rhona's yesterday,' he said instead, 'and she was fine, although well pissed off about being taken off the case. I went round to talk to her about the strategy meeting. Sean was there,' he added as though that made his visit more legitimate.

Silence followed, then a reluctant, 'Okay, but if she contacts you, you'll let me know?'

McNab promised that he would.

'Where the hell are you anyway?'

'Aviemore, looking for Ellie.'

That news had obviously cheered Chrissy up.

Ringing off, McNab immediately pulled up Rhona's number. He understood why Rhona might not be responding to Chrissy's calls, *until the deed was done*, but he might not get the same response.

Half a dozen rings later it switched to voicemail and McNab left a message urging Rhona to contact either Chrissy or himself as soon as possible.

'And I haven't told her anything,' he added.

Emerging from the station, he contemplated his next move and decided it would be to eat. Abandoning the original idea of heading for the Italian restaurant on the outskirts, he decided to go for the beef burger instead. Although he would take it far enough away from the West Coast tent before settling down to eat. If, as Ollie had said, Symes was somewhere in the vicinity, it would likely be there. He would have to trust the Harley Ladies to let him know if or when Ellie turned up.

Carrying his lunch back to the bike, he took a seat on a large rock that looked as though it had just rolled off Cairngorm, and set about both filling his empty belly and working out his next move.

Ollie's news regarding Symes possibly being involved in the course had intrigued him. Added to that, there had been a voicemail from Magnus asking him in no uncertain terms to give him a call.

McNab took a slug of the large coffee he'd bought to accompany his food, knowing that although there was a lot of liquid, it was less caffeine than he needed. He'd have to locate somewhere he could get a proper shot.

From memory he'd passed a real coffee shop opposite the supermarket on his ride through the village. McNab decided to go there, top up his current drug of choice then give Magnus a call.

Fifteen minutes later, the caffeine headache had been replaced by thoughts which were equally taxing. Magnus had been openly agitated, something McNab hadn't encountered since the first job the profiler had been brought on board for.

The one he screwed up on.

Among the psychology speak, McNab had caught a possible truth. At least one that rang with him.

He scrolled through the notes and rough sketch of the area around Glasgow University which Magnus had sent in the aftermath of their one-sided conversation.

Note the geographical cluster

Claire and Jackson both lived in West End close to park and university.

Jackson attending sleep clinic at university.

Marshall's funeral parlour on upper Sauchiehall Street in the vicinity.

[HD Bike shop near Mitchell library]

The likelihood is that the perpetrator lives/works in the same vicinity.

Perpetrator

Both deaths were non-sexual with no bodily interference, bloodless, no evidence of violence.

Intelligence and forensic knowledge on display.

He managed to draw both victims to the chosen locations, so well planned and thought through.

Symbolism of bread and wine was used as a marker, but for what purpose?

Neither body was actively hidden.

McNab pulled up short there. 'What about the bloody tunnel?' he mouthed to the screen.

I believe it was the perpetrator who alerted the police to the body in the tunnel. The first kill was out of his/her geographical area because Jackson was drawn there by the Cosworth. If Ellie was right and there was a pulse, the perpetrator was possibly still at the locus. The arrival of the girl bikers was (probably) a surprise, although if he/she had a plan, which they undoubtedly did, then they would have already noted the bike tracks round the wreck. Harleys have very distinctive tyre treads specially made by Dunlop for each model. Was he/she aware of this? Is there a Harley connection?

McNab halted and waved at the waiter for a refill, his heart upping a beat.

There is therefore a possibility that he/she saw Ellie and could recognize her again. Ellie will know by now that Jackson's death was murder. And that Claire Masters (who probably saw the perp) is his/her second victim. It's imperative you locate Ellie Macmillan for her own safety.

Rhona

How did the perpetrator gain access to Rhona's DNA and the type of PPE suit she favours?

He/She works close to Rhona or attends the course or is a personal friend or acquaintance or knows someone who is?

He/She has gained access to Rhona's flat by invitation or otherwise.

71

The fall had achieved one thing in her favour. It had loosened the gag enough for her to spit it out.

It had also knocked the wind from her and it had taken until now for Rhona to fill her lungs enough to even attempt to call out.

And shout she did, even in the knowledge that she was wasting her time. Whoever had shone the torch in her direction was long gone.

It hadn't been her captor. Rhona was pretty certain of that. Had it been, surely they would have known about the drop and, finding her missing, used the torch to check it out?

It seemed someone else had been wandering around down here. Probably one of the Urbex explorers Chrissy had talked about. Someone who could have freed her from her bonds and helped her out of here.

So, in her panic, she'd simply escaped one prison for another smaller and wetter one, her fall having been cushioned by soft soil through which a stream of water ran. A stream she was now sitting in.

Leaning back, Rhona rested her head against earth this time rather than rock. The idea that she was in an old railway tunnel was dissipating. Tasting the damp soil on her lips, Rhona imagined she could detect metal or maybe charcoal. Glasgow was pockmarked by old mine workings. This could be one of them.

If Jen had the soil, no doubt she could pinpoint exactly where they were by the constituents of the mud in Rhona's mouth.

If only.

Rhona rolled over and stuck her face into the trickling water. Letting it flow in and around her mouth, before spitting it out and taking a long cold welcome drink.

The earlier nausea had eased and she could almost think straight and form words again. What she couldn't do was remember what had happened. Well, not in its entirety, or in a way that made sense.

The demon.

She did remember the demon in the corner of the room. She'd thought she was hallucinating and the creature was a creation of her fear under the influence of the drug. The face, the red eyes, just like in the painting, but . . .

She had seen it rise, extend itself and move towards her. Then it had taken human form, with a demon face.

A mask?

Rhona recalled the figure above her as she'd lain on the glass-strewn kitchen floor. Definitely human, but male or female she couldn't say, although it had been tall, that much she did remember.

After that, nothing.

Yet she had been removed from her home and brought here, and whoever had done that definitely hadn't been a figment of her drug-fuelled imagination.

Refreshed by the water, with logical thought returning, Rhona considered her next move, which should be to try and remove her bindings. If an Urbex explorer could get in here, then she could definitely find her way out.

Rhona couldn't imagine her captor would choose to leave her here indefinitely. Surely they would return? To do what? The answer to that lay, of course, in the reason she'd been drugged and brought here in the first place.

And that had to have something to do with the Jackson case.

Feeling about in the cold water, she searched for a stone sharp enough to use on the zip tags, but felt only round ones, rubbed smooth by the action of the stream.

As her eyes grew more accustomed to the dark, Rhona began to sense the shape of her surroundings. Her prison was small, barely two yards square, she estimated. The water appeared just behind her. Bubbling from below, running under her body and past her feet, to where, she didn't know.

As Rhona moved her exploration a little further she encountered something of interest. Making a grab for it, she yelped in pain as the sharp object cut into her hand.

It was glass of some description and not blunted by the water's action.

A sudden memory swept in. She hadn't meekly submitted to the demon figure. Instead she'd grabbed at the shards of the broken bottle littered around her, although the action had done her little good. Rhona winced, remembering the angry grunt as the shard had met material, then the skin of her attacker.

She'd been thrust flat on the floor then, a foot in her back, her hands beneath her.

But not before I'd put the glass in my pocket.

72

McNab braked as the Glide approached the barrier. Supplied with a registration tag by Fran, he was about to meet his first security check. More used to producing his ID to get in pretty well anywhere, McNab had to restrain himself, while he and the bike were given the once-over.

'You heading for the camp ground?'

McNab nodded. 'Looking for a friend who's already there.'

The guy checked McNab's tag number against the bike's and, satisfied, said, 'The place is almost full. You could wander around in there for some time and never find them. I'd call them first for directions.'

How McNab would love to do that. Call Ellie and ask her where she was. Tell her he was coming and know she would be pleased.

'Thanks for the tip,' he said, before roaring through.

Having viewed the camp from a distance, he now saw up close what the guard was talking about. The large area was chock-a-block with motorhomes and tents, interspersed by bikes, loads of bikes. He could wander about in here forever.

Alternatively he could cook up a story and start asking questions. Ellie was distinctive enough with her tattoos without a photograph. Besides, it looked like most folk were recognized by their bike.

Having cruised around for a bit, McNab parked up on a grass verge and, skirting a line of young trees, walked into the camp. He'd come up with a story, and chose the first person he met to try it out on.

The tale of love and a surprise visit went down pretty well with the large bearded biker, who immediately asked what bike his girlfriend had. When McNab told him a Fat Bob, he nodded. 'Aye, the lassies like that one. You'll find a few of them around. What does she look like, this girlfriend of yours?'

McNab's glowing description brought a smile to his face.

'If she's travelling alone, she'd probably set up camp next to a group for company, and safety. We look after our own in the Harley family.'

McNab wasn't sure if the last remark was to reassure him or warn him, but he said thank you anyway then began his sweep across the field, one layer at a time, like they did when out searching for a missing person.

An hour later, he'd located six Fat Bobs and a dozen solo tents, none of which belonged to Ellie. It would have helped had he had any idea what colour and model her tent was, but since he'd scorned even thinking about camping, he didn't.

McNab checked his mobile for the umpteenth time, and this time there was a message from Fran.

A possible sighting of your girl last night in the Cairngorm Hotel bar talking to the barman. Will we check it out or will you?

McNab texted back 'Me' and, leaving the bike where it was, headed for the main street again. Dressed as he was in biker gear, with the addition of a newly purchased Harley-Davidson skull cap, there was little resemblance to his DS McNab persona. He could, McNab figured, enter and not be taken for a policeman, or be instantly recognized by Ellie or Symes for that matter. He doubted even Rhona would recognize him, he thought with a half-smile.

Cairngorm Hotel was a major drinking and music hub for the rally with a mobile stage set up in the parking lot. McNab bypassed the outdoor kiosks and headed inside. Unlike the bar at the Winking Owl earlier in the day, this place was throbbing with life.

McNab spotted the barman Fran had described behind a busy counter. McNab duly waited his turn, ordered a pint, then gave him the girlfriend story and a description of Ellie, looking suitably contrite that he was late to the party.

It wasn't difficult to tell that the guy had seen her. It was, McNab thought, written all over the barman's face, yet for a moment he contemplated denying it.

'I fucked up big time, mate,' McNab said. 'I need to fix this.'

'You should call or text her,' the barman offered with a smile. 'Maybe warn her you're here.'

'But it's a surprise.'

The barman didn't like that response and glanced at the TV screen then back at McNab.

'How do I know she wants to see you?'

It was a strange answer and one that worried McNab.

'Am I the first person looking for her?' he demanded in what was definitely a detective voice.

The guy was going to clam up. McNab did what had to be done. He pulled out his ID.

The barman looked at it, the colour draining from his face. 'What's she done?'

'Tell me what happened last night,' McNab demanded.

Emerging ten minutes later, he knew where Ellie would be. He also knew she'd viewed last night's news and not taken it well.

'I think the news scared her. The murdered girl in Glasgow. I wondered if she knew her?'

When McNab asked if anyone else had asked about Ellie, the barman had nodded.

'Who?'

'A biker had her picture on his mobile. It was from a video of the West Coast Harley shop where the staff talk about their own bikes.'

'What did this guy look like?' McNab demanded.

73

Why a demon mask?

It was easy to understand why the perpetrator would use a mask, but the mask she remembered had been the same demon as depicted in the painting Conor had shown her.

Anyone might be frightened by a demon, but to be drugged and faced with one you might recognize?

There was still a blank in her memory after her attempt at stabbing her assailant, not unusual in the case of date-rape drugs. But her rational thought was returning and with it the possibility that she might work out the identity of her assailant.

McNab had been right when he'd indicated that the perpetrator could be stalking her, and not just with the desire to outwit her forensically. A cascade of images came flooding back. The unexplained gift of red wine, followed by nausea, the headaches, the general feeling of having been poisoned. Then Tom's brush with death, the seagull deposited on her kitchen floor.

And finally the white wine.

She'd sought to blame her sickness on the early stages of pregnancy, but that hadn't been the reason, or not the whole reason. She knew that now.

Someone had tried to drug her, even poison her, and that someone must have had access to her flat and recently.

The scene in the park when she'd first met Conor now replayed in her head, but this time Rhona read it differently. This time she imagined it not as a random accident but as deliberate. Their first and subsequent meetings. The way Conor had first made contact, professing to know about her via his volunteer. His invitation to the sleep clinic where he'd shown her the painting. Then their drink together.

And he'd phoned her just when she needed help most in getting Tom to the emergency vet.

Her mind went back to the convenient flat tyre. Had Conor been responsible for that too?

God, in her present vulnerability, she'd almost accepted his invitation to dinner last night. When she'd turned him down, he'd seemed unperturbed, simply saying he would ask again when she wasn't so busy.

Rhona halted there, aware that fear and paranoia were interfering with logical thought. Conor wasn't the only one who could have accessed her DNA or entered the flat. The image of the seagull swinging in at her window confirmed this.

Sean had warned her about leaving the kitchen window open for Tom. He'd even climbed onto the roof to illustrate how easy it was for someone to gain access to her flat. If Sean could do it . . .

And a stalker would know her movements. Know all about her life. Every intimate detail of it.

The nausea rose again although there was nothing left in her stomach to regurgitate. Rhona focused on its retreat. The face of her watch was the only light in the darkness and it told her just how long she had been here in what felt like her grave.

Surely someone would have noticed she was missing by now?

Surely McNab, at least, would be looking for her?

74

The barman's description of the guy who'd already come looking for Ellie wasn't difficult to put a name to.

So Symes was searching for Ellie too.

What did that mean? That she'd told him she was coming here, then hadn't turned up at the shop?

Having ordered the barman to call him if Ellie appeared again or anyone else came in asking about her, McNab took himself outside. The crowd watching the band had grown in size, the atmosphere still good-natured despite the copious amounts of alcohol being consumed.

PC Mitchell had been right in his summation that just spotting Ellie by chance among this throng was unlikely.

Having made his decision, McNab was now on his way to the West Coast tent. If Symes was in Aviemore and looking for Ellie, then he was looking for Symes.

The entrance to the Winking Owl car park was filled with a crowd of locals queuing up to have their photograph taken on a bike that looked like the one McNab now owned. Weaving his way past the excited youngsters and those not so young, he made his way to the corner where West Coast Harley had set up shop, outside of which stood three bikes. One he recognized as a Fat Bob – maybe Ellie's?

His heart lifting at such a possibility, McNab entered the

tent, his cap down to shield his face. He spotted Symes immediately, talking to a potential customer by a rail of jackets. There were also two women in the tent, one of whom, noting McNab's appearance, made to approach.

McNab barely had time to decide how to react to any enquiry she might make, when Symes bade farewell to his customer and headed for the till. McNab followed.

'Can I help you, sir?' Symes said, clocking his presence.

McNab removed his cap and put his face in full view. 'Where's Ellie?'

A number of emotions crossed Symes's face, including puzzlement, annoyance and a flicker of fear.

'I don't know, Sergeant,' he responded in an irritated tone. 'She was supposed to be working here this weekend, helping in the shop. After she went off sick, she called me to say she would definitely turn up.' He glanced around the shop. 'As you can see, she hasn't.'

'And the Fat Bob outside?'

'That's just it.' Now the puzzled look found prominence. 'It's Ellie's bike, but we haven't seen any sign of her.'

'We need to talk,' McNab said. 'I want you across the road at the police station, now.'

'I can't just desert the shop,' Symes began, then noting McNab's expression, called one of the women over and told them he had to go out.

McNab shut the door of the interview room. The cell might not have been occupied recently, but this place had a more used look about it. PC Mitchell wasn't on the premises, but McNab had sent him an urgent message and was expecting him to arrive any minute.

In the meantime, he was drinking the strong coffee he'd

requested and observing Symes once again. There was something about this guy he simply didn't like. True, his opinion might have been formed by their meeting in the Glasgow shop, where Symes's attitude regarding Ellie hadn't helped. But it was more than that.

Symes didn't like him either, that was plain to see. Maybe that was because McNab was in a relationship with Ellie, and he'd rather it was him. Or maybe it was because he had something to hide.

McNab suspected the latter, although he had yet to prove it. He concentrated on his coffee and observing Symes for the moment, enjoying the discomfort this was causing.

Eventually Symes could take it no longer.

'Can we get on with it? I've a shop to run.'

'Big weekend for you then?'

Symes looked taken aback by the question. 'It's the largest HD rally in Europe. Of course it's big for us.' He sounded offended. 'That's why Ellie should be here.'

'You're not worried about her then? Why her bike's there and she isn't?'

Symes met McNab's eye. 'Maybe she's shacked up somewhere and forgot the time.'

The barb, aimed at him, hit home, because it might be true.

Just then, the door opened and PC Mitchell entered. McNab covered his anger by explaining who Symes was and why he was there.

Now the interview was official, McNab went for the question he really wanted answered.

'The London Street tunnel. You were aware Ellie was racing down there with three other girls?'

Of all the questions he'd expected to be asked, Symes

hadn't imagined that one. The element of surprise paid off. Symes wanted to say no, yet the glint in McNab's eye suggested he knew differently.

PC Mitchell who, as far as McNab was aware, would know next to nothing about the tunnel case, managed to maintain an expression that said he was in on whatever McNab had planned. McNab vowed to buy Ruaridh a pint for that at least.

'Yes,' emerged eventually from Symes's pursed lips.

'You knew they were down there that particular night?'

He shook his head. 'Not exactly.'

'What does that mean, not exactly?'

'I suspected, but I didn't know.'

McNab waited for an explanation for his suspicions.

'Ellie had her tyres changed. Said she wanted a better grip. The tunnel surface can be tricky at high speeds.'

'You've raced down there?'

'Yes. But not any more.'

'But you were down there that night? To watch them race.'

Symes's head went down while he decided what to answer.

'And you saw Ellie get off the bike at the Cosworth,' McNab prompted.

Symes looked up again. Either he was genuinely puzzled or he was making a good show of pretending to be. 'I wasn't down there. I saw nothing.'

'Then why call Ellie and claim the opposite?'

'I didn't.'

'But you're interested in the forensics of the tunnel case?'

'What?'

'Did you not enrol on an online forensics course run by Glasgow University?'

'Yes, but what has that got to do with Ellie?'

'So you did do the course?'

'Some of it, yes, but I lost interest. Never finished it.'

McNab observed Symes in exasperation. Everything he'd said up to now rang true, despite his own wish for the outcome to be different.

'We believe Ellie might be in danger.'

Symes looked totally taken aback by that. 'You mean because of being in the tunnel that night?'

McNab nodded.

Symes's face crumpled. 'Jesus. I didn't know.' He shook his head in disbelief. 'Fuck. That's why she didn't come in to work?'

'Probably. And why we have to find her.'

'Tell me what I have to do, Detective. I don't want anything bad to happen to Ellie.'

Once Symes had gone, PC Mitchell turned to McNab. 'So what now?'

At that moment, McNab had no idea, except for his belief that Ellie had to be somewhere in the throng out there, because she would never be parted from her bike.

Unless she was forced to.

'Let's bring the bike over here and take a look at it.'

75

The water woke her, swirling around her face, entering her nose and partially open mouth, sending her into a paroxysm of coughing. She'd been paralysed, reliving the earlier nightmare, the tentacles of roots above her, the earth splattering down to fill her mouth and eyes.

Rhona attempted to drag herself upright against the earth wall, coughing a mix of water and mud up, spitting it out, cursing herself for falling asleep, yet aware her body had had no choice, being weakened by hunger and whatever drugs were still in her system.

She'd been facing away from the stream when she'd dozed off, so for the water to have reached her nose and mouth, the level must have risen. It had been swirling around her nether regions for so long, Rhona had lost feeling there.

Dropping her hands into the flow, it was obvious that the stream had broken its banks, and now covered a bigger area with a film of water, suggesting it had been raining on the surface and she was experiencing the underground run-off from that.

Was that how this sink hole had been formed?

Rhona's mind raced with the possibility of such a thing happening again. This summer had been known for thunderstorms and torrential downpours. She imagined the water rising and her with it, to finally bring her within reach of the edge, allowing her escape.

Then reality set in. With her feet and hands bound, she wouldn't be able to tread water. She would likely flip face down and drown.

All the more reason to free herself.

Seated, knees drawn up tight to her chest, Rhona began shuffling her rear to allow the passage of her hands beneath her.

As she did so, a shower of earth and stones came flying down on her head. Quashing her instinct to cry out, she stopped what she was doing and waited, as a further scattering met her head and shoulders.

Were the weak walls of her prison about to collapse in on her?

Even as she contemplated such a frightening explanation, a light flashed on and roamed the space above her.

Someone was up there. *Her abductor or the Urbex explorer?*

This time, Rhona decided, she would take a chance and assume the latter.

The thick scratch of a shovel cutting though earth changed her mind. Whoever was up there was digging, but to what purpose?

Rhona found out the answer almost immediately as another flurry of earth and stones came hurtling into her cell.

Smothering a cry, she turned her face to the earthen wall.

76

'When Sean went round to the flat, Rhona wasn't there, and there's been a disturbance.' Chrissy was trying, but panic was obvious in her voice. 'A broken wine bottle and glass in the kitchen and blood on the floor.'

Her panic transferred itself quickly to McNab. 'You've called it in?'

'Yes, and I'm headed there now with a forensic team.' Chrissy's voice broke a little. 'I told you there was something wrong. Rhona would never stay out of touch like that.'

'She's pregnant,' McNab said. 'I thought it likely she was going to the clinic to have a termination this morning. She asked me not to say anything to anyone,' he added.

The silence that followed his announcement was more meaningful than any outbreak of cursing from Chrissy.

Eventually she said, 'Does Sean know?'

'No one knows but me and that was a mistake,' McNab said, aware at how hurt Chrissy would be at her exclusion.

'Do I tell Sean?'

'No,' McNab said adamantly. Rhona would be mad enough that he'd told Chrissy.

'You're coming back?' Chrissy was urging him.

A myriad of thoughts swept through McNab's brain, the

overriding one being that there were now two missing women linked to this case.

And I have to choose which one I search for.

The weather had shifted to match his mood.

Drumochter was overlaid by a dense and darkened sky. The rain came on halfway through the pass, beating on his helmet with a vengeance, his breath swiftly clouding the visor. McNab opened it a little to get rid of the condensation and used his gloved hand like a windscreen wiper.

The other disadvantage the bike had over his squad car, or a police motorbike, was the lack of a blue flashing light.

McNab, his beams full on, powered past any traffic he encountered, regardless. If he was caught on camera and intercepted, he would explain the circumstances. Maybe even command a squad car as his escort.

The further he got from Aviemore, the more Ellie was on his mind. Examining her bike had revealed nothing of consequence, apart from the fact that all her belongings had been removed from the paniers. Her tent too, McNab assumed.

He'd called Fran immediately after he'd heard from Chrissy and they'd hatched a plan. It was time, she said, for the Chapter to find Ellie for him.

'There's about three hundred in the Chapter. Fifty of them are in charge of the main locations like the campsite, hospitality and merchandise tents, and of course registration. All we need to do is tell that fifty we need to find Ellie and the rest will find out too.'

Fran's words had been a salve for his guilt.

'It's better this way,' she'd added. 'There are enough of us to do a proper search. I'll call as soon as we locate her.'

She'd sounded so certain, McNab almost believed her. Although it took nothing away from the realization that he'd made a choice and Rhona had come first.

How could it ever be different?

He suspected, of course, that the bastard was playing them. Orchestrating their – no – *his* movements. *He knows me well enough to set this up.*

If so, the perpetrator was much closer to the investigation than they dared believe. Close enough to know how he would react to such circumstances.

Had he done what was expected of him?

Rain splattered his visor, but McNab felt the drops inside too, running down his cheeks.

The bikes had been gathering for the mass ride-out as McNab had departed the village. An army of them, good-natured, excited, all sizes, colours, outfits, spectacularly masked or wearing only bright smiles for the crowds of spectators that lined the pavements.

'By the time we come back from Grantown, every one of the riders will know we're looking for Ellie. When we get back here, they'll tell everyone else.'

If she's here, we'll find her, Fran had finished by saying.

McNab whispered to himself, *Please God they do.*

77

Chrissy imagined Rhona there with her, her silent voice at her shoulder.

Take your time. Use every sense. It's all about context. Remember every question that comes to mind. Write them down. The story's there, all of it. You just have to read the words to make sense of it.

How many scenes had she visited with Rhona? How many deaths had they catalogued together? How many questions had they answered, actions they'd made clear together?

Forget about how the scene makes you feel. It's not about you. You don't matter. Only the victim does.

With Rhona's words ringing in her head, Chrissy still struggled to do what was advised.

All she could think about was that the kitchen where she'd spent so much time eating, drinking and laughing with Rhona had become the locus of a crime.

Read the scene, Chrissy. Remember, it's not about testing. It's about asking questions. The right questions.

Taking a deep breath to settle her racing thoughts, Chrissy attempted to do as instructed.

Letting her gaze sweep slowly around the room, she took it in properly this time, registering anything that jumped out at her. On the surface beside the slow cooker was a plate with a piece of gammon on it, uncovered. Partially gnawed at, it suggested Tom had been helping himself prior to Sean's return, when he'd been given to a distressed Mrs Harper to look after while the flat was searched.

The window had been left open, Chrissy assumed for Tom. Rhona would never listen about that window, even when Sean had tried to reason with her. *A cat needs a measure of freedom*, she'd said. *Like the rest of us*.

The floor next to the table sparkled under Chrissy's torch, bloodstains among the scattered shards of the wine bottle, the thickened base of which had come to rest under the table.

Footsteps marked the treated wooden floor, aided by the spilt wine. Stepping onto the metal protective treads laid by the scene of crime officer, Chrissy crossed to the table for a closer look.

She imagined Rhona cutting herself a slice of gammon and bringing it to the table with the bread and wine.

The bare surface, she noted, was streaked with spilt liquid that had stained the wood. A ring where the bottle must have stood. The now-empty plate with knife and fork laid on top. Alongside it, the uneaten bread.

One setting only. A single wine glass, the dregs of wine remaining.

Her last supper, Chrissy thought, her own heart frozen in fear.

She turned as his tall figure entered the kitchen. Above the mask, McNab's blue eyes acknowledged her own, then slowly swept the room. She could read his stance clearly, the tenseness, the anger, the horror at what he was looking at.

He looks, she thought, *exactly the way I feel.*

He followed the treads to the window and from there to the table and its surrounds. McNab was reading the runes, just as she had. Asking the questions they raised.

He took his time and Chrissy could almost hear his brain working. McNab had been a scene of crime officer in the past, and a good one. What he was asking himself was as important as anything she had.

He came to stand beside her and put his gloved hand lightly on her arm in support. It was a gesture that almost floored her. Chrissy took refuge in anger.

'You were right,' she muttered. 'The bastard's been stalking her, waiting his chance. My best bet is he went onto the roof and got into the flat via the open window. When exactly isn't clear. Rhona went back to the lab last night after hours, so maybe then. She sent samples off to Toxicology asking them to check for taxine.' Chrissy looked at McNab. 'The samples came from a dead seagull I found in the lab fridge. Someone,' she continued, 'tried to poison Tom. And maybe her.'

McNab gave an almost imperceptible nod in acknowledgement of her interpretation, his eyes still moving about the room.

'Reading the pattern,' Chrissy continued, 'I think something caused Rhona to rise suddenly from the table, knocking the wine bottle over. It rolled off and shattered and Rhona stood barefoot on the broken glass.'

McNab winced as though experiencing it for himself.

'That's when he appeared?' he said, almost to himself.

'Or –' Chrissy paused – 'when Rhona realized something was wrong with the wine or the food.'

McNab approached the slow cooker. 'Sean brought in

the ham while I was here. He would have put it on to cook before he left.' He crossed now to the fridge. 'The white wine was in the door. I saw it when Rhona went in for something. Maybe half a bottle.' McNab looked to Chrissy.

'We have samples to test,' she said.

'If it was taxine . . .' McNab halted.

Then Rhona may already be dead.

His unsaid words hanging in the air between them, McNab crouched next to the broken glass as Chrissy gathered herself and continued her interpretation of events.

'From the bloodstain pattern, Rhona either collapsed at that point or was pushed to her hands and knees by her attacker, who . . . has left us a partial footprint.'

McNab met her eye, and Chrissy read in his look a reflection of her own doubt.

'From the pattern on the sole I think it's a Harley-Davidson boot, but bigger than the one in the tunnel.'

78

All was silent apart from a steady drip of water from above. Her gravedigger had gone.

Turning from the earthen wall, Rhona shook her hair and spat out the soil that had forced its way past her pursed lips.

If the bastard was planning to bury her, he would have to try harder than that.

Rhona anticipated his actions had succeeded in raising the floor level by a few inches and disrupting the underground stream, although its rise in power and volume would soon clear a path through the added soil.

Moving as far out of the water as she could, Rhona set about freeing her hands. Working the tag round to between her wrists, she bent over. The tie tags had loosened a bit and might not have sufficient tension to break. To get enough force, she would have to raise her arms as high as possible, despite the pain in her shoulders.

Bracing her head against the wall, Rhona brought her wrists down hard on her buttocks, the resultant thump knocking the air from her lungs.

The snap signalled the release of her wrists, although her shoulders screamed their discomfort at having been twisted for so long behind her back.

Rhona took a series of quick breaths and swung her arms until they felt truly back in their sockets.

As she now set about loosening the zip tag on her ankles, she wondered why her abductor hadn't used a better method of securing her, like a decent set of handcuffs at least. He must have been aware that once the grogginess wore off she would have the wit to get free.

He came back to check, but I'd solved his problem by falling in here. Or that's where he'd intended to put me anyway. Why else bring a shovel?

Still in darkness, but with her mind clearer now, Rhona paced out her cell. Her estimate had been close to correct, although she now located the exit and entrance of the stream more accurately. Both appeared and disappeared below a restricting block of solid rock, which meant that should the water level continue to rise, her cell would fill up fairly rapidly.

Reaching up, Rhona tried to judge the distance to the top of the wall, knowing instinctively that it was a good six feet above her head.

There was no easy way out of here and any attempt to climb the walls, she suspected, would result in them crumbling down on her.

Weakened by her efforts and lack of food, Rhona sank to the floor again and, scooping up handfuls of water, tried to satisfy her empty stomach. She could last for some time on water alone, but she would get weaker and definitely less able to figure a way out of here.

The darkness moved in on her again, blinding her mind to hope. Surely they would be looking for her by now? But how would they trace her to her burial here?

Buried and hidden bodies, ironically her speciality.

Maybe McNab had been right to study the dissertation titles. If so, her initial suspicions over Conor would be unfounded.

Another face now came to mind. A face that had been at the busy autopsy for Andrew Jackson. There were a number of APTs on her course. And an APT would be in a prime position to collect her DNA, and be aware of all the processes involved in her dealing with a body at a locus.

She shook her head. The truth was they had no real lead on the perpetrator. *As well he knows.*

Rhona moved her hand to cover her belly. In the dark silence surrounding her, she imagined for a moment that she could feel a flicker of life. Not scientifically possible, she reminded herself. And yet . . .

She recalled another video clip that had come up in her internet search about early pregnancy. It had featured the bright flash of light emitted at the precise moment a sperm met an egg. She'd watched the sequences in wonder at such a scientific development, while also thinking, *Does the light signify the moment life begins?*

She shifted in discomfort at the memory. Surrounded by a deep darkness, the moving water caressing her body, the beat of her heart in her ears, her prison cell resembled a womb.

But how long would her captor choose to keep her, and the tiny light she carried, alive?

79

McNab stood in his kitchen, the bottle of whisky he'd almost consumed before visiting Mary, *a lifetime ago*, still standing on the table.

There was nothing else he could do tonight, he reasoned. And sometimes whisky gave him insights he didn't have when sober.

Ignoring the voice that asked *Who are you trying to kid?*, McNab broke the seal on the bottle and poured a measure. His stomach was empty and he should order pizza before he indulged, but then again, food would lessen the impact of the single malt.

McNab took in the aroma, reminding himself that he'd survived Mary's attempts at getting him drunk and, he suspected, into bed. Which suggested he could control what he drank tonight.

But not if I allow myself to think.

An image of Rhona's kitchen rose to confront him again. Dr Mackie had arrived swiftly after Chrissy's call, brushing aside her apologies at the lateness of the hour.

She'd gone immediately to the footprint. 'Is this the only one you've found?'

'The only distinct one, yes,' Chrissy had confirmed.

Jen's eyes had moved about the room, just as his own had done. 'And you think he entered via the window?' She took herself over there and looked back towards them. 'The spilt wine could have precipitated the partial print, but there will be other deposits of similar soil wherever he's been in the flat.' She drew their gaze back to the window. 'Plus whatever fell from his clothing – pollen, vegetable debris – if he entered through here.'

Having said her piece, Jen suggested he and Chrissy both leave. 'I have my usual police minders.' She indicated the two officers who'd been assigned to her.

Chrissy's eyes had been red with fatigue and worry, so McNab had added his voice to the suggestion that she go home.

'You too, Detective Sergeant,' Jen had ordered.

'We let Rhona down,' Chrissy had said as they'd exited the building together.

McNab had wanted to state how he'd tried to warn Rhona of the danger. Voice his attempts to make Sean stay there with her. But what was the point of repeating something Chrissy already knew?

He stood waiting while Chrissy got into her car and drove away before he approached the bike. Below, the park was painted black, with only a hint of the movement of trees in the darkness.

The search team would be out at first light and the park would be their first port of call. But if her abductor had succeeded in getting Rhona out of the flat unmarked, as it appeared he had, then the likelihood was he would transport her, either dead or alive, as far away from here as possible.

The rain pattering his helmet as he'd roared off, McNab's thoughts had returned to Drumochter and his hurried flight south. There had been no word from Fran since his departure, so he had to assume they'd hadn't yet located Ellie.

Having made Rhona his choice, it appeared he'd lost them both.

McNab moved a chair to face the window. The chances of him sleeping tonight were, he thought, zero. So why waste good drinking time trying?

From here he could see the Street Glide, parked under a lamp, the splendour of its form hidden below its raincoat. It made him think of Ellie arriving at Davey's dinner party dressed in leathers, only to reappear in all her inked glory.

God, she'd looked beautiful that night.

He was sliding into moroseness, McNab knew that, but didn't care. Any thought that the whisky would provide him with insight had been replaced by the stark reality of his failures. McNab stopped fighting and let it happen.

The sound of someone demanding entry broke into McNab's nightmare. He'd been reliving the scene in the wood, Claire's empty eyes, the fury of feasting flies becoming the buzz of the intercom.

He eventually roused himself, swearing about late-fucking-nighters and their pizza deliveries. Dragging his brain back into gear, he knew he had no choice but to respond, because whoever had their finger on the button wasn't about to give up.

He pressed to release the front door and took himself back through to his chair. The whisky bottle stood alongside, half consumed. He'd been right about no food, he thought. *And I need less to achieve the desired effect.* Settling himself back into the chair, he was surprised to register a knock on his own front door.

Fuck it. What now?

It wouldn't be the first time he'd been asked to help gain entry to a flat from a keyless bloody student. McNab's first instinct was to ignore it, but . . .

His angry response at the ready, he threw open the door. Her back was turned to him as though she was about to give up and he knew instantly by the jacket markings who it was. She turned, her helmet still in place as though shielding her identity, but he could see her eyes and that was all that mattered.

McNab drew her inside, enveloping her in his arms, praying she wasn't a figment of his imagination.

Neither of them spoke, in words at least. McNab felt the tenseness flow out of her body, as it did from his. Gently, he undid her helmet and lifted it free, drawing her into the flat, banging the door shut behind her.

Ellie was here and she was safe.

80

In her dream Rhona was watching the excavation of her own grave.

Arc lights blazing down, the camera recording every few seconds, Chrissy was following the grid laid out on the tunnel floor, cutting small sections or spits and bagging the soil until the body, *her* body, would be fully exposed.

From her vantage point, Rhona watched as Chrissy followed the procedures she'd been taught.

I trained her well.

Then her nightmarish world flipped over.

Now she wasn't above, watching Chrissy at work, but below in the grave, eyes open, looking up through the earth at Chrissy's face.

Rhona, seized by terror, ordered her hands to dig herself free. Begged her mouth to shout out, tell Chrissy it was she, Rhona, who was buried there. But no sound emerged, her hands refusing the order to dig.

Then she saw why.

The pressure on her chest wasn't the suffocating weight of earth, but the demon from the corner of her kitchen, the red eyes of the mask leering down at her.

The paralysis suddenly lost its hold and her body jerked into movement. The pressure on her arm was released and replaced by a pricking sensation. The demon face wavered above her then rose as though floating upwards to escape her cell.

She heard the rattle of metal steps, as the accompanying headlamp that had briefly illuminated the mask moved upwards. Then Rhona was plunged into darkness again.

But she wasn't dead or buried yet, she reminded herself.

As her head began to swim in response to whatever he'd pumped into her arm, she realized that this was to be his means of restraining her.

The administered opioid was already doing its work, the *mu* receptor softening the aches in her arms and legs and especially the pain in her head, accompanied by a breaking wave of pleasure and well-being.

Rhona allowed her eyes to drift closed, and enjoyed the welcome but brief sensation of fearlessness, interrupted almost immediately by a shower of dirt and stones hitting her head and chest.

Turning her face to the wall, she listened for the scrape of the shovel, but heard pounding instead, while above her the head torch did a frenzied dance as her abductor broke loose the soil from the upper walls of her cell to rain down on her.

Rhona, of all people, knew how easy it was to collapse the walls of a grave.

81

McNab's eyes jerked open.

The dream had been so real that he could still taste the terror that had accompanied it.

But it was just a dream.

Ellie was there beside him, her hair spread across the pillow, her face peaceful, although behind her lids, her pupils moved as though she too was dreaming.

Raising himself on his pillow, McNab watched her in silence, a smile finding his lips. He still couldn't believe it. Opening the door to give grief to whoever was knocking in the early hours of the morning, he'd found Ellie there instead.

After pulling her inside and wrapping her in his arms, praying that she was real and not a figment of his imagination and a half bottle of whisky, they'd adjourned to the bedroom, the few words spoken only concerned with what they both felt at seeing one another again.

Explanations could be left until the morning.

Registering the time, McNab rose and went through to the kitchen. He didn't need a nightmare to remind him that the search for Rhona would begin again with daylight and that his presence in the operations room would be required.

But before that, he needed to question Ellie.

Carrying the coffee through, he set it down, then gently

roused her with a kiss. Immediately her eyes flew open and for a moment McNab glimpsed fear there too, before she registered it was him, and relaxed.

'We need to talk,' McNab said gently.

He'd brought Ellie with him to the station, as much for his own peace of mind as for her to be interviewed. He had, McNab believed, already heard the whole story from the moment the four girls had entered the tunnel to when Ellie had turned up in the middle of the night on his doorstep.

And I believe every word she said.

McNab wasn't used to hearing what he believed to be true and the relief that had brought him had been like salve on an open wound.

But that didn't mean there wasn't something she'd missed. Something Ellie hadn't deemed significant enough to mention.

His talk with her hadn't been an interrogation, rather a chance for Ellie to unburden her soul. McNab had found it difficult to listen to in part, especially when Ellie had spoken of her young brother and her failure to 'save' him.

She'd broken down at that point. 'I should never have left that man in the tunnel.'

Knowing the story of her brother, McNab's heart went out to Ellie. 'You couldn't have saved him whatever you did,' he told her honestly. 'Andrew Jackson was dead from the moment he ingested the taxine. There is no antidote. And,' he added, 'everything might have been different, if I'd just listened when you called me.'

Ellie had been grateful for that, her half-smile acknowledging that she wasn't the only one with regret about that night.

McNab now stood behind the two-way mirror, observing as DS Clark and DC Fleming entered the interview room. It had been at his suggestion that the DC had been included. He'd been impressed by her approach to the professor, and her determination to offer more to the investigation than the routine tasks she'd been assigned.

And she'd stuck up for his role in the Stonewarrior case, something Magnus had also told him about. But more important than both of these were her early suspicions that they were being played by the perpetrator, which suggested to McNab's mind that DC Fleming had the makings of a real detective.

Settled now, opposite the two policewomen, Ellie looked reasonably at ease, although McNab knew her well enough to recognize the nervous movement of her hands.

Asked to describe that night in the tunnel, Ellie, glancing first at the mirror, took a deep breath and did as requested. Both officers listened in silence, with only an occasional request for clarity on timing.

During the initial run-through, Ellie had seemed assured, McNab observed, probably because of the practice run with him earlier.

But when asked for a repeat, her determined tone had faded, a weary, frightened voice taking its place, the nervous hand movements multiplied.

McNab gripped his coffee cup more tightly. They were going for her now. Something he couldn't have done, but understood why it was necessary.

If Ellie's story was true, then she was, apart from Rhona, the only person to have engaged with the perpetrator and heard his voice.

'Tell me again about the phone call,' DC Fleming ordered.

Ellie was staring into the middle distance, reliving the call once again.

'He said, "I know what you did." I . . . I said,' she stumbled, 'I didn't harm him.'

Her voice changed, as though morphing into her memory of the caller. *'No, but you felt a pulse. You felt something.'*

Her own voice replied, afraid and sorry, 'He was cold. He was dead.'

The caller's voice became wheedling like a guilty conscience. *'But you're not sure of that, are you? You could have saved him if you'd called the police. You could have saved him.'* A pause, then, *'I know what you did,'* again.

The same words used to Rhona, McNab thought. *I know what you did.*

Ellie raised her head and looked directly at DC Fleming. 'There was a torch beam. He was watching me. He knew there was a pulse. Faint, but there.'

The interview over, McNab accompanied a pale and tired-looking Ellie to reception.

'You did grand,' he said, fighting his desire to hug her. 'Go back to my place and have a sleep.'

Ellie looked surprised. 'You never wanted me staying there before.'

'Well, I do now,' McNab said sharply, unable to disguise his fear that she might disappear on him again.

'I'm going into work. Mannie's expecting me.'

McNab realized she was giving him her movements to allay his fears.

'I'll call you,' he promised. 'Let you know when I'll be home.'

Ellie shook her head. 'No point. They took my mobile,

remember? I'll head for the Rock Cafe after work. I'll see you there.'

It was a compromise of sorts and at least at the cafe she would be safe.

McNab saw Ellie off, then headed back inside. Her return should have made things easier, but he realized she was as much on his mind now as when she'd been missing.

He went by the coffee machine on his way to the strategy meeting and relived the moment when Ellie had turned the tables on DC Fleming.

She thought Ellie was lying, or at least making up part of the telephone conversation.

She'd challenged Ellie as to why her voice changed when she repeated the caller's words, *as though you're reading from a script,* she'd said.

'I know his voice by heart,' Ellie had told her. 'I've replayed it so often.'

'And how did you do that?' DC Fleming had demanded.

'I have an app that records incoming calls.'

That had completely thrown DC Fleming. McNab smiled, remembering her expression.

Maybe she wasn't a real detective quite yet.

'Clever girl,' McNab said to himself. 'You kept him talking and he made his first mistake.'

82

Dr Mackie was already in full flow as McNab slipped in at the back.

'The convent garden,' she was saying, 'is the most likely way the abductor gained entry to the property.'

There was silence in the incident room as they waited to hear why the soil scientist believed this to be the case.

'August is part of the summer–autumn season which involves a second flowering of the nettle family, plus pollination of herbaceous plants such as beet, chard and wild spinach. Three of these can be found in the convent garden close to the intervening wall. The small area behind Dr MacLeod's building is grass only.'

She replaced the image of the convent garden on the screen with one of Rhona's kitchen window.

'We retrieved evidence of nettle pollen and wild spinach round the window casing, the suspected entry point to the flat. Also, similar pollen samples were found on the rear steps of the stairwell leading to the back door of the tenement and hence the garden. That door isn't kept locked.'

McNab had fretted about the open window, but he'd never considered the back entrance or the convent as a potential weak point. *How often had he seen Rhona stand at that window looking out on what she called 'her oasis of calm'*. While he, McNab, had sought his peace in a bottle of Scotch.

'There's one further indication that the garden of the convent played a role in Dr MacLeod's abduction.' Dr Mackie brought up another image. 'The intruder brushed this willow tree as he made his way between the two properties,' she told them. 'The willow, important in both Celtic and Christian mythology, also symbolizes the will to endure the most challenging of situations.'

A metaphor, McNab thought, for Jen Mackie's belief that wherever Rhona was, she would be focused on surviving. If that hadn't been her intention, it had had that effect none the less, judging by the expressions around him.

'We retrieved soil samples from the back stairs and the metal ladder leading onto the roof, confirming DS McNab's theory that that was the route used to access the top-floor flat from the convent garden.

'How Dr MacLeod was removed from the building is less obvious. Chrissy has reported that an analysis of the white wine indicated it had been doctored, so the likelihood is that Rhona was semi-conscious and bare-footed. As such, we assume there was a vehicle parked close by to transport her.

'It's now accepted that the perpetrator has forensic knowledge and is using it. But to what degree? He wasn't wearing protective clothing on entering the flat, otherwise we wouldn't have discovered the pollen deposits. That may have been to avoid generating interest or perhaps there's a limit to his knowledge.' She paused. 'The footprint in the kitchen may reveal that limit.'

As Dr Mackie stood down, a rumble of talk broke out in the room before DI Wilson silenced them and ordered them back on the job.

After which he gestured to McNab that he wanted a

word in his office. McNab followed him inside and DI Wilson shut the door.

'I'm glad Ellie's back safe and sound,' were his opening words.

'Thank you, sir.'

'So, how did the interview go?'

When McNab explained about the recording, the boss looked mightily pleased.

'She says it's not great quality,' McNab added, 'but Tech will do their best to clean it up.'

DI Wilson nodded, preoccupied now, McNab knew, by the more pressing issue of Rhona's disappearance.

'Chrissy told me . . . about Rhona's condition,' he finally said. 'I understand she spoke to you about it before she disappeared?'

'She did, in confidence, sir,' McNab stressed.

DI Wilson gave him a swift look. 'It will go no further than me, Detective Sergeant. And when we find Dr MacLeod safe and well, there will be no reason to tell her that I know.'

McNab nodded, relieved by that.

'But,' DI Wilson continued, 'her condition makes it even more imperative that we locate her, and soon,' he stressed. 'So let's hope whatever Jen Mackie comes up with via the soil samples gives us a possible lead on Dr MacLeod's whereabouts.'

'Wherever Rhona is, sir,' McNab heard himself say, 'you can guarantee she'll be doing her damnedest to set herself free.'

83

The rising water had been busy.

Rhona had assumed that the space beneath the rock would get blocked by the extra earth her captor had shovelled in, but instead the water channel had narrowed and its increased flow had dug deeper into the floor of her prison.

Rhona, feeling her way towards the gurgling water, slated her thirst.

The opioid was wearing off, leaving her with a dry mouth and trembling limbs as the cold water took its toll on her body.

The feeling of drug induced pleasure was gone, dropping her back into cold reality with a vengeance, but her brain was clear enough now to consider what her chances truly were.

Her abductor had kept her alive until now, Rhona reasoned, but for what purpose? Only to terrify her with the prospect of being buried alive? Or had she been taken as yet another forensic test for the investigation team?

Abduct an expert on buried and hidden bodies, and see if they can find her?

Rhona recalled the test demo she and Jen Mackie had videoed for the class. Rhona had donned wellie boots and walked in a well-known but unnamed Glasgow park.

She'd presented the boots to Jen and, for the benefit of the class, asked her to demonstrate how she might track the soil to its point of origin.

It had been a popular event, especially when Jen had got to within yards of the spot where Rhona had stood.

Was that what her own capture was about?

The more she considered that possibility, the more likely it seemed.

Rhona tried to relive the scene in the kitchen, but her recall always stopped at the moment she'd tried to stab the glass splinter into her attacker's leg. Whatever had happened after that had resulted in her being transported here. Obviously a vehicle had to have been used, but what about once inside the tunnel?

The thought that it might have involved more than one person crossed her mind. Might they be dealing with a duo rather than a lone perpetrator? Although she'd only heard and seen one up to now.

If they both wear demon masks, how would I know the difference?

Rhona turned her thoughts back to here and now. She'd got free of her restraints and her gaoler had countermanded this with the opiate. But to administer it again he would have to enter her grave to do it.

And this time she would be ready for him.

84

'So everyone on the main diploma course viewed this video featuring Dr Mackie identifying the location of the soil on Rhona's boots?' DI Wilson asked.

'It was also made available online to the MOOCs students and the part-timers,' Jen told him.

McNab was bristling, but trying hard not to show it. A swift look from the boss enforced this as the correct strategy.

'However,' Dr Mackie was saying, 'what we gave them was fairly superficial. The soil map of Scotland, the way we eliminate areas, focusing in on possibilities only.'

McNab could restrain himself no longer. 'Then the mud conveniently left behind is a red herring.'

Jen Mackie shot him a look that suggested he might be right, so McNab cut off what he planned to say next and waited for her response.

'The partial print could be explained by the spilt wine which loosened the soil, or as DS McNab suggests, it may have been put there for a reason. The lack of other identifiable footprints in the flat or on the stairwell might indicate the intruder's own footwear was covered.'

McNab came back in. 'So we waste our time and effort looking in the wrong place?'

*

McNab parked the bike at the top of the steps leading from the park to Rhona's flat.

From his vantage he noted that the search team, who'd begun at dawn, were still combing the dense undergrowth that led down to the park.

It was a slow and laborious business, but it had to be done, he conceded, although the only way they would find Rhona there was if she was already dead. Something he didn't believe was the case, yet.

Of course, the perp might have already killed her and buried her body, in order to enjoy watching them search for her remains. But then, McNab reasoned, Rhona would be merely another victim, whereas *she's the opponent he needs to defeat.*

His mind went back to Ellie. He'd thought Ellie a prospective victim because someone had seen her with the body in the tunnel.

An organized killer liked to engage with the investigation, directly if possible. When Ellie had been identified, possibly via the Harley connection, the next move was to inform her that she'd been seen, and only the perp would have known that Jackson might not yet have taken his last breath.

Anyone watching Ellie would have soon learned about her connection with him, the detective. *How much pleasure that must have given the perpetrator*. Even more so when Ellie did a runner.

His recent conversation with Fran had established they'd located Ellie via the ride-out, but before they could reach out to her, she'd left Aviemore.

'I'm really glad she's safe and back with you,' Fran had said, relieved. 'I thought we'd let you down.'

So the perpetrator hadn't gone looking for Ellie. That had all been a ruse to take their eyes away from his real goal. Rhona.

He doesn't want the game to end, McNab thought. All that planning and practice, working up from interfering with dead bodies, to a kill, heavily marked as suicide. Then Claire. Claire wasn't planned, just required, probably because she could identify him.

Calling Ellie had been the perp's first mistake; having to dispense with Claire his second.

He'd tried his best with the second locus, tarting it up to match the theme, the signature, but it had been hurried. He got the evidence on the hanging wrong. He must have known that the fact she'd been strangled would be revealed at the post mortem.

Claire's murder wasn't half as accomplished as his first effort.

How long had he been watching Rhona, studying the pattern of her life? Weeks, months, longer, planning her abduction?

To achieve his goal, he would have had to get sufficiently close to Rhona to be allowed entry to her flat. Only then would he have known about her habit of keeping the kitchen window open for the cat.

85

He and Sean Maguire hadn't always seen eye to eye, but despite their history, McNab liked the guy. At this moment, he also pitied him. McNab doubted if Maguire had shut his eyes since Rhona had disappeared.

They were seated at her kitchen table, meeting here at McNab's request. He could have asked Maguire to come to the station, although DS Clark had already spoken to him. Interviewing partners was routine with any 'disappearance'. When someone went missing, the partner was always on the radar.

So there was nothing odd about Maguire having been the first port of call.

McNab wondered how he'd felt about that. Someone you really care about goes missing in what appears to be violent circumstances, and you're the first one the police interview.

And here he was back again.

'How are you doing?' McNab found himself saying.

Maguire set down the freshly brewed coffee in front of McNab before answering.

'Probably about the same as you, Detective Sergeant.'

They sat in silence for a moment, then McNab opened the proceedings.

'Would you be able to list everyone you can think of

who might have had access to the flat, this kitchen in particular?'

Maguire threw him a quizzical look. 'This is Rhona's place. I don't live here.'

'But we can't ask Rhona,' McNab said, the tetchiness obvious in his voice.

At this, Sean rose and went to the cupboard McNab knew to be home to the whisky. Motioning to the bottle, then at McNab's mug, Sean asked the silent question.

McNab nodded, then watched as a decent measure was added to his coffee. Maguire, he knew, was trying to bridge the divide between them, for Rhona's sake if nothing else.

Then again, the poor bastard doesn't know what I know.

McNab briefly considered revealing the pregnancy. At least then he could stop feeling guilty about knowing about it. *And start feeling guilty about not keeping his word to Rhona?*

'I take it you want a list of names?' Maguire was asking. 'The ones I know about anyway?' he added, a slight edge to his voice.

McNab nodded and pulled out his notebook.

'As you probably know, Rhona didn't do entertaining, so no dinner parties. She always said she wouldn't have people here she didn't like.'

Maguire's voice caught in his throat and McNab realized the guy was closer to breaking down than he thought.

In recognition of this, McNab tried to soften his own tone. 'Let's think recently. Last couple of months maybe. Did you arrive to find anyone here with Rhona?'

Maguire threw him a penetrating look. 'Apart from you, you mean?'

'Apart from me.'

'The guy from the sleep clinic, Dr Williams. He's been here a few times. Helped Rhona with Tom, but you know that already. Someone left her a bottle of red wine at the door. She didn't seem to know who.'

'And the white wine in the fridge?'

'Rhona thought that was me, but it wasn't. Not this time anyway. I told DS Clark that already.'

'Is that everyone?'

'There's a new guy moved into the neighbouring flat. He seems friendly. Came to say hello, but I don't know if Rhona invited him in. I thought you'd interviewed the other residents?'

The guy Maguire was talking about, name of Craig Robbins, worked at the Kings Theatre and rented out a room through Airbnb. According to his interview with DS Clark, he'd never been inside Rhona's flat. That couldn't be verified, of course, without Rhona.

'Then there's Mrs Harper who's looking after Tom, but I assume you've spoken to her.' He paused. 'Shouldn't you be checking out the folk on her course, and those she worked with? It had to be someone who at least knew about forensics?'

'Whoever it was had to know about the cat and the open window,' McNab reminded him.

'Well, anyone watching from the flats to the rear or the convent could have spotted the cat, or even me, climbing onto the roof.'

'You've done that?' McNab said, surprised.

'I was trying to scare Rhona into shutting the window at night.' Maguire shook his head. 'A big mistake. Lecturing Rhona on what to do has the opposite effect from what's intended. But then you're probably aware of that.'

He met McNab's eye, his own a mix of fury and despair. 'Who the fuck has her, McNab? Is Rhona even alive?'

86

Her watch and its luminous dial was her sole grip on reality.

That and the aching cold that sent her muscles into increasingly frequent bouts of shivering. It might be August above ground, but being constantly wet and in the dark was lowering her body temperature to approaching dangerous levels.

The answer, of course, was to keep moving.

Free from her physical restraints, she could at least stand up and walk about now the opiate had worn off.

And she could dig.

The swiftly moving water had helped her, discarding stones near the outlet which she could throw free of the channel. Now able to slide her arm through the widened gap, Rhona registered open space on the other side, although there was no way of knowing if it was big enough for all of her.

Rhona imagined her captor shining his torch down and finding her gone. What would he do? Assume she'd managed to climb out herself or even been rescued?

That would scare the shit out of him.

Would he come down the ladder to make sure?

Rhona tested the slither of glass now back in her

possession again, and felt a warm trickle of blood run down her finger in anticipation.

There was, of course, another scenario. Her captor could choose not to return. Or if he did, it might only be to throw more earth into her grave.

Weariness swept over her and a realization that the shivering wasn't only caused by being wet and cold, but was possibly her body's attempt at combating a rising temperature.

Rhona brushed the sweat from her eyes as a shudder ran through her body.

She had a plan, but would she have the strength left to carry it out?

She positioned herself more firmly in the space she'd created, the swiftly rising water swirling about her. Whatever part of Glasgow lay above her had experienced one of the sudden tropical downpours that were becoming more frequent of late.

The thought occurred that should the level rise too high, she might drown here, wedged in her carefully excavated cave, only to be discovered sometime in the future by Urbex explorers.

If that were the case, Rhona found herself imagining what would be left of her. She'd excavated sufficient graves to know what lasted and what didn't, due to time, the surrounding environment and circumstances.

The air she was breathing wasn't fresh, but neither was it foul. There were plenty of insects calling this place home. She'd felt them investigate her body, running over it, tasting her sweat and blood loss. No death flies had as yet come calling, but they would eventually appear to feast on her decay.

Two lives could end down here, she thought. *One barely begun.*

The flashes of light that had signified the beginning of existence had been revisiting her at regular intervals. Much like the imagined paralysis and the demon eyes.

A fevered mental fight between life and death? Or self-imposed guilt at what she'd planned to do, had she not been abducted?

She'd been close to the death of others so often. Serving the dead by cataloguing the manner in which they'd died had given her a purpose, and a way of emotionally disengaging from the reality of it.

Contemplating her own death was something else entirely.

The water rushing towards her was full of small sharp stones that scratched at her arms and legs, but not, she thought, her stomach.

She had been protecting that part of her, she realized, from the moment she'd fallen into this pit.

If I am allowed to live, then it will be too.

When she heard her name called, Rhona thought she'd imagined it. The second time, she almost responded, so long had it been since she'd heard her name spoken out loud.

Then the torch was back, sweeping her cell, seeking her presence. As Rhona pressed herself further into the space she'd created, the beam lit up the floor, then one by one the walls.

At the third and more urgent call, Rhona thought briefly that she might recognize the voice. Then it changed, became muffled, and she knew the mask was back in place, distorting the sound.

The light was on again, flickering over the moving water, skimming past her cave.

He can't see me.

Then came the rattle of the metal ladder. The sound of footsteps descending. The splash as his feet hit the water.

Rhona waited, the thump of her heart so loud that she was certain he must hear it. Standing in front of her now, all she had to do was grab his legs to topple him.

87

Dusk was descending as McNab exited Rhona's flat.

Sean had indicated he intended to stay there until Rhona returned. His declaration had sounded to McNab more like a desperate plea for him to find her.

'Rhona always said she could trust you with her life,' had been Sean's parting words.

It was a well-aimed blow, but McNab knew the truth of it. How often had he said the same of Rhona?

And she had saved him, on more than one occasion. His sanity, his sobriety and his career.

McNab glanced at his mobile, thinking to check up on Ellie, while not wishing to look like he was stalking her.

That thought led to another. Rhona had accused him that night in the tunnel of doing just that. Taken aback, he'd insisted she was wrong, while at the same time wondering if there wasn't some small degree of truth in her accusation.

Then again if he'd been more diligent about it, things wouldn't be as they were now.

The search of the park had come to nothing, verifying McNab's belief that wherever Rhona was, it wasn't close to home.

Snatched women were usually taken away by car, their bodies either dumped on open ground or buried, often far from the place they'd been taken. But this wasn't what was happening here, McNab reminded himself.

Rhona's abduction was a test, one it seemed they were failing.

As he fired up the bike, McNab looked up to see Maguire standing at the bay window, the current downpour distorting his image.

The guy was as demented about this as he was.

As McNab signalled to draw out, a white van suddenly appeared behind him. Passing dangerously close, it deluged him with surface water in the process. McNab gave the finger to the fast-disappearing vehicle, and like all good officers made a mental note of the number plate.

He would find out who that fucker was, he promised himself.

The longer she was missing, the more likely she was to be dead.

Why did he not believe that to be true?

McNab had never given credence to clairvoyants, and he'd seen a few offer their services on the job. None, to his mind, had been successful. The only story that had ever really bothered him had happened during the Stonewarrior case, when the mother of the victim, a young male student, had been told at a meeting in a spiritualist church not far from here that her son was dead, barely an hour after it must have happened.

That he hadn't been able to explain.

Neither could he explain the feeling that, despite everything, he thought – no – *knew* that Rhona was still alive.

McNab came to an abrupt halt, realizing he was at the

top of the steep steps that led down to the park, to Sauchiehall Street and to the church that had been on his mind.

He could go the long way round, he thought, or he could take the shorter and definitely more challenging, bone-rattling route, where he could test if he really could control the bike.

The upstairs bar of the Rock Cafe was heaving, the beat of the music thrumming McNab's body as he weaved his way through the crowd and headed for the stairs. Hunger assailed him as the smell of food met his descent, but McNab's first thought was for Ellie. He scanned the room, his heart rising and dipping as he thought he spotted her, then was disappointed.

McNab made for the bar to find the same guy as on his earlier visit.

'Seen Ellie?' he tried.

The response was, as before, non-committal.

'Not sure. We're busy as you can see.'

McNab ordered the same food as before, a double helping to share and a pint, then took one of the few remaining tables. Waiting for his meal to arrive, he scanned the room again and, this time, he spotted her.

She was standing in a corner, and there was someone with her. A guy leaning in on her in a manner McNab didn't like.

Recognizing who it was, McNab made his way swiftly through the crowd.

'Sergeant McNab.' Symes stepped away from Ellie. 'Good to see you again.'

McNab didn't respond, but looking straight at Ellie, said,

'I've a table over there, with food arriving. For two,' he stressed.

Ellie nodded and, turning to Symes, said, 'I'll see you tomorrow, Roddie.'

The food had provided a welcome distraction. Now that they'd cleared the plate, a conversation would have to begin, and Ellie didn't look like the one to do that, McNab thought.

In that he was wrong.

His weak opening salvo of, 'Mannie must have been glad to see you back,' was swiftly interrupted by, 'I want to help you catch the killer,' from Ellie.

She was looking straight at him, her eyes challenging McNab to respond positively to her statement of intent. Recognizing he was on dangerous ground, and definitely not wanting to piss Ellie off again, McNab swallowed his stock reply that it was the job of the police to do that.

'Okay,' he managed instead. 'Is there a way you think you can help us more than you've done already?'

She looked relieved by his reaction and he caught the faintness of a smile before she said, 'I may have seen him.'

McNab absorbed this before he replied. 'But you said you only saw his torch in the tunnel?'

She nodded. 'I did, but . . .' She hesitated. 'I kept having the feeling someone was following me. That's why I left Glasgow.' She met his eye. 'I'm sorry, I should have told you.'

'If I'd looked like listening, you would have.' McNab reached out and squeezed her hand in encouragement.

'If I could look at footage from CCTV at the places it happened.'

'Which places?' McNab said.

'Near the bike shop and the Ink Parlour. And maybe my flat.'

88

He was face down in the water and thrashing, but it had taken what little strength Rhona had had to topple him.

And he would stay there only seconds.

As he broke the surface Rhona realized that the latex mask covered all of his head. Lit up by the torch, it looked like an exact replica of the goblin from the painting.

Her feet fighting the flow, Rhona launched herself at him, rock in hand. Her initial plan had been to try and wound him again with the broken glass, but she'd decided instead to try and stun him enough to give her time to get up the ladder.

Aim for the jaw or the middle of the chin.

Which was easier said than done.

The weight of water going in the opposite direction was pulling her away from her goal. Rhona swung the rock, imagining it to be the thick fist she didn't have.

His head jerked left on impact, but the latex had obviously absorbed some of the force. Before she could repeat the action, he was pushing himself up and out of the fast-moving water.

Then it struck her. The all-encompassing mask had only slits for eyes and a small opening for the mouth. Hence the voice distortion. His coughing and spluttering confirmed this fact. Water had got in, but how did it get out?

The demon might be her saviour after all.

Rhona scrambled towards the ladder. Perhaps anticipating another blow, and surprised by her move, he didn't react quickly enough.

As she pulled the ladder free of the wall, a shower of soil and stones rained down on them both.

Ducking behind the freed ladder, Rhona pushed it over. For a moment she thought she'd miscalculated and it would meet the far wall, but no.

Its sudden descent had him swiftly back underwater, pinned there by the ladder and her weight on it.

If she stayed here like this, he would likely drown . . . and she would be free.

She thought of Andrew Jackson's body, laid out in the tunnel, of Claire hanging like a rag doll from that tree. Whoever was behind that mask had killed twice already, and she was destined to be the third.

Rhona revisited that terrible night at the stone circle. The night when McNab had used exactly the same reasoning for why that perpetrator had to die.

But I'm not McNab.

Rhona lifted the ladder and set it back against the wall. Released, his head turned, and the demon face broke the surface.

Was he alive?

Rhona knew she should wade over and check, but if he was . . .

Turning for a last look, she saw the open eyes, lifeless and fixed upon her.

89

The incident room was packed. For a moment McNab thought there might have been a breakthrough, but none of the expressions round him suggested that. He joined the boss near the front with Dr Mackie. Behind her on the screen was a map of Glasgow but not a version McNab had seen before.

As he approached, DI Wilson called for quiet, then reminded them who Dr Mackie was before asking her to take over.

'We need to consider the underlying geology and the soil texture characteristics of the samples taken from the partial print lifted in Dr MacLeod's kitchen. I should say, at this point, that the footwear has been identified as a size ten Harley man's boot.'

A murmur of interest greeted this declaration.

'Harley boots have a variety of distinctive orange-coloured patterns down the centre of the sole, with the Harley insignia placed in the instep and a further pattern on the heel. An example of this type is to the right of the screen.'

Jen Mackie continued, 'The pattern is designed for grip but the deep, narrow spaces in the tread are ideal for retaining soil. Added to that, they run in different orientations which is also good for retention. In the case of our print, the top layer of material we've identified as originating in the area marked here.'

Dr Mackie indicated a cross on the soil map marking an area south of Partick and close to the River Clyde.

'However,' she went on, 'we also retrieved material that we traced to here.' This time she indicated the Gilmorehill area of the university. 'Some of the buildings such as the Joseph Black chemistry building stand on or next to old mine workings, which run down to the River Kelvin.

'Our sample contains soil information to reflect such a location, for example, evidence of mine workings and feral animal faeces.' She paused to let the significance of this sink in. 'Also in the vicinity is a portion of the disused Kelvingrove Park railway tunnel, which emerges near the bridge carrying Gibson Street over the river. The tunnel is fenced off, but Urbex explorers usually find a way in, as the online photographs of the sections under the park demonstrate.'

So they had two, maybe three possible locations derived from the boot, with every reason to suppose that they might all have been planted.

When McNab said as much, Dr Mackie nodded. 'Although I believe an attempt has been made to wipe the sole prior to the most recent layer.' She gave a half-smile at this point. 'As with blood deposits, perpetrators rarely realize the level to which we can both identify and analyse evidence.'

She allowed the appreciative murmur at this point to die down before she continued.

'Now, let's take another look at the second locus.'

McNab had no wish to look again at Claire's body against the trunk of that tree, but that's not what appeared. This time the view was of an identified route taken from the tarred path through the undergrowth leading to that terrible spot.

'I spoke to Dr MacLeod near the second locus, shortly before her disappearance, and told her we'd collected prints suggesting Claire approached from the park, and whoever she met with used the path from the university. That was, she informed me, the route she used on her way home.

'The prints we collected in the undergrowth weren't made by the same footwear as identified at the abduction point. However, they were the same size and likely made by the same person, suggesting that whoever killed Claire Masters and abducted Dr MacLeod favours the outer edge of heel and toe when he walks.'

As the boss began organizing the search teams for the areas discussed, McNab took himself into the corridor to answer a call from Ollie.

'Jeez, where have you been, Inspector?'

'I was demoted, it's Detective Sergeant,' McNab reminded him. 'What is it, Ollie?'

'Can you come see? It's easier than trying to explain. DC Fleming's here,' he added as an afterthought.

DC Fleming? McNab thought as he headed to IT. He was aware her donkey work had been CCTV-related, but she'd been involved in Ollie's world too?

They were seated together, apparently avidly viewing his collection of screens. Neither turned on McNab's approach to acknowledge him.

When McNab cleared his throat to indicate his presence, DC Fleming immediately rose and said, 'Sir.'

'You've found something?'

'Magnus—' DC Fleming began.

'Magnus?' McNab interrupted her.

'Sorry, sir,' she said, not looking sorry at all. '*Professor Pirie* sent you his profiling notes, sir.' Fleming hurried on as though expecting McNab to interrupt again. 'Working with Ollie here, we've come up with the theory that there's another location which should be included in the geographical cluster he laid out.'

'And that is?'

'The mortuary, sir.'

'The mortuary?'

Ollie came in then. 'Though distant from the university, it fits the criteria for access to Dr MacLeod, both DNA and the suits she favours. There are also a number of mortuary technicians on the forensic course. If the perpetrator wants to control the investigation, the mortuary would be a key place to be.'

'Okay,' McNab said, accepting the logic of that.

Ollie hesitated. 'So. Combining Professor Pirie's profile notes, accessibility to Dr MacLeod, plus what I've retrieved from Ellie's mobile, and the recent footprint evidence, we've come up with a list of possible suspects who fit geographically, personally and physically to the profile.'

McNab followed Ollie's eyes to the first screen and ran down the list of names, images and matching profiles. There was only one name on there that he recognized. His heart skipped a beat, his throat closing on the exclamation that name brought to his throat.

Ollie was watching him, attempting to read his expression.

'They're not all taking the course?' McNab managed.

'But that doesn't mean they don't have the necessary forensic knowledge.'

'Has the boss seen this?'

'Not yet, we wanted to speak to you first,' Ollie said, looking relieved that he hadn't been shot down in flames. 'And this is the recorded call to Ellie's mobile.'

The voice was heavily distorted but McNab could make out what it said, and it was just as Ellie had reported.

'Can you make it any clearer?' he said.

'This version's slightly better.'

McNab listened again, trying to match the voice to the known name on that list, but couldn't.

'What's causing the distortion?' he asked.

'The quality these apps produce isn't ideal. Then again the caller may have disguised his voice by restricting the mouth space in some fashion.'

'Ellie Macmillan didn't tell DS Clark and me the whole story, sir.'

McNab contemplated the young woman before him. When DC Fleming had insisted on leaving IT with him, it was plain that she had something else to say. Maybe out of Ollie's earshot.

Challenging him about Ellie in front of Ollie would have been a mistake, so in that she'd been right.

Deciding not to bite right away, McNab wondered at the same time whether Janice had been made aware of what DC Fleming was now saying.

As though reading his mind, Fleming said, 'DS Clark and I agree on that, sir.'

She was growing impatient with his non-response, evidenced by what she came out with next.

'I know she's your girlfriend, sir.'

'Bad move, Constable,' McNab said.

Fleming shut her mouth at that, and McNab watched as she revisited what she'd planned to say.

'Sorry, sir.'

Why did he think that Fleming's rendition of 'sir' was always either an afterthought or said under duress?

God, she reminds me of myself, McNab thought, facing up to the boss.

So what would the boss do in such circumstances? 'Okay, Detective Constable, enlighten me.'

She's close to the truth, McNab thought, as he listened. Had Ellie not confided in him last night in the Rock Cafe, DC Fleming's view on this would have been a revelation.

'I take it Ollie was involved with all of this?' McNab said when she'd finished.

'When you went to Aviemore, sir, he knew you were worried about Ellie's safety, so as well as looking for her mobile signal—'

'He checked her movements on CCTV in and around her place of work and home.'

'To see if someone was watching Ellie, someone who might scare her enough to make her run.'

McNab nodded. 'She asked me last night to get hold of anything we could, featuring the days between the tunnel and her escape north. Has DS Clark seen what you've got?'

'Yes, sir.'

'Okay, we'll bring Ellie back in and see what she makes of it.'

By Fleming's expression, there was yet more she wanted to say and he could hardly deny her that now.

'Spit it out, Constable.'

'Which name on that list did you recognize, sir?'

90

Rhona halted, drawing air desperately into her lungs.

She should have been brave enough to remove the head torch before climbing out of the pit. Without light, she could well be going round in circles.

Despite the vacant eyes, she wasn't sure he was dead, and in her desperation to escape she'd failed to pull up the ladder. If he was alive, he could be following her even now. And he did have light.

And footwear. Her bare feet had grown cold and numb in the muddy water of the pit. Up here she couldn't see, never mind avoid the stones under her feet, and every hurried step was pretty well agony, only endurable because the option of not running was worse. *Stop and think*, she told herself. *Get your bearings.* She'd run in the direction she'd seen the first torch beam. At least she thought she'd come that way. But who could be sure?

Her throat was parched and she longed for a drink. Water had been her only sustenance in the pit and she hadn't eaten for how long?

The hunger pains that gnawed at her belly had grown stronger with no liquid to help abate them. If she was to keep going she would have to find something to drink.

Rhona reached out to the wall to find moss fed by trickling water. Her first instinct was to put her mouth to the wall and let the water run in, but her knowledge warned her not to. If this was part of an old mine or railway tunnel, who knew what its walls ran with.

She let the water wet her fingers, then put them gingerly to her lips.

The result was immediate and horrible. Rhona spat out what little she'd tasted, her stomach heaving in the process.

Sliding down the wall, she sat hunched as icy shivers seized her body and rattled her teeth.

It's delayed shock, she told herself. She'd seen it countless times on the job. Experienced it herself.

Just breathe and listen.

The air was fresher here, she acknowledged, with maybe some movement. And she could hear the rush of water somewhere in the distance. There was plenty of lying water in the tunnel, she'd splashed her way through it. But this was different. Could she be near a river?

If she'd been hidden close to home, she might be listening to the Kelvin; even the Clyde wasn't that far away.

The shivering hadn't stopped, but concentrating on something else had taken her mind off it. Rhona rose on unsteady legs and, turning her face to catch any imagined movement of air, set off in that direction.

91

Dr Conor Williams had been a surprise entrant on that list. Geographically, he was in the cluster. He was also a recent acquaintance of Rhona's. How exactly they'd met, McNab wasn't sure, but he guessed Chrissy would know.

McNab had waited until DC Fleming had left his company, without an answer to her final question, before he'd given Chrissy a call.

'Rhona met him in the park. Apparently he ran into her on his bike,' Chrissy told him. 'He called her at the lab afterwards. Explained that he'd been treating Andrew Jackson at the sleep clinic. Rhona went to talk to him about that.'

'How did he get Rhona's number?' McNab said.

'He said his assistant mentioned he was taking her diploma course, so he checked on the university contacts list. Why the big interest in the doctor?' Worry echoed in Chrissy's voice. 'You think he has something to do with Rhona's disappearance?'

McNab couldn't lie to Chrissy and had no wish to anyway, even if they were all clutching at straws. 'He's in Magnus's geographical cluster,' he said.

Silence followed before Chrissy said, 'He turned up miraculously when the cat was poisoned. And he's been to the flat a few times.'

'I know,' McNab told her. 'I met him there.' McNab recalled the tall figure on the landing.

Dr Williams had willingly come forward to be interviewed about his connection with Andrew Jackson. *And he'd made a big point of the possibility of suicide in Jackson's case,* linked, he'd implied, to Jackson's sleep paralysis. He'd even given an explanation for the wine and the bread, linking sleep paralysis to perceived sins.

McNab stopped himself there, knowing he was merely fitting Williams to the crime, because he'd come forward with information. It was a valid reason to consider him, but hardly damning. Anyone studying Rhona's comings and goings from a top-floor flat with its accessible roof could probably work out how they might gain access. Besides, Rhona was naturally suspicious and not easily fooled. And she didn't invite just anyone into her home. He had to assume she'd trusted Williams.

McNab switched his attention back to the list Magnus had supplied from the dissertation titles. Chrissy had mentioned that Williams had made contact with Rhona because his assistant was on her course.

McNab located the list he'd viewed in Magnus's office at the university and ran his eye over it again and there was Ray Howden's name – the title of his dissertation being 'Buried and Hidden Bodies: A Study in Soil Science'.

Too obvious a pointer?

McNab returned to Ollie's list. No sign of Howden's name on that, but were Ollie or DC Fleming even aware of Howden's existence? Had they somehow missed him among the myriad of participants, full-time and part-time diploma, and MOOCs?

Despite all his efforts, McNab knew he was lost in a

maze of conjecture. They had nothing on the killer, except that he wore size ten boots, if even that were true.

And while he ran up every blind alley, Rhona was out there, in the clutches of a psychopath or perhaps already dead.

92

The tunnel had opened out, forming a square. Rhona felt her way round it. If this was an old railway tunnel then this section might indicate a vent somewhere above her which could account for the fresher air?

Underfoot was wet, and becoming wetter by the minute, which must mean surface water was getting down here somehow, just as it had in her cell.

Thinking of her prison brought back a stark image of the masked face below the head torch, the open eyes staring blindly out at her.

The eyes were blue.

If only she'd had the courage to pull up the mask and view his face, but if she had, would she have escaped and still be alive?

Rhona leaned against the slime-covered wall as another pain gripped her. With no drinking water and no food, the problem of nausea had gone, replaced by something almost worse.

Her watch had failed, having been infiltrated by water in the fight in the pit, and she had lost all sense of time.

As she moved forward again, Rhona suddenly discovered her feet on drier ground, the sense that she was on a gradual incline taking hold. In a few more minutes she would detect daylight, she promised herself, if it was still day.

Her toe hit the bricks first, followed by her bent head. The knock stunned her, so unexpected was it. She'd thought she'd learned to read the dark, to make out obstacles in her path. She'd been wrong.

Blood trickled into her eye, warm and salty, as Rhona tried to make out the obstacle she'd come upon so suddenly.

Had she missed a curve in the road?

Her hands felt across the wall, first right then left. The rough surface of the bricks was dry, the mortar between them crumbling a little under her fingers.

She was, she decided, in an old railway tunnel as she'd thought, and this was likely its bricked-up entrance.

She walked its length, her hand trailing the wall, seeking metal, just in case there was a door like the one under London Road. Her fingertips, raw from digging in the pit and wet with seeping blood, scraped across the rough surface, desperately seeking some sort of exit, and finding nothing to suggest its existence.

Reaching the far end, she turned and did the same on the way back, just in case, already knowing there was no door and no way out, here at least.

She had no choice but to turn round and go back the way she had come, and likely straight into the arms of her attacker.

If I'd held him under the water for a moment longer, I would have been sure.

Then she could have taken the head torch and found her way out safely. She couldn't bring Claire and Andrew back, but by finishing the job, she would have prevented him from killing her and the fragment of life within her.

Which you had planned to extinguish anyway, a small voice accused her.

That was before. This was now.

Rhona sank to the ground, her back against the wall. She needed to gather her strength and try to remember anything on the way here which suggested she might have taken a different route.

A sharp point of light appeared to dance behind her in the dark, as what sounded like a single pair of feet splashed through the deep puddles in her direction.

He was coming for her.

Her heart pounding, Rhona rose on unsteady legs. If she could stay out of the light, might she go unnoticed?

The beam had halted. No longer coming directly towards her, it swung left then right. Rhona ducked to avoid it, then moving as quietly as possible towards a side wall, lay flat on her face.

If he spotted the bricked-up end, he might turn, thinking she had gone another way. It was a forlorn hope, but it was all she had.

He was back on the move and it was towards her. He was taking no chances. He planned to make sure. Rhona lay as dead, much like a wounded animal, her only hope being that he would miss her stretched-out shadow huddled against the wall.

It was the sudden and searing pain that gave her away, all attempts at smothering a moan failing. As Rhona drew up her knees, she felt the wetness of where she lay, but warm now instead of cold.

'Dr MacLeod,' a voice called, 'is that you?'

93

'Where?' McNab said.

'Old Kelvingrove tunnel, under Gibson Street. They're bringing her out now.'

'She's alive?'

'Yes, sir, but in bad shape. She's being taken to the Death Star.' Sergeant McIvor, immediately regretting his choice of Glasgow's name for the new flagship hospital, quickly corrected himself. 'The Queen Elizabeth. Who else should I let know, sir?'

'I'll do that,' McNab said.

Mounting the bike, he said a silent fucking thank you – to who, exactly?

He should let Maguire know right away, his conscience told him sharply. Chrissy too, but he wanted to see Rhona for himself first. Know that she was alive, before anyone else got there.

If he'd been on a police bike, he could have turned on the flashing lights, raced his way through the traffic. McNab did that anyway.

So Dr Mackie had been right about location. The dirt on a boot she'd analysed had taken them to the right place, despite the fact the perp had tried to fool them. McNab felt a sense of elation. Rhona was safe and they would get the bastard who'd done this.

McNab took the bike directly to the emergency entrance next to the ambulances. If the Street Glide had been towed by the time he emerged, *who the fuck cared?*

The Death Star was as big as its fictional counterpart and twice as confusing, unless he was on his way to the mortuary, which thank God he wasn't. Brandishing his badge and with repeated enquiries, McNab eventually found his way from Accident and Emergency to the ward Rhona had been taken to.

Sitting outside the door was a PO he didn't recognize but who obviously knew him.

'Has anyone spoken to Dr MacLeod yet?'

He shook his head. 'The doctor said to wait until she comes round properly.'

McNab shut the door quietly behind him and crossed to the bed.

Her eyes were closed, although they moved behind the lids as if in a dream. She was attached to the usual array of instruments and tubes, and McNab watched as Rhona's heart beat its reassuring rhythm across the screen.

Only then did he allow himself to truly believe her alive.

He registered the paleness of her skin and the parched lips, the wound above her right eye, the badly torn hands that lay on the cover. They'd found her underground – had she been trying to dig herself out?

McNab found himself horrified at the thought.

He touched the hand nearest him, stroking it lightly, and for a moment he thought Rhona's eyes might open in response, then the heartbeat steadied again in its rhythm.

McNab turned as the door opened and a female doctor entered.

'Can we speak outside?' she said.

Introducing herself as Dr Gordon, she explained that she'd advised that Dr MacLeod wouldn't be well enough to interview until she'd recovered sufficiently from the anaesthetic.

'You had to operate?' McNab said worriedly.

'There was some internal bleeding.'

'What did the bastard do to her?' McNab said, trying to control his rage.

Dr Gordon, seeing this, said, 'You're a close friend of Dr MacLeod's?'

'Very close,' McNab stressed.

'Then you may be aware . . .'

McNab knew what was coming next.

'Rhona's pregnant,' he finished for her.

'I'm afraid she was in the process of miscarrying when we admitted her.'

McNab tried to assimilate this news. *Was it bad or perhaps for the best?* More importantly . . .

'Does Rhona know?'

'She was bleeding heavily when they found her, so I think she will have suspected. When she comes round, we can tell her.' She paused. 'I take it you're not her partner?'

'No. I'm about to call him,' McNab said. 'As far as I'm aware, Mr Maguire didn't know about the pregnancy, yet.'

'Okay.' She nodded her understanding.

McNab took himself into a quiet corner and made the necessary calls.

94

Light had returned to her world.

Behind her lids it shone in a motley mix of pinks and blues. She was no longer in the pit where it had been always dark, whether her eyes were open or closed.

As her senses began to return, the smell of the cold dank tunnel was replaced by warmth and disinfectant, the echoing sound of running water with the swish of hospital scrubs.

She was alive and in hospital.

Rhona savoured the moment, but didn't open her eyes immediately, for fear she was experiencing the opiate-induced dream from before.

She searched for and located her right hand and felt for what lay beneath it. No longer stones and wet earth, but the softness of a sheet against the broken skin, worn raw with digging.

A voice spoke to her, although it seemed very far away. Rhona strove to answer, but couldn't.

A gentle hand encased hers, large and warm and comforting.

'Rhona,' the male voice tried again, and this time she recognized it, and her eyes flickered open in answer.

His face swam above her. The dark hair, the deep blue eyes.

'Rhona, it's Sean.'

'Sean,' she repeated, or tried to.

His face moved and settled into place. She knew who this man was.

'You're safe now,' he was saying. 'You're going to be all right.'

The real world was coming back. Where she was now, where she had been. What had happened?

Rhona attempted to drag herself up. 'Did they find him? I left him in the pit in the water.'

A face materialized behind Sean.

'Do you feel well enough to talk now, Rhona? To tell us what happened?'

Sean hadn't wanted to leave the room, and McNab definitely hadn't wanted him to stay. For one important reason which had nothing to do with asking Rhona about her assailant.

McNab waited until the door closed behind the Irishman before he said outright, 'You were bleeding when admitted, Rhona. You know that, don't you?'

A shadow crossed her eyes.

'You didn't get to the appointment you made at the abortion clinic. Whatever happened in the tunnel caused you to miscarry and they had to operate. I take it Sean still doesn't know you were pregnant?' McNab said, then watched as her eyes began to clear and understanding set in.

'You have to tell him. It's not our secret any more.'

She'd asked McNab to give her five minutes before he sent Sean in. He was right of course. Sean had to be told, but more importantly she had to make peace with herself first.

Rhona kept her hands where the imagined light had been, devoid now of life other than her own.

In her deepest, darkest moments in the pit, she had vowed to keep them both alive.

And she had failed.

'I'm sorry,' she whispered.

McNab forced himself to step away from the intervening glass. He didn't want to see or hear her revelation. Nor did he want to observe Maguire's reaction.

The whole thing was a fucking mess.

Her tears when she'd interpreted his words, the hands that had reached for her abdomen. The sorrow in her eyes. All of that suggested to him, at least, that something had happened in that tunnel which may have made Rhona change her mind.

About telling Sean? About having an abortion?

Two coffees later and after a long call to the boss, McNab returned to find Maguire gone. The look Rhona gave him on entry, the slight shake of her head, indicating whatever had happened between her and the Irishman was not to be discussed.

'Have they found him?' she demanded.

'They've found the pit and the abandoned ladder, but no body, drowned or otherwise,' McNab told her.

'So he isn't dead,' she said, sounding almost relieved.

'Do you feel like describing what happened that night?'

'Yes,' she told him, a determined look on her face. 'At least as much as I can remember.'

95

They would discharge her soon, probably tomorrow.

Could she return to the flat or was it still a designated crime scene?

She could stay at Sean's, something he'd already suggested. Although, after what had happened between them, Rhona couldn't imagine doing that. And by his expression, neither could Sean.

So what did she want?

To turn back time. To make different decisions. To prevent Claire's death.

To tell Sean, but not after it was all over.

Rhona recalled the turmoil of emotions that had crossed Sean's face when she'd revealed the unplanned pregnancy. Then, in halting words, her decision to have it terminated.

'That's what you and McNab were talking about when I walked in on you that day at the flat.' Sean had shaken his head as though in disbelief. 'And I thought there was something going on between you two.'

'McNab found the tester in the bathroom. I didn't tell him by choice.'

Sean had given a half-smile. 'He was pretty good at covering for you, as I remember.'

'He asked me to tell you,' Rhona had said, remembering

McNab's desperate attempts at doing just that, including recounting the tale of his own missed fatherhood.

At that point, Sean had started putting the pieces together.

'That's why he sent me out as soon as you regained consciousness? To remind you of what you had to do?' He'd looked to Rhona for confirmation.

'Yes,' she'd admitted, feeling sick inside at what she now saw as betrayal.

'So, if this hadn't happened . . . I would never have known?'

Sean had sounded so sad and lost at that moment, that Rhona had almost told him about the flashes of light video, her change of heart in the tunnel in the face of what had seemed like imminent death.

But I didn't.

'You could have died down there,' Sean had said.

A little bit of me did.

'So, where do we go from here, Rhona?' he'd asked.

A question she wasn't able to answer.

Rhona looked up as another visitor arrived.

Chrissy stood in the doorway, her face a mix of emotions. Elation and fear being only two of them.

'Jesus, Rhona. I've never prayed so hard in my whole life.'

'Me too,' Rhona said.

Chrissy came to give her a hug. It was a bit like being smothered with love.

'The number of feckin' candles I lit.'

'Well, somebody spotted them,' Rhona said with a half-smile.

Chrissy settled herself beside the bed.

'You fucking scared me. Big time.' She sought Rhona's hand and met her eye. 'How are you really?'

At that moment Rhona wanted to tell Chrissy the truth. That she was a mess, both inside and out. That she'd lost all sense of herself in that pit. That she too had tried to bargain with whichever God would listen. That she'd revisited all her sins and regrets, shouting them to the enveloping darkness.

Instead, she said, 'I'm okay, honestly.'

Chrissy made a face as though knowing that would always be her reply.

They lapsed into a silence heavy with unspoken thoughts.

Eventually, Rhona said, 'I told Sean.'

Chrissy, who was normally never at a loss for words, merely registered this with a nod. The worry about what they should next say was solved by the door opening and the entry of another pair of hospital scrubs.

The man came forward and, holding out his hand, said, 'Dr MacLeod, Nick Gallagher. We met at a recent post-mortem here.'

Rhona only had a vague recollection of the blue-eyed, masked figure of the new APT. Not to be rude, though, she acknowledged him with a smile.

'Dr Walker sends his regards. As does Dr Sissons. They hope you'll be home soon.'

Rhona thanked him. 'Tomorrow, probably.'

'Great. Well, I have a body to collect,' he said, as though it was necessary to explain his visit further. He gave her a smile. 'Not from this ward, fortunately.'

'Who was that?' Chrissy asked when he'd left.

'Dr Sissons's new APT. He was at the Jackson post-mortem,' Rhona said as Chrissy's mobile buzzed.

Chrissy checked it and rose. 'I have to get back to work.'

She avoided saying where, but Rhona knew anyway.

'If they let you out tomorrow, go and stay with Sean. Please,' Chrissy pleaded.

Rhona nodded despite having no intention of doing any such thing.

96

The tunnel was brightly lit by arc lamps, the walls resounding with the steady throb of the generator. The perp's ladder had been transferred to the forensic lab, an alternative now giving access to the pit.

McNab surveyed the scene of Rhona's incarceration, trying to imagine what it must have felt like down there in the dark, bound and gagged, earth being shovelled in on you.

He'd faced death himself on a number of occasions, but had never experienced the feeling of being buried alive. And for that he was grateful.

The tunnels around here, he knew, had been badly flooded some years ago, after a particularly wet November when the River Kelvin had burst its banks. The deluge of water had found its way down more than one disused tunnel, to eventually flood the Glasgow Central railway line.

Since that time, remedial work had been done to prevent a repeat, including, according to Jen Mackie, a partial backfill of the south end of the tunnel, as well as a higher bank outside the Kelvinbridge portal.

'That deluge probably created the hole Rhona found herself in, aided by the underground stream. The only positive thing about her prison was the fact it had running fresh water,' Jen had added. 'If Rhona had been stuck down here without that, she might not have survived.'

Rhona had related to McNab how she'd got into the hole on her own volition when she'd mistaken an approaching torch for her captor.

'He had no intention of supplying her with water,' McNab had told Jen. 'I'm not even sure he planned to keep Rhona here long-term. Alive or otherwise.'

'Well, he definitely left us soil clues to follow. I assume he was watching to see which ones we would choose,' Jen had said.

And they were back in the realms of the watcher. The perpetrator who was always there, following the investigation. Perhaps even adding to it.

Chrissy had spent a great deal of time in the pit and had apparently little to show for it. The most recent tropical downpour had, according to Chrissy, raised the water level sufficiently to wash away all evidence of Rhona's imprisonment.

'But we do have the ladder,' Chrissy had told McNab. 'He didn't take that with him when he went.'

So Rhona's fear that she'd drowned the perpetrator had been wrong. In fact, it seemed certain that having got out of the pit, he'd followed Rhona for a while. Jen had found footwear imprints matching his size and preferential wear pattern as evidence of that.

'Something stopped him, though,' Jen had said. 'Possibly the arrival of the search team.'

'Rhona's given you a description?'

'Five ten. Slim build. Demon mask.'

It wasn't much. Her captor had apparently spoken her

name clearly only once when he'd thought she'd escaped from the hole.

'If I heard his voice again,' Rhona had told McNab, 'I would recognize it.'

McNab wasn't so sure about that.

Rhona had ID'd the demon mask online but multiple sources offered it for sale, so little chance of pinpointing a particular buyer.

He tried to imagine the scenario from the perpetrator's perspective. If Rhona's abduction was the ultimate test, what result had he wanted from that?

For Rhona to die and never be found?

Or what was now the case? The airwaves filled with how clever he had been in outwitting them all.

According to Magnus, the perpetrator craved recognition – for his forensic knowledge, for his skill and intelligence, for the police's inability to catch him.

Rhona's escape, McNab began to see, may well have been part of that plan. And Magnus, when challenged on that, had appeared to agree.

Emerging above ground, McNab heard the mobile ping an incoming message.

It was from Rhona's replacement phone, the original still missing just like both Claire's and Jackson's.

I'm back at the flat. Can you come and see me, now?

97

The kitchen was a mess, the surfaces dusted for prints, the forensic markings still littering the floor. It looked like the crime scene it was.

God knows what Rhona thinks every time she comes in here.

McNab wondered if Rhona had left it like this as an aid to memory, in case something occurred about that night which she'd forgotten. Or perhaps she didn't have the heart or the energy to clean it up.

At least the cat had been reinstated, he thought. It had run to greet McNab on entry, winding itself round his legs, meowing in an agitated fashion, as Rhona had led him through the flat to the kitchen. Tom was back, but not Sean, as evidenced by the empty bedroom, McNab had noted on passing.

So whatever had been said in that hospital room had led to him moving his stuff out.

As for Rhona herself, McNab had had to cover his shock when she'd opened the door to him. Pale as a ghost, apart from the vividly coloured bruise above her eye, the hands still scratched and swollen from digging.

Rhona had caught his expression and read it.

'I look like shit, I know, but I'm okay, really,' she'd insisted.

'You shouldn't be here alone,' McNab tried again, remembering the last time he'd said those words.

Rhona dismissed his concern. 'They've alarmed the place at Bill's insistence and they've given me a tracker. You won't lose me again, even if I do get past DC Watson and Co. Plus –' she pointed to the closed kitchen window – 'the roof's off-limits to Tom. For now, at least.'

Heading for the cupboard, Rhona brought out the whisky.

'Will you join me?' she asked.

When McNab nodded, she poured them both a double measure, her hand, he thought, a little unsteady as she did so.

'Is this about Sean?' he tried.

'Yes and no,' she said, her brisk tone belying the trembling fingers. 'Firstly, something I didn't tell you, although in truth I thought I'd lost it, until they gave me back my clothes in the hospital.'

McNab accepted the open evidence bag Rhona handed him and took a look inside.

'It's from the broken bottle.' Rhona indicated the marked-up floor with the bloodstains still evident. 'I tried to stab his left leg through the trousers that night, and I think I pierced the skin, although,' she said, looking down at the blood spots, 'I doubt whether I did enough damage for any of those to be his.'

She went on, 'I hid the splinter in my pocket. I had planned to stick it in his neck when I got the chance. The way, I suspect, you would have done.' She gave him a half-smile and shrugged. 'In the end, I didn't, and as you know, he's still alive. And free to kill again.'

McNab was pleased about the glass. If it did have the perpetrator's blood on it, it would be the first DNA sample they had on him, although if, as she'd described, it had been in the mud and washed clean by the water . . .

However, judging by Rhona's demeanour, McNab wasn't sure that was why she'd brought him here, instead of simply handing the glass over to Chrissy at the lab.

Noting his puzzlement, Rhona continued.

'No one can understand what it feels like to decide between killing and being killed, until you're faced with the choice yourself.' She met his eye. 'I know that now. I learned it in the dark, in that pit. Just the way you did that night on that hill among the standing stones.'

'I'm sorry,' McNab said.

'So am I,' she said with a small smile.

And with those words and that smile, McNab knew, the business between them regarding Stonewarrior was over.

That was why Rhona had asked him to come here, he realized, but now having had a glimpse of her state of mind, including 'the kill or be killed' scenario, he was even more certain she shouldn't stay here on her own. At least not until they picked up the perpetrator.

He said as much, adding, 'It would be better if you went to Sean's.'

'I know. And I may do that. He has offered and it would save on a sentry here.' She forced a smile.

She hadn't touched the whisky and McNab sensed she'd only poured it to make him feel at ease. There was, he realized, something else Rhona wanted to say, and eventually it came.

'I have a favour to ask.'

'Anything,' McNab said.

'I'd like to go home to Skye for a week, maybe more, and I'm not sure I'm up to driving yet. Will you take me?'

He briefly considered Ellie's reaction to such an arrangement and decided she would be for it. She had a great deal of time for Rhona, knowing what had happened in that pit. And they were, as she'd said, both victims of the same attacker. 'Although Rhona was braver than I could ever be,' had been Ellie's exact words.

'Of course,' McNab said swiftly. 'When d'you want to go?'

'Once this is all over.'

98

Rhona stood behind the door, waiting for the sound of McNab's footsteps to fade from the stairwell. In truth she'd been tempted by his offer to come back later, even stay for tonight, if, as he'd said, she chose not to go to Sean's.

But she had other plans for the rest of her day and maybe the evening too. And it wasn't to stay with Sean.

A ping from her phone indicated an incoming return message from Ellie agreeing to her suggested meeting. Rhona smiled. It was good to be doing something positive. Anything was better than being regarded as a victim.

Dressed and ready to go out, she pulled the door shut on Sean's empty room as she passed, almost locking Tom in there. The cat, she acknowledged, was fond of Sean, and would probably choose him over her if given a choice. She would have to ask Sean to look after Tom again, of course, when she went to Skye.

I'm always asking Sean for something, she thought. *And he rarely asks me for anything in return.*

He'd been deeply hurt by the secret of the pregnancy. Recalling his face, the confusion and hurt in his eyes, stung Rhona yet again.

He couldn't dispute her right to make such a decision, Sean had told her. Just that he'd wished she'd given him the chance to tell her that.

Even then, Rhona hadn't been able to bring herself to reveal her change of heart in the pit. Her vow that if she survived, then maybe . . .

But that was past history now.

Pulling the door closed behind her, she double-locked it and set off down the stairs.

Her current minder was waiting outside. Giving him a bright smile, Rhona explained that she was heading out for a couple of hours and she had her tracker, as requested.

'I plan to go to the jazz club and stay with Sean Maguire tonight. So as far as I'm concerned, you're off-duty.'

PC Watson looked a little taken aback by that. 'But DI Wilson said—'

Rhona cut him short. 'Let DI Wilson know where I'll be. No point you guarding an empty flat.' She smiled. 'I'm sure you have more useful work you could be doing.'

Not waiting for a further response, Rhona headed for her car. She checked all four tyres first, then finding all was well, got in.

Ollie had been surprised to get her call, but when she'd explained what it was about, he had readily agreed.

'I don't want DS McNab to know about this yet,' she'd said. 'It's just an idea. Nothing more.' She had ended the worried silence by adding, 'If anything comes of it you can tell him immediately.'

That had seemed to placate him.

In truth, experiencing daylight and a feeling of being in charge again, of where she went and what she was doing, was exhilarating. Even driving through traffic gave Rhona a sense of control. The claustrophobic darkness of the pit had been horrific. Even afterwards in the hospital she hadn't been able to shake off the feeling of incarceration.

As for the flat, it too was tainted by association.

Rhona wondered if she could ever regain her love for the place. Could she ever look out of that kitchen window on the convent garden and experience a sense of calm? Could she ever let Tom onto the roof again?

A rush of fear swept over her once more and her hands shook on the wheel.

Would this ever go away? The bursts of remembered terror, her fear of sleeping and the demon face that featured in the inevitable nightmares?

That was why she'd decided to go west for a while. It was a journey she had always taken when life seemed too much for her. Maybe it would weave its magic again.

But before I do that.

She had met Ollie only briefly, usually when he was called to give evidence at strategy meetings, but she had heard a lot about him from McNab.

When Rhona told him so, she could have sworn the poor guy blushed.

Ellie was already seated beside him and she and Rhona exchanged hellos.

'Thanks for letting me join you on this,' Rhona said.

The last thing she wanted in return was for Ellie to tell her how sorry she was about what had happened to her. Perhaps reading her expression, Ellie didn't do that.

'I told Michael I wanted to help find the killer, just like you do,' she said with a fierceness of purpose that perhaps matched her own.

Rhona nodded her understanding.

The repeated shaking bouts such as the recent one in the car, and her guilt at what she had or hadn't done, were, Rhona knew, typical with any victim of crime. The liaison officer who'd accompanied Bill to the hospital had talked her through what they could do to help her. There were support services available and a worried Bill had urged her to make use of them.

Rhona knew herself well enough to think that unlikely, although she hadn't told Bill or the LO that, because she had had other plans for her time and her efforts.

And that was to relive her experience as often as possible, in the hope that she would remember every single second she had spent with her attacker.

The flashbacks that accompanied the shaking were vivid and growing increasingly more revealing.

Now she could recall his legs as they descended the ladder in the dancing light of the head torch. All of it suffused with the smell of her own fear. In the hospital, McNab had asked her to describe her attacker, and she'd given him the bare minimum, because that's all she could remember at that point.

Not any more.

Now she knew the eyes behind the mask had been blue. Not the deep colour of Sean's eyes, or even McNab's, but paler. The way he'd moved as he'd descended the ladder was imprinted on her memory like the bad dream it was. He'd led with his left, she thought. Both his first foot on the ladder and his hand too.

The way people moved, Rhona knew, was as distinctive as a fingerprint. And a mask couldn't hide that.

'So,' Ollie brought her back. 'You want to start with the captured footage?'

Rhona nodded, her throat suddenly dry. 'Then I'd like to hear the phone recording.'

'Run it again,' Rhona ordered.

The grainy image was like an old noir movie, the time of day playing along the bottom. Ollie had strung three clips together. Each one featured a guy dressed in a dark-coloured hooded top and jeans. In the first he was checking out the window display of possible tattoos at the Ink Parlour. In the second he almost went into the Harley shop, then decided against it. In the third recording, Ellie emerged from the shop and walked away, glancing back as though conscious of someone's eyes on her, and the hooded man turned his face away.

According to Ollie, the super recognizer, all the sightings were of the same guy.

'You haven't got one of him descending a ladder?' Rhona said jokingly to ease the tension. 'That's about all I saw him do.'

Ollie cast her a sympathetic look. 'You said you thought he was left-handed?'

'Yes.'

'So's this guy. Watch his hands. He uses the left hand to push open the door, before he decides against going in. He uses his left hand to rearrange his hood. His gait also suggests he's leading with his left.

'So he's one of ten per cent of the population,' Rhona said. 'That narrows it down.' She glanced at the two anxious faces beside her. 'Sorry. I just thought I would know if it was him by the way he moved.'

'Shall we try the recording?' Ollie offered.

Rhona nodded. She had all her hopes now pinned on

the voice, and the voice along with the demon mask was what traumatized her most.

Ellie sat rigid beside her as the replay started. Rhona would have reached out and taken her hand, but knew that her own trembled too much.

A wave of nausea hit her as the taunting voice began to weave its sinister web. Ellie had committed a sin and should be punished for it. That was the message. They were back in the realms of the sin-eater.

Rhona searched desperately for a face she might recall to match that distorted voice, but all she could visualize was the demon, crouched in the corner of her kitchen, looming over her as she lay drugged on the floor.

'He must have had the mask on when he made that call,' she said. 'It's too distorted to recognize.'

Ollie, who'd been leaning forward in his eagerness, slumped back in disappointment. 'I've cleaned it up as much as I can,' he apologized. 'Did he speak to you at all without the mask?'

Yes.

Rhona forced herself to remember. A white door, the metallic noise of it being opened. *The back door of a car? No, the double doors of a van*. A smell had hit her as the door had opened. It had been the smell of the pit.

Now she was reliving her time in the van, rattling against the bare floor as it took off, the jolts bringing her back intermittently from her drug-induced stupor. The drug had made her vomit, and hearing her from the driver's seat, her abductor had turned and swore at her, his voice no longer disguised by the mask. The same voice she'd heard in the pit.

'Rhona.' It was Ellie's worried voice that broke into her revisited nightmare. 'Are you okay?'

Rhona pulled herself together. 'I heard his voice twice clearly, apart from the phone call. Once from the back of the van he used to abduct me. And again when he called out to me in the pit.'

'And you would know that voice again if you heard it clearly?' Ollie said.

'I don't think I'll ever be able to forget it.'

99

Grabbing the duvet from her bed, Rhona took it through to the sitting room. Tom, thinking this was the first sensible thing she'd done since he'd arrived back, came to nestle beside her on the sofa. The August evening was warm, but even under the duvet, Rhona shivered.

She had placed her hopes on viewing the footage and hearing the recording and she'd been wrong. It had been too distorted.

Anyway, a voice wasn't enough to accuse someone. There had to be more. *Means, motive and opportunity.*

On her return to the flat, she'd gone straight to the kitchen, stopping short at the door. In her preoccupation with what had just happened, she'd forgotten that the kitchen was still in such a state. If she ever wanted to eat in there again, that would have to change.

'Tomorrow,' she promised herself. 'I'll start tomorrow.'

Rhona pulled the cover up round her. Any notion she'd had about food had dissipated. She thought of Ellie's worried face as they'd parted company earlier.

'If you need to talk, just call me,' she'd said.

Rhona had watched her roar away on her bike and hoped that she and McNab would find a way to stay together.

The sun was setting, its reddened glow filling the room. In normal times, she would have gone to the big bay window to admire the view. Rhona wondered if she'd ever seek that image again without her eyes being drawn to the place where Claire's life had ended.

She admonished herself for that thought. *You work with death, all of the time. Just because in this instance it almost touched you . . .*

The insistent buzz of the intercom broke into her ruminations. Her first thought was that it might be Sean, and she hesitated at the prospect of facing him again. The alternative could be McNab of course, and she wondered if Ellie might have told him about what had happened earlier.

The voice on the intercom proved to be neither of them.

'Rhona, it's Conor. May I come up?'

Conor was trying not to stare or show any reaction to her face, but wasn't succeeding.

'I saw the story on the news. I'm so sorry, Rhona.'

She brushed aside his concerns. 'I'm okay, as you can see.'

She'd led him into the sitting room where Tom was now intent on ingratiating himself with the visitor.

Rhona studied Conor's valiant attempt to deal with the cat's determined attentions.

I'm not afraid of him, she thought. *Nothing about him suggests I should be*. And yet . . . from the moment they'd met *accidentally* in the park, he'd been within her range. Supplying information on Jackson, arriving the moment she needed help with the cat. Appearing again, when she'd been investigating the roof. Means and opportunity, but motive?

Feeling her eyes on him, Conor met her studied look, his left hand still stroking the cat.

'I've given details of my movements and a DNA sample,

as requested by DS McNab. Ray tells me they're asking the same from everyone on the forensic diploma course and from anyone who knew the victims.' A look of pain crossed his face. 'You have nothing to fear from me, Rhona. I hope you know that?'

Rhona smiled, as though she agreed with him.

Taking the smile as a positive, Conor reached in his pocket.

'I work with victims of violence at the clinic. I know how difficult it is to sleep after a major trauma. I thought you might need some help with that.'

He handed her a memory stick.

'I'm not planning on sleeping much,' Rhona told him. 'But thanks anyway.'

Conor had something else to say, something he was uncomfortable with.

'What is it?' Rhona asked.

'They're calling him the sin-eater. The press, I mean. There was an image in the newspaper of a painting.' He hesitated, perhaps looking for a reaction. When there was none he continued, 'It reminded me of the painting I showed you, *The Nightmare*. I wish I'd never done that. It's haunted me.'

Rhona gave a brief nod. She wished he hadn't either, then a sudden and penetrating thought occurred. 'Did you show it to anyone else?'

'Ray and I use it in the sleep clinic with anyone who suffers from sleep paralysis. Sometimes knowing others down through the ages have shared the same horrors helps. And, let's face it, who is without sin?' he said with a wry smile.

'Are you on duty tonight at the clinic?' Rhona said as she led him to the door.

'Yes, for a while at least. We have a number of new patients to manage. We've become a little famous through all of this,' he said apologetically.

'The first recording you gave me. Does the new one have the same voice?'

'It does,' Conor said with a smile.

'Is it you?'

'Only in the intro,' he admitted. 'Ray does the sleep sequences.'

After he'd gone and she'd double-locked the door, Rhona fetched her laptop. Plugging in the new memory stick, she selected the file named 'victim support' and pressed play.

The room was already in shadow, the thick curtains she'd now pulled across cutting out the light from the street.

Rhona closed her eyes to deepen the darkness.

The voice that introduced the session, she took a moment to relate to Conor. It sounded different in the recording. But, as he continued to speak, Rhona's brain began to match his face to it, in the park when they'd first met, then later in the pub where they'd shared a drink and talked of the importance of sleep.

The words he spoke were of trauma and how to use sleep to overcome a feeling of victimhood. How to be a survivor and take back control.

As the introduction drew to a close, a second voice entered.

Decidedly hypnotic, it washed over Rhona like a warm rush of water. She attempted to map that voice to the one that had called out to her in the pit and in the van, unhindered by the mask. The voice that had repeated the muffled words, 'I know what you did,' over the phone.

100

She got away and I was impressed, although I imagined it might happen. She is nothing if not resourceful.

She could, of course, have ended it there. She had the opportunity but chose not to do so.

Was I surprised by that? Not really. Some people are too weak to take a life, even when their own life depends on it.

I listened to her in the pit, babbling on in her drugged state about her guilty sins. When I said on the phone that I knew what she'd done, I was of course referring to the planted DNA.

Were I to call her now, there are other 'sins' I could mention.

It's illuminating how a near-death experience urges us to confess our sins.

I had intended to devour all her sins like the others. That would have been my parting gift to her, but circumstances prevented me from doing that.

Mainly the fact that she is still alive.

They've begun taking DNA samples from the participants on the course, and others in the vicinity of her place of work and home.

I have a decision to make, and soon.

Do I complete my task or not?

101

Rhona shivered a little as she met the night air. August was almost over.

She thought of the winding road west she would take when this was all over. She thought of stepping out of the cottage and looking across the Sound of Sleat to the mainland.

The air would be different there. She would be closer to the sea and to the mountains, and at that thought a great longing rose in her.

Maybe she would be there soon.

She glanced down the steps. She'd taken time to make her decision after listening to the recording. By now Conor would be at the sleep clinic, preparing his patients for hopefully a good night's sleep.

Getting into the car, she pulled out the replacement mobile and brought up McNab's number. Would he take her at her word that she might go to Sean's or would he check with Bill or her minder?

Rhona put the mobile away. If she told McNab what she planned, he would only try to prevent her.

Ellie, on the other hand, had understood why she might need to do this.

'This clinic. You won't be alone there with him?' she'd asked when Rhona had explained.

'Dr Williams will be there.'

'So you're just going to check out his voice?'

'The sleep recording. It sounded like him,' Rhona said, already beginning to question herself about that.

'I'll come there,' Ellie had told Rhona. 'Give me directions.'

Ellie would be here soon. Rhona knew she should wait and let Ellie come in with her. That's what they'd agreed.

And yet . . .

It would only take a few moments for her to be sure. Not by his face, but his movements and his voice.

If she was wrong she would simply make some excuse about looking for Conor and then leave.

And if her instincts proved right, what would she do then?

A woman approached and, giving her a smile, asked Rhona if she needed help to get into the building. Seized by indecision, Rhona murmured something about visiting the sleep clinic.

'Maybe they're sleeping and didn't hear the buzzer,' the woman joked. She pressed the security keypad, and when it crackled into action, she said, 'Visitor for the sleep clinic,' and the door clicked open.

'Are you one of the sleepers?' she said as she walked Rhona to the lift.

Rhona found herself nodding.

'Sweet dreams, then,' the woman offered as she got out at the second floor.

As Rhona watched the doors close behind her, she realized she was moving into panic mode again. In that moment, every sense in her body was warning her that this was a mistake. The small enclosed lift space only exacerbated that feeling. What if the lift stopped and she was shut in here in a space the size of the pit?

In an effort to countermand the panic attack, she tried to focus on the reasons why she'd come, but the logical list she'd convinced herself with seemed tenuous now, suggesting her poor mental state had been the culprit, and not scientific evaluation.

Now she accepted that she should have contacted McNab, rather than Ellie, after she'd listened to the recording. Told him she thought she'd recognized the voice. They would have talked it through. He would have come here with her if she'd asked him to.

I'm losing it, she thought.

As the lift stopped at the fifth floor, Rhona stood hesitant. Maybe she should go back down. Wait for Ellie to arrive and they could decide whether to come up together. Or maybe she would ask Ellie to call McNab and have him join them.

McNab would know. He would decide. She would trust his judgement. McNab knew her better than anyone.

The lift doors opened and, as Rhona hesitated, a man appeared and got in, his back to her, and pressed for the ground floor.

Rhona, calmer now that she'd made her decision, found her heart begin to slow.

As the door pinged open, Rhona waited for the other occupant to exit, then followed him outside.

102

McNab knew the flat was empty as soon he opened the door. Wherever Ellie was, it wasn't here.

It appeared that neither of the two women he wanted to protect required him to do that.

As McNab entered the kitchen he spotted a note on the table.

'Out with Izzy . . . racing! Be back later.'

McNab smiled. He'd been wrong. Ellie did intend staying here tonight after all.

Sticking his ready meal in the microwave, he set it to high. He would eat, then have a drink.

He headed for the shower first and, under the pounding water, contemplated Rhona's request for him to take her to Skye. He'd assumed she'd meant for him to drive her there, but now pondered the idea that she might be persuaded to go on the Street Glide.

What would Rhona make of such a suggestion?

Probably reject it out of hand was the first response that came to mind. But, then again, if your object was to escape your old life, what better way to do it?

McNab heard his mobile buzz as he exited the shower. Hoping it might be Ellie, he grabbed a towel and went to look. Checking the screen, he found a picture message which appeared to come from Rhona's missing mobile.

His heart upping a beat, he opened it to discover an image of Ellie on her bike, taken outside the Harley shop, seemingly catching her unawares. The caption below turned McNab to ice.

Bye bye biker girl

Swiftly pulling up Ellie's number, McNab listened as it rang out unanswered.

She'd said she was racing. But where?

It couldn't be back in the London Road tunnel. So where else did the four women go to race their bikes? McNab tried to recall any conversation they'd had that had centred on that topic.

Ellie had always been cagey about it, suggesting it was better that he didn't know.

'We don't endanger the public. That's why we were using the London Road tunnel.'

With the mobile unaccounted for, they had to assume the perp had it. So this message and photo had to have been sent by him.

McNab rang Ollie. 'Find Ellie's mobile,' he demanded. 'And I just got a message from Rhona's missing phone. Someone has it and I want to know where it is.'

Ollie spluttered and said okay, then told McNab something he didn't want to hear. Something that suggested Rhona and Ellie might well be together.

'Dr MacLeod said she didn't recognize the voice on the recording. She was upset about that. Ellie was trying to help her, sir.'

Next up, McNab checked in with Rhona's minder.

PC Watson sounded apologetic. 'She sent us away when she went out, sir. Said she was going to the jazz club in

Ashton Lane and would stay with Mr Maguire tonight. Told me to inform DI Wilson of that.'

'Have you checked her tracker recently?' McNab demanded.

There was an embarrassed silence. 'I think she's switched it off, sir.'

'Jesus, Rhona,' McNab screamed at the wall as he pulled up the number of the jazz club. Sean wasn't the one to answer but he came on the line soon enough.

'She never came here,' he said, his voice panic-stricken. 'Why would she say that?'

McNab tried to reassure him. 'You know Rhona. She didn't like being watched. She felt trapped. She's maybe with Chrissy.'

Chrissy was his next try.

'She wasn't okay when I spoke to her in the hospital. She was haunted. God, you've got to find her.'

He has us running again, McNab thought, as he climbed on the bike. *In all directions.*

Only that could explain what was happening.

Keeping Ollie on speaker, McNab headed for Rhona's. If Ellie was with Izzy and the others, surely one of them would take a call.

There's four of them, he kept saying to himself, and they're on bikes. He can't isolate one of them, surely? Would he even know which was which?

Even as he thought that, McNab remembered the individual leather markings on their jackets with clarity. The perpetrator knew which one was Ellie. He'd seen her in the tunnel.

At the same time he realized how easy it was to take a

bike off the road. A single chosen swerve would do it, similar to what had happened to him when he'd almost met his maker via the white van outside Rhona's in the rain.

Exiting Sauchiehall Street, McNab turned in the direction of the park and the quickest route to the hill. If he could descend the staircase from Park Circus on the bike, he could drive up it too.

Rhona hadn't been happy about the tracking device being on, especially if she had 'a posse' as she'd called it sitting on the doorstep. Maybe she just wanted rid of them. Maybe she was back inside the flat even now.

Then why not answer her bloody phone?

McNab buzzed his way in via Mrs Harper and headed up the stairs.

'What's wrong?' she asked anxiously from her open front door.

'I want to check if Rhona's home,' McNab told her. 'She's not answering the buzzer or her phone.'

Mrs Harper looked stricken. 'Dear God. I have a key for feeding the cat. I'll get it.'

McNab had already noted from the street below that Rhona's car was missing, and there were no lights on in the flat, but he had to try anyway.

The flat was empty. McNab knew that as soon as he crossed the threshold and the cat came running towards him. He went for the kitchen first, but it was as he'd left it.

In the sitting room, the sofa was draped with a duvet as though Rhona had been lying there. Beside it, her laptop was open, a memory stick attached. On the screen a file entitled 'victim support' was open and had been running.

'Has Rhona had any visitors today?' he asked Mrs Harper.

'Apart from you, Detective Sergeant, only one. The tall man from the university. He's been here before. Rhona said he was a sleep specialist.'

'Conor Williams,' McNab said under his breath. Maybe there was a remote chance she was with him.

Williams answered McNab's call almost immediately.

'Is Rhona with you?' McNab demanded, praying she was.

'No. Should she be?'

'What happened when you came to see her?'

'We talked.' Williams, picking up on McNab's anxious tone, rushed on, alarm obvious in his own voice. 'I gave her a new recording to help her sleep.'

'Called "victim support"?'

'Yes, that's the one.' Williams prattled on about Rhona asking who'd made the recording. 'I told her it was Ray.'

'Ray who?' McNab demanded.

'Ray Howden. He's a volunteer at the sleep clinic.'

McNab had a memory of Rhona's determined expression when she'd told him she would know the voice of her abductor again, despite McNab's doubts.

'Where can I find this guy?'

'You think Ray had something to do with all of this?' Conor sounded horrified. Not waiting for an answer, he added, 'God. I told him before I left that Rhona had asked whose voice was on the recording.'

103

'Okay,' Ellie signalled. 'Let's go.'

Izzy's face was much as it had been in the tunnel, alive with excitement. Gemma, she could tell, was up for it. Mo, not so much.

The park was devoid of traffic and pedestrians, and provided a clear run to the university precinct.

She'd told McNab she was racing tonight, and in a way she was.

Travelling in twos, they entered by the gates below Park Circus and swung west to cross the Kelvin. Someone hearing the roar of motorbikes crossing the park might report them to the police, but if Rhona was right and the police turned up, that wouldn't be a bad thing.

When they'd watched the CCTV footage together earlier in the day, Rhona had studied that man's movements over and over, asking Ollie to anticipate his height, weight, whether he was left- or right-handed. Ellie had been amazed at how seriously Ollie had taken her questions.

'She's right,' he'd said. 'How a person walks is as unique as their fingerprints.'

At the time Rhona had indicated she hadn't recognized the guy or the voice in the recording, then later when she'd called, it seemed she thought she now had.

Ellie had been immediately concerned for her, recognizing

in Rhona's voice the same desperation she felt when she thought of the killer still out there.

They were approaching a set of bollards placed to stop cars from using the tarred road through the park.

But just like the obstacles in the tunnel, it won't stop the bikes.

Ellie checked behind her. Izzy was hot on her heels and keen to pass. She knew where they were headed so there was no reason not to let Izzy win this race.

As Ellie moved to one side, the Bluetooth connection buzzed again inside her helmet.

It would be Michael. If she didn't answer soon he was likely to put the police on her tail, she realized.

'Michael?' She kept her voice upbeat.

'Where the hell are you?' he demanded.

'I told you in the note. I'm racing with Izzy,' she said as the main gate loomed up in front of them.

'The perp sent me a photo of you from Rhona's missing mobile.' When McNab repeated the caption, a shiver of fear went through Ellie.

'It's okay. I'm fine,' she said.

'Do you know where Rhona is?'

Ellie hesitated. Rhona had asked her not to say what she planned to do. Then again . . .

'Ellie.' McNab's voice brooked no argument. 'She's not at her flat and she lied about where she was going. Plus her tracker's off. If you have any idea what she's up to, you have to tell me. Now.'

104

The small square was empty apart from her own car and a solitary van in shadow on the far side.

Rhona checked her watch. She would call Ellie from the car. Feeling better, she headed for her vehicle.

Her rising panic in the lift had subsided now she was outside again. She halted and took in a deep breath of night air, catching the scent of roses from a display outside one of the terraced buildings that lined the square.

Noting the van was still parked, she assumed that the man who'd shared the lift with her had been on foot and had probably taken the walkway that led down to University Gardens.

Glancing up at the building she'd just left, Rhona thought she spotted a figure at the fifth-floor window, which might just be Conor.

God, now she felt foolish.

In fact, this whole idea of coming here tonight was beginning to look like a mistake. Tomorrow she would talk to McNab about Ray. They would interview him, and probably clear him of any wrongdoing. After all, she'd even had her doubts about Conor.

Her stalker, whoever they were, was definitely connected to both her professional and personal life. Even Dr Sissons's new APT had briefly crossed her mind. He was the right height and build, and had blue eyes. Then he'd spoken to her in the hospital and that suspicion had been put to rest.

Worst of all was the knowledge that her abductor had had access to her flat. And for how long? Long enough to learn everything about her? Certainly long enough to collect her DNA.

A sudden and shocking thought now occurred to Rhona.

Could her stalker even have found out about the pregnancy and her decision to abort?

God, that would have been one for a self-styled sin-eater.

As she clicked the remote to unlock the car, Rhona suddenly noticed a shadowy figure in a nearby doorway. Its back turned to her, there was, she registered, something odd about the shape of the head.

Then the figure swung round and stepped into the circle of light from the nearest street lamp, and she saw her *shadow man*. Her own personal demon.

'Rhona,' the same distorted voice caressed her name, as hypnotic as in the sleep recording. 'You didn't think I would give up on you, did you?'

In that moment Rhona prayed that this terrible image was merely a figment of her imagination. That the panic now gripping her body might be presenting her with the image she feared the most.

But of course it wasn't. The figure approaching her now was real.

Rhona, aware that if she tried to run it would be over in seconds, wrenched at the door handle instead.

If she could just get inside the car.

For a moment she thought she might make it, but with

only one foot in, he was on her and even the open door between them wasn't enough to shield her.

Seeing the needle approach, Rhona twisted her head desperately in an effort to thwart its impact, but the point hit home anyway. The power of whatever concoction he was pumping into her was swift.

She felt the surge of the drug enter her bloodstream and she was suddenly back in her kitchen, the same demon face above her, her body refusing her commands to move, to walk, even to cry out. The disassociation complete, she now departed her stricken body to merely observe what was happening from above.

This must be what dying is like, her brain mused.

You're a fool. You convinced yourself you were going mad. That nothing you believed was sane. That trauma had confused your senses.

She had lost faith in herself, yet she'd been right.

Too late now.

The nightmare had returned. The darkness and the smell. The rattling motion of the van, the desire to vomit. Feeling around her current space, Rhona encountered the rubbery touch of the mask, the metal blade of the spade, with remnants of soil still on it from her last incarceration.

Were his plans to bury her again?

Fear swamped her and she was back in the blackness of the pit, with the memory of soil raining down on her.

She couldn't, wouldn't, let that happen again, she resolved. She dragged herself up into a sitting position. Whatever he'd managed to pump her with, it hadn't been enough. Her fight to avoid the needle had resulted in that at least.

And, in his hurry to depart the square, he'd left her hands free.

Rhona listened.

The close proximity of surrounding traffic, the repeated stops and starts, had definitely grown fewer, suggesting, she thought, that he'd left the inner city, and by the new pattern of sound was possibly on the motorway heading out of Glasgow.

Where was he taking her?

It would likely be somewhere remote this time. A body buried in the wilds of Scotland was unlikely ever to be found. She imagined him planting forensic evidence to further confuse their search.

Now that she'd discovered his identity, the challenge was different, but it wasn't necessarily over. He could dump her and disappear, to kill again.

Something that must not be allowed to happen.

Rhona checked her pocket for her mobile, knowing there was little chance it would still be there.

No matter, she thought. There was another way to communicate her position.

105

The four bikes were clustered in front of the sleep clinic building. The three girls still perched on their Harleys observed McNab's approach with obvious trepidation.

Izzy tried a 'Hi' but the other two remained silent.

'Where's Ellie?' McNab demanded.

'She went inside,' Izzy told him.

'Alone?' he said, worried by that.

'She insisted.' Izzy shrugged as though McNab should know by now what Ellie was like.

McNab found the front entrance wedged open, no doubt in anticipation of his arrival or Ellie's quick getaway. Entering, he took the stairs two at a time. When he arrived slightly breathless on the fifth floor, he found one of the three doors on that level also wedged open.

'Ellie,' he shouted, his voice echoing down the dimly lit corridor.

A face appeared at the end, but it wasn't Ellie's. Not at first anyway.

'Michael,' her voice called as she appeared behind Conor.

Both came together to meet him.

'He's gone,' Conor said. 'Ray was supposed to be on duty tonight, but he's not here.'

McNab looked at him. 'The bastard has Rhona, and it's

your fucking fault,' he said. 'When you told him about the recording, he knew she would come here. He was waiting for her.'

'God, I'm sorry. Rhona never said anything that suggested she suspected him.'

'Okay, who is this guy?' McNab said as they headed for the exit. 'I know he's a volunteer, but what does he do on his day job?' he said, trying to get a handle on the man they sought.

'He's a trainee anatomical pathology technician in his first year. He—' Conor halted mid-sentence. 'It was Ray who suggested I contact Rhona in the first place about Andrew Jackson.'

'And he was doing the forensic course with Rhona,' McNab exploded. 'And you never fucking thought about that? Okay,' he said, trying to get his anger under control. 'What does he drive?'

Conor looked bewildered by the sudden question.

He's a fucking cyclist, McNab thought. *He doesn't care about models of cars.*

Conor surprised him by coming up with an answer of sorts.

'It's a van. Small and white.'

'Okay.' McNab tried to stay calm. 'A white van. Registration number? Make?'

Conor shook his head. 'I'm sorry, I have no idea.'

They were outside now, all four girls back on their bikes, waiting for someone or something to chase, but what and who?

McNab put his helmet back on, noting the Bluetooth connection had been humming.

'Ollie?' he said on high alert.

'She's back online, sir.'

McNab gave a whoop. 'Where?' he demanded.

'Currently on the M8 heading south over the Kingston Bridge.'

Jeez, they were well ahead.

'Can you see the cameras? We think they may be in a small white van. Make and registration number not yet confirmed.'

McNab turned to the others. 'Okay, we have a tracker on Rhona.' He told them the location. 'I'm heading there. The rest of you should go home. This is police business.'

'Fuck that,' Izzy said. 'Just you try and lose us.'

McNab had no wish to argue with Izzy or Ellie, whose expression suggested she felt the same. If they kept up, well and good, but he wasn't about to hang around waiting for them.

Conor's frightened face flashed in the headlights as the five bikes, led by McNab, circled before exiting the square. He acknowledged McNab's thumbs-up, signalling that at least they knew where they were headed, and raised his own hand in response.

Poor bastard, McNab thought, *I've only dispensed some hope.*

McNab took the shortcut, roaring down the steps to meet University Gardens. A short walk away and they would be in Ashton Lane and the jazz club where, according to PC Watson, Rhona had planned to spend the evening.

If only that had been true.

McNab put his foot down and heard the roar behind him as his posse did the same.

The traffic was thick on the Kingston Bridge, headlights running like a string of Christmas lights. They were travelling in convoy. Him in front, followed by Ellie, then Izzy close on her, taking, he realized, every opportunity to try and overtake.

Fucking hell.

'Tell Izzy to fall back,' McNab relayed to Ellie.

'There's no way she'll do that.'

The traffic was peeling off into lanes as they approached the far side of the bridge. They could really screw up here, if they chose the wrong slip road.

The massive granite landmark of the old Co-op building loomed up on their left. It was decision time.

'Ollie,' McNab demanded. 'We need to know which way?'

In the interim, McNab zigzagged his way through the bunched-up traffic, skimming cars, dodging into spaces, checking behind him periodically to see if his female posse was still with him.

'For fuck's sake, Ollie. Hurry up.'

'Okay,' the voice finally came back. 'They've taken the M8 west, and it's a white van, registration number—' he began.

McNab interrupted him at the fourth character. 'I bet that's the van that almost put me off the road outside Rhona's.'

He forced his way right across the carriageway to the sound of multiple honking horns. Ellie was close on his tail, hotly followed by Izzy. The other two he'd lost in his rear mirror.

They were already breaking the speed limit and without doubt they would have police bikes on their tail soon. All well and good.

He switched the Bluetooth connection to Ellie. 'We keep going,' he told her. 'Whatever happens.'

106

He wasn't driving erratically, nor was he going too fast.

He has me, and he has a plan, Rhona thought, *as indicated by his steady driving.*

Rhona could see nothing outside from where she sat, although the intervening glass lit up periodically with the beams of oncoming traffic.

They were, by the frequency of such lights, likely heading west or maybe south, the eastern route to Edinburgh being much busier. Either of those directions would bring him into empty country fairly swiftly, where he could leave the main road and its traffic cameras and wind his way to the remote location he had in mind.

As soon as he stopped the van and came for her, the game would be over.

She had to be prepared for that.

Rhona felt about in the dark again, looking for the shovel and finding it. The space was limited and swinging it at him when the doors opened wouldn't be easy. Something smaller and sharper would be better. If she did manage to disable him, she could commandeer the van.

It was a nice thought, much easier in the planning, she feared, than in the execution.

He'd been a worthy adversary up to now, Rhona

acknowledged. There was no reason to believe he wouldn't continue to be.

Turning her head towards the intervening glass, she spotted a sign, partially obscured, suggesting they were on the M8.

So, he was headed west, or should he choose to recross the River Clyde via the Erskine Bridge, he might be intending to go north instead.

Even as she thought this, Rhona was suddenly flung to the right as he made his choice.

Bracing herself against the side of the van, and shifting round, she caught a glimpse of the oncoming panoply of lights that outlined the upward curve of the approaching bridge.

Something had happened to spook him, she realized, as his ever-increasing speed pressed her against the metal side. Rhona checked her tracker, praying under her breath that it was because he now suspected they were being pursued.

The roar of a fast-approaching motorbike, quickly followed by another, resonated like thunder inside the van. At first her captor seemed to take no notice and Rhona knew he was assuming the bikes would soon overtake, leaving him clear again.

She had no idea how her captor had known she would turn up at the sleep clinic. She had to assume that something Conor had said had alerted him to that possibility.

What she did know was that Ellie would have turned up there and found her missing. Ellie and her pals were supposedly racing tonight. That was her cover story with McNab, which meant there were four of them.

Assuming Ellie had contacted McNab when she found

her missing, maybe they would have followed her tracker. That, Rhona's heart soared, could explain the increasingly deafening noise that thrummed the sides of the van and vibrated the metal beneath her.

How many Harleys did it take to make that sound?

A sudden sharp swerve threw her to one side, and she realized her abductor was now attempting to break free of his cortège, unsuccessfully it seemed.

The noise had changed. The bikes were, Rhona suspected, now up front, to the right and behind, effectively corralling the vehicle.

The scream of an approaching siren, then another, filled the air, indicating the cavalry were about to join the advance party.

Rhona's moment of elation was short-lived as her abductor made one last bid for freedom. With a sharp swerve to the left, he crashed against and then through the barrier onto the accompanying walkway, smashing into the outer railing that had been the launch pad for a string of suicides since the bridge had been built.

107

She was physically here. She was alive and breathing. The space about her was safe.

Yet, still she shook. Still she remembered. Still she relived.

Compartmentalize.

That's what everyone on the front line did.

Soldiers, police officers, fire crew, doctors.

If you were consumed by every life you lost, every killer you didn't catch, you would never save a life, nor bring a killer to justice.

The problem was . . . the wall she'd built between what she did and who she was had collapsed.

Back again, standing at the kitchen window, in the room that had made her buy this flat, looking out at the view that had secured the sale, Rhona couldn't help but regard it differently now.

The convent garden looked the same, but now she read it differently – the plants, the trees, the pollen that had clung to her abductor's clothes. That garden had allowed him access to her home.

How could she ever look down on it again and rejoice in its peacefulness?

But I'm alive, she reminded herself. Count your blessings.

You survived and, remember, Andrew Jackson and Claire Masters did not.

Why me?

That was the question uttered by every survivor. She'd known that to be the case, yet never properly understood the sentiment until this moment.

She'd also imagined she knew what she would do in her deepest darkest moment, and she'd been wrong.

You are what you do in any given circumstances. Not what you think you might do.

All those months of castigating McNab for what had happened at the end of Stonewarrior, she'd never considered his state of mind, the torture he'd been put through in the hours before he'd done what he had.

It had been on the night of the tunnel discovery that they'd had their latest argument about it. She'd been so angry with him when he turned up later at the locus. She'd even accused him then of stalking her.

Rhona turned from the window.

Thank God he'd ignored her on that front.

Unsurprisingly, it had been McNab's face she'd first encountered as the back door of the van had been opened. McNab who'd led her to the waiting ambulance and helped her inside.

He always has your back.

Dazzled by the beams of the Harleys, and unsteady in her still-drugged state, Rhona had barely registered the faces of her rescuers as McNab had led her to the ambulance, but she knew Ellie was among them.

She'd attempted an apology then for not telling him what she'd decided to do. For involving Ellie in the plan.

'We'll talk later,' was all McNab had said.

Rhona turned to survey the sparkling kitchen, all evidence of it as a crime scene gone.

This had been her first move to try and regain her life, but she knew there was something more important she needed to do. Something she'd been avoiding but could do so no longer.

If she was ever to be comfortable in this kitchen again, she would have to unmask her demon and look him in the eye.

108

McNab was shaking his head in disbelief at her request. Bill, on the other hand, regarded her with questioning eyes.

'I have to confront him, properly,' Rhona said. 'Otherwise I will always recall him as the demon of my nightmares.'

'You saw him on the bridge,' McNab began.

'I was still drugged,' she responded. 'I saw a figure being bundled into a police car.' Rhona halted for a moment. 'I know his voice. I know how he moves. I have never seen his real face. Not properly. I want to see him. I want to speak to him.'

When there was no response except a determined negative look from McNab, she went on, 'I have to confront him, otherwise he'll continue to haunt me.'

'You'll see him in court,' McNab said.

Rhona shook her head. 'No. I don't want to wait that long.'

A quick glance at the boss suggested that he might, just might, be on her side. McNab not so much.

'You can't see him alone,' Bill said. 'McNab could sit in with you.'

'No,' Rhona said quickly. 'Not McNab. That wouldn't work.'

McNab's face was like thunder, but Rhona tried her best

to ignore that. If McNab was to be in there with her, she would be consumed with fear, not of her attacker, but of how McNab might react.

Perhaps picking up on this, DI Wilson gave a small nod. 'Another officer, then?' he suggested.

'I'd like it to be Magnus,' Rhona said swiftly.

She had thought this through. If anyone should observe any interaction between herself and her abductor, then it should be the psychologist.

Bill was considering this and, Rhona hoped, coming round to the idea. McNab wisely was keeping his mouth shut, although with difficulty, Rhona noted with a half-smile.

Bill looked to McNab. 'Okay, Detective Sergeant, let's contact Professor Pirie and set this up.'

'You okay?' Magnus's concerned look almost brought a smile to her face.

'I am,' Rhona assured him, although she had no idea if that were true.

The interview room smelt of previous occupants and disinfectant, only slightly masked by the scent of the coffee Magnus had brought in with him. The officer who stood by the door gave her a reassuring nod as the door opened and a figure appeared and was handed over.

Rhona kept her eyes on Ray Howden as he was ushered to the seat across the table from her.

Magnus introduced himself and indicated that they would be recording anything said in the meeting. Ray nodded, a smile curving his lips.

He wants this as much as I do, Rhona registered. *It makes him feel important.*

Rhona took some moments to study the man before her. So this was her personal demon, minus the mask. No longer one of Conor's shadow men, but flesh and bone, with pale blue eyes and dark hair. Ordinary and unremarkable. Someone she'd hardly noticed at the sleep clinic, and even now couldn't recollect from her lectures.

His knowing smile, as he met her eyes, suggested that he knew her a great deal better than she did him.

'Dr MacLeod,' he said, finally taking the initiative. 'You'd like to know why, wouldn't you?' He smiled.

Magnus had warned her of how this might go. That a perpetrator like Howden would want to control both her and the interview.

When Rhona chose not to respond, a flash of what looked like anger crossed those eyes.

'Because the sins of the dead,' he said, the smile back on his lips, 'are all-consuming.'

'Bullshit,' Rhona said under her breath and, catching Magnus's eye, indicated that the meeting was at an end.

109

Arriving afterwards at the lab, she'd met the scent of fresh coffee and the smell of filled rolls, accompanied by Chrissy's welcoming face.

'You're not ready to come back yet,' Chrissy said in her forthright way, when Rhona explained what had just happened. 'You've taken a step, but there's a few to go yet.'

At this point Chrissy had reached out for one of Rhona's still-bruised hands.

'McNab said you planned to go west when this was all over.'

'It's not all over,' Rhona reminded her.

'Your part in it is. Once the bastard goes to trial, that's a different matter.'

When Rhona didn't looked convinced, Chrissy came back with, 'We've been through this before, remember? When McNab got shot.' She gave a rueful smile then, as though remembering. 'Back then, I was the one tortured by guilt and you were the one telling me what to do about it. We survived then and we will again.'

Rhona had mooched about the lab after that, her gaze constantly focusing on the thick tree cover below, her eyes drawn to the spot where she knew the yew tree must be.

'Okay,' Chrissy said, coming to stand beside her. 'Begone.

Get packed. McNab's coming for you in a couple of hours' time.'

And with that Rhona was summarily dismissed.

Tom had already departed, having been picked up by Sean shortly after she'd called him. During his brief visit, they'd spoken of nothing but her trip west and how long she might stay on Skye.

'Tom's fine with me for as long as you need,' Sean had said. 'Just keep in touch, promise?'

Rhona had duly accepted his hug and given her promise.

In no man's land, she had no idea if she could or should resurrect what she'd had with Sean. Or even if he would want her to.

Rhona glanced at her watch. McNab would be here soon, so she should be ready.

She fetched the small bag she'd prepared from the bedroom, then systematically walked round the flat, checking the windows were secure and the burglar alarm Bill had had installed was switched on.

The advancing roar of the motorbike took her to the sitting-room window. When McNab had suggested she abandon the idea of him driving her to Skye, Rhona had imagined he was merely trying to get out of the job.

She'd been wrong about that.

Rhona waved to him, indicating she would come straight down.

If she was to leave her old life behind for a while, maybe McNab was right, and this was the way to do it.

Epilogue

There were many ways to head into the west.

They might have taken the route described in the traditional song, 'The Road to the Isles'.

Sure by Tummel and Loch Rannoch, and Lochaber I will go.

McNab had chosen instead to travel via Stirling, Callander and Glencoe, informing Rhona he'd discussed the bike route with Ellie and was following her advice. Rhona knew this way well too, but didn't tell him so.

Better that McNab found out what it was like for himself.

Reaching Glencoe, McNab stopped briefly, suggesting he needed to stretch his legs, but Rhona knew how overwhelmed he was by the place, like most other first-time visitors before him. The sense of ominous history loomed above them on either side and Rhona could never travel through here without thinking of the haunting story of its past.

They went by way of the Great Glen, weaving through the summer traffic, before emerging at last to climb and look down on Loch Garry stretched out like a veritable map of Scotland. Then it was Glen Shiel and its mini Alps and a brief stop at Eilean Donan Castle.

Rhona laughed to see McNab taking photographs on his mobile to send to Ellie, as though she might be the only person who hadn't encountered an image of that particular famous castle or watched the movie *Highlander*.

But Rhona really came alive when she saw the curve of the bridge ahead of her. The bridge that would take her home to Skye.

Acknowledgements

The character of Dr Rhona MacLeod was inspired by a former maths pupil of mine, Emma Hart, from my home village of Carrbridge. Her enthusiasm for forensic science was transferred to me and thus the pupil became the teacher. This led me to take the Diploma course in Forensic Medical Science at my former university of Glasgow, where I had initially studied mathematics.

There were two writers among the audience of seventy professionals on the evening course – myself and my pal and co-founder of Bloody Scotland, Alex Gray. You can guess who had their hands up all the time.

Throughout the course we made many friends, who are of course the real people in the world we choose to write about. Without their expertise, this, and all the other books in the Rhona series, wouldn't have been possible.

In particular, for *Sins of the Dead* I'd like to give thanks to . . .

Professor Lorna Dawson of The James Hutton Institute for inspiring the creation of soil scientist Dr Jen Mackie.

Dr James H. K. Grieve, Emeritus Professor of Forensic Pathology at Aberdeen University, who is more than generous in answering my queries about modes of death.

Glasgow Tigers for a fabulous day out at Ashfield, which inspired the role of the Tigers in the story and reminded me how much fun I had supporting the team when a student at Glasgow University.

The idea for *Sins of the Dead* was conceived at the annual rally of Harley-Davidson enthusiasts who gather every August in the neighbouring village of Aviemore. Known as Thunder in the Glens, it's organized by the Dunedin Chapter of Harley-Davidson.

A big thanks must therefore go to Alex Glen, the Director of the Dunedin Chapter Scotland (9083), and to Fran and Jim Anderson, chapter members in Aviemore, for their expertise in all things Harley-Davidson and of course in the running of the hugely successful and friendly Thunder in the Glens.

In *Follow the Dead* I introduced the character known as Mary Grant, inspired by the real Mary Grant from Carrbridge, who kindly gave money to Cancer Research to get to know McNab a little better.

I liked the character so much she reappears in *Sins of the Dead*. You'll have likely read the book by now, so you'll already know what she's been up to this time, and that a Harley-Davidson played a role in that.

Paths of the Dead

By Lin Anderson

Paths of the Dead *is the thrilling ninth book in Lin Anderson's Rhona MacLeod series.*

It was never just a game . . .

When Amy MacKenzie agrees to attend a meeting at a local spiritualist church, the last person she expects to hear calling to her from beyond the grave is her son – the son whom she'd only spoken to an hour before.

Then the body of a young man is found inside a Neolithic stone circle high above the city of Glasgow, and forensic scientist Rhona MacLeod is soon on the case. The hands have been severed and there is a stone in the victim's mouth with the number five scratched on it. DI Michael McNab is certain it's a gangland murder, but Rhona isn't convinced. When a second body is found in similar circumstances, a pattern begins to emerge of a killer intent on masterminding a gruesome Druidic game that everyone will be forced to play . . .

The Special Dead

By Lin Anderson

The Special Dead *is the thrilling tenth book in Lin Anderson's Rhona MacLeod series.*

When Mark is invited back to Leila's flat and ordered to strip, he thinks he's about to have a night to remember. Waking later he finds Leila gone from his side. Keen to leave, he opens the wrong door and finds he's entered a nightmare; behind the swaying Barbie dolls that hang from the ceiling is the body of the girl he just had sex with.

Rhona MacLeod's forensic investigation of the scene reveals the red plaited silk cord used to hang Leila is a cingulum, a Wiccan artefact used in sex magick. Sketches of sexual partners hidden in the dolls provide a link to nine powerful men, but who are they? As the investigation continues, it looks increasingly likely that other witches will be targeted too.

Working on the investigation is the newly demoted DS Michael McNab, who is keen to stay sober and redeem himself with Rhona, but an encounter with Leila's colleague and fellow Wiccan Freya Devine threatens his resolve. Soon McNab realizes Freya may hold the key to identifying the men linked to the dolls, but the Nine will do anything to keep their identities a secret.

None but the Dead

By Lin Anderson

None but the Dead *is the thrilling eleventh book in Lin Anderson's Rhona MacLeod series.*

Sanday: one of Britain's northernmost islands, inaccessible when the wind prevents the ferry crossing from the mainland, or fog grounds the tiny, island-hopping plane.

When human remains are discovered to the rear of an old primary school, forensic expert Dr Rhona MacLeod and her assistant arrive to excavate the grave. Approaching midwinter, they find daylight in short supply, the weather inhospitable and some of the island's inhabitants less than co-operative. When the suspicious death of an old man in Glasgow appears to have links with the island, DS Michael McNab is dispatched to investigate. Desperately uncomfortable in such surroundings, he finds that none of the tools of detective work are there. No internet, no CCTV, and no police station.

As the weather closes in, the team – including criminal profiler and Orkney native Professor Magnus Pirie – are presented with a series of unexplained incidents, apparently linked to the discovery of thirteen magic flowers representing the souls of dead children who had attended the island school where the body was discovered. But how and in what circumstance did they die? And why are their long-forgotten deaths significant to the current investigation?

As a major storm approaches, bringing gale-force winds and high seas, the islanders turn on one another, as past and present evil deeds collide, and long-buried secrets break the surface, along with the exposed bones.

Follow the Dead

By Lin Anderson

Follow the Dead *is the thrilling twelfth book in Lin Anderson's Rhona MacLeod series.*

On holiday in the Scottish Highlands, forensic scientist Dr Rhona MacLeod joins a mountain rescue team on Cairngorm summit, where a mysterious plane has crash-landed. Nearby, a climbing expedition has left three young people dead, with a fourth still missing.

Meanwhile in Glasgow, DS McNab's raid on the Delta Club produces far more than just a massive haul of cocaine. Questioning one of the underage girls found partying with the city's elite, he discovers she was smuggled into Scotland via Norway, and that the crashed plane may be linked to the club.

Joined by Norwegian detective Alvis Olsen, who harbours disturbing theories about how the two cases are connected with his homeland, Rhona searches for the missing link. What she uncovers is a group of ruthless people willing to do anything to ensure the investigation dies in the frozen wasteland of the Cairngorms . . .